"DO YOU NEED SOMETHING ELSE?" LUCAS ASKED SOFTLY.

He pushed away from his desk and walked toward her.

Tessa took a quick breath, and despite his better intentions, he watched the rise of her breasts beneath her shirt.

"No. And if you ever try that again, you can bet I'll make you regret it."

After two weeks of her avoidance and icy silences, even threats were progress. Of a sort.

"You didn't always mind my kisses."

She arched a brow and said coolly, "I was young and easily impressed."

Lucas almost smiled, not sure which he admired more: her poise or her guts. She lifted her chin, and his gaze again dropped to her lips. Then he stepped closer—and closer still as her eyes widened.

She should have remembered he never, ever, backed down from a challenge.

Other Avon Contemporary Romances by
Michelle Jerott

ABSOLUTE TROUBLE
ALL NIGHT LONG

Michelle Jerott

A Great Catch

AVON BOOKS

An Imprint of HarperCollins*Publishers*

This is a work of fiction. Names, characters, places, and incidents are products of the author's imagination or are used fictitiously and are not to be construed as real. Any resemblance to actual events, locales, organizations, or persons, living or dead, is entirely coincidental.

AVON BOOKS
An Imprint of HarperCollins*Publishers*
10 East 53rd Street
New York, New York 10022-5299

First Avon Books paperback printing: September 2000

Avon Trademark Reg. U.S. Pat. Off. and in Other Countries, Marca Registrada, Hecho en U.S.A.
HarperCollins® is a trademark of HarperCollins Publishers Inc.

Printed in the U.S.A.

QW   10 9 8 7 6 5 4 3 2 1

One

Port of Milwaukee

"**N**o, no . . . you've got it all wrong. You two need to be *together*. Like this—big buff dude in back, cute chick here in front."

The photographer clamped his hand around First Mate Tessa Jardine's arm and positioned her so that her shoulders bumped against the hard chest of the man standing behind her.

The instant their bodies made contact, her muscles tightened, and the tension shot like a rocket straight to her temples.

God, her head pounded, and the blinding-hot sun and rhythmic slapping of waves against ship and shore didn't help any—nor did the ever-present, screeching cacophony of the gulls.

Heavy humidity was slowly melting the creases of her white dress uniform, and each time the photographer squeezed her arm and called her "cute," she wanted to slug him.

"Oh, my . . . that's perfect," the photographer gushed. "*Love* the contrast. He's so much taller than you, and it emphasizes his manly-man looks—and you're just marvelous, so cute."

"I'd prefer that you don't call me cute," Tessa said in the firm voice she used to advise men twice her age or size to pay attention. "And I don't like being handled as if I'm some bimbo selling beer with sex."

The photographer snorted. From his shaved head, nose ring, and goatee to his baggy, overlong pants, he epitomized "trendy young artiste."

"Your boss's whole angle is sex, honey. Sex sells, and I can make anything sexy. You want attention, right? You want to pack that old bucket with passengers, right? So go over the top—be daring. I don't do ho-hum, I do sizzle and snap."

He snapped his fingers in front of Tessa's face. She jerked back in reflex, bumping into that warm chest again. She eased away—or tried to.

"Oh, no you don't, missy." Oblivious to her warning glare, the photographer poked her backward with an index finger to her shoulder. "Now, it's like this. The captain here, he's male with a capital *M*. I see power. I see authority. I see chicks drooling. And you're just marvelous—"

Tessa's fingers twitched.

"—with those sexy kitty-cat eyes, and your mouth makes me think of a young Bardot. You're not blond, but hey! Nobody's perfect. I can't get over just how cu—whoa!"

Tessa yanked him down by a fistful of his black-knit shirt. As his eyes popped wide, she enunciated very clearly: "Please don't call me cute."

The photographer's mouth pinched tight. When he

cleared his throat pointedly, Tessa let him go. "That, young lady, wasn't very nice."

"Being nice," intoned a deep voice behind her, "isn't part of her job description."

On a heated rush of anger and embarrassment, she almost turned, but didn't. "Why, thank you *so* much. Captain."

"You're welcome." The body behind her bent down as he murmured, "Miss Jardine."

At the touch of his breath against her ear, Tessa shivered and looked straight ahead, focusing on the gray-and-white ship rocking gently at anchor.

I can work with this man. I can, I can . . .

"A bit skittish, are we?"

At the faintly condescending question, Tessa glanced at the photographer again. He was staring at her with an expression of distaste.

Skittish just about summed up her mood at the moment—and she prayed the dampness under her arms had everything to do with the heat and nothing whatsoever to do with the man at her back.

Her commanding officer.

The perfect manly-man.

The perfect bastard.

"How much longer will this take?" Tessa asked with a sigh.

"Just give me a few seconds, and I'll finish with the publicity stills. I have a job to do here, you know," the photographer retorted.

"Don't we all," Tessa said, as the kid again pushed her back against that warm, unyielding chest. At once, the scent of spicy cologne enveloped her.

Sandalwood . . . potent and earthy. A scent that shot straight to an ancient, murky part of her brain, triggering vivid flashes of images and sensations: a slow finger sliding down the pale skin of her belly, a husky laugh, lips tasting thickly sweet of rum and coke, a beard-rough chin.

Tessa took a long, steadying breath to clear her head as the photographer said, "Now, I want Captain . . . Paul, is it?"

"Hall."

"Is that your first or last name?"

"Captain Hall."

A silence followed, and Tessa almost smiled. The "big buff dude" wasn't happy about all this posturing, either.

"My, aren't we a friendly bunch," the photographer muttered. "Okay, *Captain* Hall, put your hands on her shoulders."

Tessa stiffened. "I don't think that's appropriate."

The photographer rolled his eyes. "Chill, okay? I want a cozy, one-big-happy-family shot, just in case your boss isn't interested in a sexier angle. Now stand still and you put your hands here . . . yes, exactly. Oh, I love it, *love* it!"

Hall's hands rested lightly on her shoulders, as if he didn't want to touch her any more than she wanted to be touched. The heat of his skin penetrated the fabric of her shirt, the press of his hands somehow intimate and heavy.

From the corner of her eye she could just glimpse strong, broad hands and very capable-looking fingers. A scar—one she didn't remember—cut across the knuckles of his left hand, and with the exception of a plain watch, he wore no jewelry. Not even a ring.

The photographer tilted her chin, putting an end to her discreet survey, then moved one of Hall's hands closer to her neck. "Now," he said in a tone usually reserved for temperamental toddlers. "Let's all smile and look happy to be here. Captain, a little lip action would be nice, thank you."

Despite her irritation and pounding headache, Tessa couldn't help but smile at the irony of that particular comment.

This kid had no idea . . .

"Praise the gods, she smiles at last!" The camera clicked three times in quick succession before the photographer straightened. "That's it. I'm outta here. It's been *such* a pleasure, people."

He snatched up his equipment and stalked off, leaving Tessa with her back still pressed against her captain. To her relief, the weight of Hall's hands lifted from her shoulders, freeing her to step away. Raising her chin, Tessa turned at last to face him—and took an instinctive step back, swallowing.

From the tips of his polished shoes up to the gleaming black visor, he looked as if he'd stepped right out of a recruitment poster. Not a single wrinkle marred the navy blue jacket and pressed trousers, or the white shirt he wore buttoned to the neck with an expertly knotted tie. He still kept his dark hair military short, and a beard shadowed his square jaw. While that infamous killer smile was notably absent, he still carried himself with all the hotshot arrogance she remembered.

Tessa ignored her damp palms, as well as the flutter in the pit of her stomach she hoped came from her missed lunch. "Mr. Sizzle-and-Snap is right. You do fill out that uniform very nicely. Sir."

Lucas Hall looked past her toward open water, legs braced wide, hands clasped behind his back as if he were already on the rolling deck of his ship. He paid her no more attention than he would a gnat.

After several moments she tipped her head toward

him, smiling sweetly, and murmured, "Stop ignoring me. People will notice."

"And you think nobody's noticed you've been ignoring me since you arrived here two weeks ago?"

"I haven't had time to socialize. I've been working my butt off fitting out this ship on time for—"

"You've been avoiding me." He turned at last, staring at her from light hazel eyes. Eerie, wolfish eyes—and about as warm as Lake Superior in January. Tessa went still, unnerved, but a flash of color caught her eye before she could respond.

Oh, joy. The boss had arrived.

"Show time. Get ready!" The whispered command followed in the swishing wake of pink silk, glittering gold, and floral perfume. "The cable crew will want to talk to you both next. Remember, act professional, answer *only* as you were instructed . . . and Miss Jardine, I don't want you standing so close to Captain Hall."

Which in Pink Widow language meant: *He's mine. Back off.*

Like that would ever be a problem.

As the woman breezed through a knot of reporters, the appreciative gazes of some dozen men—including Hall's—followed the pitch and roll of her hips. The frank stares reminded Tessa of snatches of gossip she'd heard from her crew over the last few weeks, and her mood darkened.

"At her age, I expect she's plenty experienced, but maybe I could give her a few pointers on your techniques," Tessa said tightly as she stepped away. "Especially that 'disappearing into thin air without so much as a good-bye' trick."

Hall shifted his gaze back to her, and the already humid air grew a little hotter and stickier under his glare. "We'll discuss this later, Jardine, but not here."

Bull's-eye. She'd finally rattled his icy calm.

Tessa turned her attention to the ship awaiting its ceremonial christening, and the sight of her high prow and sleek lines, so different from the huge, bulky freighters she was used to, eased her tension.

Such a pretty ship. Every minute she'd spend on those freshly painted decks would be worth taking orders from Hall and putting up with the crew's inevitable distrust or harassment.

A gull's plaintive cry sounded high above her, and she looked up at a pair of gray-white birds wheeling gracefully against a blue sky high above the *Taliesen*.

It was almost a perfect day, and she wished her family were with her to help celebrate. But her father was loading taconite at Marquette, and by now Everett was downbound on the St. Mary's River. Steve had hoped his ship would make it to Milwaukee on time, but she didn't see him, and Matt—

Sudden tears stung her eyes as Tessa realized what she was doing. Swallowing away the lump of sadness, she glanced around the bustling dock, filled with a small crowd of ship buffs, media types, workmen, and several dozen suits. They'd all gathered this afternoon to watch Roland Stanhope's sleek widow launch her own venture, compliments of old Rolly's Great Lakes shipping fortune.

A cheerful shout sounded behind her, and Tessa turned to see the mayor walk past, a pack of reporters at his heels.

"Captain Hall, we need you over here," called Harry Kowalski, the company's PR rep. He motioned impatiently. "The *Sentinel* photographer wants a shot of you with the mayor and Dee, with the *Taliesen* in the background."

The gathered crowd—especially the women—

watched Hall with rapt attention as he strode toward the mayor. An anemic blonde actually sucked in her breath as he walked past.

But Tessa couldn't help watching either as people made way for him, moving back without a word or even a signal. Tall and broad-shouldered, Hall radiated power and authority. The entire package dazzled; so much so that she wondered if anybody else noticed how his easy grace barely disguised the slight hitch in his walk.

The crisp uniform likely covered other scars, and the thought caused her a twinge of regret. So many memories today—and impossible to avoid them.

"Miss Jardine!"

Tessa glanced at Kowalski, who motioned for her to join the group in front of the ship. With a soft sigh, she headed toward him and smiled at the mayor, who'd been drawn aside by several of the company's investors and board members, sweating in their expensive suits.

Upon joining Kowalski, Hall, and Dee Stanhope— who managed to look cool and elegant despite the heat and brisk wind—Tessa caught sight of a handsome black man standing with them and nearly groaned out loud.

Darryl Pointer, host of the local cable program *City Beat*, went after controversial subjects with the single-mindedness of a pit bull.

"I want a quick interview here on the dock," Pointer was ordering. "Then after the christening ceremony, we'll head over to the ship and shoot some footage there. How does that sound?"

Perfect," Dee answered. "Why don't you interview Captain Hall first, then talk to Miss Jardine. You can save me for last. I don't have anything very interesting to say, I'm afraid. Everything I do is behind the scenes, you know."

Pointer made a *tsk-tsk* sound. "Mrs. Stanhope, I'm certain I'll find everything about you absolutely fascinating."

Dee Stanhope—fortysomething and the owner of a thriving commercial shipping company—blushed prettily. She shrugged and fluttered a hand as if to say: *Oh, this old ship? Just a little something I whipped up the other day in the boardroom.*

The sharp gleam of interest in Pointer's dark eyes told Tessa he hadn't fallen for Dee's demure act. "So, Captain," he said, turning to Hall. "Ready to answer a few questions?"

"Yes."

At the terse response, Pointer's brows shot up. "No call to be nervous. If it helps, pretend the cameras aren't here."

"I'm not nervous," Hall said in a clipped tone, and Dee touched his arm, flashing a brilliant, gushy smile. After a moment, he smiled back and visibly relaxed.

Startled by the familiarity of the exchange, Tessa dropped her gaze to the polished tips of her shoes. So much for rumors: Hall really *was* sleeping with the boss.

Anger spiked, sudden and hot. It had taken her over six years of hard work and struggling against blatant sexism to finally land the job of first mate, and all Lucas Hall had to do was unzip his pants and—

"Yo, Darryl," yelled the cameraman, interrupting Tessa's thoughts. "It's hot, man. Let's get this show on the road."

Pointer squared his shoulders, donned a jaunty smile, and stared into the wide black lens. The cameraman focused, then made an okay sign.

"Sun-drenched skies," Pointer said in his deep, pleasant voice. "Sparkling blue water. The pounding of the surf. A cruise ship, rocking quietly at anchor. The Caribbean? The Bahamas? Well, would you believe . . . Milwaukee, Wisconsin?"

He paused for effect, widening his smile. "If it seems a world away from the typical ocean cruise, you're right. I'm here today with Captain Lucas Hall, First Mate Tessa Jardine, and Stanhope Shipping's owner, Mrs. Dee Stanhope, to talk about risky business."

Pointer turned toward Dee, who stood with an indulgent smile as the breeze fluttered her pink skirt. "Risky business as in purchasing a century-old steamship, which today will be rechristened the *Taliesen*. Many are questioning the financial wisdom of a cruise ship sailing Lake Michigan. In these tough economic times, is the *Taliesen* doomed to sink, figuratively if not literally, before she even sets out on her maiden voyage? Mrs. Stanhope, would you care to comment?"

Sink?

Tessa stared at Pointer. What a jerk!

"Getting the *Taliesen* back in service has long been a dream of mine," Dee answered, unflustered. "She's a tribute to a way of life that's all but disappeared. These days, people are so intent on getting somewhere fast that I wanted to reintroduce the joys of leisurely travel. Stop and smell the roses, that's my motto."

"But do you—"

"However, dreams and business don't mix, so I've spared no expense in restoring this ship from the keel on up. I've handpicked stellar officers and a dedicated crew, all of whom will make sure this ship is not only safe, but who'll treat each and every passenger like royalty. And at a very affordable rate. Unlike that *other* Great Lakes cruise line."

"But you acknowledge there's a risk?" Pointer said quickly, before Dee could interrupt him again.

"Of course. But without risks, life would be so dull, don't you think?"

That clearly took Pointer by surprise, although the man didn't miss a beat. "Captain Hall, you're a Coast Guard veteran, are you not?"

"Yes, sir. Nearly twenty years of service."

"And you've also received quite a few medals, including several commendations for valor?"

Hall nodded once in acknowledgment as a muscle in his jaw tightened. "That is correct."

"So modestly stated, sir." Pointer smiled. "But our area viewers will recall you also played a key role in one of the worst maritime tragedies of the past twenty-five years."

Here it comes.

Tessa's gaze shifted toward her boss. Dee's pink lips tightened a fraction, and Kowalski had turned purplish.

"Since the loss of the *Edmund Fitzgerald* in 1975, the Great Lakes has maintained a good safety record," Pointer continued. "Until the tanker *Robert D. McKee* exploded and sank nearly two years ago. Captain Hall, some people find it ironic that you're now working for Stanhope Shipping, the company that owned the ill-fated *McKee*. Has this been an issue for you?"

"No, sir, it has not."

Tessa darted a glance at Hall. He stood straight and proud . . . and an unexpected pang of sympathy stole over her, even if he was the last person she should feel sorry for.

"And is this true for the first mate?" Pointer turned his inquisitive dark gaze on her. "Miss Jardine, you lost a brother on the *McKee*. How does it feel to work with the man who was partly responsible for sending your brother, and the four men with him, to the bottom of Lake Michigan?"

A heavy, awkward silence followed.

"Mr. Pointer, please," Kowalski said with a sigh. "This is *not* an appropriate question. Captain Hall was cleared of any wrongdoing, and with the Yarwood lawsuit still pending in court, you know we can't publicly discuss the *McKee* incident."

"I was only asking Miss Jardine to share her feelings with our viewers."

Tessa would've gladly done so, but snarling "Up yours!" wouldn't go over well with Stanhope's board of directors. After all, she symbolized the company's equal-opportunity savoir faire and had a part to play today.

"I have the utmost respect for Captain Hall, both as captain of the *Taliesen* and as the officer who tried to carry out his sworn duty, even at the risk of his own life," Tessa said, as she'd been told. In her own words, she added, "Shipboard employment can be dangerous, but as you pointed out, accidents are rare. I've worked for Stanhope Shipping for years, and I have no complaints—obviously, or I wouldn't be here."

"Hiring Captain Hall also set off a rumble of anger in the union." Pointer didn't take his gaze from Tessa. "Some claim he was hired over more experienced men as compensation for the injuries he received during the botched rescue attempt, which forced him to retire from active service. Is this true?"

Stunned by the insensitivity—it was *her* younger brother who'd died in that "botched" rescue attempt—Tessa forced herself calmly to return Pointer's stare. The effort kept the pain at bay; it would look bad if

Stanhope's token female first mate burst into tears on camera.

"My company is well within its right to hire outside the unions," Dee cut in, her tone civil but cool. "And Captain Hall is more than competent, Mr. Pointer."

"Maybe the captain would like to comment for himself?" Pointer turned to Hall.

"I'm very good at what I do, sir."

"Of course you are, but I see a big difference between commanding a passenger ship and chasing drug smugglers or illegal aliens," Pointer said, his eyes bright with pleasure at so obviously hitting a nerve. "And Miss Jardine has only worked as a junior officer on freighters. We've heard a lot of negative press lately about the safety of the cruise industry. Why hire a captain and senior officer who lack experience with passenger vessels? Isn't that just asking for trouble?"

Dee smiled, shaking her head. "Play fair. You can't compare a foreign cruise ship to one owned and operated in the U.S. We've passed stringent Coast Guard inspections and Miss Jardine coordinates a first-rate safety program. The complaints, Mr. Pointer, are just sour grapes. Now, shall we get on with the christening of my ship?"

"Certainly." Pointer signaled the cameraman to stop filming, then grinned. "You're one tough lady, Mrs. Stanhope."

"Please, Darryl, call me Dee. It's so much shorter, and we have a busy afternoon ahead of us." Dee rested her hand lightly on the man's shoulder. "I don't consider myself tough, but the *Taliesen* is my baby, and we both know a little controversy is always good for business. Within reason."

Pointer laughed out loud, and Tessa yearned to shove him into the water. She glanced at Hall, half-afraid to see what emotion, if any, lurked in those hazel eyes—and found him watching her. Unnerved by the intensity of his gaze, she quickly looked away.

Kowalski herded everyone toward the *Taliesen*'s prow, where the mayor and his suit-wearing party waited with barely concealed impatience. No doubt they wanted to climb into their air-conditioned cars and head back to their air-conditioned downtown offices.

Tessa could well imagine their reactions to the sooty boiler room and the sweating firemen who loaded black coal into the orange-red inferno of the boilers. The women, with their heels and manicured fingernails, didn't look like they'd enjoy getting down and dirty, either.

She wished she were below deck right now, trading insults with the chief engineer, listening to the sound of hissing steam and the well-oiled thud and clang of massive piston rods, or the crew's curses and laughter hanging in air thick with the acridly sweet smell of burning coal.

A trickle of perspiration rolled down her back, itching beneath her white cotton bra. She ignored the itch, standing still while the mayor made his speech. Dee followed, keeping her own remarks brief, then she swung the bottle of champagne against the ship's repainted hull and christened the *Taliesen* in an explosion of pink bubbly.

Cameras popped and flashed, the crowd cheered and clapped, and Tessa smiled until her cheeks ached— staying as far away from Hall as possible.

Keeping her distance wasn't difficult; the guests and reporters, especially the women, found him far more interesting than a lowly first mate—not to mention controversial. After all, she hadn't been accused of blowing up any tankers while there were men still alive inside.

How had her perfect job ended up such a mess?

Over and over, she'd told herself that turning down a promotion like this because of anger would be foolish—but a hell of a chasm lay between theory and reality.

"Miss Jardine, we're heading to the *Taliesen* now." Kowalski's low warning brought Tessa back to the present.

The mayor departed along a line of shaking hands, while half the media group followed Dee up the ship's ramp for a private tour. The sound of their voices and laughter drifted down, mingled with the slap of water against the *Taliesen*'s hull.

Kowalski followed, guiding the rest of the group toward the main deck, which left Tessa and Hall to bring up the rear.

Hall was watching her. Again. With the brim shielding his eyes, she couldn't read his expression—and it made her defensive, uncertain.

"What are you staring at?" she demanded.

"I'm not staring. I'm waiting." After a moment, he motioned toward the metal gangway. "Ladies first."

Tessa narrowed her eyes. "In this uniform, Captain Hall, my gender doesn't mean squat. You think of me as just one of the guys. Got that?"

Two

Not while he still had balls and a heartbeat.

Lucas watched Tessa march up the ramp to the deck, her hips swinging with irritation and drawing his attention to how her white trousers fit snug against her bottom, showing a hint of panty lines: high-cut panties, the kind that would make the most of the great pair of legs hidden beneath her uniform.

He briefly closed his eyes, until the scent of her baby shampoo drifted away on the breeze. After all this time, he still couldn't smell that powder-sweet scent without remembering a nineteen-year-old Great Lakes Maritime Academy cadet whose fingers and mouth had been anything but babyish.

Somehow, he expected she'd have grown beyond baby shampoo. God, the rest of her sure had grown up.

Quickly killing that thought, Lucas grasped the metal rail and followed his mouthy mate.

If they didn't find neutral ground, and fast, one of

them would have to leave this ship. It sure as hell wouldn't be him, and he suspected nothing short of death would get Tessa off the *Taliesen*. It had been a long time, but some things a man didn't forget.

Just then, she shot a snotty glare at him over her shoulder.

And there were some things a woman wouldn't forget, either. Or forgive.

On deck, he made his way toward the sound of Kowalski's smoke-roughened voice relaying the *Taliesen*'s history.

"... was built in 1908 and converted to a metal hull in the forties. She was retired from service in 1974 when the cost of maintaining her became too expensive. Mrs. Stanhope purchased the ship six years ago and began the restoration project with the help of public donations ..."

While Kowalski rattled out trivia, statistics, and amusing anecdotes, Lucas kept away from the crews toting cameras and sound equipment, and the half dozen local television and newspaper reporters.

He'd rather corner a desperate Colombian smuggler with an AK-47, or even turn back a boatload of miserable refugees, than face another question about the *McKee*.

Lucas glanced at his mate, at the proud lift of her chin and wind-tousled dark hair—and wished to God the reminder of every stupid mistake he'd ever made in his life wasn't wrapped around the luscious, neverforgotten body of Tessa Jardine.

Guilt shot through him, and an all-too-familiar knot tightened in his belly. What he really needed was a grueling, mind-numbing swim. How could he have thought he'd prepared himself for this?

"We're heading to the pilothouse. Are you coming?"

At Kowalski's questioning voice, Lucas looked up. Everyone, including Jardine, stood staring at him. Waiting.

"My apologies." He caught Jardine's gaze. "I was just admiring the view."

Jardine's dark, thick-lashed eyes widened, then she spun on her heel and walked stiffly away. As Kowalski and Dee guided the media up to the pilothouse, Lucas followed, his mood grim.

He shouldn't have let his temper slip loose, but if Jardine wanted to poke sticks through the cage of his self-control, it was only fair to warn her he would grab that stick and poke right back.

As everyone squeezed inside the small room overlooking the bow deck with its neatly stacked lounge chairs, Lucas positioned himself far away from her. The pilothouse still smelled heavily of varnish and paint, and the window frames gleamed with a suspicious wetness.

Dee had moved the *Taliesen*'s launch forward with relentless force, despite the controversy surrounding the Yarwood trial's accusations of negligence against Stanhope Shipping in the *McKee* accident. The best way to deflect negative publicity was with something new and exciting and equally controversial—like hiring as captain the key player in that same accident.

"Captain Hall." The *Milwaukee Journal Sentinel* reporter's voice cut across Lucas's thoughts. "Would you mind explaining the purpose of this equipment?"

As Lucas came forward, everyone made way for him without his having to ask.

"The ship's wheel, of course." He grasped the polished wood and gave it a twist back and forth, then laid his hand on the instrument beside him, the brass cool beneath his fingers. "This is the engine order telegraph, or chadburn, which transmits speed and directional orders to the engine room. As Mr. Kowalski explained earlier, the *Taliesen* is equipped with a quadruple expansion steam engine. She's one of the last steam-fired passenger ships on the Great Lakes."

"Will we get to see—"

"Miss Jardine will take you below deck for a tour of the engine department," Kowalski assured the *Sentinel* reporter.

Lucas then pointed out the GPS, gyrocompass repeater, magnetic compass, radar, radio, and chart room. Using the simplest language possible, he explained the line of gauges mounted near the ceiling that measured wind direction and speed, rudder angles and engine RPMs, while several of the men nodded as if they understood.

"Amazing," said Pointer when Lucas had finished. "Guess this means I shouldn't complain about driving my Saturn on cruise control down the I-94."

His comment garnered several laughs and smiles, then Kowalski led the group out of the pilothouse. Single file along the narrow corridors of airy aqua-and-ivory hues, gleaming chrome trim, and tan carpeting, they trooped through the public areas: the dance floor and bar, cafeteria-style dining room and retro-looking soda fountain, movie theater, children's play area, gift shop, even the ship's museum. All stood empty and quiet, but within a few days, these rooms and halls would once again ring with the sounds of passengers and crew.

Kowalski allowed the reporters a peek inside the private rooms, from the economy Pullman cabins to the larger, pricier suites located on both decks.

"It's not as fancy as a luxury liner," said a petite blonde in a red suit. She sounded disappointed.

"The *Taliesen* wasn't meant to compete with luxury ocean liners, but to provide comfortable, affordable travel on the Great Lakes," Dee replied. "All those fancy interiors you saw in the movie *Titanic* wouldn't work here. Wooden decks and walls are against Coast Guard regulations. Fire hazard, you see."

"It's still pretty nice," said one of the cameramen. "Bet you couldn't build a ship like this today without spending a small fortune. Man, look at that bar!"

They'd returned to the dance lounge, gathering before its focal point: a vintage Art Deco black-and-silver bar shaped like a crescent moon.

"We've restored the *Taliesen* to what she would've looked like during her heyday, which is why the passenger areas have an Art Deco Modern appearance," Dee explained, her eyes shining. "I compared paint chips and fabric swatches myself, and hired a company to reproduce the original furniture designed by Warren McArthur. I spared no expense for authenticity. Of course, we've had to make changes to bring the ship up to modern safety standards. I've also modified the crew and officer quarters and converted one car deck to another berth deck. But otherwise the *Taliesen* is largely unchanged. She's not only a working ship, she's also a museum."

That spawned yet another discussion on economics and the shipping industry as the group trooped back up to the pilothouse, where Lucas sought out Jardine again. She stood at the back of the room, stifling a yawn.

With her attention elsewhere, he let his gaze linger. A full mouth complemented her exotic slanted eyes, olive-tinted skin, and dark hair, which she wore much shorter than he remembered. She looked indecently good in the practical shirt and trousers of her uniform—as well as natural. She carried herself with a confidence that said she'd found her place in the world.

Lucas felt a small, sharp twinge of regret that he couldn't claim the same thing.

His perusal moved upward, following the curves of a body no uniform could disguise—and met Jardine's eyes. He didn't look away. What did she see when she looked at him?

He had a pretty good idea, since her attitude spelled it out—and he'd hardly expected otherwise. As she'd avoided being alone with him over the past weeks, his hopes had faded that they could ever put the *McKee*—and her brother's death—behind them.

"Captain, can you tell these people about navigation on the *Taliesen*?"

Glad for the distraction, Lucas turned to Kowalski. With his back to Jardine, Lucas spent the next ten minutes explaining basic navigational techniques, until Dee ordered Jardine to fetch a sextant from the chart room and demonstrate how it worked. Then Jardine had no choice but to stand close to him in the hot, sweaty press of humanity crammed into the pilothouse.

The scents of starch and baby shampoo drifted his way. The sunlight added an auburn tint to her hair, and its softly polished sheen invited a touch.

Shifting back from her as much as he could, Lucas clasped his hands behind his back, his fingers tightening.

"A sextant provides the basis for all celestial navigation," Jardine said, holding up the instrument. She didn't look at him, totally oblivious—thank God—to his line of thought. "It measures angles in degrees, minutes, and seconds. The angle between the star and the horizon is called altitude and—"

"Isn't that interesting," interrupted Ms. Red Suit.

"But what I'd really like to know, Ms. Jardine, is how it feels to work on a ship full of men."

After a short silence, Tessa put down the sextant on the wheelsman's empty stool. Her arm brushed against Lucas, since she had no room to move away. "I'm asked that question a lot, actually. If it helps, think of my work as similar to corporate middle management. In addition to directing the ship's course on my watch, I handle the daily paperwork, cargo and inventory, personnel, and resources-management tasks. It's like an office job, except my office happens to float."

"Oh, I see. So it's like he's the boss," Red said, pointing a long, painted nail at Lucas, "and you're his secretary."

"No, that's not what I said." Jardine's body went stiff beside him. "I carry out the captain's orders, but I also issue orders and delegate responsibilities to other crew members. I'm a deck officer, ma'am, not a receptionist."

Red Suit pondered that for a moment, a faint frown on her face. "But do you ever feel overwhelmed? Do the men obey you as they would a male officer?"

"We've moved out of the Dark Ages," Dee cut in smoothly. "Orders are orders, regardless of the officer's gender."

"So sexual discrimination isn't ever an issue?" asked Pointer, plainly sensing a potential hot spot.

Now there was a loaded question. Lucas glanced from Jardine back to Dee, who stood watching him with a small smile.

"The older generation can be a little slower to warm up to change," Jardine answered in a carefully neutral tone. "But most crew members judge me by my abilities, not my gender."

"In addition to Miss Jardine's comment," Dee said,

"I'd like to add that personal relationships *are* against Stanhope's company policy."

"Always?" Pointer leaned forward, bright interest in his eyes. "Didn't you say your chief cook is married to one of the men in the engine department?"

"Married crew members of the same rank aren't an issue, but we don't allow relationships between officers and subordinates."

"What about between officers?" Red Suit asked. Lucas didn't miss the woman's quick glance down his body and could almost see her mentally stripping away his uniform. "Captain Hall, are you married?"

"No, ma'am, I am not."

Beside him, Tessa twitched.

"Miss Jardine, are you?"

"No."

Lucas's gaze shifted briefly to Jardine's clasped hands, even though he'd already noticed the lack of a diamond twinkling on her ring finger.

"This isn't relevant," Dee interrupted, giving the petite reporter a cool look. "Personal relationships between officers are against policy for the same reason officer and subordinate relationships aren't allowed— it's a conflict of interest and complicates the chain of command. Now, I think we've covered everything we need to up here. Mr. Kowalski, Miss Jardine, please take our visitors down to the engine department."

Jardine nodded and motioned toward the door. "This way, please."

"Are you coming along, Mrs. Stanhope?" Pointer asked.

She turned and smiled at Pointer. "I'll wait here with Captain Hall. It'll be a little crowded if we all go."

When everyone had ducked through the hatch, Lucas turned and held back his irritation. Whenever possible—the inevitable public functions aside—he avoided being alone with Dee.

"So," she said once the footsteps and voices faded away. "I think that went well. How about you?"

Lucas leaned back against the wheel. "Not bad. The ship looks good. You charmed them, and Kowalski impressed them with his stories and barrage of statistics."

She walked closer, saturating the room with the scent of an airy floral perfume. "The business with the *McKee* went better than I expected. Tessa did well."

Lucas's inner alarm went on full alert. Interacting with Dee Stanhope was a little like swimming through shark-infested waters, so he played dead, letting no emotion show in his eyes or voice. "Jardine strikes me as the type who always gets the job done."

Dee moved closer, her body almost touching his. "You're certain the *McKee* incident won't be a problem between you and Tessa?"

Although he didn't move back, Lucas glanced out the window bay, tracking an orange forklift lumbering along the dock, and told Dee what she wanted to hear.

"She's a professional. Whatever personal gripes she has with me, we'll work through them."

"I expect you will." Dee rested her hand on his arm, long enough for him to feel the warmth of her skin, but not long enough to be outright suggestive.

Lucas looked back at her, catching the faintly amused, assessing look in her eyes.

"This is my baby I'm placing in your hands. My dream," Dee said softly. "I need my crew to work together, or I'm going to fail. Do you have any idea how many of those nice, smiling businessmen out there today would love to see Old Rolly's Folly fall flat on her face? One mistake is all it'll take, and my investors will pull out and we all go down."

"I won't make any mistakes."

"I suppose not." Her expression was thoughtful as she stepped away with a final pat to his shoulder, slender fingers lingering. "You can't afford to, can you?"

"No," Lucas said, smiling humorlessly as an inner anger burned. "I can't."

Against her expectations, Tessa enjoyed touring the media through the bowels of the *Taliesen* and talking about her favorite subjects. At least she didn't have to stand near Hall any longer, or feel his stare boring through her back.

How convenient, though, that the Pink Widow had stayed behind alone with him—especially with the captain's cabin just off the pilothouse.

"You're frowning." Darryl Pointer's voice interrupted her thoughts. "Is something wrong?"

"No, I . . . have a headache, is all. It's been a long couple of weeks."

Pointer smiled. "And now you're stuck baby-sitting us. If it helps any, the sacrifice is appreciated."

She still hadn't forgiven him for his earlier interrogation, but managed to smile back. "Thank you."

"Ms. Jardine, these boiler things *are* safe, right?"

Tessa looked over at the blond, red-suited reporter, who picked her way carefully through clanging pipes, throbbing hoses, greased gears and shafts, and sweating crewmen who weren't shy about eyeing her legs or breasts.

They didn't look at Tessa like that. Or if they did, they were smart enough not to get caught.

"Extremely safe, ma'am. Steam engines have evolved a long way from the ones that used to blow up the old paddle wheelers."

The group didn't linger in the engine room, although there was a moment of aghast fascination as they watched the firemen demonstrate how a conveyor belt delivered coal to the boilers, the inferno within glowing red-hot and blasting heat.

"It's like stepping back in time," Pointer said once they were on deck again. He tugged his tie loose, and his dark skin gleamed with sweat. "Are you sure that job's legal? You don't chain those poor guys in there like slaves, do you?"

Kowalski made a dismissive motion with his hand. "The shift rotates often, four hours on duty, eight hours off. It's not the classiest job on earth, but without the firemen and coal tenders, the *Taliesen* goes nowhere."

"Man, you couldn't pay me enough to work in there," Pointer said with feeling. "It gives a whole new meaning to the word sweatshop, you know what I'm saying?"

"Which underscores the crew's dedication toward making the *Taliesen* a success," Kowalski said smoothly. "I believe this wraps up our tour, ladies and gentlemen, so unless anyone has additional questions, I'll escort you all back to the business office. We have drinks and a buffet waiting."

No questions followed; just a murmured "thank you" here and there.

Kowalski nodded. "Good. Miss Jardine, please let Mrs. Stanhope know we're returning to the dock."

"On my way," Tessa said.

She took her time, enjoying her first unhurried look at the ship since she'd first arrived in Milwaukee to begin fitting her out. While she wasn't personally a fan of the industrial look, it suited the *Taliesen*. The clean, uncluttered lines and light colors opened up the ship, and made her look and feel bigger than she really was.

When Tessa stepped back inside the pilothouse, she was relieved to see Hall nowhere in sight, although her boss stood propped elegantly against the magnetic compass, her hips framed by the compensation spheres.

"I take it the tour is over?" Dee asked, examining a long, pink fingernail.

In spite of herself, Tessa couldn't help checking for signs of a quickie—but not even a single hair was out of place on Dee's head. And the woman was still standing; a sure sign nothing had happened in the captain's cabin, unless Lucas Hall had lost his touch over the years. And that was highly unlikely, seeing as how nothing else about him had changed.

"Yes, ma'am. Kowalski asked me to tell you they're heading back to the dock office."

"Good, I'll join them." Dee looked up. "But first, if you have a minute, I'd like to talk with you about this thing between you and Captain Hall."

Tessa hesitated, suddenly uneasy. "I'm sorry, ma'am, but I'm not sure what you mean."

"What else could I mean, Miss Jardine? I'm referring to the *McKee* incident, of course." The Pink Widow cocked her head to one side, her delft blue gaze direct and discomforting. "You handled the reporter's questions well, thank you. But I sensed a certain . . . tension between you and the captain. You assured me your brother's death wouldn't be an issue. Has that changed?"

Tessa tamped back her rising temper. What did the woman expect, that she'd blithely forget? As if she could ever put it behind her, working day after day with Lucas Hall as a reminder.

"I can keep my professional and personal feelings separate."

Dee smiled. "You're my kind of woman, Miss Jardine. So dedicated and ambitious."

Coming from anybody else, it might've been a compliment. But with Dee Stanhope, Tessa didn't know what to make of it.

After a brief silence, Dee said, "Have I ever told you how much I admire your willingness to give up a traditional lifestyle in order to pursue your dream?"

Where the hell was this heading? "No, but thank you."

"I chose the more time-honored route to my own dreams."

Right—as if marrying a rich old man could be called "time-honored" in this day and age.

"Some people don't approve of how I did it." Dee smiled, as if she'd read Tessa's thoughts. "But Rolly understood my needs, even if he wasn't the most enlightened man. If he were still alive today, you never would've been hired as first mate."

"I know that, ma'am." With an effort Tessa kept her voice cool, even as she realized where this was heading.

"And you know how important it is to me that the *Taliesen* is a success, Miss Jardine. I'm taking quite a chance on you."

"Yes, and I *am* grateful, ma'am."

"Then I trust you won't disappoint me."

"I won't."

"Good. Now, one more thing," Dee said, stepping away from the compass. "Forgive my bluntness, but you're an attractive woman, and I feel a need to remind you that a relationship with a fellow officer is, really and truly, against the rules."

The unspoken implication—and threat—hung between them. Tessa hadn't gotten this far in her career by acting like a doormat, and if she'd harbored even an iota of interest in Lucas Hall, she might've argued with Dee.

But she only wanted to forget the man and everything he reminded her of.

"I understand," Tessa said. "Completely."

"That's what I was hoping to hear." The Pink Widow smiled again. The woman never seemed to stop smiling. "Now, I must be off. One more performance for the media, then we can call it quits for the day. Let's head back to the office together."

Tessa would rather roll in hot coals. "Sorry. I have to check in with Lowery on a few things first."

Not true, but it was a good enough excuse to avoid spending one more minute in this woman's company.

"Very well." Dee walked past, hips swaying, her silk skirt *swish-swishing*. At the door, she stopped and looked back at Tessa. Her smile faded. "I'd be here Friday for the launch if I could, but there's no way I can miss the Cleveland meeting. Promise me you'll take good care of my baby."

"As if she were my very own ship," Tessa said—and that, at least, was the absolute truth.

After Dee's departure, Tessa leaned back against the wheel and let out a long, low sigh.

Alright, there'd been an awkward moment or two today. Still, she and Hall had appeared together for the first time in public and the world hadn't come to an end. Maybe if she spent enough time around him she'd build up an immunity to the bad memories, and working with him wouldn't be so bad. She only had to treat him as she'd treated all her past captains: "Aye, sir" or "No, sir" or "Right away, sir."

How hard could it be to look at him as just another uniform?

Her confidence bolstered, Tessa headed out of the pilothouse and nearly collided with the short, squat body of Chief Engineer Amos Lowery.

Maybe the day's bad luck hadn't quite run out.

"I saw the boss," Lowery said, his gaze locked on Tessa's breasts. "She said you wanted me. I like the sound of that."

Once the older man looked up from her chest, Tessa stared him straight in the eye. "She was wrong. Now move."

"Hey, Jardine! How come you're never nice to me?"

Tessa pushed past him. "Bite me, Lowery. I'm in no mood to put up with you today."

The man's mocking laughter followed Tessa as she clanged down the ramp, annoyance fueling her forceful stride, and headed for the small office building off the pier.

Amos Lowery was a card-carrying member of the good ol' boys club; a man who still believed a woman's work was carried out in the kitchen or flat on her back.

Too bad Lowery was indispensable. He was one of the few existing engineers who knew his way intimately around a steam engine, hardware as outdated as the old man himself.

Really, she should be used to it by now. Discrimination and sexual harassment, subtle or outright, was a fact of life for any woman working in shipping. Every year she'd spent in the business had added another thick layer to her skin—but some days, even that wasn't enough.

In the dock office, Dee and her poster-perfect captain held court in one corner of the room, surrounded by most of the guests. Everybody else hovered around the food tables.

Tessa's dark mood lightened. Nothing relieved stress

better than a full stomach. Unfortunately, these days most of what she ate seemed to mutate instantly into fat cells on her hips.

Several people smiled a greeting at her, and Tessa grabbed a can of Diet Coke and smiled back. For the next half hour or so, she didn't have to do anything more taxing than smile, make small talk, and munch on fussy hors d'oeuvres.

She was contemplating the number of calories in a dollop of shrimp sauce when Rob Shea, the second mate, ambled over to join her. He, too, wore his dress uniform, his sandy hair was neatly combed, and he smelled a bit strongly of cologne. "Hey, Tess."

"Where were you earlier?"

"Kowalski wanted me to stay in the office in case any of our guests showed up late."

"You missed all the fun."

Rob shrugged. "Darn."

Tessa's attention shifted across the room toward the Pink Widow, who was laughing, her blond head bent close to Hall's. Bothered by the intimacy of the exchange, Tessa looked away. The small window air conditioner wasn't keeping up with all the body heat being generated in the room.

"I'd sure like to know how that woman manages never to sweat," she grumbled.

"She's plastic," Rob said with a grin, then added, "Your brother won't put in this afternoon. I just heard the *Houghton* set out from Gary a day behind schedule."

"Figures." Disappointing, but pretty much business as usual. She popped the shrimp-topped cracker into her mouth, her attention drifting across the room once more.

Dee had her hand on Hall's forearm and then, to

Tessa's surprise, she reached up and straightened his tie.

What a . . . wifely gesture.

Feeling tired, sweaty, and hopelessly inelegant in her permanent-press uniform and steel-toed safety shoes, Tessa made a show of glancing at her watch. Her headache was throbbing again. "Time for me to head out. See you tomorrow morning at six."

"He sure knows how to land on his feet."

"Who?" Tessa followed the direction of Rob's gaze toward Dee Stanhope and Lucas Hall. "Oh. Yeah, I guess some people are lucky that way."

"You don't like Hall?"

Tessa glanced back at Rob, noting his arched brow. "What difference does that make? He's the skipper. You know the routine."

"You're not going to forgive him about Matt, are you?"

Good old Rob; always blunt and to the point. They'd been friends since their days at the academy, and had dated briefly not long ago. Rob knew her too well for her to bluff him.

"Even if Hall gave that rescue attempt his best effort, the sister part of me—" Sudden grief hit her, still sharp and strong, as if two years hadn't passed since Matt had died. After a moment, she finished softly, "The sister part will always feel he should've known better."

Rob frowned. "He made a mistake."

True enough. Unfortunately, Lucas Hall seemed repeatedly to make his mistakes in *her* life.

"I worry about bad blood between you and the skipper. It'll cause nothing but trouble."

Again, Tessa glanced toward Hall—and met his gaze head-on. Even from across the room, the intensity of that look sent a jolt of shock through her. After a moment, he lifted his plastic punch glass in a mock salute.

Cheeks burning with anger, Tessa turned back to Rob, but didn't meet his blue eyes as she gave him a comradely jab to his shoulder. "There won't be any trouble. We're the ones who have to do all the work. He just has to stand around and look good."

Three

*F*riday morning arrived windy and warm, with filmy rays of sunshine seeping through a cloudy sky. As Lucas pulled his Jeep Cherokee into the employee parking lot behind the Stanhope port office, he could see his ship waiting quietly at anchor.

"This is it," he muttered.

Lucas grabbed his duffel bag as he got out of the car. He rubbed his damp palms against his dark blue trousers and made his way toward the *Taliesen*, thinking the refitted passenger steamer looked as out of place amid the bulky commercial freighters as he felt.

But she sure was a sight to behold.

The *Taliesen* was a grand old girl, if well past her prime, and there was nothing quite like a shiny new coat of paint to hide the years of wear and tear.

Unless it was a new uniform. Thank God for the familiarity of a uniform.

"Morning, Captain!"

Lucas raised an acknowledging hand at a group of deckhands gathered outside the ramp leading to the ship's cavernous car deck and cargo bay. They sat on empty dollies, enjoying an early-morning smoke and coffee from the ship's galley.

"You're here early," an older man said.

Lucas stopped beside them, not so much because he wanted to, but because it seemed he should. "I wanted to check her over one last time."

A young man with shaggy dark hair dug into the pocket of his gray uniform shirt, then held out a pack of Camels toward Lucas. The familiarity caught him off guard every time, even though he knew the hierarchy and code of conduct he'd lived with for half his life had no place here.

"No thanks," he said. "I don't smoke."

The man shrugged, tapped out a cigarette, and lit up. "She'll pass any test you can give her," he said, puffing with gusto. "The mate's been riding our asses all week. We got you a fine ship."

Lucas eyed the group. "Has Jardine been working you hard?"

The men laughed, and someone muttered: "She can work me hard anytime."

A grinning deckhand turned to Lucas. "Yes, sir, she sure knows how to crack that whip."

Again, the men laughed.

Lucas felt a stab of irritation at their sexual innuendo, and almost warned them against such talk. But Jardine wouldn't appreciate his effort, and his intervention would undermine her authority more than it would help.

"And where is Jardine?" he asked instead.

"In the hold, bitchin' out one of the greenhorns."

"We have a busy day ahead of us," Lucas said

evenly. "I'm sure you all can find work to do."

The smiles faded, and a few men shoved their hands in the pockets of their trousers or coveralls.

"Yes, sir. We were just finishing up our break."

With a curt nod, Lucas headed for the *Taliesen*'s hold. Behind him, a low voice murmured, "Stuck-up bastard, ain't he?"

He could've turned and barked out a stinging rebuke, but a man didn't wear these captain's stripes unless he'd earned the right to do so, and that meant projecting a façade of control and confidence. Whether he felt it or not.

No mistakes, he reminded himself.

The metal ramp clanged as he strode into the car deck, refusing to let his stiff leg slow him down. The place smelled of decades-old layers of oil and grime no amount of paint could disguise.

Although still mostly empty, the hold would soon be packed with not only passenger's vehicles, but cargo. Dee Stanhope, nobody's fool, refused to rely solely on passenger profits.

Once in the hold, Lucas didn't have to look for his mate—he could hear her. For a moment, the sound of her voice wrapped around him, uncomfortably intimate in the dim light. Her raspy, low voice perfectly matched her sultry looks. The first time he'd met her in that noisy Traverse City college bar, her voice and challenging, frank stare had sent a jolt of hot lust straight through him.

"Your name's Marshall, right?" that same voice was demanding, still alluring, still a siren's call to something bone-deep within him.

"Andy Marshall, yes, sir . . . I-I mean, ma'am."

A brief silence. "Are you nervous, Marshall?"

"Some, yeah. It's my first time out."

Lucas moved forward quietly until he could see the two of them. The "greenhorn" under fire, blond and wiry, couldn't have been much more than eighteen or nineteen. He stood stiffly in front of Jardine, who sat perched on a crate, clipboard resting across her lap. She wore a thin-lipped look of annoyance.

Poor kid.

"Marshall, do you understand what 'in trim' means?"

"Yes, ma'am. It's, like, about balance?"

"Right. And if the ship is out of trim, it's what?"

"Listing," the kid answered firmly.

"Excellent, Mr. Marshall. Now, keeping that in mind, please explain why you've arranged all twelve tractors back there"—she jerked a thumb over her shoulder toward Lucas, but didn't turn—"against the starboard hold?"

"Because Mr. Sherman told me to?"

Jardine sighed. "And you didn't think it was strange?"

The kid shifted uneasily. "I didn't want to look stupid, or bother the officers with too many questions."

"Mr. Marshall, my officers and I don't consider questions stupid. Answering questions is part of our job. I like questions. I like a trim ship and a happy captain. Okay?"

"I'll ask next time."

"Good. Right now, move six tractors to port. We have a lot full of cars and trucks to load according to point of departure, and that doesn't include the cargo and other vehicles we'll be picking up in Chicago. It's going to be tight in here."

"I'll get right on it, Miss Jardine." The kid headed for the tractors, where Lucas stood watching the exchange.

"Hey, Marshall," Jardine called.

When he saw Lucas, the young deckhand froze, the panicky expression on his face as readable as a neon sign: what to do first, answer the mate or acknowledge the captain?

"Hi, sir." The kid almost saluted, but stopped himself. "Yes, ma'am?"

Jardine twisted around, a frown creasing her brow when she saw Lucas. Her gaze cut toward Marshall, softening a fraction. "There's a lot to remember at first about working on board ship, but you're doing fine. Go take a break. You've earned one."

The kid bobbed his head. "Yes, ma'am."

Lucas waited until the sound of Marshall's footsteps faded away before walking toward Jardine. The dim lighting left her face half-shadowed—but the shadows gentled the fierce thrust of her chin and unwavering stare, and added a graceful flair to the straight back and wary tension of her muscles.

Still 200 percent female, no matter how hard she tried to hide it or deny it.

Damn; here he was, alone with her for the first time in two weeks, and instead of trying to talk to her and face this anger between them, he was checking out her curves.

The silence stretched on for several awkward seconds before Lucas cleared his throat, the sound echoing loudly. "You handled that well."

"Thank you."

Silence fell again. She slowly came to her feet, holding the clipboard against her breasts as if it were a shield.

"I've been watching Marshall. He's a hard worker and smart, which is why some of the guys are playing pranks on him." She hesitated, then met his eyes squarely, and asked, "Is there something you need from me?"

Plenty; but nothing you'd willingly give me ever again.

He took a quick, sharp breath. Where the *hell* had that thought come from? "I'm doing a final walk-through on the ship."

"She's ready. I've gone over every square inch of the *Taliesen* myself."

If she got any stiffer, she'd shatter on the next puff of breeze.

"I'm sure you have," he answered mildly as he moved closer. "But this is my ship, and the safety of every single one of her passengers and crew is my responsibility. It's not that I don't trust you, but I still intend to look her over myself."

Jardine's chin inched higher—but she didn't back away. "You're one of those hands-on kind of captains, huh?"

"I've always been a hands-on kind of guy." He held her proud, angry gaze, and added softly, "Remember?"

Her eyes darkened, and a flush stained her cheeks.

He instantly regretted his words, but the hostility radiating from this serious, straight-backed company robot, who wasn't anything like the woman he remembered, kept tripping up his good intentions.

"Look," he said, suddenly weary of the games, the guilt, "let's cut through the bullshit. I know you've got problems with me. Which one am I dealing with here: that I walked out on you years ago, or that I sent your brother to the bottom of Lake Michigan?"

She flinched, and grief briefly shadowed her eyes before she fixed him with a steely stare. "All of it. I've always been an all-or-nothing kind of gal. Remember?"

At her mocking reply, his muscles went taut as sharp desire curled deep in his belly. The tension thickened between them until he could almost taste it.

"Tessa." He touched her stiff shoulder before he could stop himself, and she recoiled immediately. He drew his hand back. "Walk the ship with me. We need to talk."

She shook her head, backing away with the clipboard crushed to her chest. "I've got too much work here to do."

As if on cue, the echo of male voices sounded nearby—no doubt the deckhands, returning to work as he'd ordered. Frustrated, Lucas glared over his shoulder, but couldn't very well order them back outside.

He turned back in time to catch a look of relief cross Jardine's face. "Get Shea to handle the cargo."

"I'd rather not. Unless that's an order, sir?"

The deckhands shuffled to a stop, watching the exchange with curious expressions.

He had the authority to force her to go with him, but doing so held no appeal—and not only because he didn't want to give the crew something to gossip about. Years of rising through the ranks had taught him to pick his battles.

"It's not an order, only a request." He waited a moment longer, in case she changed her mind. When she didn't, he added tersely, "Carry on. I'll see you topside in an hour."

"Yes, sir," Jardine said, her tone subdued.

He gave a brief nod to the staring deckhands, then climbed the narrow, steep ladder up to the salon deck.

Somehow they'd have to get beyond it all, and for the next week, as they circled Lake Michigan, he'd give her a chance. If she still hadn't come around by the time he docked the *Taliesen* at Milwaukee again, he'd pin her down for a talk. Without revealing more than he had to, he'd let Tessa Jardine know in no uncertain

terms that he needed this ship as much as she did—
maybe even more so—and he wouldn't put up with
her hostility.

Lucas leaned back against the railing and breathed
in deeply. The morning air smelled fresh and new, and
the strong wind—southeasterly, about eighteen to
twenty knots—felt cool against his face after the stifling
heat of the hold.

He'd be sailing the ship through a few six-foot
waves. It wasn't what he'd wanted for the old girl's
launch, not with a green crew and four hundred passengers, most of whom had probably seen the movie
Titanic a half dozen times apiece.

He walked down the starboard deck, running a hand
along the bottom of the lifeboats secured above him,
all freshly painted blaze orange. Neat rows of life vests
hung from the lines strung through metal eyelets on
the overhead—just as they had when she'd sailed in
her heyday, over fifty years ago.

The ship lay quiet, except for the low thrum of the
banked engine and an occasional shout from a deckhand. Standing back against the rail again, he ran his
gaze from the smokestack to the mast and pilothouse.
Colorful ensigns, strung along the mast, snapped and
billowed in the wind.

The ever-present knot in his belly twisted tighter, but
he paid it no mind and headed below deck to the engine room. Ducking through the low hatch, he found
the hot, cramped areas in turmoil. Chief Engineer
Amos Lowery stood yelling at his engineers, mechan-
ics, oilers, wipers, and firemen, sending them scurrying
along the deck and catwalks.

"Is there a problem?" Lucas asked, pitching his voice
above the noise.

The chief—a crusty old-timer who made no secret of

his contempt for the Coast Guard and its officers, retired or otherwise—barely glanced his way. "Nope.
Just a bunch of lazy asses thinking they can stand
around all day drinking coffee and eating donuts. Shea
called. The coal truck's here. We got work to do."

Which meant it was time to start boarding passengers.

Unneeded in the engine room—and unwelcome—
Lucas circled back through the two bustling cabin
decks. He returned the shy smiles of the housekeepers
as they moved between staterooms, checking to make
sure the beds were neatly made and all the amenities
in place. He stopped in the aft galley for a cup of coffee
and a jelly donut as the cooks and stewards rushed
around in a chaos of last-minute preparations. He
sniffed the air, and his stomach growled loudly.

"Smells good," he called over to the chief cook.

"You want me to make you breakfast?" she yelled
back, beaming, her round cheeks shiny with perspiration. "Eggs or bacon? Pancakes?"

Lucas shook his head, holding up his cup and donut.
"I'm all set, thanks."

After leaving the galley, he walked along the narrow
corridor between staterooms, trailing his fingertips
along the bulkhead, feeling the pulse of his ship and
listening to the language of her creaks and groans as
she rocked at anchor.

The beeping of his pager cut across his satisfied perusal. He glanced at the number, pulled out his cell
phone, and dialed the dock office.

"Hall here," he said.

"Miss Jardine has cleared the ship for boarding, sir.
We're waiting your word."

"Go ahead. I'm giving the salon deck a quick inspection, then I'll head for the pilothouse."

Lucas slipped the phone back in his jacket pocket and made his way through the main lounge and cafeteria and went topside to the salon deck.

Outside, all the chaise lounges were neatly stacked. Inside, the raised dance floor, cordoned off by a white railing decorated with cast-iron seashells, awaited its first dancers. Under overhead spotlights, the bar's curving bands of silvery chrome gleamed against contrasting black laminate.

Lucas almost expected to see Humphrey Bogart belly up to the bar and order a whiskey on the rocks. The bartenders—two college boys on summer break wearing white shirts and black trousers and vests—laughed as they polished and stacked glasses.

When the bartenders saw him, their joking stopped, replaced with a wary, respectful silence.

Lucas hesitated, and in an attempt to put them at ease, he asked, "Everything ready to go?"

"Yes, sir," quickly answered the tall blond. "This is the best-stocked bar I've ever worked. We've got everything from raspberry ale to Jack D, just like Mrs. Stanhope wanted."

With a nod, Lucas headed out on deck again. Once there, he watched passengers thread their way up the ramp and onto the main cabin deck, where Chief Purser Jerry Jackson and his team would be greeting passengers, collecting tickets, and dispensing instructions with cheerful efficiency.

Lucas ducked through the hatchway leading to the pilothouse. He took the steep, narrow steps two at a time, slowing only when he saw a familiar figure waiting for him.

For an instant, as their gazes met, he had a crazy need to find out if her lips were still as soft as they looked, and if she still made those little sighing sounds when kissing.

"I was wondering when you'd show up," Jardine said, those full, kissable lips pursed. "It's almost time to get under way."

He stepped closer until his body almost touched hers. She went very still, eyes widening in alarm. He held her gaze for a moment longer in a silent warning, then brushed past her without a response.

Wheelsman Kip McNulty came to his feet. Second Mate Rob Shea turned from the radar and nodded a greeting. As they watched him, bodies taut and eyes bright, Lucas sensed a charge of expectancy in the air— excitement mingled with launch-day jitters.

"We'd better fire up the boilers," he said. Taking hold of the engine telegraph's handle, he swung it briskly and set the telegraph at STAND BY. A moment later the engine room rang back, signaling it had received the order. Within minutes, the ship's pulse accelerated and the thrumming grew louder.

Lucas turned toward Tessa. "Are we ready for cast off?"

"The anchor detail's on standby. Rob just got word the last passenger is on board. We're ready on your order." She added stiffly, "Sir."

Lucas caught Shea's raised brow before he turned away and radioed a warning to the engine room that he was starting the motor generator setup. To Tessa, he said, "Weigh anchor and cast off all lines."

"Weigh anchor, aye."

He faced the wide window bay, and moments later the ship started to vibrate beneath his feet. The lights dimmed and flickered as the windlass strained to raise its huge anchor.

Hundreds of spectators had braved the heat to give

the *Taliesen* a proper send-off. They lined the dock, service roads, parking lots—even the walkway of the breakwater. The passengers crowding the railings smiled and waved.

The ship shuddered a final time, and a loud, metallic *clang* reverberated through the ship, signaling that the anchor was stowed.

"The watchman's on board," Jardine said from behind him. "All the mooring lines are in."

Grasping the steam whistle toggle above him, Lucas gave it a firm yank. The deafening blast reverberated over land and water. Babies and toddlers burst into tears, children clapped their hands over their ears, and adults cheered and waved.

"Time to take this old girl for a ride," he said. "Let's see what she's still got."

Lucas let off the whistle, and as a rush of anticipation and pure exhilaration swept over him, he looked at Jardine—and caught an answering gleam of excitement in her eyes, a faint hint of color on her cheeks.

"Mr. McNulty, I'll steer her out of port myself."

McNulty stepped silently away as Lucas set the telegraph at ASTERN SLOW. The bow thrusters slowly eased the ship away from the dock. As he swung the wheel, its smooth wood vibrated from the powerful thrum of the engine and the responding tension of her rudder.

"Atta girl," he crooned.

God, it was good to feel a deck pushing beneath his feet again. All the whispering doubts and fears slipped away as the *Taliesen* slipped from her berth, her bow swinging toward open water. He ordered the engine AHEAD SLOW.

Now the passengers and spectators along the breakwater waved in earnest. Even the deckhands and officers from nearby freighters and tugs hailed the *Taliesen* as she steamed past, escorted by a Coast Guard utility boat.

Lucas checked the compass, and rudder and wind gauges. Outside, a noisy chorus of gulls contended with the low roar of the wind and waves, and he glimpsed the splash of foamy white spray as the *Taliesen*'s bow sliced through the water.

It was the most beautiful sight in the world; one he thought he'd never see again. And as the *Taliesen* began to ride the waves, something deep within him suddenly loosened.

The laugh broke free before he even knew it was coming. Shea let out an answering whoop, punching his fist into the air in a victory salute, and McNulty stood grinning from ear to ear.

At the radar, Tessa turned.

For a moment, nothing else registered: not the live feel of the ship in his hands, not the beckoning blue horizon, or even the faces and voices of his crew around him. Only her eyes, and within them the spark of some deep emotion he couldn't quite read.

Lucas looked away and sounded the master's salute on the whistle—one long blast, followed by two short ones. On cue, the Coast Guard boat let loose with the ceremonial water cannon, directing a playful spray of water from their firehose up toward the huge bow of the *Taliesen*.

"Looks like an ant spitting at an elephant," Lucas said, grinning.

He glanced Tessa's way again—and this time a wide, gamine smile illuminated her face. Dazzled, he didn't remember where he was for several seconds—or what he should be doing. He forced himself to look away and focus instead on the wide blue horizon opening before him.

Four

When Lucas's rich laughter rippled over her as the bow cleared the breakwater, and a raucous cheer rose from the passengers crowded on deck, Tessa fought back a hot press of tears.

If the guys caught her crying, she'd never live it down. Even though only someone with a heart of stone would be untouched by the moment, crying would brand her as weak, and out here the weak didn't survive very long. She hastily wiped a tear from the corner of her eye, then blinked several times to clear away the last bit of telltale moisture.

Ahead lay miles and miles of turquoise-blue lake, a vast watery expanse roughly three times the size of New Jersey that reduced a 380-foot steamship to an insignificant dot.

And here she stood on that insignificant dot, with the last man on earth she'd ever wanted to see again.

Did she know how to have a good time or what?

A sudden curse cut across her thoughts, and she shot Lucas a questioning look.

"What's that kid doing hanging over the rail?" he demanded. "Where the hell are his parents? Get someone to—"

"Marshall's on it," she interrupted, pleased to see the young deckhand step forward. He hauled the enthusiastic boy safely to the deck, then hunkered down to eye level and spoke. The kid nodded earnestly, and Marshall ruffled his hair just as an elderly woman seized the boy's arm and dragged him off.

Lucas's scowl eased into a frown. "Mr. McNulty, take the wheel and keep her at one-seven-two."

"One-seven-two, aye."

Lucas raised the microphone to the shipwide speakers. "Good morning, ladies and gentlemen. This is Captain Hall welcoming you aboard the *Taliesen*. As we get under way here, I'd like to remind you that for your safety no one is allowed to climb on the rails, especially children. The water's colder than it looks, and I'd rather not have to swim today, thank you."

No sooner had his words echoed over the ship than people eased back from the railings and parents either tightened their holds on their children or pulled them down to the deck.

"Much better," Lucas muttered, then keyed the microphone again. "The travel time to Chicago, our first port of call, is approximately seven hours. It's windy today, so please see the nurse or purser in the main lounge for help with any discomfort you may experience. Thank you, and on behalf of myself and the crew, enjoy your stay on the *Taliesen*."

"You sound like a flight attendant," Tessa blurted as he replaced the microphone—and immediately wanted to kick herself for saying something so inane.

He suddenly grinned, twin dimples deeply grooving his cheeks. "I feel more like a bus driver, but right now I don't give a damn. This old girl's still got what it takes."

Flustered by his smile, and those irresistible dimples, Tessa stood, uncertain what to do next, as Lucas shrugged out of his uniform coat. Turning, he tossed it on a nearby chair. Tessa tried not to watch, but couldn't help noticing the pull of his muscles beneath the plain white shirt—and the lines of a sleeveless T-shirt.

An unwelcome warmth spread over her, and she quickly looked away. Obviously he'd kept up with his swimming, and as she knew all too well, there was nothing like a tank top to showcase a swimmer's powerful chest and shoulder musculature.

"It's a little warm in here. Rob, can you crank open the window, please," she ordered, and surreptitiously fanned her face with the clipboard. Still very aware of Lucas's gaze on her, she avoided glancing his way.

"Better?" Rob called on a refreshing blast of moist breeze.

"Yes, thanks." Tugging her tie loose, Tessa backed away from Lucas, her movements deliberately casual.

Funny, how a laugh could leave her so shaken and bring so many memories rushing back.

She only had to close her eyes to conjure up that long-ago night: a crowded bar, dim lights barely cutting through the haze of cigarette smoke, the suffocating scents of stale beer and perfume and sweat. Through the pounding decibels of rock music from the speakers by the tiny dance floor, and over the wavering wail of Stevie Nicks, she'd heard a deep, rowdy laugh and sought out its source.

A pool cue in one hand and a beer in the other, he'd stood leaning against the wall, smiling. He'd worn tight jeans and a sleeveless, ribbed tank that displayed a body no sane woman could ignore, but she'd learned to recognize an off-duty Coastie on the prowl. When he noticed her staring, he'd winked—and knocked the bottom out of her world right then and there.

A hand suddenly passed in front of her eyes. Startled, she jerked straight. "I'm sorry, were you talking to me?"

Lucas frowned. "I said, what's the report from the lookout?"

"Lookout. Right. I'm on it." Hurriedly, Tessa hailed the lookout on her two-way radio, then answered, "All clear."

Lucas eyed her for a moment longer, standing far too close again for her comfort, before turning away. He headed to the telegraph and signaled the engine room to increase speed to HALF. "What's our bearing?"

"Southbound at one-seven-two as ordered, straight for the Rawley Point Light."

Trying to look busy and efficient, Tessa glanced at her clipboard. "Our waltz-club passengers have the dance floor reserved this morning for a party, and the captain's scheduled right now to meet with them. Rob has the eight-to-twelve watch. Dave relieves him at noon."

"I know the schedule," Lucas said. His cool, clipped voice brought Tessa's attention abruptly back to him. "I'll be on my way to play the dutiful figurehead in a moment. Right now, I'd like to spend a moment on the bridge and enjoy the ride." For a moment, she swore his gaze touched on her lips, moved lower, then up again. "It's been a while."

In the sudden silence that followed, Tessa felt a stinging heat beneath her cheeks. He couldn't possibly have meant what she thought he meant. Could he?

A quick glance around the bridge showed Rob oddly intent over the radar. The wheelsman didn't take his gaze off the rudder gauge. Just then, the lookout and watchman walked through the door, laughing over some joke—but their laughter stopped the instant they sensed the tension in the pilothouse.

"Do you need me for anything?" Tessa asked at length, as if nothing was amiss.

"No."

Another heavy silence settled over the room.

"Okay . . . I'll get the weather reports together before I head off watch." Stiffly, without looking at Rob or the other men, Tessa turned and walked to the small chart room, which held a table overrun with charts and papers on one side and a small desk and computer on the other.

She stared down at the familiar navigational charts, at the shorelines, depth markings, and landmarks, willing herself to get a grip on her composure.

She caught McNulty's bemused stare and quickly looked away. Hall's voice droned on, quiet and deep. She glanced down again and skimmed the weather printouts, forcing her thoughts back where they belonged.

The reports were encouraging: windy, but no storms projected for the rest of the week. They could expect clear sailing from Chicago to Grand Haven.

Here was something to be thankful for, at least.

"I'm heading to the dance lounge."

At the sound of Lucas's voice, she glanced up, tensing. Despite her best intentions, she couldn't help drawling, "Have fun. Sir."

Lucas stopped and spun sharply. Although he said nothing, the look he gave her should've lowered the temperature in the room by a few degrees. Tessa let out her breath in a soft puff of relief as he turned again and left the pilothouse.

Glancing down at her hands, she saw they were shaking.

Rob gave a low whistle. "Hey, what was that about?"

McNulty glanced up from the wheel, and the watchman and lookout eyed her with a wary curiosity, too.

"It's nothing."

"Nothing?" Rob repeated. "It must've just been me then, and the tension between the two of you wasn't thick enough to cut."

Tessa tightened her mouth. "Don't worry about it."

"Nobody knows who opened that hatch, Tessa—and even if a lot of people have pointed fingers at Hall, a board of inquiry cleared him of any fault. You know that." Rob fixed her with a direct look, his usual smile absent for once. "At least it was quick . . . or would you rather they slowly burned to death?"

"Drop it," she warned him softly. "You're out of line."

After two years, the pain had faded, but visions of her brother's last moments still haunted her. She couldn't help wondering what had gone through his mind before that final explosion, and no board of inquiry's findings could take away the pain of losing the brother she'd all but raised from babyhood.

"You've worked hard to get here," Rob said, stepping up beside her. "And it sucks that Dee Stanhope hired the one guy who'll always remind you of Matt's death. But it's not fair to the crew or passengers if you can't do your job with a clear head. You know that."

As quickly as it had come, her anger faded, replaced by a twinge of guilt. Rob was only stating the truth, as much as she hated to admit it, and she had no right to rip him a new one for that.

"I hear you. Thanks." After a moment, she asked, "Anything else to report before I head out?"

"The *Norton* radioed to say hello and wish us luck."

Tessa smiled; she'd shipped out with the *Norton*'s skipper when she was a cadet. "Tell the *Norton* we're much obliged."

"Already did."

Her smiled widened. "Hey, you guys are good."

Rob and the other crewmen grinned back, breaking the tension. Tessa rolled her shoulder muscles, then rubbed at the stiff muscles at the back of her neck.

"I'm going down to the galley. I've been up since three this morning, and I need coffee. I'll bring you guys a thermos on my way back to my cabin."

From the dance floor, Lucas faced fifty-odd people dressed in tuxedos and gowns while the orchestra set up behind him. Chairs scraped, voices murmured over the sound of string instruments being tuned, and the organ wavered and throbbed while an oboe made a reedy run through a course of notes.

For a moment, it seemed too surreal and alien; as if he'd walked into somebody else's life. Tuxedoes. Oboes. He was back on a ship, back in a uniform, and back in command—but this edgy sensation of being out of place wouldn't go away.

That last skirmish with Tessa didn't help his temper any. One minute she was smiling, and he'd start to relax a bit, then the next minute she'd hit him between the eyes with cold animosity.

Lucas shifted and glanced around the dance lounge. A man toward the front of the gathered group caught his attention. Tall and silver-haired, he wore his tuxedo with an air of comfortable elegance.

The man smiled. "Pardon me, but I was just thinking that you look pretty young to be a captain of a ship like this."

Several of the man's retiree-aged companions stared at Lucas outright while others eyed him more discreetly—but not a single person crossed the invisible barrier of two feet of polished oak floor toward him. Wearing a uniform set him apart from others, and long ago he'd learned to live with that distance.

"I'm thirty-seven." Lucas clasped his hands behind his back. "Not that young."

"Ha," exclaimed a matronly woman in pink. "A mere baby."

"It's not the years that count, ma'am," he answered, smiling. "It's the mileage."

Over the laughter following his words, a round, balding man added, "I read you used to be in the Coast Guard. You travel a lot, then?"

Small talk. Good enough. The oboe made a breathy, sinuous sound behind him. "I did, sir. The Caribbean, South America, Japan, Alaska, and the Gulf Coast."

"How fascinating!"

"I was a Navy man myself," a wiry man put in, his gruff tone tinged with a veteran's pride.

His smile fading, Lucas turned, hearing the echo of another voice—now gone—in that pride. "My father was a career Navy man, and my grandfather before him."

At that response, the wiry man brightened. "What's your father's name?"

"Captain Samuel Hall."

"Don't believe I know him."

"He died a few years back."

"Sorry to hear that, sir." After a moment, the man

asked, "With a family history like that, how come you didn't go Navy?"

With every eye upon him, Lucas carefully chose his words. "My father had hoped I would, but I wanted to go into law enforcement. The Coast Guard seemed a good compromise."

"Captain?"

Lucas turned with relief to the conductor. "Yes?"

"We're ready, sir. To begin playing. Whenever you're ready, of course," the young conductor added hastily.

Lucas inclined his head in agreement, then turned again to face the waltz club. Their numbers had grown as curious passengers stopped to investigate.

"On behalf of Stanhope Shipping, I'd like to welcome all of you aboard the *Taliesen*," he said. He automatically braced his legs against the increasing roll of the deck, hands clasped behind his back. "No music has been heard on this ship for nearly thirty years, and all I ask, as you make a small piece of history today, is that you'll have a good time while doing so."

The silver-haired man came forward. He stumbled as the deck tilted, but quickly righted himself. "Thank you, Captain, and I hope you'll do us the honor of joining us in the first dance?"

"My pleasure," Lucas said as the orchestra began playing a stately, lyrical waltz behind him.

He crooked his arm toward the man's wife: a tall woman with steel gray hair swept up into a French twist and who wore her black evening gown with the grace of a woman half her age. She smiled at him as she slipped her arm through his and rested her hand— with a huge diamond on one finger—along his forearm.

"It's very kind of you to join us, Captain," she said,

and Lucas detected a hint of a Texas twang to her voice.

"And whom do I have the pleasure of dancing with, ma'am?" he asked as he slipped a hand around her back.

"Mrs. David Hawthorne." She smiled in the flirtatious, friendly way of an older woman with a younger man. "But you may call me Betsy."

"Only if you call me Lucas."

Her pale blue eyes widened. "Oh, but that wouldn't be proper!"

"It's a direct order, ma'am." He winked as he swung her around, enjoying himself more than he'd expected. Mrs. Hawthorne laughed and rapped his shoulder lightly with her knuckles.

"You, sir, are a scamp."

"Yes, ma'am."

She laughed again, then said, "Oh, look! There's that young lady—one of your officers, I believe."

Lucas waltzed Betsy Hawthorne around until he saw Tessa Jardine. She motioned to him discreetly and didn't look happy.

Damn. Now what?

"I'm sorry, Betsy, but it looks like duty calls." He danced her into the arms of her husband, then wound his way toward Tessa through swirling tuxedo tails and billowing silk-and-chiffon skirts in a rainbow of colors. His muscles tensed with every step closer.

"What are you doing here? You're off watch."

"A message came in for you, and Rob asked me to bring it down," she said, her tone clipped, although she focused her gaze at some point beyond his shoulder.

Like hell would he stand here, in front of *passengers*, and allow her to not look him in the eye. He moved a fraction closer. "I thought you were a deck officer, not a receptionist," he said softly.

That brought her attention right where he wanted it: on him.

"The message is confidential, and it's from Mrs. Stanhope." Her full mouth tightened. Briefly, her gaze shifted toward the dance floor, then back to him. "You do have a way with older women, don't you?"

Touché.

He returned her chilly stare, but before he could respond, a high voice behind him called, "Yoo-hoo, Captain! Would you mind posing for a picture?"

Lucas set his jaw, turned, and smiled. "Not at all."

"And the young lady, too?" A heavyset woman swathed in sky-blue chiffon beamed hopefully at Tessa.

Tessa backed away. "Ma'am, I'm on duty."

That was a lie, and he shot Tessa a quick glance, noting a flush darkening her high cheekbones.

"Oh, honey, it'll only take a second, really. Without a picture, the gals back home won't believe I talked with a handsome ship captain or saw a lady officer. *Please?*"

There was no graceful way to wiggle out of the request, and Tessa knew it. Her chin rose a fraction even as she smiled, and said politely, "I'd be happy to pose for one photo, ma'am."

Her firm tone almost made him smile. Tessa Jardine could hold her own against even the most aggressive, camera-toting tourist.

"The two of you together. On the dance floor, okay?"

"Here we go again," Lucas murmured.

Tessa glanced up, and below the wariness, sudden amusement gleamed. Then, as quickly as it had come, the moment of camaraderie passed.

With a dance floor full of passengers, Lucas played his role to the hilt. He held out his hand and, after a hesitation, Tessa took it. With a half smile, his gaze holding hers, Lucas raised her hand—warm, smooth, with nails clipped short—to his lips and kissed it as she stared at him as if he'd lost his mind. But she didn't dare protest or pull away.

Laughter rumbled behind them, along with scattered applause, and Tessa's cheeks pinkened. She remained silent as he took the hand he'd just kissed and tucked it in the crook of his arm, then led her to the edge of the dance floor. The blue-chiffon lady chattered away, her words fast and high with excitement. "Pose like you're dancing," she said, the camera to her face. "Oh, Lord, the gals just aren't going to believe this!"

Lucas couldn't believe it either—that he was standing before all these people with Tessa Jardine in his arms. Despite an inner whispery warning to keep a professional distance, he slowly slid his hand down along the curve of her spine until it rested on the small of her back, just above her bottom. She stood absolutely motionless, staring straight ahead at his tie tack, her cheeks still pink.

God, she smelled so good.

Although Tessa held herself stiffly, she felt warm and soft, and her hair brushed his chin, catching on the stubble of his beard. The familiarity tugged at him, and for an instant he regretted no longer having the right to pull her closer, to slide his hand lower and skim the rounded curve of her bottom . . .

" . . . such a lovely couple."

"She *is* striking, isn't she? What a strange line of work for such a pretty girl . . ."

The low voices carried to Lucas over the music, but he paid them no mind, more shaken than he cared to admit at holding her like this, so close against him.

What he wouldn't give to take back all the pain he'd caused her. Still so familiar, the line of her cheek, the curve of her lips, and the intimate arch of her back. He spread his hand, his fingers brushing lower. Slowly, Tessa raised the fringe of her lashes and looked directly into his eyes.

The camera's flash yanked Lucas back from plunging into dark, dangerous waters. As Tessa blinked, he quickly broke their contact before he made an unforgivable mistake.

Like kissing her on the lips.

"Thank you," said their beaming photographer, unaware of the discomfort she'd caused her two models. "I do appreciate your taking the time to pose for me."

"It was our pleasure, ma'am," Lucas said. His, anyway. "Now, if you will excuse us, we have to be on our way."

Raising a hand in farewell, Lucas turned and headed toward the officers' quarters. Passengers made way for him, a few smiling, most with startled or curious looks. He didn't check to see if Tessa followed or not.

Once in the private corridor, he glanced over his shoulder. As expected, Tessa stood right behind him.

"Come to my cabin," he ordered, and continued on without waiting. The officers' deck was quiet, although he could hear the low drone of a television from one cabin.

Lucas walked into his office, which adjoined his bedroom, and shut the door. He moved to his desk and leaned against it. Then he asked, "Where's the note?"

Wordlessly, she handed over a piece of paper, careful not to touch him. Nor did he miss how her gaze darted around the room with unease before she returned her attention to him.

"Is there something wrong, Miss Jardine?" he asked. When she didn't answer, he added, "Being alone with me makes you uncomfortable."

From her startled expression he knew he'd guessed correctly, yet she shook her head.

Repressing a sigh, Lucas settled on her a look that told her not to move, then he unfolded the note and skimmed Shea's scrawl, anger rising with every word he read.

Confidential, his ass.

"Bad news?"

Looking up, he detected no more animosity than usual, which meant she hadn't read it.

"No."

Her brow arched, and he could guess what conclusion she'd reached. It did nothing to improve his mood.

"You can go," he said curtly. "The message requires no action on your part."

Tessa didn't move, and her frown drew his attention to her mouth. He focused on her lips for a fraction too long, and when he looked up, that familiar, thick tension fell between them—a tension charged with a dangerous awareness.

"Did you want something more from me, Miss Jardine?" he asked softly. Before he could think twice, he pushed away from his desk and walked toward her.

Tessa took a quick breath, and despite his better intentions, he watched the rise of her breasts beneath her shirt.

God, he was a dog.

"No, sir, I do not."

"You're certain of that?"

She folded her arms across her chest, eyes narrowing. "As sure as humanly possible. And if you ever maul my hand like that again, you can bet I'll make you regret it."

After two weeks of her avoidance and icy silences, even threats were progress. Of a sort.

"You didn't always mind my kisses."

She only arched a brow, and said coolly, "I was young and easily impressed."

Lucas almost smiled, not sure what he admired more: her poise or her guts. She tipped her head to better meet his eyes, and his gaze again dropped to her lips.

It made no sense, this attraction. He couldn't even exchange a civil word with her; why the hell did he keep thinking about kissing her?

"Tessa, we need to work together. It's time to put aside our differences. I'm offering the olive branch," he said, then added wryly, "A kiss of peace."

Her eyes blazed. "I'd as soon eat lake muck as kiss you ever again, Lucas."

She'd finally called him *Lucas*—not *sir*. And she should've remembered he never, ever backed down from a challenge.

Lucas bent closer, and her eyes widened as she realized he wasn't just goading her this time. She put her hands on his chest to hold him off and leaned back, and he found himself pressing a soft kiss not on her forehead, as he'd intended, but on her mouth instead.

For a split second, Lucas froze, then he seized the opportunity and really kissed her. She resisted for a moment, then responded. It was all his instincts needed to take her shoulders and pull her against him.

At the sweet taste of her heated need shot through him, and when a soft sigh escaped her, he slid his hands from her shoulders down to her bottom and pulled her against his stirring arousal.

Instant, hot, mindless—God, one kiss and she made him lose all control, just as she had years ago.

Tessa suddenly broke the kiss and, with all her strength—which was considerable—shoved him away.

For a long moment they stared at each other, then Tessa whispered, "Why did you do that?"

"Damn good question," he said tightly. "Maybe I wanted you to stop looking right through me as if I'm not here."

"Professional ethics—"

"This has nothing to do with professional ethics, and you know it," he interrupted harshly. "This has to do with you and me. What's between you and me."

Perhaps it *was* the mention of ethics that finally made him back away—but more likely it was the swell of emotion in her dark eyes, anger and grief and bewilderment, sharply reminding him that he'd caused her trouble enough.

"I think I'd better leave now."

He made no protest, no move to stop her. Tessa hesitated, then turned and walked out of his cabin with stiff dignity.

Lucas told himself it was for the best that she'd left when she had. Right now, with the feel of her lips still fresh in his mind and her closeness fanning the heat of an unwise desire, he needed her as far away from him as possible.

He sank down onto his leather desk chair. For a long moment, he stared at the door through which Tessa had left, replaying what he'd done, trying to understand how he could've let himself lose self-control like that.

Finally, with a low curse, he pushed the thoughts away and looked down at his desk, where Dee's note lay open. Frowning, he picked it up and read it again:

I need to talk to you as soon as you return to Milwaukee. Leave the details to me. I'll arrange a nice, quiet dinner away from all the usual restaurant hubbub. I need your advice on a matter, and only your advice will do.

He could imagine what that "advice" entailed.

Usually he liked strong, intelligent women who knew what they wanted and went after it. He appreciated a woman who didn't consider a wedding ring a measure of her self-worth and yet still enjoyed being female—but it sure wasn't a vision of Dee's blond hair or model-slender body drifting across his mind, tantalizing him with images, sensations, and possibilities.

With another curse, Lucas crumpled the note and tossed it into his trash can.

The next five days couldn't pass fast enough. And as he stared at the clock, watching the seconds tick away, he vowed to give Tessa Jardine a wide berth for the remainder of the voyage—and, when they'd both cooled down, an apology.

Five

The *Taliesen* returned to Milwaukee from her maiden voyage, and Tessa, like any sailor, wasted no time in getting off the ship. Being cooped up for nearly a week with an ex-lover who watched her so often made her all the more anxious to escape.

After the first day—and that kiss in his cabin—Lucas had kept his distance. He didn't try to corner her again, and he was civil whenever forced to share the pilot-house or officers' mess with her. But he was still *there*, his presence like a live wire crackling a warning to keep her distance—as if her own inner alarms didn't buzz like crazy when she heard his voice or merely his name mentioned.

Foolish, to go all hot and light-headed and fluttery because he'd kissed her. It had been ten years, for heaven's sake. A lot of water had passed under both their bridges. Life, experience . . . and no doubt other lovers.

It was so irritating, not knowing how to act around Lucas. Nobody had ever taught her the proper protocol for dealing with a man who'd been responsible for a brother's death, and though she'd sworn to Dee Stanhope she could work with Lucas, she now wondered if she'd made a major mistake. Theory and reality weren't meshing quite as she'd imagined.

Tessa winced as she slid into her car. Days in the sun had left the seat griddle-hot, and the air inside was heated and thick. She tossed her cap into the backseat and yanked off her tie. With the air conditioner blasting, she drove away from the port complex, determined to leave all her shipboard problems at the dock.

For a few days, anyway.

It helped that her brother Steve's ship would arrive in another hour—late, as usual—and since their schedules meshed for once, he'd asked her to dinner at his place. As the car's interior cooled and she made most of the green lights, her mood lightened. Nobody in the universe grilled marinated chicken like her sister-in-law, Nina.

It had been months since she'd seen her niece and nephew, and Amy had to be—what? Tessa frowned, counting as she roared through a yellow light. Amy was born while Steve's ship was laid up in Escanaba for repairs last August, which made her almost eleven months old. Soon she'd celebrate her first birthday.

When had time started to fly by so quickly? Lately, she couldn't seem to keep up with all she needed to do, and thoughts about her own approaching birthday left her feeling a little panicky and restless.

Thirty. Good God, she was nearly thirty!

Fifteen minutes later, that restlessness still lingering, Tessa pulled up to a cozy, older house nearly identical to the others surrounding it.

The place looked typical 1950s: two stories, fenced yard, and detached garage. It couldn't compare to the yuppie palaces in the suburbs, but it was close to the port— and when a guy only had a few hours to see his wife and family before shipping out again, every minute mattered.

Tessa shut off the engine and ran a hand through her windblown hair, making a mental note to get it cut soon. She shut the car door, and spotted her nephew, in shorts and grubby T-shirt, kicking a red ball around the front yard. "Hey, Tommy!"

The boy looked up, beaming. "Mommy, Auntie Tessie's here!"

The minute she cleared the gate, Tommy launched his skinny, six-year-old body against her legs. Laughing, Tessa scooped him up and swung him upward. He howled with laughter, his dark hair tumbling into his eyes.

"Hey, Tess!" Her sister-in-law stood in the doorway, dark hair in a ponytail and wearing shorts and a T-shirt, the baby perched on her hip. Even as Nina smiled a greeting, her gaze slid past Tessa toward the street.

Tessa recognized that expectant look; it was one her mother had worn far too often before she'd finally had enough and traded in her sailor husband for a nine-to-fiver, leaving her four young children in care of a paternal aunt.

"Steve's ship is late," she said. "The *Houghton* put out of Gary an hour behind schedule."

"What's new," Nina said with a sigh.

Tessa looked away from the disappointment in Nina's brown eyes. "Oooph, Tommy, you weigh a ton."

She deposited her nephew on the front step and followed Nina into the house.

"Wow, look at you," Nina said, shutting the door. "I feel a salute coming on here. Great to see you, *ma'am*! Where the hell have you been, *ma'am*? Have you forgotten how to dial a phone, *ma'am*?"

"Enough with the guilt thing," Tessa said with a grin. "I had three days to move down here from Duluth, and Stanhope hardly gave me any time to fit out the *Taliesen*. For the past few weeks, I've been living on tuna fish and crackers and four hours of sleep a night."

Nina rolled her eyes as she headed toward the kitchen. Tessa followed, sniffing the aromatic air. Garlic. And—thank God!—something definitely, blissfully chocolate.

"Tess, honey, what you need is a house-husband."

"As if I'll ever find a guy like that in the dockyards or on board ship. What I really need is to win a five-year supply of Lean Cuisine. Ack, look at these hips!"

Nina cast a critical eye over her. "News flash: you're a woman. You're supposed to have curves."

"I could do with a few less, thank you very much." Tessa sat at the table, next to a pan of freshly baked frosted brownies. She sighed. "And I'm just a girl who can't say no."

"Tell me something." Niná turned, her expression curious as she shifted Amy in her arms. "What's the point of this female empowerment stuff if you can't do a so-called man's job while acting and looking like a woman?"

Taken back by the question, a moment passed before Tessa shrugged. "That's the way it's supposed to work. In theory, anyway."

"Then it shouldn't matter if you have hips. You look great, by the way. Hey, don't touch," Nina warned as Tessa hooked her index finger over the pan and pulled it closer. "You know how territorial Steve gets about my brownies."

Tessa inhaled a mist of moistly warm brownie scent, and gave a little shiver. "I bet these aren't low-fat."

"You know, some things in life shouldn't be faked. Like chocolate." Nina grinned. "And sex."

With a laugh, Tessa pushed away from the table and helped Nina prepare dinner, chopping vegetables, sharing family gossip, and listening to Nina talk about her new day-care job. After they'd finished, Tessa scooped up the baby and raced Tommy out to the small backyard, where Nina was firing up the gas grill.

While Tommy kicked his ball around the yard, Tessa leaned back, the grass prickling her elbows, and coaxed her niece to creep toward her. Amy pulled herself up using Tessa's shirt and intently examined her shoulder boards. Breathing in deeply, Tessa took in the scent of freshly mown grass, baby powder, and grilling chicken. A yellow jacket, lazy with the heat, buzzed past her ear.

She had to admit the landlubber's life held a certain appeal.

"Somebody decide to throw a party and forget to invite the man of the house?"

At the deep, familiar voice, Tessa turned. Her brother stood casually propped against the back doorframe, still in his work coveralls, a grin stretched across his sun-darkened face.

"Steve!" Joy lighting her face, Nina let out a squeal and ran toward him. He moved quickly down the steps and caught her in his arms, lifting her high off the ground as he wrapped her in a fierce embrace and brought his mouth down on hers.

Oh, boy.

Tessa watched the kiss, embarrassed and wistful and

knowing she should turn aside and give them a moment of privacy—but she couldn't move. God, it was just so *romantic*! The last time she'd been kissed like that . . .

Had been only a few days ago.

Her face burning at the memory of Lucas's kiss and her response to it, Tessa watched as Nina slid down Steve's body, kissing him hungrily and holding on to him by a fistful of fabric as he ran his hands with a slow, lazy intent over her curving bottom.

Overwhelmed by a sudden sense of emptiness, Tessa looked away. She stood and picked up Amy, and squeezed her eyes shut as she rubbed her cheek over the baby's fine, flyaway hair.

Tommy yelled, "Daddy!" and Tessa listened to the rapid thud of his racing footsteps. Laughter and giggles sounded behind her, and loud smacking kisses as father and son greeted each other.

How did Steve do it? A good job as a second engineer, a great wife, and two beautiful kids. He'd missed Amy's birth, and would miss a lot of birthdays, anniversaries, and other family events over the years, but somehow he and Nina made it work.

The chances of finding a husband who'd put up with her own schedule weren't very good, as several failed relationships had already proven. Even if she married someone in shipping, that didn't leave much of an opportunity to raise a family; not with one or both parents out for days on end.

"Hey, Tess." Steve's voice cut across her morose thoughts. "Is that my best girl you're hiding over there? You can turn around now. We're done with all that mushy stuff."

Smiling again, Tessa turned to face her brother.

"Mushy? I expected to see the grass singed black and still smoking."

Nina colored, but Steve only grinned. He gave Tessa a quick kiss on her cheek, then reached for Amy. The baby at once stuck out her lip and turned her face into Tessa's neck.

Steve knew better than to push it, and settled for running a hand over her back. Despite the flash of disappointment in his eyes, he smiled. "She's too little to understand why this big noisy guy keeps poppin' in and out. Hey, it's Daddy, sweetheart. You didn't forget me already, did you?"

"After a few minutes I'm sure you'll have her cooing."

"Yeah, I have that effect on women, don't I?" Steve turned toward his wife, winked, and picked up Tommy. "That chicken of yours ready, babe? I'm starved."

Nina's eyes shone bright. "Almost. You guys head on in."

Halfway through dinner, as Amy cried, Tommy chattered nonstop, and Nina and Steve kept making eyes at each other, the phone rang. Steve answered, and after a brief conversation punctuated by laughter, he yelled, "Tess, it's Dad. He's calling from Marquette. Wanna talk to him?"

Tessa met Nina's gaze before looking away. "Nah. Tell him I don't have anything new to say since the last time we talked."

It was a blatant untruth and didn't fool anybody. When Steve sat at the table again, he said, "I wish you wouldn't do that. In his own way, Dad's proud of you."

Tessa cut off a chunk of chicken, but didn't respond. The tense silence stretched on a little longer before

Steve added, "So . . . what have you been up to? You and Rob Shea still dating?"

"No, and I don't think we ever qualified as *dating*. We only went out for dinner a couple of times."

"You don't sound too broken-up about it."

Tessa met her brother's gaze across the table. "It worked out for the best. He's second mate on the *Taliesen* now, and Dee Stanhope doesn't like her officers getting too cozy."

"You'll never get serious with a guy who's in your same line of work."

"Now who sounds like Dad?" Tessa shot her brother a warning look. "I appreciate your worry, but it's unnecessary. I made a decision to focus on my career, and that's what I'm doing."

Steve eyed her over his glass of milk. "You weren't even twenty when you made that decision. Ten years is a long time, and you're a woman—"

"What does that have to do with it?" she interrupted.

Steve scowled. "What I was going to say, before you jumped down my throat, is that unlike us guys, women can't wait too long to have kids, and you're always telling me you want kids."

Tessa glanced toward the high chair, where Amy sat smearing Spaghetti-Os over the tray—and an undeniable pang of longing shot through her.

"I plan on having a family, but not right now. The timing's not right," Tessa said, her tone putting an end to the subject. "And I'm not ready, anyway."

After dinner, everyone gathered in the living room to watch the news on TV, just in time to catch the brief coverage of the *Taliesen*'s triumphant return to port.

At the inevitable mention of the *McKee*, and a brief close-up of Lucas Hall standing on the deck looking the part of the strong, stalwart captain, silence fell over the room. For a while, the only sounds heard were those of Amy nursing and Tommy's growling roars as he played with a toy monster truck his father had brought home as a present.

Tessa glanced away from the television, and her gaze fell on Matt's high-school graduation portrait hanging on the opposite wall. Above it, Nina had arranged a spray of dried flowers taken from the memorial ceremony. In the photo, Matt was smiling, bright-eyed and fresh-faced. So young; expecting so much of life. He hadn't lived even long enough to attend his first high-school reunion.

And to die the way he had . . . sometimes, even now, she couldn't hardly bring herself to think about it.

"I wish they'd let the *McKee* rest," Steve said, his voice tight, and Tessa turned back. "It was bad enough when those divers took pictures of the wreck last year, and people starting calling again, asking questions. Why drag it up every chance they get?"

"It's a burial site now," Nina said, reaching over with her free hand to squeeze his in comfort. "There won't be any more dives. Those poor men can finally rest in peace."

Steve looked toward Tessa. "Did they ask you about it?"

"That guy from *City Beat* wanted to know how I felt about working with the man who blew up my brother."

Steve swore softly. "Dee Stanhope was out of her mind to hire Hall. Even a pinhead like her should've known how hard it would be for you to work with him. What the hell was she thinking?"

"That he looks hot," Nina murmured, a brow raised. She inclined her head toward the television, which showed Lucas and Dee standing side by side. "I've been watching them together on the news for weeks now, and they make a pretty couple. Her husband's been dead for what, three years?"

"Hall is experienced," Tessa said after a moment, shifting her focus away from the image of Lucas and the Pink Widow. "Not that he needs defending from me, but it's true."

"Come on," Steve scoffed. "All you know about the guy is what you've read in the newspapers, and hauling a tub full of refugees back to Cuba isn't experience with a passenger vessel in my book."

Tessa looked down at her nephew, watching his cheeks vibrate as he made motor noises.

Wounded pride had prevented her from telling her family about her affair with Lucas. After years trying to forget she'd been such a fool, now wasn't the time to confess she knew a lot more about the man than anyone thought.

God, what had she been thinking, to let him kiss her? What had *he* been thinking?

"I heard a few rumors at the dock today," Steve said, interrupting her thoughts. "Is he sleeping with Dee Stanhope?"

Tessa glanced up. "They seem awfully chummy, and she's always touching him, so I suppose the gossip's true."

Which made her kissing him back even more disgusting. Dammit! She should've slapped his arrogant, handsome face.

"Great. And my sister's taking orders from a man whose major qualification is the size of his dick. How can you stand working with the guy?"

The anger in his question brought a fresh rush of guilt. "This isn't the first time I've worked with a skipper I didn't like. The job's important to me. Please don't think I'm selling out Matt for a promotion."

"Aw, Tess, I didn't mean for it to sound like that." A few moments passed before he shot her a lopsided smile and poked her with his elbow. "Hey. Did I tell you what a babe you are in that uniform?"

The teasing remark snapped the tension. Nina burst out laughing, and Tessa jabbed Steve back.

"Jerk," she said with fond exasperation as she pushed up from the couch. "I'd better get going. The two of you keep looking at the clock, and I know what that means."

"Yeah." Steve flashed a roguish grin. "I haven't seen my wife for nearly a week and it's almost bedtime."

"Daddy, no," Tommy wailed. "I don't wanna go to bed; I wanna stay up and play with you!"

"Once he learns to tell time, you'll have to come up with a better fib." Tessa kissed her nephew's cheek, then Amy and Nina. "Thanks for the doggie bag. Steve, if I don't see you before the *Houghton* ships out tomorrow, have a safe trip."

"Same to you," Steve called after her. "And stay out of trouble!"

"You look like something left for dead."

"So take the hint and walk on by." Lucas didn't open his eyes. "You're standing in front of my sun."

The pier's weatherworn boards creaked as Kevin Carter moved. Sunlight fell warmly across Lucas's bare chest and legs again, its golden light penetrating his closed lids.

Lizards and turtles had the right idea, lazing around in the hot sun, listening to waves lapping against the shore, dragonflies buzzing by, and the wind whispering in the trees. The air smelled sweet and musty.

For the past two years, his life had been like this—drenched with peaceful sensations, sounds, and scents. After a week like he'd just had, he was almost sorry he'd left it at all.

"UV rays cause cancer." Kevin's voice broke across his thoughts again. "I can think of quicker ways to kill yourself, if that's what you're aiming for."

"Thanks. I'll keep your offer in mind."

"Things didn't go so well, huh?"

"Nope."

"That woman still giving you a hard time?"

Lucas cracked open an eye and stared up at his brother-in-law. With the sun behind him, Kevin's brown hair had a reddish glow.

"Which woman?" Lucas shut his eye again, trying to recapture the peace he'd had only moments before. "The one who wants to screw me, or the one who wants to gut me?"

A long silence followed. "You sure know how to get yourself into tight spots, Luke."

Since there was nothing to say to that particular fact of life, Lucas didn't answer. But with his peace flown, he slowly sat up and eyed the calm, blue water of the lake. Another hard swim might tire him out. He had to catch some sleep tonight.

"Are you going to do something about it?"

Lucas shifted, and looked up. "About what?"

Kevin snorted. "She's rich, a looker, and willing. If she wants to get to know you—"

"Dee Stanhope has no interest in getting to *know* me," Lucas said dryly. He'd considered telling Kevin about his "date" with Dee, but now thought better of it. Kev would only get the wrong idea.

"So? A bit of recreational sex would do you some good. What can it hurt?"

"She signs my paycheck."

"That doesn't seem to bother *her*."

Lucas looked out across the water, squinting against the sun sparkling across its surface, as another woman's image flashed to mind: dark hair and eyes—and a lush, soft mouth. "I have enough problems right now without adding to them."

"You can always come back to work for me," Kevin said.

"I appreciate the offer, but I can't."

Working on Kevin's fishing boat the past two years had meant long hours filled with hard, dirty work. At the end of each day, he'd been too exhausted to do more than crash into bed and snatch a little sleep before waking again before dawn. At the time, when he'd needed a reason even to get out of bed, working on the *Katie Lee* had given him one.

"We made a pretty good team."

Lucas smiled. "Yeah, we did. Even if you were a goddamn slave driver."

Kevin grinned back. "You haven't given up the idea of owning your own boat and opening a charter business, have you? I thought for a while there you'd go for it."

Lucas turned his attention back to the water. "It was all talk, about the boat. Just spinning a bunch of crazy ideas."

"Didn't sound so crazy to me."

At the time, it hadn't sounded crazy to him, either. Then Dee Stanhope had called, and he'd put aside all those half-formed plans. He looked back up at his brother-in-law. "I made my choice, and it's the right one. I'm doing this for me."

Kevin rocked back on his heels, hands on the waistband of his swim trunks, and asked, "Thinking of going for another swim before Diane and the kids get back from their walk?"

"Maybe."

The dark calmness of the water beguiled; its waves whispered. He sensed movement and looked over at Kevin's extended hand. Lucas grasped it and pulled himself stiffly to his feet. Almost without thought, his fingers found the long scar on his right leg and massaged it.

His leg ached most on wet, cold days. No amount of swimming seemed to help, and he had a bad feeling that with the next foggy morning, he'd be hobbling about the *Taliesen*'s decks like Captain Ahab.

Not the dashing image Dee Stanhope was shooting for.

"When are you shipping out again?" Kevin asked.

"Friday."

Two days was all he had; precious few hours of lying in the sun, trying not to think, soaking up enough peace to get him through another voyage—without any more stupid mistakes like kissing his mate.

"How long will you be gone again?"

"Nearly a week. We hit Chicago and Grand Haven, then head up along the Traverse Bay resort towns to Mackinac Island." Lucas slipped on his T-shirt, the cotton dry and hot against his skin. "Then I take the ship to Green Bay before we return to port in Milwaukee. If the weather holds and we make good time, we have a few days off before shipping out again."

"Sounds like you've got a busy summer ahead of you."

"We're booked solid through mid-October."

October. Three months of seeing Tessa Jardine on a

daily basis, with that damn kiss simmering between them.

"What's the matter?" Kevin asked.

"Nothing."

"So why the pissed-off look?"

Before Lucas could answer, the sound of childish squeals erupted behind them, and he turned to see his four nieces and nephews—like nesting dolls in height, each no more than two years apart—come on the run toward the lake.

He watched as one after the other jumped off the pier into the water. Even the youngest, three-year-old Sarah, could swim like a fish. Kevin and Diane owned a prime piece of lakefront property with a modest vacation cabin—which Lucas was now renting from them—and all their kids had learned to swim before they could walk.

"Hey, Luke! Are you going to jump in after them?" asked his youngest sister, Diane.

She'd put on weight over the past few years, and wore a skirted swimming suit designed to disguise it. Her full breasts, pushing against the Lycra, revealed a deep V of cleavage.

More than once, Lucas had caught Kevin leering at his wife—and after ten years of marriage and four kids, Lucas considered a healthy lust like that pretty damn amazing.

"Maybe." As he kept a sharp eye on the splashing kids, Lucas stretched, feeling like a lazy cat in a sunbeam. "I went on my two-miler a while ago. But I can always use the exercise."

Diane eyed his chest as she leaned comfortably against Kevin's wiry body. "Like you need it. We could scale fish on your belly."

Smiling, Lucas returned his attention to the lake. The

bottom was fairly shallow for a good twenty-five feet out, but by habit he kept the children in his field of vision.

Counting heads, he suddenly went still. Where was Kyle?

"Help!"

The high-pitched scream cut across the peaceful quiet. Icy fingers of fear closed hard around him, and Lucas spun toward the source of the cry.

"Help! Lizzie, help me!"

Oh, God, mister . . . please! Help me, don't let me die . . .

Go . . . go now! All he had to do was dive, and swim fast and hard toward his flailing nephew—but a paralyzing fist of powerless fury held him locked in place.

The cloying sweet scent of gasoline filled his lungs, even though he knew it wasn't real. Sweat beaded on his forehead, his upper lip, and slicked his palms. The roar of rushing blood pounded in his ears.

Despite it, he forced himself to take a step, then another. As he pounded to the end of the pier at a run, a giggle sounded and he jerked to a halt.

"Fooled ya, Liz!" Kyle splashed around, playfully kicking up sprays of water. "Got you back, stupid!"

A joke. Jesus, just a joke . . .

Lucas squeezed his eyes shut, and a violent shudder ripped through him. His knees gave out, and he sat heavily on the sun-warmed wood. Breathe. In, then out; deep breaths from his belly, filling himself—toes first, then slowly upward until the intense anxiety was pushed aside by the cleansing air.

Face it. See it. Cage it. Control it. . . .

"Kyle!" Kevin's yell cut across Lucas's regimented thoughts. "How many times do I gotta tell you not to pull crap like that, especially with Uncle Luke here!"

The laughter and playful splashing stopped. Behind

him, Diane sighed. Silence followed, heavy with discomfort.

To hide his shaking hands, Lucas rubbed at his leg—up and down that long pale scar.

"Hey." A hand, callused and warm, rested on his shoulder. "Luke? You okay?"

Okay? He'd never be "okay" again, and they all knew it.

Lucas set his jaw and glared at Kevin—and the look on his face. "Lose the pity, dammit!"

"It's not pity, you idiot, it's concern." Kevin glared back, then made a sound of frustration. "It's not too late. You don't have to do this. We're behind whatever decision you make, but you know there's a hundred other guys who'd be happy to take your place on the *Taliesen*—"

"No."

Diane turned away, busying herself with folding beach towels so that she didn't have to look at Lucas—good thing; she cried too easily—and the kids huddled together, wide-eyed and solemn.

Lucas swallowed, his throat dry. "I'm going to beat this. I won't let it keep me down."

"We're right here behind you," Kevin repeated quietly. "No matter what happens. Remember that."

Lucas stood, looking down as he backed away, fingers clenching as he fought against emotions too close to the surface. If anyone touched him now, the thin shell of his self-discipline would shred and he'd lose it. Just lose it, and come apart in a million humiliating pieces.

"Time for a chat with that idiot boy of mine," Kevin said grimly. "If he pulls a stunt like that again, he's grounded for the rest of his natural life."

"I'm going to shower up. I have a meeting in Milwaukee soon." As Lucas padded barefoot down the pier toward the cabin, a sudden resolve took hold of him.

It was way past time to tie up loose ends. And since his peaceful day was already shot—because of a ten-year-old boy's pranks and the battle of wits he'd face with his dinner "date"—he might as well finish off the day with a bang, and corner Tessa for a talk.

Six

"**A**re you sure you wouldn't like some wine? The house brand is exquisite."

Lucas raised his hand, declining the wine bottle the waiter held out. "No thanks. I don't drink."

After the waiter left, Dee raised a brow. "Really? How very nonadventurous of you."

Leaning back in his chair, Lucas surveyed the intimate, posh downtown-Milwaukee restaurant Dee had chosen. The place was all shining gold and reflective glass, accented in black and gray—an attractive showcase for Dee's pale beauty and icy pink sheath dress that showed a lot of her trim, tanned legs.

"I was plenty adventurous in my younger days. You could say I adventured myself out."

"Given your particular problem, I suppose there's the danger of giving in to the urge to self-medicate."

He sipped his lemon water, eyeing her. "Play nice, Dee."

Tipping her head to one side, she studied him with interest. "That was a compliment, actually. I've always thought drunkards and drug addicts were of weak character to begin with, and I doubt very much there's a weak bone in your body."

Slowly, her gaze slid down over his traditional dark suit and basic striped tie. Annoyed, Lucas glanced away—and caught the stylish, middle-aged couple at the next table staring at him with curiosity. He stared back until they looked away.

"No games," he said coolly, turning his attention back to his dinner partner. "What do you want from me?"

She smiled at him over a glass of Sauvignon Blanc. "Didn't you read my message? I need your advice."

He returned her perusal, no more subtle than she'd been. With the careless unconcern of a woman comfortable with her body and its usefulness, Dee sat back, arranged herself for maximum male appreciation, and let him look.

Her skin glowed with youthful vitality, although the restaurant's lighting didn't disguise the faint lines around her eyes and mouth. Still, not a single strand of gray showed in her golden hair, and she had high, round breasts and a slender figure unmarked by childbirth.

Beautiful, and about as perfect as a woman could get—if a guy went for that Trophy Wife look.

"You could've just called me up," he said.

"I didn't feel comfortable talking about it on the phone." At his pointed look, she cleared her throat, looking faintly embarrassed. "I think someone is . . .

trying to scare me. You've dealt with the criminal element in your past. I thought you could tell me if it's something I should worry about or not."

Masking his surprise, he said, "You better be playing straight with me."

"Of course I am! What did you—" She stopped, shooting him a look of disbelief. "You think I'm making up some silly story so I could lure you here, make you feel sorry for me, and then seduce you."

"The thought crossed my mind."

"Trust me, darling, if I'm going to seduce you, you're going to know it. I don't do ambiguity."

Lucas couldn't help but smile. To his surprise, a blush stole across Dee's cheeks, the first real hint at warmth he'd noticed since she'd hired him on months ago.

"It's not funny! Here, read these." She pulled two folded squares of paper from her evening bag and handed them to him. "My secretary at the Milwaukee office found them under my door."

He opened the first, frowning as he skimmed over the laser-printed note:

Knock, knock.
Who's there?
Ice.
Ice who?
Just ice.

" 'Just ice.' " He looked up. "That doesn't make sense."

"It obviously made sense to whoever wrote it," Dee retorted as she took a quick gulp of her wine. "Read the other one. It's even lovelier."

When she returned the glass to the table, hand trembling, a little spilled onto the black tablecloth. A nice touch—and she seemed paler than usual—but he knew Dee wasn't above dramatics or using a dirty trick or two. He opened the second note:

Rock-a-bye pretty baby on the sea-saw
When the wind BLOWS AWAY the cradle will crack.
When the bough-wow breaks,
The cradle will fall, and
Down will go baby, cradle and all.

A chill settled over him. "Shit."

"Yes, it's rather difficult to be blasé about creepy, unsigned knock-knock jokes and nursery rhymes, isn't it?" She tossed back the rest of her wine. "Do you think someone is threatening to kill me? 'Blow me away' or 'ice' me? Isn't that the usual slang of street thugs?"

"Could be," Lucas said. "And I don't think I'm the one to help you here. This is beyond my experience. You need to talk to the police."

"What if the police just brush it off?" Dee asked, as the waiter brought their salads. "Sometimes, people don't take women like me very seriously."

Once the waiter had departed, Lucas sat back. "Maybe they would if you showed a little less skin."

Her blue eyes narrowed. "Excuse me?"

"I don't get why you stick with this blond-bombshell act. You're a sharp businesswoman. You don't need to play the vamp to your board of directors or investors. By now, don't you think you've proven you're more than Old Rolly's Folly?"

"People have expectations of me. I deliver." She smiled, her gaze cool. "And it's easy for you to pontificate, darling. You're a man in a man's world. All I ever did, and still do, is fight my battles with the best weapons I have."

"So use your brain this time." He stabbed at his lettuce. "The police will take you seriously. You're worth a lot of money, and wealthy people end up as targets for nutcases all the time. The cops can ask questions where you can't, and talk to you about security options."

Dee nodded, her expression thoughtful as she nibbled on a small carrot, taking it between her pink lips bit by bit.

Lucas marshaled his rapidly shredding patience. After a moment, he asked, "Do you know anybody with the initials *I-C-E*? A ship? Another company?"

"Not that I recall."

"What about your husband?"

She frowned, taking a sip of water now that her wine was gone. "I'll have my staff check into it. Rolly knew a lot of people, and not all of them were friendly with each other."

Lucas refolded the notes and slid them across the table into Dee's hand. He hesitated, then gave her cool fingers a brief, comforting squeeze. "Go to the police."

After a moment, she nodded.

The rest of the dinner progressed as Lucas expected. When she wasn't trying to shock or arouse him, Dee proved an amusing companion and easy to talk to, although she continued to smile, lean his way, flip her hair, and flatter him with attention—letting him know without a single word that he could take her to bed tonight should he so choose.

Knowing the best defense was a good offense, he made certain to pick up the tab.

After dinner, Lucas drove Dee to the sprawling Queen Anne-style house the Stanhope family had owned for nearly a century. She referred to it wryly as the "lake cottage," and stayed there when in Milwaukee on business.

After passing through the security gate, Lucas parked by the door and escorted her up the front walk. At the door, from the shadows of an entry arch dripping with ivy and climbing roses, she turned, and said, "Thank you for listening to me tonight."

In the fading sunlight of an early-summer evening, Dee looked soft and inviting. She knew it, too, as surely as she wanted him to kiss her. The awareness of it hummed between them.

"No problem. That's what friends are for."

Dee watched him. "Is that what we are? Friends?"

"That's all we can be."

"I see." Her breathing sounded slow, regular. "Is there another woman?"

A vision of exotic eyes and windblown hair came to mind, but Lucas shook his head as he headed down the steps, hands in his trouser pockets. There'd be no women until he got his head straightened out, and even when he did, Tessa wasn't in the running.

"I'm not seeing anyone, and I'm not looking, either. Good night, Dee."

"Lucas, wait!"

Almost to the car, he hesitated before turning. She stood on the top step, arms wrapped around herself as if cold. An act or not, she looked small and vulnerable—and alone.

"Can you be here when I call the police tomorrow morning? I'd feel better about it if I had a friend"—her lip curled upward on the word—"with me."

The request and its grudging tone surprised him, but he took care not to let it show. "If you need me, I'll be here."

She laughed, then sashayed down the stairs toward him. "Spoken like a true hero."

Even knowing what she was up to, Lucas refused to back down as she leaned into him, sandwiching him between her warm body and his car door.

"Oh, for Christ's sake, Dee, leave off the—"

"If you won't kiss me good night," she interrupted, twining her arms around his neck. "I suppose I'll have to take care of matters myself."

She gave him a pleasant kiss, her lips softly pliable, but it caused no answering fire; no hot need raking at his guts. Her kiss left him with nothing more than a cozy warmth and an appreciation for a pretty woman. Nothing at all like those few moments of a stolen kiss in his cabin. Even with this woman's body pressed against his, he could still feel Tessa's soft curves in his hands, the taste of her mouth.

Dee pulled back. "I see you're going to take a lot of work."

Her words filled him with annoyance. He was no longer flattered even mildly by her persistence, and cursed himself for letting her maneuver him into this untenable position.

"Dee, I'm not interested in going to bed with you."

She arched a brow. "Really? You know, I've read that people with your . . . condition have a decreased interest in sex. Is that what's wrong with you?"

The question, its implication, stirred his anger—and a thin sliver of fear. "There's nothing wrong with me."

"Good. It would be a pity if a man looking like you turned out to be a dud. Now I'm going to tell you a little secret: I like sex and I like men," she said in a mater-of-fact tone, as if discussing her favorite color. "But I'm . . . fussy. I was faithful to Rolly for twenty-five years, and I've only had one lover since he died. I want you to be my next lover. I can make it worth your while."

"I don't negotiate for sex," he said, easing away as he tamped down hard on his anger. "And you're my employer."

He'd given her a graceful way out, and Dee was smart enough to take it. She unwound her arms from his neck and stepped back.

"What difference does that make?" Her voice mocked. "You're not one of those macho types who feels unmanned by a woman with more money and power, are you?"

"You hired me to be the captain of the *Taliesen*, not your piece on the side."

"Oh, that's rich." Dee laughed. "Look at you. So big and strong. A decorated hero. Who'd believe you couldn't just say no to little old me?"

"It takes a lot to make me lose my temper, but you're getting damn close to crossing that line," he said evenly. "Keep this up, and you can find yourself another captain."

"You won't quit on me. I've given you the chance no one else would, no questions asked. You owe me."

Lucas returned her challenging stare, knowing she was partly right—but not as right as she liked to think. "If you want to play rough, I'll play rough. But take it too far, and you'll regret it," he said.

"Is that a threat?"

"You bet. And here's another one while I'm at it: Leave Tessa Jardine alone. She didn't deserve what you did to her."

Surprise flashed across Dee's face, then anger. "What do you care? Jardine doesn't even like you."

"Exactly. I've caused the woman enough pain, and I won't be used." He swung open the car door and slid inside, cranking the engine. "People aren't game pieces you can shuffle around for a headline and an extra buck, Dee. That'll just make you enemies—and from what you showed me earlier tonight, I don't think you need any more enemies. Including me."

Seven

After leaving Steve and Nina's house, Tessa drove back to her apartment. It wasn't fancy, but what it lacked in size it made up for in convenience, situated fifteen minutes from the port.

The mail carrier had left a week's worth of accumulated mail, and she sorted through it as she walked up the stairs, her duffel bumping against her hip.

Inside, she dropped the bag to the floor, turned on the light, and sank gratefully onto her sofa.

She'd never get rich on maritime pay, even as an officer, but she could afford all the niceties she needed to make her private space as different from a ship as possible. The pictures on her walls displayed nary a sailboat or seascape, and she'd indulged her passion for deep jewel colors and extravagant ornamentation in her living room and kitchen—and in the bedroom.

Head resting against the high-back sofa upholstered in navy-and-burgundy stripes, Tessa smiled to herself as she imagined the shocked looks on her crew's faces if they got a gander at the froufrou and frills in her bedroom.

Not that any of them would ever see it; her secret life as a lover of the Victorian Country look was safe.

With a groan, she pushed herself up from the soft cushions. Time to get out of her clothes. Wearing a uniform was the *Taliesen*'s only drawback; when she'd worked on freighters, she'd worn jeans and sweatshirts. But she didn't miss the slippery deckwash or getting socked by icy waves, either. She'd gladly trade the wet and cold and long monotonous hours for the tidy, lively *Taliesen*, even with Lucas Hall underfoot.

No.

From now until she had to board the ship again, no thinking about *him*.

Tessa eased her feet from her work shoes, kicked them aside, and began unbuttoning her shirt. A bath, with bubbles up to her chin, would be heaven.

As she walked toward the bathroom, a knock pounded on the door, firm enough to rattle the hinges.

Frowning, she turned. Who on earth . . . ?

She headed back, refastening one button for decency's sake as she peered through the peephole—and froze.

"Open up, Tessa," came a terse, too-familiar voice. "I know you're in there."

She glared at the door, trying to ignore the sudden rush of heat, the fluttering of her stomach.

"I saw you walk into the building. Now let me in."

Almost without thought, conditioned to obey after just a week of working with him, she opened the door—but only a crack.

"It's my day off," she said. "You'd better have a good reason for bothering me at home."

"We need to talk."

She didn't buckle under the intensity of his stare. "Whatever we have to say to each other can wait until we're both on the clock."

"Not this."

That fluttery feeling solidified into a heavy lump of dread. At a loud thud, she looked down to see the shiny black toe of his dress shoe blocking her door.

Slowly, she raised her gaze, the fact that he wore a suit only now registering.

"Either let me inside," he said flatly, "or your neighbors get an earful of things I'm sure you don't want them to hear."

Tessa still didn't open the door. "Do I look like a woman who can be bullied?"

He stared back at her, face expressionless. "You and I are going to sit down and figure out how to work together, or I go to Dee Stanhope and ask for another mate."

"On what grounds?" she demanded. "I'm a good officer, and you know it."

"I'm the captain. My word goes."

She stepped away from the door, deciding she didn't want her neighbors to hear any of this, after all.

"Meaning Dee Stanhope will side with you?" Tessa shut the door behind him.

"Meaning I have the authority to make that kind of decision if I feel it's necessary. It's up to you whether or not I'm forced to do so."

"*Forced*?" Tessa repeated. "As if you wouldn't find it real convenient to get rid of me."

In the middle of her living room, she returned his wary regard. His tall, broad-shouldered body and aura of authority overwhelmed the welcoming comfort of the room—and reminded her with an unpleasant jolt of what happened the last time she was alone in a room with Lucas Hall.

Lucas's gaze shifted toward her sofa, obviously waiting for her to invite him to sit, as if he were some old chum dropping by to gossip over a cup of coffee.

Well, he could just go rot!

After a moment, he looked back at her. "I can't help wondering how you manage under the weight of that chip on your shoulder."

She glared at him in disbelief. "Get out. Now."

"Too late. I'm here until we hammer out this problem, even if it takes all night."

His calm response filled her with anger—an anger edged with unease.

"You want to talk? Fine. Let's start at the very beginning: why did you dump me, without even saying good-bye? Excuse me for being upset over it, but what did I do to deserve that? What did I do that was so wrong?"

"You didn't do anything wrong." Lucas rammed his hands into his trouser pockets. "I thought I was doing you a favor by making a clean cut. You were just a kid, and I knew you had . . . strong feelings for me."

How quaintly phrased. She'd had a near-lethal case of puppy love. The embarrassment of that memory still made her want to crawl into a deep hole and hide.

At length she asked, "And that's it?"

"Pretty much."

"I see." She continued to stare at his expressionless face, resentment overtaking her anger. "How incredibly arrogant, to think you could decide something like that for me."

She expected him to go on the defensive. Instead, the tension in his shoulders eased a fraction. "You should've put it behind you by now, Tessa."

"Who says I haven't?" A restless silence fell between them, and then she asked, "Or did you come here expecting me to cheerfully forgive what you did? Or maybe you think you can kiss me again, and I'll forget everything?"

"I'm not going to kiss you again, and as I recall, I did a lot. Maybe we should work through them one at a time."

His voice revealed nothing, not wariness or regret. God, how she wanted to see an emotion—any emotion like *she* was feeling—on that granite rock he called a face.

"It's not like I pined away for you," she said, needing to make that clear, even if it sounded defensive. "I cried a few tears, said a few bad words, and got over it. I met a nice guy at a Christmas party that December and moved in with him."

Nothing. Not a raised brow, a glint of surprise in his eyes, or an offended, "Glad to hear you found me so easy to replace." Considering how he'd kissed her in his cabin, she expected more than this blank expression.

"I shouldn't have ended things the way I did. And I was wrong, to kiss you the other day. I was angry, not thinking straight. I apologize for that."

His quiet admission and apology caught her off guard, and she didn't like that. A dark, hazy instinct warned her to hold tight to her anger.

She sighed. "I need a beer. You want one?"

"No, nothing for me, thanks."

Tessa went into the kitchen and grabbed a can of Miller Lite from the fridge. When she returned, she flopped down on the sofa. "You may as well sit down and get comfortable."

He hesitated before taking the chair opposite her, sitting on the edge of the cushion. She noticed the weary lines of his face, and guilt pricked her.

"You can take off your suit coat if you want. Why are you all dressed up, anyway?"

He didn't take off his coat. Instead, he rubbed the back of his head. "I had dinner with Dee."

Surprise hit like a cold fist. Not that she cared, but actually hearing that he and Dee were—

She wouldn't let herself finish the thought. "You always did like to walk that fine line. You're as reckless as ever. I suppose some things never change."

He eyed her, gaze cool. "We're not here to talk about me, but about us."

"There is no 'us,' Lucas. Not now, not ever again." She popped the top of the can, filling the room with a strong, yeasty scent. A long silence passed, tight with tension, before she asked, "Do you know how I found out you'd left?"

He shook his head; a barely perceptible motion.

"It was Friday night. You do remember those Friday nights, don't you? How you'd drive down to Traverse City, and then we'd spend hours making love?"

His eyes met hers. A raw, sexual awareness pulsed between them until Lucas looked away. He shifted on the chair. "I remember."

As did she, too much. Several seconds passed before she felt sure enough of her voice to continue. "You didn't show up that night. Hours passed by. You didn't call. I was worried, certain you were bleeding to death in a ditch somewhere. Finally, I called your station house."

He went still, not looking up from his clasped hands.

"Some yeoman told me you'd transferred to Miami. Imagine that." She paused. "How long had you known you were leaving?"

"Since before we met."

Lucas looked up, but she didn't want him to see the hurt his words had caused, and lowered her head, focusing on her feet. "You must've figured that if I knew you weren't going to stick around, you'd never get me in bed."

He said nothing.

Tessa let out a long sigh. "I was just a quick lay to you, wasn't I? Nineteen and naive. God knows I made it easy. All you had to do was smile, and I fell into bed like a—"

"Tess, don't. We had good times, too."

"I pretty much just remember the sex," she said bluntly, hating the bleakness that leaked into her voice.

She understood what he was trying to do, but she wanted him to grovel. At least a little, even if it was ten years too late. She deserved that much.

"It wasn't like that and you know it," he said sharply. "We had a lot in common. You came from a Rogers City sailing family and I was a Navy brat. How about all those times you called me after you'd had a fight with your old man?"

"It was easy talking to you." Tessa looked away again. "My brothers always laughed at me when I cried. You didn't."

"That's right. I knew what you were going through, because my father didn't approve of my choice of career, either. Tessa, look at me."

Reluctantly, she did so, torn between wanting to keep the anger between them and wanting to let it go.

"It went both ways. When I had bad days, I called you and we'd talk for hours. I could tell you things I couldn't tell the other officers."

Tessa suddenly remembered a call he'd made at 4 A.M., after an exhausting two-day search for a missing ten-year-old girl ended with the recovery of her body. She'd never forget the thickness in his voice as he told her how his crew had gently taken the girl's body aboard the cutter, talking to her as if she were still alive: *There you go, sweetheart. We've got you . . . gonna take you back to your mom and dad now . . .*

It was always the worst, he'd said, when they lost a kid.

Unexpected tears stung her eyes and reminded her that even if she wanted to think of him as a cold-hearted bastard, it wasn't that simple. Nothing ever was.

She looked away, and her gaze settled on her bookcase, filled with a haphazard collection of romances, mysteries, and history books. Interspersed were family photos, including a small grouping of pictures of Matt, from babyhood up to one of the last pictures of him taken before he'd died.

The rational part of her knew it was absurd to feel like a traitor by having Lucas here, but the guilt would not let her go.

"Remember the nights on Traverse Bay, Tessa?" Lucas asked. "When we bundled in beach towels, watching the stars in the sky. All the talking."

She nodded, remembering more than talking, but she wouldn't speak of it: his lips on her skin, kissing her while his fingers stroked her between her legs and she'd trembled from the cool night air as much as the hungry passion.

"We used to spend hours boating on the bay and walking along the dunes," he continued in that same quiet, low voice.

Sand, hot and dry between her toes, and ending up in her clothes, everywhere. A blush warmed her cheeks as she recalled how he'd helped brush it all away, along with her clothes, and her breath.

"What about the summer fair? The funnel cakes and hot dogs, and how you screamed on the roller coaster."

"I hated roller coasters," she said vehemently.

"But you liked the Ferris wheel."

Tessa didn't look away, all too aware of the golden brown warmth of his gaze. When he turned his full focus upon her, as he did now, she could almost feel as if she were all that mattered in his world, that it was only the two of them. He had a way of making a person feel singled out, and special.

"You liked kissing on the Ferris wheel, Tessa."

Heat wound through her—colored with more than embarrassment. If he didn't leave right now, she was afraid she'd end up saying or doing something she'd regret. "Lucas, this is a bad idea. I don't want to—"

"I'll never forget the sound of your voice on the phone in the middle of the night," he interrupted relentlessly. She saw anger in his eyes, as if he didn't want to remember, either. "The feel of my heart pounding as I drove to Traverse City, hitting ninety and hoping the state troopers were busy, because you were waiting for me and I wouldn't slow down."

The kitchen clock loudly ticked away the seconds. The sheer force of his presence, the intensity of his gaze and commanding sound of his voice immobilized her. She clenched her hands in her lap, fighting the relentless pull of his attraction.

God, it would be so easy to just let go, and let the currents take her where they might.

"I wanted every minute I could have with you," he added, in a voice so low she could hardly hear it.

Yet he'd left her, without warning, without an explanation.

Tessa took a quick sip of beer, her mouth gone suddenly dry. As if it were only yesterday, she recalled the touch of his hands on her skin, the heat of his mouth on her breasts and his low groans as her own eager hands explored him, delighting in the hard strength of his muscles, the ready erection. How it had been to take him inside her body, the heady discovery of her female power over him. The same force he'd held over her, making her forget anything and everything.

Putting the beer aside, she glanced up—and the darkly intent look in his eyes told her he remembered, too.

Her gaze lingered on his face, on the few strands of gray at his temples, the lines at the corners of his eyes, around his mouth. Only now did she accept just how much time had passed. How much he had changed. How much she had changed, too.

She glanced at the photographs again and sighed. Even if she wanted to go back to the way things had been with them—and that was a mighty big if—the shadow of Matt's death stood between them. Surely he had to see that.

"I remember it all because you were my first lover," she said at last. "But to you I was, what? Girl number twenty by then? Why should you remember?"

A muscle in his jaw tightened. "Look, I've been trying to apologize."

"That's not an answer, Lucas."

"How close are you to getting your master's license?"

She blinked at the abrupt change in subject. "Pretty close. What does that have to do with anything?"

"You were smart and determined. You told me that following in your family's footsteps, getting your master's license by the time you were thirty, was all you wanted."

Tessa lowered her lashes. "I was nineteen. I had a lot of big dreams."

"So did I. I wanted to leave behind my father's disappointment, to do something that mattered . . . something more than freezing my ass off breaking ice. Transferring the hell out of that district was all I'd wanted. I couldn't stay, and I knew you wouldn't leave the academy. End of the story, Tess."

"That's your excuse? For knowing all along that you were leaving me, but never saying a word about it?"

"I was wrong, but I can't go back and change what I did."

To her mortification, tears stung her eyes. "I want to hate you for it."

He didn't look away. "I know."

She shook her head in disbelief, still not understanding. "Why? Were you afraid I'd cry? Embarrass you? It shouldn't matter, not after all this time, and that I'm still so angry about how you left me . . . you can't believe how much this pisses me off!"

At her outburst, he let out his breath. "All I can do is try and patch up things so we can both do our job. I know being first mate on the *Taliesen* is too important for you to risk losing it over an affair that was dead and buried long ago. You're too smart for that."

Tessa finished off her beer and gave a short nod.

"I also wanted to tell you . . . being captain of the *Taliesen* is—" He stopped, mouth thinning to a straight line. "It's important to me. And . . . there's the *McKee*. Your brother."

His halting words surprised her, but she shook her head sadly, and said, "Nothing can bring Matt back, or change the fact that if you hadn't opened that hatch, he might have lived. It's not something I can forget."

Lucas clenched his hands together, knuckles white. "I'm still sorry. For what happened."

With his discomfort so painfully obvious, Tessa wanted to say something; anything to let him know she understood his regret, and that she'd never expected he'd felt otherwise. Before she could find the right words, Lucas continued talking.

"I should have contacted you after I left the hospital, but I wasn't—" Again, he cut himself off. "I feel bad about what you had to go through last week. With the reporters, all the questions."

Fresh tears burned at the back of her throat at this unexpected concern for her feelings, and she could only nod. *Oh, Lord, don't let me cry, not in front of Lucas.*

"You better go," she managed to say calmly enough. "What we're dragging around between us will take more than a day or two to clear up. But you're right; I've been unreasonable. I'm sorry for that. I'll . . . act like a professional officer from here on out."

Thankfully, Lucas didn't pursue the matter. He stood, nodding. As she pushed herself to her feet as well, he said, "I'll see you Friday morning and we—"

He stopped abruptly, his gaze lowering—and Tessa remembered her unbuttoned shirt. A quick glance showed the gaping placket held in place by one precarious button.

Heat stinging her skin, Tessa raised her chin. She wouldn't act like some bashful virgin. So she had breasts; he could damn well deal with it.

"I was changing out of my uniform when you knocked."

His gaze shifted from her face toward her chest, then away again. A muscle in his jaw tensed.

"It's no big deal," Tessa added. "We're ancient history, dead and buried . . . and we've agreed that I'm just one of the guys when I'm in this uniform. Right?"

Except she was half out of that uniform. What was she doing, antagonizing him like this? What was she trying to prove? It wasn't as if she wanted him to kiss her again, or even look at her as if she were a woman. . . .

Lucas's eyes locked with hers, and Tessa took a quick breath. She couldn't mistake the desire in his eyes, or explain away the heat between them.

"Besides," she added in a tight voice that betrayed none of her inner turmoil, "you're hardly a free agent. Sounds to me like you've been pretty busy with a widow in pink."

Tessa suddenly found herself pinned against her living-room wall, between the rough plaster and Lucas's warm body. He'd moved so fast she'd never seen it coming.

His gaze shifted down toward her chest—and the plain sports bra partially revealed by her open shirt.

His hands rested on her shoulders, a hot and heavy weight. Her body pressed against the hard length of him, and the unmistakable ridge of his arousal. He angled his face close to hers, so close that their lips almost touched.

Panicked, Tessa tried to twist away, and Lucas suddenly lifted his hands from her shoulders. She tensed, prepared to stop him but went absolutely still when he gathered the front of her shirt in his hands. Bracing herself, she waited for him to rip it wide.

Lucas yanked it closed.

"I am not," he said quietly, fastening the lowest button, "sleeping with Dee Stanhope."

Lucas's knuckles brushed against her breasts as he moved up to the next button. Tessa sucked in her breath at the sweeping, aching desire, and her nipples tightened.

His long, sun-browned fingers lingered on the swell of her breasts—only for a fraction of a second—before fastening the next button.

With his breath stirring her hair, he murmured, "And I am never going to think of you as one of the guys."

By the time he reached the last button at her throat, his fingers brushing her chin, she'd all but stopped breathing.

Lucas stepped away, and she sagged back against the wall, speechless.

When he closed the door behind him, she slid down the wall to sit on the floor.

Running an unsteady hand through her hair, Tessa moistened her dry lips, and whispered, "Wow."

Eight

*L*ucas headed up the *Taliesen*'s ramp at a brisk pace, half an hour behind schedule following his meeting with Dee and a detective from the Milwaukee police department.

After talking with the detective—an old guy who'd acted unimpressed by Dee's wealth or the hot pink suit she'd worn with a tight skirt a good six inches above her knees—Lucas figured he'd left her in capable hands.

That was about the only thing that had gone as planned these past few days. He didn't look forward to facing Tessa again after this latest blunder between them, and his mood darkened with every step up to the pilothouse.

As he stood outside the hatch, the sound of his crew's laughter drifted his way. Tessa, Shea, and McNulty were trading jokes. McNulty rarely said much whenever Lucas was in the pilothouse, but now the man was cracking off-color jokes.

"Hey, what's the look for?" McNulty's voice demanded in mock offense. "You're not blond."

"It's a sexist joke, Kip," Tessa retorted.

"Rob's laughing at it."

"And it's a well-known fact that Rob has no taste."

"Hey, it's a guy thing," Shea cut in. "You girly-girls don't understand."

"I don't know why I put up with you," Tessa said, but with an undertone of humor.

Squaring his shoulders, Lucas cleared his throat and stepped into the pilothouse. "Good morning."

The relaxed atmosphere vanished, and smiles melted away. McNulty nodded a greeting as Shea turned, and said, "Morning."

Never one to avoid a challenge, Lucas met Tessa's gaze head-on. An instant awareness rose between them, of that moment in her apartment when he'd almost kissed her again.

Tessa held her clipboard in a death grip against her breasts, her chin cocked at that angle he was beginning to recognize as pure bullshit.

"Miss Jardine."

"Sir."

"Let's get under way," he ordered, then sounded a long, loud warning blast on the whistle.

Shea, although officially off watch, stayed on the bridge as the *Taliesen* left port. With an eye to the strong wind and thick fog, Lucas eased his ship toward open water, blasting the fog warning signal every couple of minutes as Tessa kept a sharp eye on the radar and stayed in close contact with the lookout at the bow. Nobody wanted to start the trip by slamming into the concrete breakwater wall, or running over any small boats that might have strayed into their path.

Once the ship moved into open water, the fog eased, and Lucas ordered the speed to HALF.

That was it, his task completed, and now for the next five days, the safety and well-being of over four hundred passengers and crew were his sole responsibility.

Massaging his stomach, he asked, "What's on the radar?"

Tessa turned. "The *Arthur Anderson* downbound and a barge upbound. We'll pass the *Anderson* in an hour or so."

He walked up behind her to see for himself. The quick look she gave him told him she didn't appreciate being checked on.

"What's the weather in Chicago?"

She shifted back as much as she could and retrieved her clipboard. "A fog warning's been issued, but it'll clear by the time we put in. Other than that, we've got partly cloudy skies, winds north to northeast at ten to fifteen knots."

Fog. God, he hated fog. "I'd like to see the reports."

Her mouth thinned, but she handed over the papers. Quickly, he thumbed through them, finding everything just as she'd said.

Lucas handed the papers back, aware that he stood too close to her. He could feel her heat, smell her sweet, fresh scent, and his body responded on instinct. "Looks good. Steady as she goes, then, Miss Jardine."

"Yes, sir."

Shea sent a quick look at Tessa, then Lucas, before returning his attention to the window bay, a faint frown on his face.

"I'm going to my office," Lucas said.

"Can I get you to sign off on some paperwork?" Tessa asked.

Lucas halted just outside the hatch, and nodded. Tessa retrieved her clipboard and brought it to him. She stood at a conspicuous distance, and as she held out the clipboard with invoices, bills of lading, and logs, he had to reach for it.

"You can come closer, Miss Jardine. I don't bite."

Her chin rose. Again, their eyes met—and he didn't miss the wariness on her face. Admittedly, he preferred the wariness to her hostility, but not by much.

"Sorry," she said. Then added, "Sir."

Holding back a retort, Lucas signed off on the half dozen forms and handed the clipboard back to Tessa.

Without another word, he left the pilothouse—but he hadn't gone far before he heard a whistle, then Shea's low voice, in a mocking tone: "*Miss* Jardine . . . Christ, he's a tight-ass. And you're no better. What's with all this *sir* shit, anyway?"

"Aren't you off watch?" Tessa asked, an edge of irritation to her voice.

"I'm telling you, Tess, that beef you've got with Hall, you'd better get it out of your system."

After a short silence, she said, "Look, I'm trying to find my way toward dealing with this, but give me a little leeway, would you? He wasn't your brother, he was mine. A day doesn't go by that I don't miss him."

"But the board of inquiry—"

"It doesn't matter what they said. Whether anybody can prove it or not, Hall made a critical error in judgment, and it cost five men their lives." Tessa's voice was closer, and Lucas stepped back.

"Chances are they were already dead, Tessa."

On a painful stab of guilt, Lucas briefly closed his eyes.

"Nobody knows that for sure," Tessa murmured.

"Right. Just like nobody knows for sure if it was Hall

who opened the hatch, or somebody else. I gotta tell you, this is turning into a problem bigger than just between you and Hall. His attitude isn't making him any friends with the crew—"

"He's the captain. He doesn't have to make friends."

"I know that, but some of the crew don't like him much. They think he's arrogant and doesn't respect their work."

"That's ridiculous."

"Maybe, but the rumors that you and Hall are feuding aren't helping any. It's bad enough half the guys think he got this job by noodling Dee Stanhope, and the other half aren't sure what to make of you yet, since you're a woman, and it makes the guys nervous that the captain and mate—"

"I get the picture, Rob," Tessa interrupted, her tone cool. "This is only our second voyage. It'll take time for the crew to get used to each other and work out the kinks. I'm not feuding with Hall, and he isn't noodling the boss."

"How do you know that?"

"He told me so, and I believe him."

"He told you?" Shea repeated, incredulous. "When did—"

"Would you leave? I've got a ship to run, and you know my feelings about gossip."

Lucas quietly walked to his office and shut the door just as Shea's footsteps pounded down the stairs before fading away.

For a moment he stood before his desk, grappling with frustration and that increasingly familiar feeling of having crash-landed in somebody else's life.

In the Coast Guard he'd always had tasks to occupy his time, and at least a bus driver drove his bus the entire distance of the trip to keep busy. Lucas didn't even have that much, with his crack crew handling everything, leaving him hours to do nothing more than sit and think.

Not something he wanted to do at the moment.

With a sigh, he sat at the desk, pulled out the log, and opened it—but instead of making the usual entry, he sat back in his chair, frowning.

That crew morale wasn't exactly at a high point didn't surprise him. Tessa was right; the crew was green and wary of each other. The college kids working for the steward department didn't mix with the licensed crew members, often viewing each as alien invaders. The deck department personnel considered themselves superior to the engine department personnel—and vice versa. It was typical rivalry and would work itself out.

But he should talk more with the crew. His rank set him apart from everyone on board ship, but this wasn't the service; fraternization wasn't an issue. He had to remember this.

As for Tessa, he'd be more patient with her. She was under close scrutiny, her performance subjected to harsher judgment than if she were a man. She had to be under a tremendous amount of pressure—and the last thing she needed was for him to complicate her life with old mistakes, old grief. Old passions.

Lucas drummed his fingers on the desk surface. He'd bet he wasn't the only person who'd unfairly screwed her over, and if she wasn't as bright-eyed and eager as he remembered, if she didn't laugh as much and seemed harder, she had good cause. The years couldn't have been easy on her. She'd achieved her dreams, but not without a cost.

The sadness in her voice whenever she talked of her brother was warning enough. No matter that he was as attracted to her now as when they'd first met. He might earn her forgiveness for leaving her, but she'd never forgive him for the *McKee*.

Lucas tossed a thick boat catalog—his dream book, as Kevin called it—onto his desk, then leaned back in the chair to stretch his cramped muscles. A quick glance at the clock showed it was closing on midnight. The *Taliesen* should be nearing Grand Haven.

Standing, he massaged his thigh to ease the ache that warned him a storm front was moving in. The usual remedy for stiff muscles was a long swim, but a walk around the deck would have to do.

Shutting the cabin door behind him, he walked up into the pilothouse for a status report. Third Mate Dave Compton stood by the chart desk.

Anything to report?"

Startled, Compton swung around. In his mid-twenties, he was short and heavyset, freckled and red-haired. He'd pulled off his tie and rolled up his sleeves. "Nothing much. It's been a pretty dull night."

Lucas nodded, yet walked to the radar. Even with modern technology, a bridge crew had to remain alert. Lake traffic was busy that time of year, with ships downbound for the industrial ports clustered at the southernmost end of Lake Michigan.

The radar checked out; the latest weather reports looked good. The wheelsman sat on his stool, wide-awake and drinking coffee, and Compton had the course plotted correctly. If the mate altered the course by so much as a few degrees, the gyro repeater in Lucas's cabin would start clicking in warning.

"Is everything alright, sir?"

Lucas turned to the third mate, noticing the man's

high color. "Looks fine, Compton. Good job."

"Thanks," Compton said with a brief, wooden smile.

"I'm heading out for a walk. Need me for anything?"

"No, sir. I do believe I have everything under control."

Lucas hesitated, sensing resentment, but said nothing as he left the pilothouse. He couldn't explain his feelings of danger, of things out of balance. Even though he knew it was a lingering symptom of his "condition," as Dee put it, and knew the danger wasn't real, he found it hard to ignore such feelings.

Real danger or not, his mantra remained: *no mistakes*.

Lucas headed down the corridor between the officer's quarters. As he passed Tessa's cabin, next to his own, he heard no sounds from within, not even a TV.

Maybe she'd headed to the galley for a quick snack. It was what he'd do if he had the twelve-to-four watch. Lucas continued on his way, shifting from side to side with the ship's motion. This late, the *Taliesen* was quiet, with only a handful of night owls hanging out in the bar and a few couples lost in each other, stealing kisses on deck or on the dance floor.

Passing through the lounge to the muzzy strains of a cello, violin, and muted trumpet, he raised a hand in greeting to the tall blond bartender, who was busy restocking glasses fresh from the galley.

"How's it going, Scott?"

"Pretty good, sir. Are you looking for Miss Jardine?"

"Not really, why?"

"Oh. Just thought you might be. She came through about ten minutes ago."

Surprised she was on deck, he asked, "Headed where?"

"Aft, I think."

Lucas nodded his thanks and headed to the back of

the *Taliesen*. It was a cool, windy night with a round moon hanging low over the water, half-obscured by dark clouds. Between the running lights and the moon, the deck was well lit, and it didn't take him long to spot her.

He stopped, allowing himself the quiet pleasure of watching her in the soft, hazy light. She leaned against the rail, seemingly deep in thought, and his breath caught at her beauty. Dark, exotic, strong—she wasn't like any other woman he'd ever known.

After a moment, Lucas crossed the deck. She didn't hear his approach, and jumped when he stepped beside her. As she turned, desire coiled through him, tight and hot and undeniable.

"You have the next watch?" he asked.

He knew she did, but he couldn't think of what else to say. Thirty-seven years old, and as tongue-tied around a pretty woman as any seventeen-year-old.

"Not for another fifteen minutes," she replied.

He frowned at the familiar rigid line of her back. "I thought we were working on this anger thing."

Tessa sent him a brief, unreadable look. "We are."

"So what's with the 'back off' body language?"

She sighed. "It's not about anger, exactly."

Lucas mulled that over for a moment. "So what's it about?"

"Nothing I want to talk about."

"Okay." He moved closer. "Then can I ask what are you doing out here?"

"Admiring the view. Gorgeous, isn't it?"

He leaned at the rail beside her, listening to the ever-present roar of wind and waves. After another glance at the moon, he turned back to her. The wind tangled strands of her hair across her eyes, but she didn't bother pushing them aside. He had a sharp, sudden need to trace the high cheekbones of her face, slide his hands through her hair, and to see her dark eyes regard him with something else beside wariness.

It's not about anger.

Remembering her earlier conversation with Rob Shea, he had a pretty good idea what it was about.

"Absolutely beautiful view," he agreed at length, quietly.

"Whenever the stress is too much or I'm having a bad day and wondering if all the crap I put up with is worth it, nights like this tell me it is," she said, unaware of how his gaze slid slowly down her body, then upward again to linger on her firm chin, the full lips turned up slightly in a soft, dreamy smile. "I love this job."

He wished he could say as much, and so easily. He needed this job, but that wasn't the same thing as wanting it.

After a moment, watching the wind ruffle her hair, he said, "You wear your hair shorter than you used to."

She looked at him, startled, before she turned away. "The first thing I learned at sea was to keep my hair short."

Although her posture remained casual, her hands closed tightly on the rail—and with some surprise he saw that she held a pink carnation in one hand.

But before he could question her about it, she asked, "Don't you like my hair this way?"

"You're as beautiful as ever, Tess," he murmured.

Unlike Dee Stanhope, Tessa couldn't hide her emotions, and her surprise—and alarm—showed plainly on her face.

"Um . . . I think I'd better go now. Whenever we're alone together, strange things start happening and—"

"What's with the flower?" he interrupted, and when she stepped back from the railing, he shifted to block her.

She sent him an uneasy glance, but didn't try to squeeze around him. "I was only . . . it's nothing."

Tessa didn't look at him as she tossed the flower over the rail and into the dark water churning in the *Taliesen*'s wake. The bloom bobbed along, a spot of pale color growing smaller and smaller with each passing second.

Lucas watched it for a moment longer, then said quietly, "Memories are worth much more than nothing."

Some of the wary tension eased from her face, and she sighed. "He wasn't much for pink, but it's all I could find in the dining room today, and I felt like coming to say hello."

Lucas closed his hands tightly over the rail. "You used to call him Matt the Brat."

She smiled. "Yes, I did. I'm surprised you remember."

Lucas looked out over the dark water. Somewhere out there, hundreds of miles away yet, lay the wreck of the *Robert D. McKee*, twisted from the force of the explosion that had sent it to the bottom—with a little help from him, some still claimed.

He had to live with that every day for the rest of his life. How could she think he'd not remember? Did she think him such a callous bastard?

"You used to tease him," Lucas said at length. "About his bad jokes, and how he was always telling the punch line first."

"Matt rolled through life like it was one big party, and he made friends with everybody. Not even his ex-girlfriends ever held a grudge against him. He had this smile . . . you couldn't stay mad at him." Her own smile fading, she added softly, "It's been almost two years since he died. My God. Two *years*."

A familiar, sharp dread pierced him, and his muscles went rigid in response. Focusing on the water, he sucked in several slow, cleansing breaths.

Once the thrum of anxiety ebbed, he glanced at Tessa, still looking past him. Thank God; she hadn't noticed.

He moved closer, until her warmth seemed to touch his cold skin. "How's it been for you, these past two years?"

"I'm exactly where I want to be in my career, and I'm happy with that."

"I meant about your brother's death."

"Oh." She looked down, and sighed. "Some days are better than others. Now and again, I still look for him in a crowd, or expect to hear his voice when I answer the phone. I know he's dead, but sometimes my mind plays tricks on me."

They leaned against the rail in silence until she turned to him, her expression troubled. "Don't take this wrong, okay? But you look like you could use some sleep. Maybe you should go to bed. It's almost midnight."

Stung, he glanced down, hiding his face. "I'm not tired."

"So what are you doing out here? Another inspection? Checking up on your crew?" she asked. "You don't have to do that. They're all well trained. Trust them. And me."

He looked up. "I'm a hands-on kind of captain. Remember?"

Frowning, she said, "Lucas, about what happened the other night, I—"

"I shouldn't have said what I just did. Forget it. And

forget the other night even happened," he said, his tone harsher than he intended.

"I see." Tessa rubbed the bridge of her nose. "Well, I'd better get up to the pilothouse. It's almost a quarter to."

"Tessa . . . ah, shit, wait a minute, would you?"

She'd taken only a few steps away. She stopped, but didn't turn. "I really should go. Whenever we spend any time alone, one or both of us ends up doing or saying something we end up regretting."

He came up behind her. "We need to talk about the *McKee*."

Her shoulders tensed, then slowly relaxed. She turned, and moonlight illuminated her face, the sheen of her eyes.

Were those tears? Lucas clasped his hands behind him to keep from touching her face and seeing if his fingertips would find the salty moisture of her tears.

Hurt was all he seemed to bring her, no matter how hard he tried to rediscover and mend the friendship they'd once known.

"What's there to talk about? In our line of work, we all risk dying out here." She motioned to the vast darkness of the lake surrounding them. "A series of mistakes sank the *McKee*. She was an old ship, and the repairs made to her hull the previous season were sloppy. When her fuel line ruptured, she lost her steering, foundered on a reef, and sank."

"With a little help from me."

For a long moment, she held his gaze, then looked away. "You did what you could. And twenty-five men did survive."

"But it's the five—or the one—who didn't that you can't forget." It wasn't a question.

Tears of grief, of anger, shimmered in her eyes. "And

what about you, Lucas? Are you able to forget?"

"What do you think?"

"I have no idea what's going on in your head right now . . . any more than I understand what the *hell* were you thinking when you opened that hatch."

In response to her low accusation, his anger blazed, hot and irrational—and edged with a dark fear. "Nobody knows how the hatch opened, and I didn't know there was a gas leak."

"Oh, God, Lucas, don't . . . you *knew* her cargo was gasoline!"

"Yes, I did," he snapped. "I suspected a leak, but didn't know it for a fact. There were a lot of things that should've happened, but didn't—starting with the *McKee*'s captain not sending out a call for help the minute he hit those rocks. And if somebody had told me they suspected a fire in the engine room, I might've acted differently."

"You can remember all this, yet you claim not to remember who opened the hatch. Why is that?"

"As I have stated a hundred times already to the Coast Guard and the NTSB, I can't remember anything after I climbed on the aft deck. The explosion rattled my brains around pretty hard, you know."

The silvery moonlight glinted on a single tear slowly rolling down the curve of her cheek. "You almost died."

He didn't think that tear was for him, despite her words. "Did you ever wish I'd died in place of your brother?"

She flinched. "That's not a fair question, Lucas. And I'm not going to answer it."

"That's answer enough."

"What do you want me to say?" She turned to him, fists clenched against her side. "People keep telling me to deal with it, and I agree it's a damn good idea, but you tell me how . . . how I'm supposed to move on, to forget!"

"Nobody's telling you to forget, Tessa. Least of all me."

"When my mother ran off, Matt was two years old. I was only nine when I found myself raising my brothers. Matt . . . he was so little when she left, he didn't remember her. I was more like a mother to him than a sister. Dad always said that Matt went to work on ships because he thought it would make me proud."

"He was an adult and made his own choices. You can't blame yourself for that, and neither can your old man." He hesitated, then glanced away, digging the heel of his palm into his belly, over the deep ache inside. "Tessa, if you had such a problem working with me, why did you take this job?"

"Because nobody really knows what did happen. There was enough of a doubt that I thought I could learn to deal with it. And I'm trying, Lucas . . . it's just so hard. Seeing you every day like this is a constant reminder. I don't want to be like Jason Yarwood's father, spending years in court pointing fingers and laying blame. I want to move on, and to really believe what I keep telling myself: that accidents happen and you were only doing your job."

In the silence that followed, she made a show of checking her watch. "And I have a job to do, too. I have to go relieve Dave."

As she walked past, he said, "Does this mean you won't ever forgive me?"

She stopped abruptly, then looked at him over her shoulder for a long, tense moment. "The board of inquiry said there's nothing to forgive."

Except for the little matter that he'd lived, and her

brother and four other men had not, a guilt for surviving that no board of inquiry could absolve.

"Maybe I don't feel that way."

Her brows drew together. "Do you need my forgiveness?"

"Yes," he admitted quietly—but it wasn't just the *McKee* he referred to, and he saw the moment understanding dawned in her eyes.

"Forgiving you would be the worst thing I could do for myself right now."

The despair on her face hammered the guilt home. "Tessa—"

"No, Lucas. I have to go. What you want from me . . . it's too much, too soon." She wiped her eyes with the back of her hand, and squared her shoulders. "Dammit! I can't go around crying like this all the time. Just leave me to deal with this on my own terms. Please!"

Nine

Midway through her voyage and shortly before noon, the *Taliesen* put into port at Mackinac Island, a resort reachable only by ferry, where cars had been outlawed since the early 1900s.

Tessa stood on the bridge, giving orders to the wheelsman while Lucas looked on.

"Do you have to stand so close behind me?" she asked through her teeth. "You're making me nervous."

"I need to see what you're doing."

"Fine. Just stop breathing down my neck. I've done this before, you know."

"Didn't get enough shut-eye last night?" Rob asked. "You're not exactly a little beam of sunshine today."

"And *you* can just shut your mouth," she said, but amiably enough.

"Hey, I'm here watching and learning. I wanna grow up to be just like you, Tess."

She shot Rob an exasperated look, and ordered, "Kip, hard right."

"Hard right, aye," her wheelsman said, grinning, as he spun the wheel. The *Taliesen*'s bow slowly angled toward the port, crowded with sailboats and pleasure boats, and her waiting pier.

"Line her up straight with that sign. Perfect." She waited a moment longer, then signaled the engine room to SLOW. "Her bow's a little squirrelly today."

"Strong cross breeze," Lucas said from behind. "Not north–south like usual."

Tessa glanced again at the wind speed and direction gauges. "Keep her on this course until we drop anchor."

"Steady as she goes, aye."

Twenty minutes later, with a little maneuvering of engine speed, rudder angle, and wind direction, Tessa docked the *Taliesen*. She turned, satisfied, to see Lucas smiling.

She couldn't help smiling back. She'd done a good job, and knew it.

After their difficult talk on the aft deck, Lucas had kept his distance. She felt bad for saying that forgiving him would be disastrous; but he seemed to understand her feelings that any acceptance of him would be like a betrayal to Matt.

"Not bad," Lucas said.

"I did damn good," she retorted, avoiding the warmth in his eyes, which only made her feel more guilty. "And no smart remarks about woman drivers, either."

Hands on his hips, Rob stood before the windows, gazing out toward the harbor where the incongruous timbered battlements of Fort Mackinac loomed above the modern harbor. "I wonder if that cute little tour guide is still working at the fort."

Tessa eyed his back. "I didn't know you went for women in hoop skirts."

"I have this Scarlett O'Hara fantasy—"

"Which I really don't want to hear," Tessa interrupted. After retrieving a pile of papers from the chart desk, she held them out toward Lucas. "Before you go anywhere, I need you to sign payroll forms."

As Lucas took the sheaf of papers from her, their fingers touched, warm skin to warm skin. Startled, Tessa jerked her hand back, and scattered the papers across the floor.

She stared down at the mess. "Sorry."

Rob turned, his gaze moving between Lucas and Tessa, his eyes bright with interest.

She bent to pick up the papers. Lucas bent at the same time, and nearly collided with her head. She stood. He stood. She bent again, and when he moved to follow, she burst out, "Oh, just stay put! I dropped them, I'll pick them up."

The heat of a blush spread across her face as she wondered what the bridge crew thought of her sudden clumsiness.

"After you do so, bring everything to my office. I'll sign the forms there," Lucas said. Without giving her an opportunity to respond, he turned and walked off.

After a moment, she followed, with a scowl at Rob's widening grin and speculative gaze.

In Lucas's office, she noticed again how much the room suited him: the blocky, muscular chairs and spare, industrial lines of the desk and tables fairly oozed power and testosterone. This was the captain's territory. When his door was shut, no one dared interrupt or even put through a call, unless it was an emergency. But Lucas had made almost no attempt to personalize the room. His coat and hat hung from hooks near the door, and a pile of books and magazines, most of them fishing-related, were neatly stacked on his desk.

She glanced through the open door of his bedroom as he continued to sign the payroll forms. It had the same uncluttered lines as his office, masculine in tone: aqua and gray, with technical-looking artwork on the walls and tall, thin torchiere lamps. Though her cabin was bigger than the other officers' cabins, it wasn't as big as this, and hers was done in peach and brown tones. She still hadn't adjusted to the vintage abstract print of her porthole curtains, which she feared had come from the era of *Lost in Space* and *The Jetsons*.

God, she was a closet Victorian marooned in Retro Land.

"What's the sneer for?" Lucas asked. "My bed's fixed."

Tessa swung her gaze back to Lucas. "I wasn't looking at your bed!"

Lucas slid the signed forms across the desk toward her, a smile tugging at his lips.

She ignored it and stood quickly, realizing they were alone again. Not a good idea. "Are you staying here?"

"Yes, I have a few phone calls to make and paperwork to finish."

"I'm not back on watch until eight tonight. Is there anything you need before I go?" she asked with a touch of caution. So far, they seemed to be conducting a fairly normal conversation.

"No. Just shut the door behind you when you leave."

Deciding not to push her luck, Tessa quickly turned and left, and headed to her cabin to change.

Standing before her narrow locker, she debated what

to wear for a day playing tourist. Not counting her extra uniforms, she had a pair of jeans, a couple of T-shirts and sweatshirts—and a purple knit sundress.

Probably not an option. Probably she hadn't shoes to match; only her work shoes or a ratty old pair of sneakers.

A quick glance showed a pair of sandals—the strappy kind with heels—crammed into a far corner, under her duffel.

Tessa chewed her lip as she pulled out the dress: a short flirty skirt, a bodice cut to hug curves. Dare she wear it? Maybe. Unless it needed ironing; then forget it.

A critical once-over showed the knit was only a little creased and, being knit, it would smooth out. She couldn't decide if this pleased her or not.

She fingered the fabric; its soft texture, its rich plum color. Even with such simple lines, the dress would bare a lot more skin and curves than her uniform.

But the lure of being free of trousers, shirts, ties, and clunky steel-toed shoes for a few hours held a strong appeal. She also had a good idea about what else lay behind this sudden longing to dress like a woman for a change.

Reluctantly, she glanced at the framed photo of Matt she kept on her small desk. He was sitting in a chair, his girlfriend on his lap, and Tessa had her arms wrapped around him in an affectionate hug. She was smiling, Matt was smiling. Even now, looking at the photo, she couldn't help smiling.

"Oh, Matt," she said with a sigh. "He just has this effect on me . . . and I don't think it's really so bad, is it?"

If Matt were here he'd probably give her a shoulder a playful shove, laugh, and tell her to go for it.

Not that she'd let anything like *it* happen. Even if she was having trouble getting her brain and her hormones to agree with each other, Dee's threat still hung over her head like an ax—and Lucas wasn't worth her career. Not after she'd come so far.

Tessa stared at her reflection in the small mirror above her sink, holding the dress against her. Eyes full of indecision stared back at her.

Coward, those eyes also said. *It's just a dress.*

Right. And so what if wearing a dress meant she'd catch a few smart-ass comments from the crew? They shouldn't be shocked to see she had legs and breasts. Most of the crew and officers were married—they knew what the female body looked like.

With renewed determination, she scrounged around until she found her one tube of lipstick. If she had to put up with the teasing, she might as well go all out.

Tessa wiggled into the dress and smoothed it out across her stomach. Then she pulled the neckline a little lower, and looked in the mirror.

Whoa. Too much cleavage!

She yanked the neckline back up and debated taking off the delicate gold chain she wore—its tiny horseshoe charm rested on the swell of her breasts, drawing attention there—but she left it. A dress needed jewelry.

After fluffing her hair with her fingers, she applied the conservative rose shade of lipstick, slipped her feet into the sandals, and donned a pair of sunglasses with small round lenses.

How absurd, all this worry over wearing a simple dress. She'd been working with men a little too long . . . it was time to remember she was a woman.

Without looking in the mirror again, Tessa grabbed her shoulder bag and backed out of her cabin before she could change her mind—and her bottom instantly contacted with a warm, solid body.

Startled, she turned. Lucas stood behind her, a donut and a steaming coffee cup in one hand, which he held up to keep from spilling. With obvious surprise, his gaze moved lower, then up again with deliberate slowness, pausing at her chest.

Why, oh why, did *he* have to see her first?

Hands fisted at her side, Tessa lifted her chin. "What are you staring at? Haven't you seen a woman in a dress before?"

"Excuse me, do I know you?"

For a stunned instant she thought him serious, until she caught the gleam of amusement in his eyes—and unmistakable male appreciation.

If he laughed, if he made so much as one smart remark, she'd kick him! If she didn't die of humiliation first.

Focusing on the bulkhead beyond his shoulder, she said coolly, "Very funny. Now please move—you're in my way."

But he only continued studying her with an unwavering gaze that left her feeling downright naked. She struggled to keep her breathing normal, thinking she might escape if she could just squeeze between his body and the bulkhead—except touching him was absolutely, positively out of the question.

What would Dee Stanhope do in this situation? Certainly not get all hot and panicky under a man's stare, that was for sure.

"You look great, Tessa."

At his quiet pronouncement, her nervousness eased enough for her to casually say, "Thank you."

"Going out?"

"I'm playing tourist—when in Rome, and all that.

I'm going to the Grand Hotel's seven-hundred-foot veranda and gawk at all the rich people playing golf. I'll have lunch, do a little shopping, that sort of thing."

Dammit, she didn't blather like this when she was in uniform and on the bridge.

After a moment, when he still hadn't moved, Tessa cleared her throat. "Is there something you wanted?"

"You don't want me to answer that," he said, his voice low, his meaning unmistakable.

So much for normal breathing. He stood too close, his stare too direct. He smelled warm, musky, and male. She began to take in a long, steadying breath—only to freeze when he reached toward her with his free hand and lifted the horseshoe charm on her necklace. His fingers brushed her skin.

Don't move. Act calm.

Spots danced before her eyes, and she quickly filled her air-starved lungs before she keeled over. "Lucas, please!"

His eyes met hers, and she couldn't look away, struck anew by their beautiful golden brown shade, the thick black lashes. After a moment, he said, "You still wear this."

Grateful for an excuse to break eye contact, Tessa looked down. Against the paler skin of her breasts, his hand looked large and dark and rugged. "It's my good-luck charm."

He nudged the charm with his thumb, and she startled at the rough feel of his skin. "I thought you might have thrown it away."

"I wouldn't be so childish." She guiltily recalled the pictures of the two of them she'd snipped to pieces long ago—but she hadn't the heart to get rid of the necklace he'd bought her. After a moment, she added,

"It's fourteen-carat gold. You don't just throw away anything valuable."

Emotion briefly shadowed his eyes. "Not if you're smart."

It took a moment before his meaning sank in, but before she could respond, a cabin door down the hall opened, and she went still. Her first impulse was to run, but it was too late for that. She looked up, meeting Lucas's narrowed gaze.

"Shit." It was Dave; no doubt with a fine view of Lucas holding her necklace, his fingers against the swell of her breast. "I do *not* see this."

Lucas shifted, his broad shoulders blocking her from Dave's view, but she still managed a glimpse of a wide-eyed Dave as he whipped back into his cabin and slammed the door shut. Only then did Lucas drop her necklace and pull away. Seizing her chance, Tessa darted past him.

Lucas watched her, his expression angry—but whether at her, at Dave's interruption, or at himself, she couldn't tell. And she didn't care. Right now, she needed to get away from these confusing emotions his gentle touch had caused, raging inside her like the worst November gale.

She all but ran, and emerged onto the deck and the strong sunlight. The touch of Lucas's fingers still seemed to burn on her skin, and her hands were shaking—and she didn't think it was just from fear of having Dave find her in a position with her captain that could be all too easily misunderstood.

She dredged up a smile and walked down the ramp past the crewman on security duty, and pretended not to notice his openmouthed stare.

At the bottom of the ramp, Tessa spotted a familiar figure trudging back to the ship.

"What's up, Andy?" she asked, slowing. "You're off the clock. You should get out and spend some time uptown."

"I already did." He stopped and peered at her over the top of his sunglasses. "Hey, you look real nice today, Tessa."

A tingle of warmth washed through her; pleasure and shyness tumbled together. "Thanks," she said with a breezy nonchalance. "Where'd you go?"

"To a few shops. I wanted something for Sherri."

Sherri was his girlfriend, and from past conversations she knew that Sherri was eighteen to Andy's nineteen and they'd been dating for three years.

"Did you find anything?"

"Yeah."

Tessa frowned. Glumness was not the look he usually sported when talking about his pretty girlfriend. "Is something wrong?"

He sighed, pushing his sunglasses back up the bridge of his sunburned nose. "No."

"You seem upset. If you want to talk about it, I'm all ears." When he shifted, looking down, she added, "Or you could talk to the captain, if you'd feel more comfortable talking to another guy—"

"Hell, no!"

"So there *is* something wrong?" As Andy nodded, Tessa moved closer. "The hands often talk with a captain when they have problems. Sometimes, he's like a father and a priest all rolled into one. Don't feel shy about it."

"I'd rather talk to you," Andy said. "The captain . . . man, he just don't seem like he'd understand, he's so almighty perfect."

A complaint she was hearing far too often, and she

was torn between wanting to warn Lucas about it and letting him deal with it himself.

Motioning for Andy to follow, Tessa walked back to her cabin in silence. Once inside, Andy sat in her arm chair while she sat at her desk. Shifting uneasily, he looked everywhere but at her.

She leaned forward and smiled to put him at ease. "Now, why don't you tell me what's wrong?"

Looking down at his feet, he said, "I called Sherri, and there's, like, this problem."

"She's okay, isn't she? Nothing's wrong with her or your family?"

He shook his head and his hair, bleached almost white by the sun, fell over his forehead. Impatiently, he shoved it aside. "No, Sherri's okay. I mean . . . not really okay, but not sick or anything. I guess."

Tessa waited, a growing suspicion replacing her alarm.

"She's pregnant," Andy finally said in a near-whisper.

Suspicion confirmed. Tessa sighed, eyeing him with both exasperation and sympathy. "Oh, Andy."

He made a noise of disgust, but she sensed he was close to tears; tears of frustration, anger, and shock. He was just a kid . . . although obviously old enough in a few crucial areas.

"We had a fight, and she was crying." He shifted on the chair. "She hasn't told her parents yet. She wants me to be home when she does."

"Sounds like a good idea," Tessa agreed.

"Sherri's dad . . . man, he'll kill me."

"I doubt that—but I'm really sorry to hear this."

He glanced up then, looking very young and scared, and Tessa ached to pull him into her arms and hug him, like she'd done with Matt. For all his sunny personality, Matt had been so easily hurt, and he'd been fair game to the neighborhood bullies.

"Sounds like you'll need time off when we get back."

"I hate to ask, being so new and with everyone real busy, but I need to see Sherri."

"I have to clear it with the captain, but I doubt it'll be a problem. We can get someone to work relief if necessary."

"Thanks." Andy slumped back on the chair. "I feel so stupid. I mean, it's not like I don't *know* about birth control, but we were celebrating that I got this job, and—"

"No explanation needed; we all make mistakes. Don't be too hard on yourself, okay? Accidents happen."

"Yeah, but not *this* accident," he insisted, his expression darkening. "I knew better. Now I'll have to leave the *Taliesen*."

Tessa frowned. "Why? You pull a decent salary and you're a good worker. You'll move up through the ranks fast at the rate you're going. I'd hate to lose a deckhand like you."

"It can't be easy to have a baby and be alone. She'd be alone a lot if I stay with the ship."

"Both my brothers have families, as do a lot of my friends, and they manage. I'm not saying it isn't tough. Wives get lonely and kids miss their fathers, but you can work it out if you try."

"Is that what you'd do, if you had a husband and kids?"

Tessa stared at him, taken by surprise. A logical question, yet she hadn't seen it coming. "It might be a little different for me."

"Why?"

He was still young and innocent enough to ask why.

"For a woman, the rules are often different." To ease the sarcasm in her voice, she smiled and added, "And can you see me pregnant? Lumbering along the decks of the *Taliesen* with my stomach sticking out to here?"

"It would look kinda weird," Andy admitted. "Is that why you're not married? Because it's too much trouble?"

Tessa's smile faltered. "Something like that."

"Sorry. Didn't mean to be nosy. It's just that most of the crew think you're hot-looking and say things about why you don't hang with guys."

"I can imagine what they're saying, but don't worry. I'm used to it."

Andy flushed. Taking pity on him, she leaned over and patted his shoulder. "Ask some of the married guys for advice. You'll find a lot of them have experiences they're willing to share. Especially Dave Compton. He and his wife separated a couple of times when they first married, but they patched things up and are expecting their first baby this winter."

He nodded as he stood. "I'll do that. Thanks for listening, Tessa."

Tessa also stood. "No problem. I always have time for talks like this . . . and Andy, one more thing."

At the door, he turned.

"I bet Sherri's scared right now, especially if you two argued on the phone. It would help if you called her tonight and told her you loved her and you'll be there for her. Trust me, a woman appreciates knowing that a man will stick with her."

Tessa walked the tourist-crowded streets of Mackinac Island, enjoying the sunshine. The last time the *Taliesen* had stopped there, she'd had little opportunity to explore. Now she took her time wandering along Main and Market Streets, where shops and eateries were interspersed with municipal buildings, old houses, and bed-and-breakfasts. She bought fudge at Mays, snitching pieces of it as she walked, and picked up a yo-yo for Tommy and a wooden puzzle for Amy at a toy store.

The shops were pricey, but since the islanders had to squeeze in as much tourist season as possible before the lakes froze and the ferries stopped running, she couldn't blame them.

After roaming through a dozen gift shops, Tessa settled on a hand-painted T-shirt for Nina. She finished up at the bookstore, buying a sexy romance, then caught a horse-drawn buggy to the Grand Hotel for lunch in the tearoom, where a string quartet played softly in the background as she read.

Before heading back to the *Taliesen* to unload her loot, Tessa strolled across the expansive veranda, admiring the huge, white-painted building that had changed little from when it was built in 1887. The view of the busy harbor, and the clear blue expanse of Lake Michigan beyond, was so beautiful it nearly brought tears to her eyes.

The guys would call her sentimental and sappy, but she hoped she'd never see the day when she took a sight like it for granted.

When she was back aboard the ship, the crew stared and did double takes when they saw her, although no one dared whistle or comment out loud—at least, not until she encountered Amos Lowery on the way to her cabin.

The old man let out a wolf whistle so loud it made her wince. "By God, Jardine, I always figured you were hiding a mighty fine body under that uniform."

No way would she let the little creep ruin her good mood. In a bored tone, she said, "Get a good look now, because this is all you're ever going to see."

"Yeah, that's a real nice dress." Lowery swaggered closer, his eyes gleaming with a perverse mix of lust and dislike. "Dressing up for the captain, eh? I noticed how he watches you."

At her cabin door, Tessa turned to the leering chief. Alarm prickled, raising the hair on her arms.

"And you watch him back," Lowery added, grinning. "Uh-huh, lots of watching going on."

The last thing she needed was Amos Lowery watching her every move and spreading rumors. He'd do it, too, whether the rumors were true or not. This man could make serious trouble for her if she didn't call his bluff now.

Though he outranked every crew member on board, herself included, Tessa moved closer until they stood nose-to-nose.

"Chief, I could care less if you don't like working with women or feel female officers offend your almighty manhood. But I'm tired of your stupid comments about my body, and if you so much as whisper one lie about the captain and me—just one—I'm going to scream sexual harassment." She stared without blinking into his dark eyes. "Do you understand what that means? Stanhope Shipping will turn you off this ship so fast your head'll spin."

Lowery's eyes narrowed. "Ain't that just like a woman: Gotta go cry and whine to the captain when things get a little rough in the real world. Bet he'll do what you want—if you're real nice to him."

"What's the problem here?" came Lucas Hall's terse voice.

Tessa turned and Lowery took a step back.

"Nothing I can't handle," she answered.

"That's not what I asked." Lucas came closer, his gaze locked on Lowery. "Answer me, Mr. Lowery."

Lowery sneered. "If she dresses like that, she's asking for attention. No cause for her to go crying about it when she gets it."

"I won't tolerate disrespect on my ship."

"Or you'll go whining to Dee Stanhope? Hey, what a big man." Despite the ugly tone of Lowery's voice, he backed off farther.

Lucas smiled; a thoroughly cold and unpleasant smile that reminded Tessa he'd gone head-to-head with vicious drug smugglers. He could easily handle one aging bigot.

"I don't make idle threats, Lowery," Lucas said coolly. "I'm getting complaints about you. If I hear again that you're hassling your people or showing a lack of respect to a fellow officer, I'll throw you off this ship myself."

"Try it," the old man said with an answering smile. "You ain't the only one with an inside angle to Dee Stanhope, and without me, your little ship don't go nowhere."

"Don't rate yourself too highly. We're all replaceable," Lucas said.

With a last glare, Lowery retreated. Lucas turned, scowling. "You know, there's a guy like Lowery on every ship. I usually ignore assholes like him, but for some reason, I have this urge to knock his teeth down his throat and watch him choke."

Tessa smiled. "Yeah, he has that effect on people."

"You okay?"

She nodded. "I've gotten used to it."

"It's not something you should have to get used to,"
Lucas said, his face dark with anger.

Surprised, Tessa touched his arm lightly. "Over the
years, I've learned not to judge all men by a few. But
thank you. I appreciate your concern."

She smiled and walked into her cabin. She tossed her
shopping bags onto her bunk, but when she turned to
kick off her sandals, she saw that Lucas had followed
her inside.

Her cabin seemed suddenly smaller, the air warmer,
closer. The bed loomed.

She recognized the edgy shiver of sexual desire. It
was there, beneath every glance, every touch. He didn't
hide it, and she'd be a fool to ignore it.

Lucas broke eye contact first, shifting his attention to
the bags on her bed. "You've been busy. What'd you
buy?"

Relieved, Tessa emptied a bag. "Trinkets and stuff. I
found a yo-yo for my nephew." She hauled it out of
the bag and wound its string. "Watch this."

A little clumsy, she demonstrated her limited reper-
toire of yo-yo tricks: walk-the-dog and rock-the-baby.

"Very good."

Tessa slid her gaze back to the yo-yo, self-conscious
with his smile and intimate gaze. "If I can do this,
Tommy can. His hand-eye coordination is really ad-
vanced."

"Spoken like a proud auntie. How old is he?"

"Six," Tessa answered, returning the toy to its bag.
"Steve and Everett have two kids apiece. And you?
Your sisters must've made you a proud uncle a couple
times over by now."

Lucas leaned back against the closed door, all hard
length and easy grace. It made her nervous. Maybe she
should ask him to open the door, before Lowery told

everyone he'd seen the captain go into the mate's cabin for a quickie.

"I have a tribe of nieces and nephews," he said, unaware of her worries. "My mom's in heaven about it."

"I was sorry to hear of your father's death," she said, suddenly guilty for not expressing her sympathies weeks ago.

"Thank you," he replied after a moment.

"How's your mother doing?"

"She doing great. After Dad died, I transferred back to the Great Lakes District to help her out, though I don't know why I thought she needed me. She raised four kids single-handedly while Dad was off at sea. She's the strongest, bossiest woman I know. One of them, anyway."

Tessa returned his pointed stare, not entirely certain how to respond. After a moment, he added, "But I'm glad she's got my sister Tricia close by. And you? How are your folks?"

"Same old. Dad's still skipper on the *Superior Star* and still thinks I'm a sorry excuse for a female. Mom's on her third husband and just bought a Winnebago. She wants to motor across the country. It amazes me that she ever stayed in one place long enough to have four kids."

Lucas shook his head. "I'm sorry to hear your dad still hasn't come around."

Silence settled over the cabin.

What were they doing here? Unfurling white flags in a truce? Inching back toward the friendship they'd once shared? Perhaps; but underneath it all shimmered a heated desire. Call it lust, call it unfinished business, call it a first love she'd never completely let go, but it stood between them, as forbidden and impossible as it was real.

Tessa glanced briefly at the photo on her desk, almost hearing Matt's voice: *You gotta learn to have a little fun, Tess. You're always so serious.*

Lucas followed the direction of her gaze, then he moved forward and picked up the frame. Uneasily, she watched for his reaction, but only a faint smile crossed his face.

"Looks like he was having a good time."

"Having a good time is what he did best."

"Who's that sitting on his lap?"

"A girlfriend. Her name was Vanessa." Tessa smiled, and pointed. "Here you can just see my brother Everett . . . and Dad, there. The photo was taken in February for Steve's birthday, six months before Matt died. It was the last time we were together as a family, and I'm grateful we had that chance."

Remorse flashed across his face, then was gone. "It helps me to hear about the good memories. Thanks."

"I'm heading back to the island in a moment," she said, looking away so he wouldn't see her sudden, unexpected tears. "I just wanted to dump all my bags, and go talk to Dave."

"More shopping?"

"Maybe." She smiled; a little forced, but perhaps he wouldn't notice. "There's this bar I found called Horn's, and they have a live band. The dinner menu looks good, so I'll head over about six-thirty tonight, listen to a little music, and have supper before coming back on watch."

"What are you talking to Dave about? If it's what I think it is, I wouldn't worry."

She went warm at his reminder. "I thought I'd just pretend that didn't happen. It's about one of the crew. Nothing you have to worry about."

He gave her a speculative look, but nodded as he

opened the door. She breathed a soft sigh of relief.

"Where'd you say you bought that yo-yo? I might head out later to pick up a few."

Tessa gave him the directions, and he thanked her and left, shutting the door behind him. For several minutes, she sat on her bed, staring at the door, aware of how suddenly small and empty her cabin seemed. Then she pushed herself off the bed and headed up to see Dave.

Ten

"**W**hat's up?" Tessa called as she walked into the pilothouse.

Dave turned from the window. "Well, we're still moored to the pier, which I'm sure comes as a relief to you. The *Taliesen* causes one hell of a stir when she's in port."

Tessa joined him, observing the large number of people gathered at the pier, taking pictures. It made her smile. "Never underestimate the power of nostalgia. What've you been up to?"

He grinned. "Watching girls."

"Oooh, I don't think Mrs. Dave would like that."

"Mrs. Dave doesn't mind as long as Mr. Dave doesn't touch."

Tessa made a *tsk-tsk* sound. "Sue's a much more tolerant woman than I'd ever be."

He folded his arms over his chest and inclined his head toward her. "Nice dress. Meant to tell you that earlier, but you were kinda cozy with the skipper."

Oh, damn—she could feel a blush creeping up her neck to her cheeks. She fixed Dave with a frown. "He was only asking about my necklace. No need to make an international incident out of it."

"Whatever. Your business is your business; I don't carry tales." Dave fingered the mustache he was attempting to grow, then said, "Did you drop by for a reason?"

"Yeah. Has Andy Marshall been up here to talk to you?"

"No. Is he supposed to?"

"Maybe. Between you and me, he's having some problems at home, and I suggested he might talk with you about them."

Dave's brows drew together. "What kind of problems?"

"His girlfriend's pregnant, and he's scared. He's not sure he can be married and a father, and still work on board ship. He's a good deckhand, and I don't want to lose him."

Dave grunted. "Dumb kid shoulda kept his pecker in his pants." At her stern look, he sighed, and added, "Yeah, yeah . . . I fill him in on what *not* to do in married life."

"Thanks, Dave," Tessa said, smiling as she headed out.

"You owe me," he said in a growling tone. "You know what I want, baby, and you better deliver."

"How do you want it this time?" she asked from the hatch, grinning at his nonsense.

"Five pounds. The kind with nuts in it."

"You got it," she said. "Five pounds of chocolate fudge with nuts. Though if you ask me, nuts are highly overrated."

"You wouldn't say that if you were a guy . . . hey, don't give me that look! You walked right into that one."

Tessa laughed, then left the pilothouse. When she was back on the island, she stopped first to pick up Dave's payoff fudge—snitching a bit as a delivery fee—and then spent another couple of hours shopping.

A little before six-thirty, she headed to the bar, following the sound of the music. The band was playing something loud, with a lot of bass guitar and a rat-a-tat-tat drumbeat, and she started swinging her shoulders to the music even before she walked through the front door.

She'd expected to run into a few crew members, but a scan of the dim, crowded room showed no familiar faces. It was dark, noisy, frenetic, and smelled heavily of beer—and reminded her, oddly, of the night she'd met Lucas. She shook off the feeling. After putting herself on the wait list for a table, she squeezed into an open spot at the bar. It was a little early yet for any serious partying, but you'd never know it in here.

"Hey, there," drawled a voice beside her.

Tensing, beer bottle in hand, Tessa turned toward a pleasant-faced young man in a Georgia State University T-shirt.

"Hi," she said with a brief smile, not wanting to be rude, but not wanting to be too friendly, either.

The guy said, "Good music." When Tessa nodded, he added, "Where are you from? I'm from Atlanta."

He pronounced it *Atlanna*.

"I figured as much," she answered, and at his surprised look, pointed at his T-shirt.

His eyes crinkled nicely as he smiled. "Forgot I was wearin' that. So, where you from?"

Charmed by his Southern drawl, Tessa smiled back

warmly. "I'm from Rogers City. But I work on the ship." At his blank look she added, "That big ship in the harbor. The *Taliesen*."

"Hey, that old cruise ship? You work on it, you say?"

"I'm the first mate."

He gaped at her, from her sandals, body-skimming dress, and scoop neckline right up to her face. "No shit?"

"No shit," she agreed, her tone dry.

The Georgia Peach grinned suddenly. "So, you're on shore leave, right? Like in *Star Trek*?"

Oh, boy. She eyed the three empty bottles of Molsons in front of him. "Something like that."

"Where's Captain Kirk?"

His question sounded much louder than intended, because the din suddenly ebbed in response to the tall, dark, and daunting figure that had just walked through Horn's front door.

Tessa sighed, and pointed her bottle over his shoulder. "Right behind you."

The Georgia Peach turned, then rapidly stepped back as he said, "Sheee-it!"

If she were in his place, she'd probably do the same thing when faced with six feet two inches of hard-ass authority packed into a uniform.

"I see you're mingling with the locals," Lucas said evenly.

"So I am." She noticed he carried a small bag from the toy store where she'd shopped earlier.

"Is she really your first mate?" the Peach asked, leaning closer now that he'd recovered from his shock.

"She's my one and only." Lucas glanced at Tessa, but the room's dim lighting shadowed his eyes beneath his hat visor, and she couldn't tell if he was being sarcastic or not.

"Sheee-it! Isn't that something."

A sudden suspicion forming, she asked, "Why are you here?"

Before Lucas could answer, the hostess tapped Tessa on the shoulder, smiled, and said, "Excuse me, miss? Your table's ready."

Glad for the opportunity to make her escape, Tessa excused herself, then threaded her way through people dancing everywhere, even between tables, and slid into a seat on the other side of the room.

She placed her order and waited, sipping her beer as she kept an eye on Lucas where he stood at the bar. A group of young women fluttered about him; pretty, bouncy girls with tanned, toned bodies and not an iota of shyness about showing off those bodies.

Captain's groupies, by the looks of them. Some women just lost all good sense when faced by a nice pair of shoulders in a uniform.

Some women, however, were smart and mature enough not to let it show.

Her salad arrived, but she wasn't all that hungry and she picked at it, hoping the lively press of people and the music would chase away her irritation.

Sighing, she pushed her plate away. It wasn't *all* irritation; and at times like this, she wished she could be as comfortable in her body as those young women.

"Excuse me? You wanna dance?"

Tessa looked up, recognizing her Georgia Peach's drawl. He was a little unsteady on his feet, but smiling and friendly.

She hesitated, then downed the last of her beer. A world of men existed outside of Lake Michigan, so why not take advantage of it and have a little harmless fun?

"Sure." She stood, and as he slid his large, warm

hand around her waist, she asked, "What's your name?"

"Jimmy."

"I'm Tessa."

"A pretty name for a pretty lady."

Instinctively, she stiffened, but then forced herself to relax. It was a compliment, just old-fashioned flirtation, not a summons to war. "Thanks."

While he'd had a few too many Molsons, Jimmy danced well enough and didn't step on her toes. After a few attempts to discourage him from holding her too closely, Tessa gave up. She'd never see the guy again, and he was attractive, attentive, and not obnoxiously aggressive—there really was no reason for her not to relax and enjoy herself.

Even as the thought occurred to her, she glanced toward Lucas, where the smiling girls still huddled and fluttered around him.

He smiled back at them, lounging lazily against the bar, but his hands never left his can of Coke.

Interesting.

"Your captain's one lucky guy," Jimmy shouted in her ear, blasting her with beer breath.

"I take it you're referring to his harem?" she yelled back.

"Hell, no! Because he gets to work with you."

"You're a flirt, Jimmy." But she was flattered, all the same.

"Yeah, well, I'm tryin' real hard!"

Tessa laughed, dragging his roaming hand back up to her waist—then ran hard up against Jimmy's body because he'd suddenly stopped moving.

"I'll dance with the lady now."

Jimmy eyes went round, and he released her without

a word of protest. "Yes, sir. It's been a pleasure, ma'am."

Tessa watched Jimmy disappear into the crowd—who were all staring at her, or, more accurately, at the forbidding figure in their midst—before she turned to Lucas.

"You're very good at intimidation, aren't you?"

"Years of practice."

"You know, I was having fun with him."

"I noticed he had busy hands. Don't you think he's a little young for you?"

She eyed him. "Oh, come on. How can you stand there and ask me that with a straight face while you had those coed cuties crawling all over you?"

But he only said, "Are you going to dance with me or not?"

She shrugged as if it didn't matter, and hoped he didn't notice the slight trembling of her hands as she slipped her arms around his neck. Lucas pulled her close as the band switched to a new song, a quieter, slow-dancing number.

"This is a bad idea," she said into the crook of his warm neck, enjoying far too much the hard feel of him beneath her hands, even the rough brush of his coat's fabric against her cheek. "What if somebody from the ship sees us?"

"Why do you care so much about what people think?"

"I care what Dee Stanhope thinks," she corrected, leaning back to look at him.

"We're not doing anything wrong."

Yet.

Closing her eyes against that unsettling thought, Tessa hid her face in Lucas's neck again, inhaling deeply of his scent. Mmmm . . . sandalwood.

"What are you doing here?" she asked, her voice muffled against his shoulder, which seemed impossibly broad. "I have a feeling you didn't wander in here by chance, since I told you I'd be here."

"You mean that wasn't an invitation?"

She heard the humor in his voice, but didn't look up. "No, it wasn't an invitation."

"You're sure?" When she didn't answer, he said, "Maybe I just wanted to dance with the pretty lady in the purple dress. She has nice eyes and a sexy smile."

Tessa closed her eyes, lashes fluttering against his shoulder as she smiled. "Lucas, I'm trying so hard not to like you. Liking you is very bad for my job and my peace of mind."

Although very good for her feminine self-awareness.

"So why did you say yes when I asked you to dance?"

His hands slid lower, and her breath caught as the tips of his fingers brushed just below the small of her back. He held her so close that his coat buttons pressed against her skin.

"Because I'm a weak woman," she whispered, and he only heard her words because her lips were so close to his ear.

"There's nothing weak about you." Lucas continued his slow circling movements, but pulled away to look down at her. "Do you want to stop?"

Tessa hesitated, then shook her head, not taking her gaze from his. If he lowered his head just a fraction, their lips would meet.

For a moment, she wished he would kiss her, wished she really were only a tourist in a noisy bar and flirting with a handsome man she'd never met before.

"Tessa," Lucas said, his hand tightening around her waist. "I don't want to cause you any more trouble than I already have. All I want is for us—"

"Please," she interrupted, her voice low. She wanted to hold on to the magic of this moment. "Don't say one more word—let's just enjoy ourselves. For now, until the music stops, let's forget the past. All of it."

Face expressionless, Lucas nodded. He held her close as they danced, and Tessa knew where every finger, every inch of him, touched her. She closed her eyes and gave herself over to the warmth, the contentment and pleasure, of being held in his arms. No guys from the crew were around to raise their eyebrows, poke each other with their elbows and wink, or make crude comments. For once, she didn't have to be strong and in control of her emotions—she could let Lucas be strong for her, let herself be all woman in his arms.

"What are you thinking?" His voice was low, a tickle of breath against her ear, and she shivered.

"Mmmm, that you feel nice," she murmured, without opening her eyes. "What are *you* thinking?"

He laughed softly. "You're better off not knowing."

That made her look up, and she returned his lazy smile. "You know what this reminds me of?"

"The first time we met," he answered, his smile widening. "Except you weren't wearing a dress."

"And you weren't in uniform."

She let her lids flutter shut again and pressed closer against him. Lucas shifted, easing his fingers lower until they rested on the swell of her bottom. She tightened her grip on his shoulders, slipping one hand higher until she could run her thumb over the short hair just above his collar.

"Jesus, Tessa," he muttered, but she didn't stop—and he didn't pull away.

The rest of their dance passed in silence. As the next song started, with a much faster beat, Lucas released her and stepped away with reluctance. "I'd better head back to the ship."

Tessa looked away, her attention settling on the bar and the annoyed gaggle of groupies.

Lucas followed the direction of her gaze. "I think I may have trouble getting rid of them." He grinned at her. "I don't suppose I could talk you into a quick job as a bodyguard?"

Tessa wondered if he'd asked her to dance to discourage those young women, instead of from a burning desire to hold her in his arms. But she dismissed the thought—he'd wanted that dance as much as she had. "Sure, Captain. I'd be happy to rescue you."

He grimaced. "Don't gloat, Tess. It's not nice."

"Nice isn't in my job description, remember?" she asked cheekily. "I just don't want you expecting me to scare them off by holding your hand—or kissing you."

Good Lord!

As she stood there, hardly able to believe what she'd just said, Lucas's gaze dropped to her mouth. When he slowly looked up again, she didn't misread the hunger in his eyes.

Lucas wanted to make love to her.

It thrilled her, roused an unexpected sense of triumph to see he still wanted her—but thinking about making love with Lucas was one thing, acting on it quite another. A healthy dose of self-preservation instinct kicked in, quickly cooling her desire.

"Let's go," he said, his voice low.

One look at the tight lines of his face warned her against saying anything, so Tessa nodded, then went to pay her bill and retrieve Dave's bag of fudge. On their way out, with Lucas's guiding hand on the small of her back, the groupies at the bar didn't hide their annoyance and made rude comments loud enough for Tessa to hear.

She ignored them with an effort. She was *not* old! And she didn't have a big butt. She certainly had hips—but neither Lucas nor her Georgia Peach had seemed to mind.

Outside, in the cooler air and darkening sky, Tessa and Lucas walked toward the harbor at a leisurely pace. She didn't miss the curious, admiring looks sent Lucas's way. He appeared not to notice the stares, the elbow nudges, and whispers.

Curious, she asked, "Why are you out and about?"

"I wanted to buy a few yo-yo's. Dash out, dash back was the plan," he answered with a shrug. "I didn't intend to go to the bar, but when I saw you go inside, and how all those men were staring at you, I changed my mind, in case you found yourself in trouble."

She stared at him. "That was sweet, but I can take care of myself. I work with men, and understand men. It's women I have trouble with." She sighed, then glanced at him again. "You know, if you want to blend in with the locals on these dashes of yours, you're going to have to lose the uniform."

"It has its uses."

"Like scaring nice college boys half to death?"

He shrugged again. "When you spend most of your life in uniform, you get used to it."

"I know how that is," Tessa said with feeling.

He smiled, running his gaze down her chest, then back up again. "I'm glad you wore the dress."

Tessa cleared her throat. "Thank you. I think."

As they passed through the harbor, talking about impersonal subjects, Lucas suddenly veered off and headed for a big cabin cruiser that fairly glowed with newness.

Brows raised in surprise, Tessa followed him.

"That's a great boat," Lucas called to the two men puttering about on deck.

The men stood, eyes widening, and Tessa shook her head, wondering if Lucas even noticed these reactions.

"Thank you," said the older of the two. Father and son, she guessed.

Lucas offered his hand. "Captain Lucas Hall of the *Taliesen*."

The father shook his hand first, then the son. The father said, "Nice to meet you. That's a fine old ship you have."

"She sure is, but yours is a beauty, too."

The father's gaze drifted to Tessa, who'd come to stand beside Lucas. The man smiled. Without waiting for Lucas to introduce her, she put out her hand. "I'm Tessa Jardine, first mate of the *Taliesen*."

God, that had a great ring to it, and she couldn't help but let a little pride color her voice.

Lucas and the two men were soon deep in discussion about running private charters and fishing excursions. Business cards even crossed hands. Surprised by the animated tone of Lucas's voice, and the extent of his knowledge about the business, Tessa wondered what this was all about.

After leaving the men and their charter boat, Lucas headed back toward the *Taliesen*. Tessa followed, sending him a curious look. "I didn't know you were interested in charters."

Lucas glanced at her. "Before I took this job, I'd considered starting up my own charter service."

"Sounds like you're still thinking about it," she said. He smiled. "Maybe."

Tessa waited, but he didn't elaborate. A moment later, shortly before reaching the *Taliesen's* ramp, Tessa stopped abruptly. She snagged Lucas's hand, bringing him to a halt beside her, and whispered, "Will you look at that."

The setting sun cast a pinkish glow over the ship as she sat proudly at anchor, pretty as a postcard. Every now and again, the majesty of the ship left her in awe, reminding her again that the *Taliesen* wasn't just any ship; she was a grand old queen of the lakes, and the last of her kind.

"She is something," Lucas murmured.

Tessa tipped her head to one side, a warm sense of pride and satisfaction washing through her. "I probably sound like some proud mama, but damn . . . there's nothing like her."

Lucas laughed, and she grinned as they walked up the ramp side by side.

Chief Purser Jerry Jackson, head of the steward department, stood at the curving chrome purser's desk, giving a young couple directions. At six-foot-five, with dark black skin and a shaved head, Jerry made an intimidating figure—except that he almost always wore a smile.

"I'm heading to the pilothouse," Lucas said with a nod toward Jerry, who nodded back in a respectful acknowledgment.

After Lucas and the young couple had departed, Jerry rubbed a big hand over his head, and said, "Look at you, girl. What's the special occasion?"

As Jerry was a happily married man and the proud father of three teenage girls, the mild flirtation didn't bother her, any more than the jokes and innuendos bandied back and forth between her, Rob, and Dave. The difference was respect—they never crossed the line of her comfort zone as Lowery did.

She grinned. "I wanted to dress up. And the way the

crew's acting—including you—you'd think they'd never figured out I was female."

"Oh, I figured that out sometime ago." Jerry leaned over his desk and said in a conspiratorial whisper, "You and the captain were looking pretty tight."

Tessa glanced away, then back, her smile gone. "Don't start seeing things that aren't there."

Jerry's brows shot up, creasing his broad forehead. "I'm not looking for trouble, but it sure is good to see you with him and you not wearing a face that says you want to kill the man."

Kill the man?

"Is it that obvious?" she asked, mortified.

Despite Rob Shea's warning, she hadn't wanted to believe her tension around Lucas had been visible to the crew outside of the pilothouse.

"I hear talk. Some of it's just foolish, but there's worry in some of it. Worry that the captain and the mate are feuding. We sure don't need that kind of trouble this early on. I got my hands full keeping hundreds of passengers happy, and I don't need to be reassuring my people that there's not an all-out war going on up there in the brain box."

Tessa managed a smile. "Thanks for the warning, Jer."

He nodded, his expression easing back to its usual laid-back benevolence. "Anytime."

She headed to her cabin, more determined than ever to put a stop to these less-than-platonic thoughts about Lucas. If she didn't, others would soon take notice, and start talking about something much more troublesome than a "feud."

With a sigh, she stripped off her dress and changed back into her uniform. She wanted to avoid seeing Lucas again that day, but she had to talk to him about this growing attraction. If he continued to touch her, watch her, and follow her about, all her efforts to resist temptation wouldn't amount to much.

Especially since she wasn't all that sure she wanted to resist temptation.

Eleven

*A*fter relieving Rob on watch—and frowning over a weather report of a storm front moving in—Tessa sat down at the chart desk, grabbed a donut from the box Rob had left behind, and settled in for the night.

The next several hours crawled by, and shortly before ten, the storm hit. Bored with her computer solitaire game, Tessa walked over to the window bay to watch.

Lightning snaked jaggedly across the black sky, thunder cracked and rumbled, and the rain came down in sheets. The wind roared northeasterly and although the *Taliesen* was safe in the harbor, she rocked back and forth, mooring lines taut, the pier groaning whenever her hull rubbed against it.

"Summer squall, I see."

Tessa jumped at the sound of his voice and spun. "Lucas! Jeez, don't sneak up on me like that."

He walked closer. "Sorry. I thought you heard me

come in. What's the weather report saying?"

"Nor'easter moving south at twenty-five to thirty-five knots, bringing heavy rain and possibly hail. But it'll be clear skies and seventy degrees when we ship out tomorrow."

While Lucas skimmed the report, Tessa stole a lengthy look at him. It was late, yet he was still buttoned to the neck. It troubled her, as did the weary lines on his face. More and more, as her wariness around him faded, she sensed something just under his cool, controlled surface. Something definitely wrong.

"We'll have choppy seas," he said, looking up.

"Not too bad. Winds will be more southerly tomorrow." Then, abruptly, she asked, "Are you okay?"

At the question, his brow arched. "Of course. Why?"

"You're up late."

"It's only ten." He moved closer, and she took an instinctive step backward—bumping into the window. He noticed her retreat, and frowned. "Am I bothering you?"

"Bother" wasn't quite the word she'd use to describe this warm, fluttery feeling in her chest.

Oh, Lord, he'd gotten her alone again.

"You hardly bother me," she said, hoping her cool tone disguised her sudden nervousness. "But I do sometimes feel like you're checking up on me because you don't trust me."

"Do the other mates feel that way?" When she nodded, he rubbed his jaw, and said, "I'm not checking up on you, I just need to be *doing* something."

The note of frustration in his voice surprised her. Being a captain meant giving orders and standing back while others carried them out. Lucas knew how the system worked—or he should have.

"I've wondered why you wanted this job. From what

I've heard, you led a pretty interesting life down in Miami . . . a lot of action, danger. What made you decide to command the *Taliesen*?"

Stepping back from her, Lucas folded his arms across his chest, pulling the fabric of his shirt taut at the seams. Discreetly, she admired the play of his muscles.

"I'd had enough excitement, and the *Taliesen* sounded like quiet, easy work."

"Figures," she said with a sigh. "This is my big break, but to you, it's just a nice, cushy little job."

"Not as cushy as I'd expected." With a brief, unreadable glance, he pushed away from the window. "I'm going for a cup of coffee in the galley. Do you want me to bring you back some?"

Tessa eyed him, curious about his odd statement. After a moment, she said, "No, thanks." He nodded, moving away. He'd reached the hatch when she called, "Hey, Lucas."

He turned, his expression still closed.

She swallowed. "I need to talk to you, and—"

"Come to my office when you get off watch."

"Isn't that a little late? It can wait until—"

"No," he interrupted again. "I'll expect you at midnight."

Tessa stared at the shadowed doorway where he'd been, puzzled by his insistence. Then she turned back to the window bay, frowning and deep in thought, while lightning split the dark sky and the wind howled.

By the time Dave came to relive her, Tessa had carefully planned what she wanted to say to Lucas. Everything would be very civilized and calm.

"Civilized and calm," she reminded herself as she stood outside Lucas's office. The door was ajar, and she knocked.

"Come in."

Tessa slipped inside. "Are you still up to talking?"

Lucas nodded. "Shut the door."

She hesitated, preferring to keep the door open, if just a crack, then thought better of it and pushed the door closed with a soft *click*.

He sat at his desk, appearance unchanged from when she'd seen him two hours earlier. He hadn't even loosened his tie, much less taken it off. A can of Coke sat on his desk, amid orderly stacks of papers.

"What are you doing?"

"Catching up on paperwork."

"It's midnight."

"I'm aware of that." He leaned over his desk. "I assume you're not here to discuss the time, the weather, or my work habits."

"No."

"Have a seat."

Tessa sat down, then took a quick breath and plunged ahead full bore. "Lucas, we both know that it's going to take a lot of hard work to make the *Taliesen* a success. Dee Stanhope has her work cut out for her just to break even, so she doesn't need any trouble between her officers."

"I thought we'd worked that out."

"I'm not talking about being angry with you over what happened years ago, or even about Matt." His lids lowered a fraction, and she added, "I'm here because of sex."

Lucas sat back, the leather of his chair creaking. After a moment, he said, "I do admire your directness, Tessa."

"Good, because I'm going to be even more direct." She continued in a rush, "I seem . . . as strange as it sounds, I still find you attractive. And I know this attraction isn't just my problem."

As if to prove her point, that awareness rose between them again, crackling, alive. Under his unwavering regard, she felt open and exposed. Her heart pounded.

"I already made that clear."

"You did?" she asked cautiously, trying to remember what he might have said, and when.

"That night I told you I'd never think of you as one of the guys." He leaned forward again. "What did you think I meant?"

Her whole body warmed at the memory—and the sweet aching need he'd roused within her.

Unable to meet his eyes, Tessa settled her gaze at a point below his chin. On his broad chest, and his tie—and its perfect knot. She frowned, squelching a sudden, powerful urge to slide it off his neck. "You could've been a little clearer."

"If I'd been any clearer, I'd have had you on your back on the living-room floor."

She jerked her gaze back up, shocked by his bluntness. An image of what he implied flashed to mind, and heat tingled through her. "Why didn't you?"

His brows shot up. "Are you saying you wanted me to?"

"I don't know. Maybe. I can't seem to think very clearly when I'm with you," she admitted, rubbing at her brows, too tired to be delicate or deny that she wouldn't have stopped him if he'd tried, even as angry as she'd been then. "I suppose I should thank you for not taking advantage of me."

A brief smile curved his lips. "Nobody's ever going to take advantage of you, Tess."

She narrowed her gaze, uncertain if he meant that as a compliment or not. "The point I'm trying to make, and not doing very well, is that I hadn't realized how quickly the crew picked up on the tension between us, and I don't want anyone picking up on the . . . other thing between us. That would be a disaster."

"A disaster," he repeated, his expression grim. "Don't worry. Even if I spend half my waking hours thinking about how good it would feel to make love to you again, I can control my baser urges."

How good it would feel . . .

"I'm glad we got that all cleared up." Tessa smiled brightly, hoping she looked calm and cool. "I think that if you can behave yourself, I can keep myself from pouncing on you as well."

Even if the notion made her breathing shorten, and her skin flush from head to toe—and a little voice whisper: *What could it hurt, to pounce? Just once . . .*

Silence blanketed the office as the wind outside howled, and the *Taliesen* rocked from side to side. As he watched her, Tessa crossed her legs, then uncrossed them again. Lucas steepled his hands together.

"Is that all you wanted to say?" he asked at length.

"Yes . . . well, no, there's something else." She eyed his tie again, the buttoned collar.

"Do I have a spot?" he asked, glancing down, then at her. "You keep looking at my shirt."

"Why do you keep dressing up like that?"

His face blanked. "I'm the captain of this ship. I'm expected to look the part."

"Lucas, your ship's asleep and there's nobody in this room but me. Or are you playing a part for me, too? The stalwart captain, ever in control?"

Tessa wasn't surprised when he didn't respond. She stood and crossed to his side, resting her hip on his desk as she studied his closed face. A muscle in his jaw tensed.

At this small, telling detail, she blew out a shaky breath. "Well, *somebody* needs to tell you to loosen up. It might as well be me, since you so admire my directness."

"Tessa, I don't—"

"The crew thinks you're arrogant and too good to mix with them. And that's the nice things they're saying. What are you trying to prove with this?" She flicked his tie with her finger. "Stop acting like you're some sort of superman. Nobody will think less of you if you unbutton your collar and relax."

Anger flashed in his eyes. Well, if he didn't like hearing the truth, tough. Tessa took the offending tie between her fingers. Navy silk, and soft—not the usual company polyester.

When she looked up again, his angry expression had softened to something more like wariness—or expectancy.

"Relaxing is easy. Even you uptight, controlled types can do it." Tessa tugged on his tie, then wiggled it back and forth to loosen it. "Just slide the knot down, like this. Then push this button through this hole and—"

The sensation of warm skin and crisp dark hairs at the base of his throat silenced her. A long moment passed before she finished quietly, "And doesn't that feel better?" Her fingers lingered on his skin.

As his mouth tightened, his eyes locked on hers. "It feels damn good."

Ancient, female instinct warned he was referring to something farther south of his collar. That same instinct made her take a step back, but Lucas shot out his hand and stopped her.

Tessa looked up from his hand on hers and met the full force of his gaze. She watched the play of emotions in his hazel eyes: surprise, anger—and raw, primal lust.

Shaken, she realized what she'd just done. One little button; that was all it had taken to unleash the beast he'd kept so tightly in control.

"Your mouth is telling me one thing, Tessa," Lucas said in a low voice. "But your eyes and your hands are telling me something else, and I don't like this game."

He stood only inches from her: tall, broad-shouldered, and intimidating. He'd released her, but didn't move back. Nor could she turn away. It was as if an invisible netting of need wrapped around them, and desire pooled warm and deep within her, too strong to deny.

"It's no game." Looking away from his eyes, she began working the knot of his tie, focusing on her fingers, very aware of the rise and fall of his chest.

Slowly, with a silky rustle, she slid the tie free of his collar and tossed it on his desk. "There," she murmured. "That wasn't so hard, now, was it?"

"What the hell are you doing? I could swear that just five minutes ago you told me you didn't want this to happen."

"I didn't say I didn't want it to happen; I said it would be a disaster." She let her hands fall to her side. "The problem is, I never was very good at resisting temptation—and even though I know you're bad for me, I still want you."

Outside, the wind still howled, and rain slapped against the hull like a barrage of buckshot.

Lucas moved closer, his body brushing along hers and tightening that soft, liquid inner heat into a sweet, sharp pull of desire. Again, she placed her hands on his chest, amazed at the hard heat of him. Fingers fumbling, she began unbuttoning his shirt. Halfway down the placket, Lucas closed his hands over hers.

"Just so we're clear on this, Tessa: I want you on that

desk, naked, and I want to be inside you." Their eyes met; his pupils dark and wide. Hungry. "But I need to know what you want from me."

"Bastard," she whispered, but it was more of a caress than a curse. "The Lucas I remember wouldn't have cared."

"He's learned a lesson or two since then. Now answer my question. If it's a one-night stand, fine. If you want to get me out of your system, that's fine, too. But I need to know."

Tessa sighed, then stopped fighting the need to touch him again. She played with a button just below his ribs—and slipped it open, watching his reaction. His jaw tightened, and he briefly closed his eyes.

"I guess I want what we had," she admitted. "I want back what you took from me when you walked out of my life."

Tessa freed the next button, then another, and this time, he didn't stop her, not even when she pulled the shirt from his trousers and spread it wide with a soft sigh of appreciation.

Beneath the tight ribbed knit of his undershirt, his muscles were firm, his skin hot. She ran her hands along his chest, enjoying the familiar, half-remembered feel of his body. No matter how hard she'd tried to forget, her fingers, her senses, her heart, remembered.

"I want the glow I've never found with any man but you. And I want to make you lose control and go crazy."

"I'm halfway there already." He smiled, but it didn't reach his eyes. "Want to come the rest of the way with me?"

It was a challenge; a return to the cocky, daredevil Lucas she'd known. The excitement of danger, of the forbidden, was a powerful lure, and stirred a reckless rebelliousness.

"To hell with Dee Stanhope and her threats," she whispered. "Nobody runs my life but me."

"I pity the man who ever tries to tell you what to do," Lucas said. Pressing against her, he took her face between his hands, and kissed her.

Oh, the warm, rough feel of his mouth on hers!

Impatient for more, Tessa returned his kiss with equal urgency, gathering the front of his shirt tightly in her fists, as if he might get away if she didn't hold on tight.

He made a sound low and deep in his throat, sliding one hand to the back of her head, the other down her spine, drawing her against his body, close enough for her to feel his erection, the tension of his muscles as he held back.

She didn't want him holding back; she wanted all of him.

"Oh, no you don't," she whispered against his lips, and slid her hand down the front of his trousers, cupping his weight, tracing the shape of him.

With a growl, he sat on his desk and pulled her down until she straddled his lap. Hooking a finger under her chin, he tipped her face and kissed her again. A hot, wet, and possessive kiss, holding her still with one hand as he quickly unbuttoned her shirt with the other.

Tessa felt a sudden sensation of cool air against her skin, then he tossed her shirt to the floor and his hands slid under the back of her bra.

He moved his lips from her mouth, trailing hungry kisses down her neck to her breasts. A low moan escaped her, and Tessa bit down on her lower lip, struggling to stay quiet.

When his tongue circled her aroused nipple, she sank her fingers into his shoulder muscles and tipped her head back.

"I want this off," Lucas muttered, and neatly rid her of her bra so that nothing separated the sensitive skin of her breasts from his mouth, the rasp of his beard, the warmth of his breath.

Leaning into him, she cupped his face in her hands. For an instant, she shivered at the raw need in his eyes—and the thin edge of anger that acknowledged her power over him, that she'd overrun his control.

"If you're going to change your mind, do it now," he said, his voice rough, harsh.

Tessa shook her head, running her hands down his face to his shoulders, and tugged at his shirt until he was free of it. She trailed her fingers down his chest, then up across his bare arms. She smiled slowly. "All or nothing."

He made another low sound, pulling her into his kiss. His tongue traced the line of her lips, then slid inside her mouth. With a muffled sigh, Tessa leaned her bare breasts against him, letting him inside, touching, tasting, teasing. He assaulted her with circling kisses, breaking for quick, gulping breaths before returning to the wet, warm, intimate connection again.

Still kissing her, he moved a hand down to her breast, cupped it, then circled her nipple with his thumb.

Intense pleasure ripped through her, almost more than she could endure, and Tessa arched against him. She pulled at his undershirt until Lucas finally broke away with a muttered curse and yanked the shirt over his head and threw it aside. Shoving the papers and pencils from his desk, he whispered thickly, "Lie down."

Tessa eased back, toppling the Coke can. She gasped, but the empty can fell harmlessly to the floor, clinking against the deck with every sinuous roll of the ship.

"Come here," she whispered, grabbing his belt buckle. "I'm not done kissing you yet."

She yanked his hips down and the rest of him followed, his bare skin and chest hair rough on her breasts. She rubbed against him as he kissed her eyelids, her nose, forehead, and cheeks, then finally her lips.

Softer now, slyly teasing as his hands trailed lower and pulled at her buckle. He popped the button at her waistband, and she heard the whisper of the lowering zipper and felt the cold surface of his desk beneath the flushed skin of her thighs.

Lucas kissed her neck, the hollow of her throat, then sucked and teased her nipples until she thought she'd come apart right there on the desk, with his mouth at her breasts and his hand resting against her white-cotton underwear.

She held back a desperate moan of pleasure as he trailed kisses down her belly and ran his tongue along the edge of her panties. He tugged on the laces of her shoe, then the other, peeling away her socks, her panties—and soon he was kissing bare skin rippling with goose bumps from the onslaught of sensation.

Upward he moved—first her ankles, calves, then her knees. He pushed her legs apart and she tried to close them, trembling with the need for release, yet shy in the light of the lamp on his desk, feeling too exposed and vulnerable.

Too fast; he was going too fast . . .

"You're so beautiful," Lucas whispered, his lips brushing the inside of her thigh. "God, I've spent hours thinking of nothing but this."

"Lucas, wait. I—" She gasped, and choked back a cry as the hot warmth of his tongue caressed her sex.

"Day after day," he whispered, with a soft, tickling kiss. "Wanting to taste you here. To touch you."

It was too much, this movement of his lips, this hot and delicate touch of breath against her sensitive flesh with each word he spoke. Tessa arched as pleasure swept through her in hot, liquid pulses that built and finally exploded, then finally gentled to a nearly painful pang.

Once she'd caught her breath, she pushed herself up onto her elbows, a little unsteady. "Next time . . . you better be inside me when that happens."

Lucas grinned, his pupils nearly black. He tipped his head toward his bedroom. "In case someone forgets that when my door is shut, no one so much as knocks. I'd hate to have to kill Shea or Compton."

He helped her from the desk and caught her against him, kissing her mouth again, slowly and thoroughly, as his hands cupped her bottom.

Then, without warning, Lucas scooped her up in his arms. She let out a yelp of alarm, since getting swept off her feet wasn't an everyday occurrence.

"What do you think you're doing?"

"What does it look like?" He grinned, and dropped her unceremoniously on his bed. "Don't move. I'll be right back."

Tessa stared after him, wondering what he was up to, until she heard the click of a lock. She quickly dimmed the lamp, then slipped beneath the cool sheets. As she lay waiting, doubts and fears began forming despite her determination not to let the past touch her tonight—doubts of the rightness of what she wanted, fears of what tomorrow might bring. But all doubts scattered the instant Lucas walked back into the room and shut the door.

In the soft light, he looked formidable, dark, and not a little dangerous. Secrets in his eyes, a shadowy promise in his slow, curving smile. He stood bare-chested, his trousers partially unzipped.

Tessa swallowed, unable to take her eyes from his hard-edged beauty. She recalled the mole on his lower ribs—although not that curving scar—and how the hair of his chest swirled thick before narrowing toward his groin. She remembered the terrain of his body, as familiar to her as any navigational chart.

"I see you still swim."

"Whenever I can." He kicked off his shoes, then his trousers heaped to the floor, leaving him in only his underwear, his erection pushing against the fabric.

A long, pale scar that ran nearly from groin to ankle caught her gaze—another mark that hadn't been there before. With a swell of sadness she realized this wasn't, after all, the same flawless body she'd explored with eager young fingers. She ached for him, and the pain he had gone through. She'd known he'd almost died, but seeing the scars, the extent of those injuries—

"It looks better than it did." His voice cut across her thoughts, and she looked up. He stood by the bed with squared shoulders, hands fisted at his side, eyes watchful.

"Oh, Lucas," Tessa whispered as a new, confusing grief filled her. She gently traced the scar with a fingertip, then leaned forward and kissed it, where it slashed down his thigh.

Lucas swallowed audibly, and for an instant, she thought his eyes glistened—with tears, with emotion, she couldn't tell in the dim light . . . maybe it was only a gleam of lust.

But he made no move to join her, not until she eased over in the bed and patted the mattress.

"You're going to get cold standing there. Come here, Lucas." When she noticed the small packet in his hand, she smiled. *"Semper Paratus."*

" 'Always Ready.' " Lucas smiled back—a true smile, and the deep, slashing grooves of his dimples chased away the years from his face. "Once a Coastie, always a Coastie."

"But not necessary. I'm on the pill."

He sat beside her, tossing the condom aside. The mattress dipped under his weight, rolling her against him, and he leaned over and kissed her. Gently at first, then more insistently as he drew back the sheets.

"You're all grown-up," he said, tracing a finger between her breasts and down her belly. Then his lips followed the path his finger had taken. "And more beautiful than ever."

He kissed her mouth again, hands skimming her breasts, his skin hot against her, his body heavy and hard with a tightly leashed power.

Tessa worked off his briefs until nothing at all separated them. Lucas moved quickly, settling between her legs. She looped her arms around his neck and pulled him down.

He slowly filled her, letting out his breath in a rush when she raised her hips to take him all the way in.

A long moment passed, but he didn't move, as if afraid to break the fragile moment of joining. Tessa lay as still, reveling in the sensations, in the wonder of this man inside her. For a woman, nothing spoke of her trust in a man more than letting him make love to her, to allow him within her very body. Bare, vulnerable— even this soft light left no places to hide emotions on a face, in a gaze, that was mere inches away.

Eyes locked on hers, Lucas began to move. Slower than she expected, his face tight with the effort to hold back for her sake.

"You feel even better than I remember," he muttered, lowering his mouth for another kiss.

Tessa rose to meet him halfway, her arms tight around his neck. He thrust again, kissing her as his hands slipped beneath her bottom and shifted her so that he could go deeper.

He broke the kiss and began pumping his hips with urgent intent. Tessa grasped the sheets, wrapping her legs around Lucas's hips. The liquid warmth gathered, then radiated outward again as she dug her fingers into the mattress. Sweetly thick, each deep stroke nudged her closer to release. Her muscles shook from need and anticipation as she focused on feeling each and every minute sensation of each and every stroke. Her eyes squeezed shut as Lucas increased his rhythm, his breathing louder, harsher, against her ear.

A low moan broke past her lips before his mouth covered hers. The wave of pleasure crested quickly . . . then hovered, suspended, a split, sweet second of forever before release broke over her and her tensed muscles softened, her cries caught in Lucas's kiss.

"God, Tessa," he groaned, and his final, powerful thrust lifted her body inches off the mattress.

His eyes glazed over, neck tendons straining. As the orgasm rocked his body, she glided her hands up along the rock-hard muscles of his arms and curled her fingers over his shoulders.

Lucas swayed above her for a moment before she drew him down against her, kissing his warm, damp forehead. She ran her fingers through his short, dark hair, amazed at the heat radiating from his skin.

"My God, you're hot," she whispered.

He grinned, and his voice was a low rumble as he pulled her against his chest. "That's supposed to be my line."

Twelve

*B*reathing hard, Lucas held Tessa close against his chest, feeling her cheek bunch as she smiled. He couldn't seem to move, still drained from the force of his release.

It had been a long time since he'd enjoyed her soft warmth in his arms, and now that they'd gotten that explosive need out of the way, he wanted to explore the swells and valleys of her sweet body, so familiar and yet different. She had a mature confidence, but was more reserved than he remembered. Somewhere along the line, she'd lost her youthful eagerness, her open curiosity.

He'd had a hand in that, though she was doing a good job of avoiding any mention of it.

"I can hear your heart," she murmured.

He smiled, closing his eyes as a sudden weariness swept over him. "Must be reassuring to know you didn't kill me. There'd better be no emergencies on the bridge, because I don't think I can crawl out of this bed."

She propped herself up on his chest, hair mussed, looking sexy and beautiful—and satisfied. "You had quite a workout there."

"Sex is great for cardiovascular health." He arched a brow. "An orgasm a day keeps the doctor away, I always say."

"You would." A faint frown creased her brow as she traced her fingers over a thin scar on his upper arm.

"The body's more banged up than you remember."

She glanced up. "What happened?"

He grunted. "I spent a year patrolling the Bering Sea, and it was the coldest, most miserable year of my life. I was the boarding officer on duty when we stopped a Chinese fishing trawler that had strayed on the wrong side of the boundary line. One of the crew went berserk. Bastard stuck me with a knife. Took fifteen stitches to close it, and it hurt like hell."

Tessa winced in sympathy. "So you were a fish cop for a while, huh?"

"Yeah," he said, his gaze roving along her breasts. "Being a Coastie was all glamour and glory."

"Do you miss it?"

The question took him by surprise. No one had ever asked him this before, and he absently brushed his thumb across the swell of her hip as he considered his answer.

"I don't miss getting shot at, stabbed, or pulling bodies out of the water. But I miss . . . I don't know, doing something worthwhile, I guess. I miss the routine, the high that followed when everything came together."

"The *Taliesen* must seem pretty dull in comparison."

He glanced away, toward the framed ship blueprints

lining the wall of his cabin. "Like I said earlier, at the time, I was looking for dull."

Tessa stroked a warm, soft hand along the length of him, and Lucas made a low, appreciative groan.

"You weren't looking for dull a few minutes ago."

"Nope," he agreed, as a mischievous grin crossed her face.

Tessa shimmied downward, marking every inch of his body with kisses before she straddled him. His breathing shortened with anticipation.

As the *Taliesen* rolled beneath them, she guided his erection within her. Leaning down, she kissed him as his hands caressed her breasts. She rocked with the ship's motion, biting her lip, a frown of concentration between her brows. She was so beautiful, with her lush breasts, smooth skin, and intent responsiveness.

Aroused almost to the point of pain at the sight of her above him, of the feel of being inside her tight, hot body, Lucas grabbed her hips and bucked, pushing as deeply inside her as possible. She gasped, eyes fluttering shut.

She came first, head arched, fighting back a cry of pleasure. Lucas rolled her over, eased a pillow under her hips, and entered her again, hard and deep, nearly losing control when she deliberately squeezed her moist inner walls around him.

He slipped his hand between them, rubbing her sensitive nub. As her body contracted around him, his pleasure spiked fast and hot, and with one last thrust, his orgasm hit hard.

Winded and spent, Lucas fell back on the bed. In the low light, perspiration gleamed on her skin, and he watched her breasts rise and fall with her every rapid, audible breath.

"Well, we sure wrecked your bed," she murmured.

A moment later, she added, "And it looks like we've pretty much picked up right where we left off."

A tenderness took hold of him at the wistful note in her voice. For a moment or two, he'd almost let himself believe they could go back to what they'd had, and that making love to her would leave him feeling the way he had back then—charged with purpose and conviction. A man on top of the world.

But there was no going back, and she'd realize it soon enough. In the rational light of morning she'd probably regret what they'd just shared, perhaps even hate him for it.

At least nobody could ever accuse him of screwing up small time. When he made mistakes, they were doozies.

Closing his eyes, he allowed himself to enjoy the moment for its own sake, for as long as it lasted. Her fingers stroked up and down his chest, the light scratch of her short nails lulling him. It made him want to purr like a big, satisfied tomcat.

"Lucas, did you ever get married?"

"No." He opened his eyes, meeting hers. "I lived with a woman for nearly five years, but we split right before my father died and I moved back to Michigan."

"Oh." She caught her lower lip between her teeth, worried it a moment, then asked, "What was her name?"

Lucas shifted, uncomfortable talking about another woman after just making love to Tessa. "Christina."

"Was she in the Coast Guard?"

"She was a kindergarten teacher." Christina's face came to mind: earnest, smiling, and sweet—until he recalled the hurt and disappointment in her eyes during their last months together.

"Did you love her?"

Weariness rolled over him, and he looked away. "Why are you asking me this?"

"Because I want to know."

"She was nice, always upbeat. I enjoyed being with her, but she needed more than I could give." And he'd needed more, too. He'd needed someone to talk to on those bad days, but she'd always insisted he not bring his work home, and so he'd kept it all bottled up inside. "It just didn't work out."

Tessa fell silent, and Lucas supposed she was waiting for him to ask the same questions of her. But he didn't want to know about the other men she'd been with.

He rolled to his side, propping his chin on his hand, studying her serious face. "Regrets?"

"I'm a big girl, Lucas. I wanted to go to bed with you; you didn't force it on me." She sighed in frustration. "But I can't help wonder what we might've had between us years ago if you'd just told me the truth."

"Don't go there, Tess. You were too young to make a decision like that."

"But not young enough for you to sleep with me."

He rubbed at his brows. "If I had told you the truth, what would you have done? Would you have left the academy for me?"

"I deserved to make that choice myself."

"You thought you were in love with me—"

"I *was* in love with you," she interrupted sharply. "Yes, I was only nineteen and naive, but my feelings for you were real."

"And if you'd come to Miami? Given up your career? Can you tell me you wouldn't have ended up hating my guts? I didn't want to hurt you then, and I don't want to hurt you now. I should stay the hell out of your life now, too."

"Why?"

Lucas stared at her. "Let's not fool ourselves into thinking we're some everyday, average couple, Tess. You won't be taking me home to meet the family." When she looked away, he added, "You can imagine how they'd react to me when you say, 'Hey, everybody, look who I brought home. You remember him, don't you? He's the one who blew up—' "

She stiffened, and he cursed himself for ruining the warmth of the moment. A chill stole over him, and he pulled her body closer.

"So what do we do now, Lucas?"

"Damned if I know."

He ran his finger down the length of her stomach, circled a taut nipple. She shifted against him with a quick breath, and her response left him feeling nothing but guilt.

Too much had changed between them. And he had no business tangling any woman, especially *this* woman, in his personal messes. Until he pulled his life back together, he shouldn't have so much as looked at her, much less pursued her.

He should sit her down and explain he was recovering from a traumatic stress disorder—emphasis on the recovering. She deserved to know, just as she deserved a whole man, not a part of one.

"Lucas, what's wrong?"

Now. Tell her now.

Instinctively, his hands closed tightly around her, as if to prevent her leaving. "Nothing."

The words he wanted to say wouldn't come.

"You sure?" Her concern only added to his guilt.

"Yeah," Lucas said, closing his eyes. "I'm just tired."

"Then I should let you get some rest, and leave before the watch changes. I don't want anybody seeing me sneak out of your cabin."

He nodded, and they dressed in silence. At the door, he kissed her deeply, a kiss that said everything he could not. She looked a little startled at his intensity, but gave him a sweet smile before slipping away. He listened until he heard her door click shut, then returned to the bed, with its twisted sheets still carrying her scent.

Lucas lay back down, rubbing tiredly at the bridge of his nose. Making love to Tessa might have eased his immediate physical problem, but it sure had created one far worse.

He'd bring her nothing but heartache and conflict with her family, and could very well wreck the career she'd worked so hard to achieve. The best thing he could do for her was walk away. Again.

But he was too damn selfish to let her go. He wanted her—her calmness, her humor, her strength and vitality.

Yet it wasn't a simple matter of wanting her. He *needed* her—and there wasn't anything simple about that at all.

Thirteen

*A*t seven in the morning, Tessa dragged her aching, weary body into the officers' mess. She couldn't sleep through the sounds of the ship preparing to get under way, and decided if she had to be awake, she might as well eat breakfast.

The closer she came to the mess room, the more she wanted to turn and run back in the other direction. She heard murmuring voices and laughter—but it wasn't the loud, crude banter that went on when the "old man" was absent.

Which meant Lucas was sitting at the table.

When she'd awakened from her brief, restless sleep, she'd first thought those brief, wild moments with Lucas had been only a vivid, erotic dream. Until she moved and the unmistakable ache of muscles—in places she'd forgotten she had muscles—told her she'd been very thoroughly loved.

Aromatic scents of eggs, toast, bacon, sausage, and

strong coffee filled the air as she entered the mess room. A darting glance showed Lucas slouched at the head of the table.

"Morning," said Dave.

Tessa plopped down on a chair. "Gimme coffee. Please."

"Good morning to you, too, Sunshine," Jerry Jackson said with a grin, sliding the pot toward her.

Tessa sighed as she poured, then gulped the coffee, wincing as the steaming brew scalded her tongue.

The first and second assistant engineers also sat at the table, deep in conversation about a sticky boiler valve. No sign of the chief. Thank goodness for small favors.

With her stomach fortified, she helped herself to a banana, cubed cantaloupe, a bowl of Cheerios, and a blueberry muffin. As she poured the milk on her cereal, she noticed a sudden silence and looked up to find all the men staring at her.

"What?" she demanded, quickly glancing down to make sure she'd buttoned her shirt.

"Hungry this morning?" Jerry asked, amused.

"Yes," she retorted, jabbing her spoon in the bowl. She didn't dare look at Lucas.

Dave noisily slurped his coffee, then said, "Ran into Andy Marshall a while ago. He said he wanted to talk to me later. Thought you'd want to know."

"Something up with Marshall?" Lucas asked.

Tessa had to look up at the direct question, and as she met his gaze, a blush began creeping up her neck. He looked very relaxed—and way too good this early in the morning, with his unbuttoned shirt and tie draped around his neck. She resisted a sudden, intense urge to grab the tie, wrap its ends around her fists, and slide that man across the table to her for a deep, hungry good morning kiss.

She casually sipped her coffee. "I asked Dave to talk to him about some problems he's having at home. Nothing major."

Lucas set his cup on the table, his movements languorous. "Mrs. Stanhope sent me a message last night, and I need to talk to you about it. Come to my office before you go on watch."

Her eyes met his. So much lay unspoken between them, yet she could read his desire, the concern. His eyes seemed to ask: *Is everything all right with you*?

"Will do."

Tessa doubted he wanted to talk about Dee Stanhope. More likely he wanted to get her alone in his office. She shifted on her chair as she entertained a graphic thought about what they could manage in ten or fifteen minutes.

Eyes downcast, she finished her breakfast, listening to the conversations flowing around her. The usual family stories and shop talk, jokes, teasing, and bitching.

"Hey, Lucas," Jerry said, tipping back his chair, "did I ever tell you what Tessa said to me the first time we met?"

Tessa stared at him over her cup. "Jerry, please. You've told that story a dozen times. It's really not that funny or interesting, and—"

"I haven't heard it," Lucas interrupted, folding his arms over his chest—which did wonders for those biceps she'd run her fingers over just hours before. "Tell me."

Dave leaned forward, his expression expectant, and said, "Oh, yeah, this is a good one."

Jerry grinned. "First, you had to be there to see her face when Personnel introduced us."

"Give me a break," Tessa cut in, not about to sit by meekly. "It's not every day I see a six-foot-five, bald black man on board ship. I was a little . . . surprised, okay?"

"Uh-huh," Jerry said. "That's right, and she stood there, staring at me like I was from this other planet, see, and this voice inside told me to play with her some."

"Like a cat plays with its prey, you mean."

Jerry ignored her grumbling. "So I put out my hand, and I said to her, 'How do you do? I'm Jerome Jackson, Stanhope Shipping's token black buck.' "

The first engineer sputtered. Dave gave a snort, and Lucas's lips curved in a smile.

Tessa shook her head. "I still can't believe you said that. How politically incorrect of you."

"Man, you should've seen her mouth hanging open, like this." Jerry pulled a face of comical shocked horror. "I thought I had her good. But you know what she did?"

Tessa sighed.

Jerry's grin widened. "She put her hand in mine, smashed my fingers—she's strong for such a little thing—and said, 'Hello, Mr. Jackson.' " He mimicked her voice. " 'I'm Tessa Jardine, Stanhope Shipping's token white bitch.' "

Lucas's face split into a wide grin as the second engineer hooted and drawled, "Damn!"

"From that moment on," Jerry declared, in his normal deep voice, "I have been wild in love with this sassy woman."

Tessa eyed him with the irritated fondness usually reserved for her brothers. "I didn't exactly get where I am now by being sweet, shy, and delicate," she said, feeling a need to explain. "Every man I've ever had a conflict with over the years has never hesitated to call me a bitch."

"We love you anyway, Tess," Dave declared, batting his lashes at her. She'd have kicked him under the table, but he sat too far away.

Yes, this contained community was much like a family. The same rivalries—and the same deep understanding of each other. Hiding her affair with Lucas would be impossible.

She realized they couldn't so much as touch each other again while on the *Taliesen*. What they did on their days off was nobody's business, but no sex on board ship anymore.

He wouldn't like it any more than she would, but she saw no other way to avoid getting both their butts canned. Her bravado from the wee hours of the morning had faded in the harsher reality of daylight.

Lucas stood, mug still in his hand. "I'm heading to the pilothouse."

"Later, man," Jerry said, doing a high-five thing with his captain.

Lucas passed by Tessa on his way out, and brushed against her in a private, intimate, and unmistakable signal of possession.

She took in the lingering scent of his soap and aftershave—and inhaled a muffin crumb. Coughing violently, she reached for her cup.

"Whoa, killer muffin! I got first dibs on Heimliching her," said the second engineer.

"Then I get mouth-to-mouth. She likes me better," Dave chimed in, grinning.

"Uh-uh. No way. I'm bigger and badder than all of you put together," Jerry declared.

She'd have groaned at their joking, if only she could breathe and her eyes would stop watering.

"And I outrank you all."

A surprised silence followed—Lucas had never before joined their teasing and joking. Tessa, mortified by the stares and Lucas's private meaning, made a pathetic squeak before she gave in to another fit of coughing.

"Can't argue with that," Jerry said after a moment, a slow smile spreading across his face.

"Screw you," she croaked out.

"Ain't she cute when she talks trashy?"

"Dammit!" Tessa lobbed a cantaloupe chunk at Dave, not able to hold back her grin. "I *hate* being called cute."

Lucas threw back his head and laughed—and Tessa didn't know who he'd shocked most by that rich peal of laughter, the crew or herself.

But, God, she loved the sound of it.

Lucas took the *Taliesen* out of port at Mackinac while his third mate and bridge crew talked and joked. The crew seemed more relaxed, and he didn't think it was only because of his own mood—those long, sweaty moments with Tessa had left him beyond mellow.

With some bemusement, he watched Compton, his third mate, play with a red wooden yo-yo. Tessa's purchase had inspired a trend, and now one of the toys had made its way onto the bridge. As long as his crew did their jobs, he saw no harm in letting them pass the often tedious hours of their watch in whatever way they wished.

He glanced to his left, through the window to where

Tessa stood on the narrow deck outside the pilothouse, leaning over the rail, the wind rippling her shirt, blowing her hair back from her face. She was smiling, and he hoped he'd had a hand in putting that smile on her face.

Once they were under way, he left his ship in Dave Compton's capable hands and joined her. She glanced up as he leaned beside her, smiled again, then looked back out over the lake.

Below, the decks swarmed with passengers, most lining the rails to watch Mackinac Island fade away behind them. A good many lounged on deck chairs, reading, snoozing in the sun, or chatting. A group of children spied him and enthusiastically waved. Smiling, he waved back.

He didn't feel any need to talk. Being with her was enough just then, with the sky as clear a blue as a sky could be, the water bright turquoise, the wind fresh and sharp.

Breathing in deeply, letting the vitality and beauty of the moment fill him, he leaned toward Tessa, and said, "Hey."

She turned, eyes bright. "Hey what?"

"Ain't life grand?" he asked, grinning, his tone lazy.

"Since when can you read my mind?"

"I don't have to." His gaze lingered on her face, and an immediate, intense flush of arousal swept over him. "I can see it in your eyes."

"Yeah," she admitted, leaning against the rail. She lifted her face to the wind, closed her eyes. "This is the life."

Smiling, he watched her, entranced by her matter-of-fact contentment. After a moment, he said, "Penny for your thoughts."

"They're pretty serious ones." Her eyes opened, no

longer full of humor. "I'm thinking that I want this job so much. But I want a family, too. And kids."

Lucas's smile faded as she turned to him.

"As usual, I want it all," she said quietly. "And I can't have it."

He could dismiss her words, tell her it wasn't so, but he respected her intelligence and strength far too much to do so. After a moment, he rested his elbows on the rail, and said, "Sometimes you have to settle for what you need."

"Is that what you've done?"

"Almost dying forces you to look at life differently."

She moved a fraction closer, until they almost touched. "That's not really an answer, Lucas."

"I don't have all the answers. And I make a hell of a lot of mistakes, too."

"Like this morning?" she asked quietly, watching him.

"I hope not," he said with feeling. "Was it?"

Turning back to the rail, she shook her head, a faint blush coloring her cheeks. Lucas, attuned to every creak and pitch of his ship, felt the speed increase— and wished he were as attuned to this woman's moods. In silence, they watched the *Taliesen*'s bow plow through the waves, white foam spraying, the droplets shimmering in the sunlight.

"I really do need to talk to you," Lucas said, squinting out toward the far horizon. She nodded, and followed him through the pilothouse—where Compton marked their passage with a raised brow—and into his cabin.

"Shut the door," Lucas said, once they were in his office.

Tessa hesitated, then did as he asked—but didn't

come any closer. She held herself with an unwelcoming stiffness.

Looked like they both had a bad case of morning after nerves.

"You okay?" he asked at length.

"A little tired." She rubbed at her arm, as if cold. "I think Dave suspects."

"If he does, he won't say anything. Compton's a decent guy." Since she wouldn't move, Lucas crossed the room in a few short strides and gathered her close. She tried to pull away as he kissed her, but for only a moment, then she gave in with a small sigh.

Tessa broke the embrace first, pulling back. "Is this why you wanted to see me?"

"Partly," he admitted.

"I don't think we should do that again."

He stared down at her thick, glossy hair, her small frown. "What are you talking about?"

Her gaze searched his. "Lucas, we can't . . . we shouldn't be together again while we're on board ship."

"Why the hell not?" He moved away from her and leaned back against his desk, arms folded across his chest.

"Because the crew will figure out what's going on! You and I spend hour after hour on this ship with people who know us well enough by now to read a silence, a glance . . . Lucas, I can't take that chance. And there is the issue of professional ethics."

Disappointment nipped at him, although her every word rang true. She'd also handed him the perfect opportunity to make a clean break. All he had to do was give some excuse, about having a few personal issues to work through before he could see her again.

But the memory of their time together scant hours

before surged to mind: the taste of her flushed skin, and the hot, slick feel of sliding deep within her body, her soft kisses.

Her expression was so plainly guilty that his own frustrated anger faded. Between the appeal for his understanding in her dark eyes, and his own powerful need to have her in his arms again, he couldn't turn her out of his life, even if he should.

"What about when we're off the ship? I want to see you again."

"I want to see you, too," Tessa admitted, and it took every ounce of his self-restraint not to haul her into his bedroom and make love to her again.

"My place is isolated, and I promise no one from the ship will come anywhere near it. Will you stop by?"

Lucas hoped that didn't sound as hopeful as he suspected it did. He understood her dilemma—the last thing she needed was for him to force the pace—but even that didn't ease his consuming need to make love to her.

"Tessa?" he pressed after a moment. When she didn't look at him, he went to her. He brushed a strand of hair from her eyes, then traced the curve of her face from brow to chin. "Feeling guilty?"

Immediately, she turned her face away and he knew he'd hit the truth. "I wish I could just forget."

"Believe me, there are days I wish I could forget, too."

Briefly, she glanced at him. "I tell myself it shouldn't matter so much, that whatever really did happen, you were only trying to save those men. But—"

"But you feel like you're betraying your brother with the man who killed him." She flinched, but he saw no reason to sugar-coat the obvious.

"Yes," she said softly. "I'm sorry."

No more sorry than he was; God, what he wouldn't give for the chance to go back and make right all those wrongs. "This isn't really about Matt. He's dead, and beyond feeling betrayed."

Tessa sighed as she leaned against him, and nodded. "I'm not telling you that the guilt, anger, or grief you feel isn't real. I know it is. But we have to move on."

"I won't ever forget him."

"I don't expect you to." He hesitated, feeling his way cautiously through this morass of tricky emotion. "Don't be too hard on yourself, that's all I ask."

"I'll try."

He saw no tears, no frown, just a sad confusion that made him want to hold her—and feel her arms around him. "How about a kiss?"

Tipping her face up, she closed her eyes—and it was all the invitation he needed. He pressed his lips against hers, just a soft press for a second or two until she opened her eyes, her gaze questioning, waiting. He smiled against her lips, then kissed their soft warmth with gentle pressure. He slowly glided his mouth along hers, from one side to the other, sometimes kissing her, sometimes not.

Surrendering to his teasing kiss, she let out a little sigh and leaned fully against him, arms wrapping around his neck. Lucas slid his hands down her back to her bottom and pressed her against his hips, and the hard-on he'd had from the moment she'd shut the door.

Lucas coaxed her mouth open and ran his tongue along hers. Her fingers closed tightly over his shoulders. It aroused him, just this touch of mouth and tongue, and kicked his body into high gear, muscles tensing, blood pumping in anticipation of something more.

Not that he'd likely get anything but the kiss, but it didn't matter. He lost himself to the smooth, hot feel of her skin, the rich taste of her mouth, the uneven sound of her breathing—until Tessa broke the kiss and pulled back.

"Wow," she whispered, then gave a loud, gusty sigh. "I am a weak, weak woman where you're concerned."

Hearing her admit it eased his immediate frustration, but he released her and retreated to the other side of his desk. Otherwise, he'd have her up against the bulkhead in a heartbeat.

"The other reason I asked you here, besides going crazy from not touching you, is that I do need to talk to you about the message from Dee."

"Is there a problem?"

"Not for us. A big problem for Dee." He unknotted his tie with a sigh of relief. "This doesn't go any farther than me and you. She's been receiving threatening notes at her office. The night I came to your apartment, when I had dinner with her earlier, she told me about it."

Tessa's eyes went flat. "So why call *you*?"

"She didn't know if she should be worried or not and didn't want to go to the police. She reasoned I was the next closest thing."

"Is the threat real?"

"The cops are taking it seriously enough to keep her under surveillance."

"Why are you telling me this?"

"Because I don't want you getting the wrong idea about any notes, calls, or summons that Dee sends me."

Tessa frowned, her expression still skeptical. "One of the drawbacks of being rich and flashy, I suppose. You attract attention, some of it negative."

"That's the angle the cops are taking for now."

Her eyes narrowed. "And you don't think she has ulterior motives?"

Lucas rubbed at his chin, holding back a smile. "I *know* she has ulterior motives. Among other things, Dee wants people to think I'm involved with her. She thrives on controversy."

"She's an embarrassment to the entire female gender."

"A word of advice, Tess—don't underestimate her."

"Oh, please. Dee Stanhope married a rich man twenty-two years older than she was. She has too much money, wears too much makeup, and nobody takes her seriously. I mean, for God's sake, she wears *pink* all the time!"

Folding his arms over his chest, he asked, "Do you know why she hired you?"

"I'm around to show investors that Stanhope is a wonderful, politically correct company. I'm also good at my job."

"That's part of it. But why do you think she waited until after you'd accepted the job offer to tell you about me?"

"She probably figured I'd be reluctant to work with you. Although she doesn't know the half of it." Her eyes narrowed. "Does she?"

Lucas gave a short, impatient shake of his head. "You know better than that. I've said nothing about us being lovers."

Lovers.

The word seemed to hang in the air, a tantalizing, forbidden fruit that roused that restless, hungry awareness again.

"Tessa, she hired you because the news reporters and papers would link us with the *McKee* and that would grab attention."

Tessa stared at him. "That's not true. My work record—"

"I'm not denying your competency," he cut in quietly. "But to Dee, your work record is secondary. I'm sorry, sweetheart, but I can't let you miscalculate the lengths Dee will go to get her own way. To her, the fact that you have a dead brother at the bottom of Lake Michigan and that I helped put him there is guaranteed publicity. You'll have noticed how the press loves to bring it up every chance they get."

"I despise women like her; I really do." She swallowed, eyes dark with hurt anger. "So you were *never* interested in having an affair with Dee?"

That she had to ask stung, but he returned her gaze levelly. "She's attractive, but not my type. Besides, she's my boss, and I do have morals."

"Yet you'll sleep with me, your subordinate?"

Lucas studied her, trying to gauge her mood. "You'll never be my subordinate, Tessa."

He left the desk took her in his arms. Again, she tensed, so he made a show of kissing her mouth—but at the last second kissed her ear instead.

"Hey," she said, relaxing a fraction. "You missed."

"Did I?" Lucas shifted to the right, dipped toward her lips, then pulled away as she lifted her face toward his, and kissed her nose. "Look at that. I missed again."

He teased her a while longer, until she growled, seized his tie, and yanked him down to her. Then she laid on him a hell of a kiss: full-mouthed, energetic, and full of promises.

"Take that," she said, letting go of his tie. "Sir."

Lucas watched her stride out of his office, wanting her so badly he wanted to howl his frustration—and now she'd gone and declared herself a DO NOT TOUCH zone for the rest of the trip.

Considering that he should've never touched her in the first place, the irony didn't escape him.

He sighed, scrubbing his hands over his face. Life had been a lot less complicated when he'd been fishing.

Fourteen

*T*essa glanced at the map in her hand—a map Lucas had hurriedly drawn on a scrap of paper and pressed into her hand moments after he'd docked the *Taliesen* in Milwaukee.

According to these chicken scratches—for such a masterful kind of guy, his handwriting was ungodly sloppy—his cabin should be somewhere off this fork. Peering through the thick woods, she drove slowly, partly because the dirt road was rough and partly because she didn't want to end up lost out in the middle of nowhere. Give her an open sea and a decent GPS any day over country roads that were little better than deer tracks.

Where was this cabin, anyway?

A flash of sun against glass caught her attention a moment before she saw the A-frame-style log cabin— and on the porch stood Lucas, in shorts and nothing else, waiting for her.

Tessa parked the car, squeezed her eyes shut in a hopeless effort to calm her racing heart, then grabbed her duffel and walked toward him. Despite his watchful expression, he appeared more relaxed and sure of himself than she felt.

"I wasn't sure you'd come." He folded his arms across his bare chest—and she suspected he knew exactly what effect that would have on her libido.

Slowly, she walked up the steps, not missing his lazy examination of her shorts and old STANHOPE SHIPPING T-shirt. "Halfway here, I almost turned around and drove back. I'm still not sure this is a good idea."

"But you're here."

"I can't seem to get my hormones to agree with my brain."

A faint smile crossed his face. "Difficult little bastards, those hormones."

She smiled back. "Something you know about, huh?"

He took her bag and dropped it on the porch. "Come here."

Lucas kissed her like a sailor too long at sea. Hungry, demanding, and impatient as his warm, urgent hands roamed over her bottom and breasts. She opened her mouth to his, tongues caressing as his breathing roughened.

After a moment, Lucas stepped back. His eyes gleamed. "Let's go inside."

Tessa didn't need any encouragement. He caught her hand in his and led her into the cabin, a small, rough-hewn place with an open main floor and a sleeping loft above. Her immediate impression was of lots of exposed timbers and buffalo plaids.

"Cozy," she murmured as he directed her up the ladderlike stairs to the loft.

"It belongs to my sister and her husband. I'm renting it until I settle on a place of my own."

Soon, only rapid breathing and the whisper of clothes falling to the floor sounded in the dim loft. She tumbled with Lucas onto the sturdy bed and made love, fast and furious—a powerful need demanding to be soothed after waiting a forever of days.

Afterward, lying in his arms, listening to the steady beating of his heart, Tessa murmured, "Boy, I needed that."

"I was going nuts by the time I got off the *Taliesen* today. It's been hell, seeing you and not even being able to touch you." As if remembering that he'd been deprived of that touch, he cupped his hands around her bottom.

Tessa gave him a quick kiss, then snuggled closer against him. "You know, I realized on the way over that I have no idea what you've been doing these past years."

"I already answered this question."

She frowned, then shook her head. "No, you told me you missed the service and you fished for your brother-in-law. You didn't tell me much about what you did. We have some catching up to do. I want to know what you've been up to all this time."

"Maybe I don't want to talk," he said in a low voice, squeezing her bottom again.

Tessa squirmed, and smacked his hand. "Maybe I do."

Seeing she was serious, he sighed and rolled over onto his back. "I spent most of that time in Miami and the Gulf, intercepting refugees and drug smugglers, and enforcing fishing laws, except for my stint patrolling the Bering Sea. There's nothing like finding yourself staring down a pissed-off Russian and wondering if you're about to start an international incident."

"That's not what I meant. You said you wanted to do something that would make a difference. I'm wondering if you did, that's all."

A sudden tension radiated from him, and a moment passed before he answered. "Sometimes. Sometimes not. Miami was a hell of a lot different than Cheboygan, Michigan."

Tessa sighed, her head on his chest, rubbing her fingers along his skin. "You used to talk so easily to me."

He looked down at her, then away. After a moment, he said, "I saw a lot of ugly shit. I wanted to help people, and too often, I couldn't do a damn thing. You intercepted a boatload or two of cocaine, but more always slipped through. The refugees . . . God, that was the worst. Nobody wants them, but Joe Citizen doesn't have to smell those boats, pull bodies out of the water, look in the desperate eyes of a mother, or face down a man with a machete when he sees you as the only thing standing between him and freedom."

He shifted, lacing his hands behind his head as he stared up at the ceiling, his expression distant.

"Up here on the lakes, we didn't get many search and rescues. But on the Gulf and the coasts, that changed. All those long hours without sleeping or eating, crossing back and forth and hoping *this* time you'll find them before it's too late."

"Like that little girl?"

"Yeah," he said quietly. "Like that. My last week on duty up near Alaska, we got a mayday from a fishing trawler, who said they were taking on water fast. We flew . . . man, those engines were smoking."

"You didn't make it in time?" She knew the answer; the bleak look on his face told her as much.

"In water that cold, survival is counted in minutes,

not hours." A muscle in his jaw tensed. "We found the crew dead. Some of them had almost made it into their survival suits. If they'd had even a couple minutes more before their boat sank, we might have brought a few of them home alive."

Beneath her ear, the thudding of his heart betrayed his casual sprawl and even tone. "You worked the recovery of that 747 that went down off Miami, too, didn't you?"

His heart beat faster, and his skin beneath her fingers and cheek grew damp with a sudden perspiration.

When he said nothing, she glanced up. "Lucas? Did you?"

"Yes."

Silence followed, and after a moment, she said softly, "I guess you don't want to talk about it?"

Still staring at the ceiling, he said, "Christ, I'd never seen such a mess . . . and I remember this baby."

Tessa closed her eyes, and stopped her slow, massaging movements.

"He looked like he was sleeping. I can still see his face, sometimes."

"I can't imagine what it must be like to deal with tragedies like that, over and over again." A shiver took her, and she pressed closer. "The work you did . . . I know I couldn't handle it. Not for a day, much less almost twenty years."

"I wasn't complaining." He frowned a little as he stroked her hair back from her forehead. "It was my job."

"Just like the *McKee*," she whispered. "Just a job."

His chest rose and fell as he took a long breath. "Deep down, you know you can't win every time. But you go in anyway and give it everything you've got, because you hate losing. You really hate it."

She hesitated, then said, "I did read the official accident reports on the *McKee*."

"Then you know I wasn't even supposed to be on that ship. I was on leave in Charlevoix to see my sister, and thought I'd stop by to visit the base. When the mayday came in, I was the only officer around. The cutter was out, leaving only a utility boat and a few nervous kids. I had to do something. I knew this was a bad one, and I had more experience than anybody else there."

"What you did went above and beyond, Lucas. Nobody has ever doubted that."

"It sure as hell was a mess when we got there," he said, as if he hadn't heard her at all. "Her bow was almost underwater, and she had a bad list to port. There was confusion everywhere. I couldn't ask those kids to go down into the *McKee* after the engine-room crew."

Tessa let him talk, understanding that he needed to do so, although it wasn't easy listening to him detail those last minutes of her brother's life. Still, it comforted her in a way, bringing a sense of closure and bringing to life what the dry, passionless details of an official report couldn't.

"I swam over with a bunch of life vests and climbed the ladder up to the deck, and that's when—" He stopped for a long moment, then turned his face away. "I don't remember anything after that."

"Why? You were there. How come you can't remember what happened?"

He still didn't look at her. "The doctors said it's not uncommon with a head trauma to have only a partial memory of events, or even a total loss of memory."

Tessa sensed his avoidance, but didn't know if it was simply painful for him to talk about the accident, or if he remembered more than he claimed—and refused to admit it.

She didn't press the subject. Instead, she began massaging his muscles. "It feels like you need to relax. Lie still. You've spent years taking care of people and cleaning up after their mistakes . . . Just lie back and let someone take care of you for a change."

Without protest, he closed his eyes, and she rolled and kneaded all the knotted muscles from his shoulders down to his calves. The minutes passed by in a content quiet, as she enjoyed pampering every inch of his powerful body, the warm skin and geography of muscle and sinew, the raised ridges of his many scars. With satisfaction, she felt his tension gradually ease.

"And what have you been doing?" Lucas asked after a while, his voice a low, lazy rumble. "Your turn to talk."

With a gentle push, she coaxed him over onto his stomach and proceeded to massage his back, lightly brushing the scar just beneath his ribs. She didn't need him to tell her it was from a chest tube. The reports had been graphic in detailing his injuries—including that he'd gone into cardiac arrest on the rescue helicopter.

Dear God, he had come so close to dying!

Shaken, she kissed him on his back, where beneath the skin, muscle, and bone, his heart beat strongly.

"Not much to say, really," she said when she trusted herself to speak without betraying the tears stinging her eyes.

"Tell me anyway." Facedown in the pillow, Lucas made a low sound of pleasure as her fingers worked a tight shoulder muscle.

"Life's been a lot less exciting for me. Within a couple of months after I graduated, I landed a job as third mate with Stanhope. I worked on freighters, and you know what that's like: ten months of hustling and boredom, then a couple months of winter layup. I made it to second mate after a few years, but found myself stuck there until the *Taliesen* opportunity came along."

"What about that guy? The one you replaced me . . . ow!"

Tessa dug her fingers into his ribs, but since she was sitting on him, knees on either side of his hips, he couldn't turn. She smiled, because unless she was mistaken, that comment sounded a wee bit jealous.

"Paul was a great guy. He was sweet, gentle, and treated me like I was a princess."

Silence. She continued to work the muscles of his back.

"If he was such a great guy, how come you didn't marry him?"

"Because we made better friends than lovers, that's why," she retorted. "There wasn't much zing-zip-pizzazz between us."

"Zing-zip-pizzazz?" he repeated, voice muffled.

Tessa eyed him suspiciously. Was he laughing? "He was a considerate and generous lover, Lucas." Beneath her hands, he twitched. "But we mostly just had . . . nice. I loved him, but—"

"He bored you."

Again, Tessa eyed him. "I wouldn't put it that way. It didn't help that after we graduated, he couldn't find a job. I had to make a choice between him and Stanhope's offer."

"And it wasn't that hard a choice, was it?"

"No," she admitted quietly. "And he deserved better."

"Hard feelings?"

"A little, at first, but we stayed friends. I went to his

wedding a couple years ago. He works for a shipbuilding company out of Sturgeon Bay. He has two kids now."

Kids that might've been hers. Strange, to think of it that way.

"Anybody else after him?"

"Of course," she retorted, to deflate his ego a bit. "Next I dated a second engineer with Stanhope, but we split after a year because our schedules kept us apart too much. My boyfriend after that didn't work in shipping, but in the long run, it didn't matter."

"Why?"

"I wasn't around enough, and he had problems with me working with men. I just got tired of him not trusting me." She trailed her fingers down Lucas's back to the curve of his rear, kneading its tight firmness. A fierce, sharp tug of possessiveness swept over her, startling in its intensity. After a moment, she added, "I can't ever seem to make things work. It's always the guy or the career."

"It doesn't have to be like that."

"Easy for you to say. Since when has having a career *and* a family ever been a problem for a man?" Running her hands up his back, over the muscles and bumps of his spine, she added, "But if I find a guy who'd at least try working it out with me, you can bet I'd give it my best shot." When he still said nothing, she went warm with embarrassment. "I'm not proposing to you, so don't get all freaked out."

"I'm not," he said, voice muffled in the pillow once again.

"Well, you're just lying there like a big lump!"

"Am not. I'm thinking."

Curiosity got the better of her. "About what?"

"That you just haven't found the right guy yet."

They were drifting into dangerous waters. Still, she couldn't help asking, "Don't you ever think about settling down?"

"What do you think? I'm pushing forty, and as I said before, almost dying has a way of shifting your priorities."

A small hope bloomed, but she quickly nipped it. She'd been down this road too many times before, and once already with him. She really ought to have learned her lesson by now.

"Then you know how I feel," she said after a moment. "Hope springs eternal."

The body beneath her bucked without warning. She yelped, finding herself on her back and Lucas on top of her. She squirmed, but she was good and caught, and as his fingers began a slow exploration of her body, she gave a purr of pleasure.

"Are you trying to distract me?" she murmured.

"I'm tired of talking. We can talk on the *Taliesen*. This we can't do, because you won't let me."

With his mouth on her breasts, he nudged her legs apart with his knee. Soon the smooth press of his erection brushed her inner thigh, and he slid inside her with satisfying ease.

Tessa didn't fight the pull of desire. She never could say no to Lucas. Didn't want to, anyway. God, she needed this; needed the full, heavy feel of him within her again.

"Oh," she sighed out on a long breath. "I love the way you feel inside me."

Lucas smiled, but his eyes were focused inward, concentrating on drawing out both her pleasure and his. The intensity of his control was almost frightening.

"Stop," she whispered, pushing against him. "You did all the work last time. Now it's my turn."

He turned onto his back. In charge now, Tessa teased him until a film of perspiration covered his body and his breathing grew labored. She squeezed her muscles around him and, with a great shuddering groan, he went stiff and rammed his hips upward. The power of each deep thrust brought her rapidly to a climax, and his followed before hers had even ended.

She let out her breath, her muscles heavy and shivery as she dropped down on top of him. He was hot and damp, and his arms closed around her, strong and comforting.

"I'm not twenty-seven anymore," he said. With her ear against his chest, his voice rumbled deep inside him. "I don't think I can pull those all-nighters like I used to."

Tessa smiled. "Maybe not, but I see you've learned to make it last longer. I figure that evens everything out."

He laughed, his chest shaking beneath her cheek. "You're good for my ego, Tessa."

"Does this mean we'll have to do something else while recharging our batteries?"

"How does a swim sound?" He stroked her hair away from her forehead, thumb tracing the line of her brow.

"I didn't bring a suit; sorry."

"Wear what you came in. I like wet T-shirts on a woman." She smacked him, and he demanded, "Hey, what was that for?"

"When I hear a sexist comment, my hand has this automatic slap reflex. Nothing personal."

He grinned and slapped her bottom. "Come on. Let's go cool off in the lake."

A few minutes later, Lucas had on a pair of black swim trunks that didn't cover much, and she nearly swallowed her tongue at the sight. She'd donned her T-shirt—sans bra—and underwear, and he'd eyed her unbound breasts with blatant interest. She also carried two colorful beach towels.

"Race you down to the pier," she challenged, grinning.

That brought his attention up from her chest. "I can't run like I used to."

Her smile faltered as she glanced at his leg, but only for a moment. "You look healthy enough to me, and without a bra, I'm going to have to run like a girl. That makes us even. Come on!"

She took off, acutely aware of her bouncing breasts and Lucas right beside her, not missing a single jiggle. In the end, he passed her easily, cannonballing off the pier with a whoop, a loud splash, and a deluge of wet, cold spray.

Tessa stood on the edge of the pier, gasping and dripping. "You did that on purpose, you *pig*!"

Silence.

Narrowing her eyes, Tessa searched for the outline of his body, but saw only the widening ripples from his point of impact.

He'd better not try to—

A hand erupted from the water, grabbed her, and pulled her in before she even let out a yell. That same hand quickly became very fresh with her breasts until she slapped it away.

She surfaced a moment later, sputtering. Lucas stood laughing, water rolling down his face in rivulets, his swim shorts molded against every contour of his body.

Catching the direction of her gaze, he grinned. The full-dimple grin. "Been a while since we made love in the water."

"And it'll be a while yet," Tessa retorted, swimming

away. As if she was going to make it easy for him *every* time.

Tessa rolled onto her back, floating. She knew what she looked like with the wet white T-shirt molded to her skin closely enough to see every goose bump—and a quick peek at Lucas showed him looking downright carnivorous.

She smiled with smug satisfaction. With Lucas, being all female again was just so incredibly easy.

He waded her way as she floated, face turned toward a sky darkening as the sun began to set. In another hour, the stars would be out.

Lucas stopped, grabbed her ankles, and pulled her toward him. Tessa laughed, paddling her arms to keep from going under as he drew her against his thighs. He slid his hands under her back and lifted her out of the water. She slid down his chest, slick with water, as he brought his mouth down on hers. His lips were cool, but inside his mouth, he tasted hot and smooth.

They stood kissing, deeply and slowly and lazily, until the sound of a car cut across the quiet.

With a gasp, Tessa pushed away. "Oh, God, somebody's here!" She glanced down at her wet shirt, the aroused, dark peaks of her nipples, and panic swept through her. "What if it's somebody we know? Lucas, don't let them see me!"

Lucas watched her, his expression closed. "Calm down. Nobody comes up here but my sister and her family. She usually calls first, although not always."

She shivered with sudden cold, arms wrapped tightly around herself and trying to regain her composure. Her fear was absurd; nobody from the ship had any reason to seek out Lucas.

The car suddenly backed up, turned around, and drove away.

"Guess they were lost," she said. "Sorry."

Their previous intimacy had vanished. Still shivering—more from fright than the cold—Tessa climbed up onto the pier and wrapped herself in one of the towels. What was wrong with her? She'd never been one to panic so easily.

Looking back out at the lake, she saw Lucas treading water a short distance away, still watching her.

"Come back in," he called.

She shook her head. "I want to lie here for a while and watch the sun set."

And until she stopped shaking.

"Suit yourself. I'm going for a swim." He set off before she had a chance to answer, but she didn't miss the flash of anger on his face. Best to let him work off some frustration, and not try to call him back.

After a while, she spread her towel on the pier and rolled over onto her stomach. An island sat a half mile from shore—nothing more than a tiny sandbar with a few scrubby trees. Lucas had nearly reached it, his strokes strong and fast, showing why he'd excelled in swimming events in high school and the service. She admired his hardiness. Close to shore, the water was warm, but the temperature dropped rapidly the farther out you went.

Chin cupped in her hands, she watched as he swam back toward her. Physically, he hadn't changed much, but she still couldn't shake the feeling that he was holding something back. It didn't help that every time she tried to talk about personal matters, he immediately set about distracting her.

Not that she minded the manner of his distractions, but surely he knew her better than to think she wouldn't notice what he was up to.

Once he reached the shallow area, he waded toward

her and she was woman enough to fully appreciate the mature male body beneath wet trunks, the dark chest hair flattened by the water's weight. She watched his approach with a smile. Before she'd realized what he meant to do, he'd placed the palms of his hands on the pier, which came to mid-chest, and hoisted himself up out of the water.

Tessa's mouth dropped open. His arm and shoulder muscles bulged with the effort, his chest rising and falling rapidly from the exertion of his swim.

Hot, primitive desire sluiced over her at this blatantly aggressive display. "Nice."

"Not bad for an old man of thirty-seven, eh?" He grinned, vertical dimples slashing his cheeks, and Tessa thought she'd melt into a puddle of lust right there on the pier.

"Kiss me," she ordered in a low growl.

He leaned over her, and she could feel the faint tremors of his muscles as he supported himself. His kiss deepened, demanded more, and she slowly sank down onto the pier again, rolling onto her back, away from the edge. He followed, pulling himself onto the pier, and it seemed so strange, kissing him upside down, with a beard-roughened chin where his eyes should've been.

She laughed, the sound muffled beneath his mouth. He broke the kiss to kneel above her, hands on either side of her chest.

"What's so funny?" he asked, the coolly amused tone of his voice clashing with the heat in his golden brown eyes.

"It's weird kissing you upside down. Come back over me. I'm cold, anyway."

"Bet I can do something about that," he said, shifting until he'd positioned his body above hers, palms flat on the pier above her head. Water dripped on her, each chill, delicate drop registering against her flushed skin.

"You're cold," she murmured, and shivered—more because of his tight, hungry look than because of her damp clothes.

"Warm me up," he invited, and lowered himself for a kiss as if he were doing push-ups over her.

Once, twice . . . he gave her ten quick kisses, each time going lower and lower. For the first few kisses, his body didn't touch hers, keeping only the trapped heat between them, a solid barrier of warmth. His body dipped lower with each following kiss, brushing hers, until he lingered for several seconds on the last kiss, his erection nudging her.

It made her smile. "Show-off."

"Is it working?"

"What do you think?" she retorted, watching as he raised himself again and gazed at her damp shirt and her hard nipples.

"Nice," he said, grinning.

"I am not making love out on this pier," she said quickly, right before his mouth came down over hers again for a long, breathless kiss.

He pushed himself up. "Why not?"

Just as he came down for another mind-numbing kiss, she weakened and said, "Because."

"This is private property." Down. Kiss. Hips rolling against hers. Up. "What'd you say?"

"Get off me, you big lug, and let's go inside. I don't want any slivers in a tender part of my anatomy."

He grinned, dazzling her with the sheer, over-whelming force of his presence. And then, to her shock, he continued his push-ups over her—but *one-handed.*

Blood roared in her ears, and heat suffused her entire body.

"Okay. I'm impressed. And very, very turned-on," she said, proud of her cool tone—except for its betraying breathless hitch as he came down over her on the last word. "But I'm still not having sex with you on the pier."

He was grinning, his breathing coming heavier, although he still made these one armed push-ups look disgustingly effortless.

"And if you fall and squash me, that won't do much for the romantic mood here . . . not to mention your macho image." She grinned back. "I can think of a better way for you to put all this up-and-down motion to good use before you wear yourself out."

"That's the plan." He pushed himself up a final time, then shifted to sit beside her.

She couldn't resist snuggling against him, soaking in his heat as she ran her fingers through his wet, dark hair. In the fading light, she couldn't read his expression, but he seemed strangely subdued all of a sudden.

Hoping to recapture their playful mood, she said, "It's your fault I'm soaking wet, so you'd better let me borrow one of your shirts to wear until mine dries."

"Are you spending the night here?"

"Of course." She looked at him, surprised. "Unless you don't want me to?"

"I want you to stay." He rubbed at his eyes, shifting away from her. "But I should warn you that I don't sleep much."

"Why?" she asked, concerned, trying to see his face.

The smile he flashed didn't reach his eyes. "I have better things to do than sleep when I've got you in my bed."

His tone, his posture—even the odd question of her spending the night—told her something was not right.

Then he kissed her, and for the next few hours, nothing else mattered at all.

Fifteen

*T*essa jerked awake at a shrill ringing sound, and groped for a phone that wasn't where it should be. She remembered whose bed she occupied just as Lucas's sleepy voice mumbled, "Hello?"

Yawning, she sat up and stretched. Lucas was sitting up, wearing nothing but a twisted plaid sheet, and frowning. He looked impossibly sexy with his rough, dark beard stubble, mussed hair, and heavy-lidded eyes. She snuggled against his bare warm back, her chin on his shoulder.

"Now?" He glanced at the bedside clock. "It's barely eight in the morning. Okay, okay, calm down. Did you call the police? Good. Sit tight. I'll get to your office as soon as I can."

At this last bit, Tessa came wide-awake, watching as he hung up the phone. "Let me guess: Dee Stanhope?"

Lucas rubbed at his eyes. "Her secretary found another note. I have to go."

Tessa pushed back her hair, resentment stinging. "She's a grown woman and runs her own company. Why do you have to ride off on a white horse to rescue her?"

"I'm not rescuing her. I'm the closest thing the woman has to a friend around here, and she asked for my help."

Lucas stood gazing down at her, hands on his bare hips. A small smile played at the corners of his mouth, and she wanted to grab him, tie him down in bed, and do wicked things to him with her mouth all morning long.

And he was going off to Dee Stanhope.

"Don't you trust me, Tess?"

She sent him a dark look. "Yes, I trust you. I'm . . . a little jealous, okay?" It killed her to admit this, but she'd be damned if she'd just sit in his bed and sulk. "And I don't want you to go. I want you to stay with me."

"Dee isn't playing games this time. She really is scared." His gaze roved along her body, from her bare legs to the T-shirt wadded around her hips, her breasts, then her face. Blatant lust mixed with regret in his hazel eyes and, oddly enough, it made her feel better. "You don't have anything to worry about, and I'll be back as soon as I can."

"Well, excuse me if I don't trust her," Tessa retorted, swinging out of bed. She leaned against him, arms around his waist, feeling a primal, irrational need to mark him as her own.

"I didn't say I trusted her." Lucas rubbed his thumb along the line of her jaw. He kissed her, a soft brush of lips, then more firmly. When he pulled away, he walked to the closet and pulled out a pair of pants. "Will you be here when I get back?"

Seeing he really meant to leave, she sighed. What could she expect? This was Lucas: When somebody was in trouble, helping out was automatic.

"Yes, I'll wait. I can stay through the afternoon, but I should go home tonight. Somebody from the ship might try to get hold of me, and I'd better be available."

"If they can't find you, they'll call here."

She shot him a look of unease as he pulled on his shirt.

"Don't worry, I won't blow your secret," he said, as if he could read her mind, and his voice sounded a shade cooler. "But I can tell whoever calls that I'll get the message to you. Then I'll roll over and whisper it in your ear."

She wanted very much to stay, but she was also feeling a little anxious. Everything was moving too fast for comfort, and she needed to pull back.

"The offer's tempting, but I think I'll pass. This time."

He studied her. "You're mad because I'm going to see Dee."

"A little," she admitted, annoyed at herself. "But I'm heading home because I want to. I need . . . some time alone tonight."

"What's wrong?" His question was blunt, and impatience flashed in his eyes.

Guilty, knowing she'd disappointed him, Tessa glanced down at her bare toes. "Just those doubts nipping at my heels, I guess."

Lucas hesitated, as if he might kiss her or touch her, but he moved away instead. "Maybe you should go home now. If you don't want to be here, then I won't make you stay."

Her guilt intensified. "Lucas—"

"Look, it's okay."

Tessa nodded, but she could tell it wasn't really okay. She wanted to say more, but with one last glance her way, he left the loft. Sitting alone on the bed, she listened to him shower and dress. Soon after, the door slammed, and she heard the roar of his car's engine, fading as he drove away.

Maybe they both needed some downtime. With a sigh, she fixed the bed—trying not to think about all their touching and kissing and lovemaking—tidied the kitchen, then packed her things, and drove home.

When Lucas arrived at the Stanhope building in downtown Milwaukee, his mood grim, a uniformed police officer met him at the door and escorted him up to Dee's office.

"Hey, Burton. It's Mrs. Stanhope's captain."

Mrs. Stanhope's captain?

Before Lucas could correct the young cop, a tall, wiry man approached them. He appeared in his late forties, with receding reddish gray hair, gray eyes, and lots of freckles.

"Detective John Burton." The man's grip was firm as he shook Lucas's hand. "I'm with the Dignitary Protection Unit, Milwaukee PD's Intelligence Division."

That sounded promising. "Where's Dee?"

"In the ladies' room, fixing her face," Burton said. "She's a little upset."

"She told me she received another note."

Burton's gaze was frankly assessing. "Yup. I understand she showed you the first two."

"That's correct. What's this one say?"

"Read it for yourself." The detective motioned to Dee's desk—a hi-tech affair in tubular metal and Plexiglas—where a letter lay. "We'd like to keep the details among as few people as possible, understand? You don't say anything about it. And don't touch. We'll need to process it for prints."

Lucas walked over to the desk, aware of the detective's measuring stare. Without touching the paper, he read:

TIGRESS, TIGRESS BURNING BRIGHT
NINE LIVES HAS YOUR TOMCAT?
LYNX
TIGER
COUGAR
DEADLY
R.I.P.
ARE YOU READY?

Lucas frowned. "The tone of this one is different."

Burton raised a brow. "You've got a sharp eye. What do you think makes it different?"

"It involves a second individual." He glanced at the detective. "And I bet I know what your next question will be."

"I'd read that you were a smart guy, Hall," Burton said, hands on his hips. "So you don't mind if I ask a few questions?"

"Not at all."

"Over the last few months, the *Sentinel*'s run a lot of pictures of you and Mrs. Stanhope together, going out to parties. Ditto for TV. What's your relationship with the lady?"

"She's my employer. Part of my duties as captain of the *Taliesen* requires I escort her to events that involve publicity for the ship."

"That's it?"

Lucas returned Burton's stare. "I'm not intimately involved with Mrs. Stanhope, despite what you may have heard. Or been led to believe."

Burton ran a hand over his chin, amusement glinting in his eyes. "Can you verify your whereabouts all day yesterday and this morning?"

A chill shot through him. "Yes, sir, I can."

"Somebody was with you all day and night?"

Damn. "I'd be happy to provide details. Just not here."

This time, Burton grinned. "Reading you loud and clear."

Lucas curbed his irritation, no easy task since he was dog-tired. "You think 'tomcat' refers to me?"

"The lady's not visibly involved with anybody else. The local press has made a big deal of showing you together. The notes are focused only here. So, yeah, that's my guess."

"Any more guesses?"

Burton slipped his hands in his trouser pockets. "A few, but I'm keeping them to myself right now."

"That's because he's such a pig, darling. He won't tell me, either. All this hush-hush nonsense, and *I'm* the one being threatened."

At Dee's voice, Lucas turned. She walked toward him, eyes red-rimmed and streaked with mascara. Her hasty repairs couldn't disguise her pale face or lines of strain, even as she glared at the detective.

"Watch it, Mrs. Stanhope. You're dating yourself by calling me a pig," Burton said, not looking in the least offended.

"I meant it, Detective, in the most literal sense."

After a quick, curious glance between Dee and Burton, Lucas pulled out the desk chair for her. "How are you holding up?"

She laughed, but it was a brittle sound. "As well as can be expected, seeing as how I'm being terrorized by a psychopath and surrounded by insensitive louts."

Again, Lucas looked over at the detective, who only shrugged. "What are your people doing to keep her safe?"

"We've increased the building security and we have Mrs. Stanhope under surveillance while she's in Milwaukee," Burton answered. "So far, the threats haven't involved her Cleveland, Duluth, or New Orleans offices."

"Why only Milwaukee?" Lucas asked.

"We're working on that," Burton answered tersely.

But Lucas had a good idea what this was about, and he bet Dee did as well. He rubbed at his brow.

God, he wanted to be in Tessa's arms, feeling her soothing touch, listening to her sexy voice and her laughter, and finding satisfaction in her warm, welcoming body.

Except she'd left; said she needed to be alone. He kept telling himself this wasn't a flat-out rejection or a failure. But it sure was beginning to feel that way.

What the hell was he doing wrong?

"This person isn't very sophisticated," Dee said, her voice cutting across his thoughts. She tried to sound cool, but her voice shook. "Even *I* can figure out these stupid notes."

From his perch on her desk, Lucas reached over and gave her hand a quick, comforting squeeze. No matter how much she pissed him off, he hated to see her this frightened—and he bet she detested losing control of a situation as much as he did.

"You're supposed to figure it out. It's part of the psychology and manipulation of fear." Lucas turned back to Burton. "What's your take?"

Burton shrugged again. "Somebody wants to scare

her, no doubt about that. And that somebody's getting into the building without being noticed. Which I really, really don't like."

"Brilliant, isn't he?" Dee murmured. "It gives me such confidence in our public servants."

"I'm doing my job, Mrs. Stanhope. Now, with all due respect, ma'am, button it up."

Brows raised, Lucas glanced at Dee. Two bright red spots colored her cheeks, and Lucas almost smiled. Any man who could navigate the rocks and shoals of Dee's tricks and moods was a man he could trust to get the job done right.

"I would like to talk to Captain Hall privately," Dee said, fixing Burton with a cold stare.

"Fine with me. Hall, I'll want to talk to you myself, so before you take off, please give my men a number where you can be reached."

Lucas nodded, then followed Dee down a long hallway lined with soft-hued abstracts in slender frames. The plush, pale carpeting muffled their footsteps.

After shutting the conference door behind her, she motioned him to sit. He did so, admiring as always the spacious room, with its oval oak table, state-of-the-art audiovisual equipment, and high-backed chairs upholstered in deep purple. Antique framed ship blueprints hung on these walls, and the windows overlooked the downtown skyline.

"This is about the *McKee*, you know," Dee said.

"I guessed as much."

"It's that Yarwood man. He's made several threats about making Stanhope Shipping pay for what happened."

"He's trying to squeeze ten million bucks out of your insurance carrier. That may be the only kind of 'pay' he means, Dee. The man lost a son, and that kind of grief can screw people up. It could be just wild talk."

"Do you really think so?"

"Yarwood wasn't the only one who lost a family member on the *McKee*. And I'm sure Burton's already made the connection. I bet he's keeping an eye on Yarwood."

"Do you think Burton's also made the other connection?"

Lucas frowned. "Hell, yes. He already grilled me about our so-called personal relationship. You have to stop giving people the idea that I'm sleeping with you."

She made an impatient, dismissive gesture. "Don't be dense. I'm talking about you and the *McKee*."

He sat back, rubbing his thumb along his chin. "Why wouldn't he? The newspapers and reporters bring up my part in the sinking every chance they get. If Burton thought that note was a threat against me, he'd have said so."

"Maybe," Dee conceded, her gaze troubled, her touch on his shoulder this time more concerned than sexual. "All the same, darling, I'd suggest you watch your handsome back."

Sixteen

*A*fter spending the rest of her time off alone and at home—and after a fitful night with little sleep—Tessa's alarm buzzed loudly at four on Friday morning. She banged the OFF button, eyes tired and gritty, her back and thigh muscles protesting as she swung out of bed. She stood gingerly, feeling for all the world like she had a hangover from sex. Was that even possible?

Probably. She sure wasn't nineteen anymore.

She blasted herself with hot water, working away the aches, wondering what Lucas was doing. For a moment, eyes closed against the water, she regretted her hasty departure the day before, wishing she had awakened beside him today.

She'd called him the prior evening to talk. He hadn't sounded angry, and even apologized for his abrupt departure. Still, she sensed a coolness, and he hadn't asked why she'd left. She hadn't volunteered an explanation, either.

Divided loyalties weren't easily patched up with dynamite kisses and hours of sublime sex.

The shower helped clear her head, and to finish the job of jump-starting her body awake, she slugged back a cup of black, foul-tasting instant coffee. Taste aside, it did its job of getting her out the door and to the *Taliesen*, more or less alert.

"Skipper here?" she asked as she boarded the ship.

The sleepy-eyed purser on duty shook his head. "Haven't seen him yet."

The answer brought a sting of disappointment, but with cargo and a lot full of cars to load, she'd soon be too busy to worry over Lucas, or how badly she'd bungled things.

Tessa stopped at the galley for an orange-cranberry muffin, and had wolfed it down by the time she arrived in the hold.

The guys were giving Andy Marshall a gentle ribbing—his talk with Sherri must've gone better than planned, since he was back so soon—and it took Tessa a few moments to understand he'd come to work wearing a telltale smile that broadcast the fact he'd gotten lucky the night before. She thought it sweet, in a crude sort of way.

Suddenly aware she wore a dreamy grin herself, Tessa quickly wiped it off her face.

"Hey!" she called as she walked forward. "What's this? A bunch of gossiping old ladies or the best damn deck gang on the lakes?"

Laughter and a few rude comments greeted her as she eyed her crew with fondness. "Let's get those cars loaded. Andy, I know you had a nice time last night, but let's pay attention, okay? In Green Bay, we're picking up a load of paper products bound for Milwaukee. Don't forget that when you're parking your vehicles. Allworth, help the stewards load up the groceries. The supply truck should be here any minute. Let's move it!"

She watched her crew hurry to carry out her orders, smiling with satisfaction and pride. Then, clipboard in hand, she got to work herself.

Lucas still hadn't shown up an hour later, and she began to worry. Just like in the old days, she imagined him lying dead and bleeding in a ditch somewhere.

By the time he walked through the pilothouse door, twenty minutes before sailing time, her nerves had gone beyond frayed.

"It's about time you showed up!" she snapped.

Lucas stopped dead his tracks. The wheelsman darted a look her way, brows raised, then stared straight ahead.

"I had a meeting this morning," Lucas said evenly, but his gaze warned her against asking further questions.

She nodded, feeling foolish for letting her nerves get the best of her. Lucas came up beside her, close enough to feel the heat of his body, to smell the lingering scent of the soap he'd used in the shower.

She gave him a smile, meeting his eyes to let him know she wasn't angry with him, just worried.

Once the *Taliesen* was under way and steaming toward Chicago, Tessa tried to avoid him. But he deliberately stayed close to her, making her acutely aware of his every movement. It didn't help that he went out of his way to touch her: brushing her arm when he reached for the chadburn handle, his body skimming against hers when he walked by.

When his fingers brushed her breasts as he reached

to fiddle with the radar, she glared at him and mouthed: *Stop it!*

He only grinned and mouthed back: *I want to kiss you.*

Although she wanted to be angry with him, she nearly laughed when he puckered his lips at her and kissed the air.

With a frown meant to discourage him, Tessa retreated to the chart table—more to gather her wits than because she needed to check the ship's position or weather reports. Her reprieve lasted only twenty minutes or so, and out of the corner of her eye, she glimpsed Lucas stalking her again. She promptly turned her back on him in a silent warning to stay away.

Which, of course, he took as a challenge.

The instant Lucas came up behind her, she sensed him—his heat, his scent, and the fluttery awareness he seemed to generate whenever in her vicinity. When he put his hands on her hips, and leaned forward to press a soft, warm kiss on her neck, she froze. A hot thrill of desire shot through her, threaded with annoyance and panic.

"I mean it, Lucas, stop this," she whispered as his hand slid higher toward her breast. "Someone will see!"

"The watchman and lookout went down to the galley. The wheelsman's busy behind me and can't see us," Lucas whispered back, his breath tickling her ear. She shuddered, her nipples tightening as his fingers brushed lightly down her sides. "I can't go another week without touching you, much less another hour. Come to my cabin when you're off watch."

A moment later, he released her and left the pilot-house—and for an odd moment, it seemed all the color around her had faded a little with his departure.

Tessa closed her eyes in dismay, only to have a delicious, giddy shiver roll over her. Oh, boy, was she in trouble.

Once her heartbeat had stopped its Indy 500 imitation, Tessa leaned back against the table for support and shot a quick, guilty look at the wheelsman's back. But he appeared quite unaware that she was melting into a puddle of libidinous goo behind him.

The rest of the morning passed uneventfully, the day clear blue and calm, lake traffic relatively light.

"Anything to report?" Rob asked as he came on watch when the *Taliesen* was still several hours from Chicago.

"Nope. We have three freighters keeping us company, but I've adjusted the course a few degrees to port to take us out of their way."

"Where's Hall?"

"In his quarters. I have a message to take him. Do you need to talk to him?" Tessa asked, her tone deliberately casual. But she didn't miss Rob's quick, curious look.

Did everybody suspect? Or was guilt making her see things that weren't there?

"Nah," Rob said. "I was just wondering where he was. See you later."

The door to the captain's office was open, but she didn't see Lucas. She knocked softly, and he called out for her to enter. His voice sounded as if it came from his bedroom.

After his antics in the pilothouse, she was *not* going anywhere near there. Stubbornly, she remained planted where she stood and a few moments later, Lucas walked into the office.

Meeting her gaze, he said, "Shut the door."

Flustered, she did as he'd asked. After a brief, awkward silence she risked a quick glance at him. He was leaning casually against his desk, arms folded across his chest.

Tessa cleared her throat and settled on a safe question: "What was the meeting you had this morning? Did it have to do with that call from Dee yesterday?"

Lucas nodded, still watching her. "I had to answer a few questions for the police. Routine stuff. They're questioning people connected to Dee. Don't be surprised if you get a call."

"Me? Why?"

"Because I was asked to provide an alibi, and you're it. Don't give me that look," he added as she stared at him in growing alarm. "I don't lie to the police. What I told them is confidential. Dee won't hear about it."

She let out her breath in relief, then frowned. "But why question *you*?"

"They can't rule out an employee as a potential suspect, especially when they've been led to believe I was more than just an employee."

"Oh." After a moment, she grudgingly asked, "How's Dee?"

"She's not too happy, that's for sure. But I don't want to talk about Dee now."

He pushed away from the desk and began walking toward her, only to stop when she snapped, "Oh, no you don't. You stay right there."

Amazement crossed his face—obviously, he wasn't as used to obeying orders as giving them—followed by that wary look a man wears when he's in trouble with a woman. "What'd I do?"

"You know I'm talking about what you pulled in the pilothouse earlier." With an effort, she kept her voice low. "What were you thinking? Lucas, this isn't a game. This is my livelihood, and what you did was way out of line. Don't you touch me like that again while I'm on duty!"

A dark flush stained his cheeks, and after a moment he gave a short nod. "You're right, and I apologize . . . but you're driving me crazy, Tess. I want you."

The frustration on his face cracked through her anger, and she wearily squeezed her eyes shut. "Lucas, who do you think will get the boot if Dee Stanhope hears we're sleeping together? Do you really think she's going to send *you* packing? Not likely. And if I get fired because of a sex scandal, how do you think other crews will treat me? They'll think of me as some idiot woman who lost her head over a smooth-talking guy. And as fair game. Good-bye, respect."

"So what do you want from me, Tess?" he asked after a moment. "Help me out here, because I don't know what to do."

At that, she walked to him. He made an aborted move away from the desk, then his mouth tightened and he stayed put.

"You have to let me decide what comes next." She placed her hands on his chest and could feel the beating of his heart beneath her palms.

A smile hovered at the corners of his mouth. "You're telling me you want control."

"Yes."

"That's asking a lot from me."

"I know," she admitted. "But then, I'm the one who stands the most to lose. It only seems fair."

He studied her, his expression a mix of humor and frustration. "Alright. You're in command from here on out."

Knowing what this had cost him—and what it said

for his feelings for her—Tessa whispered, "Thank you, Lucas."

"I owed you one."

On impulse, she perched beside him on the desk, then took his hand and folded it in hers. The silence stretched on and on, alive with anticipation.

"I'd like to kiss you."

"Lucas—"

"Only if you want."

"You won't get carried away?" she asked, weakening.

"Only if you let me," he said wryly, eyes gleaming in a way that warned he'd try anything he could get away with.

"I guess one kiss wouldn't hurt."

Twenty minutes later, Tessa yanked her shirt together and muttered, "Just a kiss." The purr of her closing zipper accompanied her glare. "Right. Why is it I turn into a complete idiot when I'm with you?"

Lucas swung his legs off the bed and reached for his pants. "All I did was kiss you."

All I did was kiss you . . .

Tessa rolled her eyes, then fixed him with a disgruntled look. "You should be neutered."

"I did what you asked," he retorted. "You wanted that as much as I did."

Unable to deny it, she grumbled, "I should be neutered, too."

Lucas jammed his shirttails into his pants. "Self-control isn't a problem for me most of the time. I'm damn good at it—except with you. You always made me crazy."

"Thanks. I think."

"Dammit, Tessa, I'm *trying*."

"It would help if you stopped copping a feel," she said. "That just gets us both all hot and bothered, and we know where that's going to lead."

Lucas dropped his head back, and for an alarmed moment, Tessa thought he was going to howl like a wolf.

"Five days of not touching you. Five *days*," he groaned. "Shit!"

She smoothed back her hair, watching him cautiously. Was he angry again, or just frustrated?

"I have to go."

Letting out his breath, he gave a short nod and watched her walk to the door. She could feel the intensity of his gaze boring into her back. At the door, she turned. "Lucas?"

"What?"

She tried not to smile at his cranky tone. Yes, he was most definitely frustrated. "I did have something work-related to tell you. I'm planning an evacuation drill while we're in Chicago."

"The crew'll love you for that."

"Yes, well . . . misery craves company."

He laughed, if reluctantly, and with a smile Tessa slipped out of his cabin. She quickly peeked down to make sure all her buttons were aligned and her trousers fully zipped.

Common sense warned her against having sex with Lucas, even in secrecy and the relative sanctuary of his cabin, but in his arms, it was so very easy to forget the guilt, even the worry. It was like with Nina's brownies . . . she just wasn't capable of saying no to something that damn good.

And Lucas was good for *her*, Tessa the woman—she didn't doubt that for a minute. Now, Tessa the deck officer, and Tessa the sister, that was an entirely different matter.

A long walk to work off this extra energy would be nice, but her only option was a few quick circuits of the deck, smiling at the passengers as if she hadn't a care in the world—or she hadn't just indulged in fifteen minutes of brain-melting sex.

She hoped it didn't show, and twitched her lips to make sure she wasn't smiling one of those telltale smiles.

On her way to the deck, she ran into Andy Marshall. "Andy! Glad to have you back so soon. How's it going?"

"Hey, I'm okay, thanks." His easy smile reminded her so much of Matt—and for once, the pain of that reminder didn't cut so sharply. "Me and Sherri talked, and things are cool. We set a date in October to get married, and Sherri's cousin is going to rent us half of his duplex. I talked to Compton, too."

"Good." Tessa returned his smile, pleased. "This means I get to keep you for at least another season or two?"

"Guess so. I'm kinda juiced right now. Like maybe being a father is gonna be cool. There's this little person growing, you know? It rocks."

She laughed at his nervous excitement, then continued on her way. The ship rolled from side to side, and she put a hand against the bulkhead to steady herself. Choppy seas again today.

Outside, the day was bright and sunny, the wind whipping through her hair. The passengers on deck wore sunglasses and jackets, even though it was summer, and smiled at her as she passed by. Children ran along the narrow side deck, laughing. An elderly couple made their way slowly along the deck, the wind flattening the woman's gray curls to her head.

Several uniformed stewards passed by, smiling politely, and she nodded in return. After making several rounds of the decks, she headed toward the bow, and saw Lucas, hands clasped behind his back, talking with a group of passengers.

Ordinarily, the crew from the steward department interacted with the passengers; rarely the deck officers or engine-room crew. But as captain, Lucas made himself visible. He was good with people: completely at ease, ever polite, and always willing to tour guests through the *Taliesen* when possible.

Nothing looked so right and true as the sight of him on the deck of his ship. Something suspiciously like tears stung the back of her eyes, which annoyed her to no end.

Bad enough that being with him made her incapable of rational thought; now he'd gone and made her all mushy-emotional, too.

And mushy-emotional was *not* good. By and large, the men who worked for her on these great ships weren't exactly known for being overly in touch with their female side.

Still, she had to smile as Lucas charmed a pint-sized admirer, who twirled her hair in an innately flirtatious gesture. When he hunkered down to the little girl's level and flashed that heart-stopping smile, something inside Tessa made a fluttery catch of longing.

Before he could turn and see her, she slipped away. For the rest of the trip, she sat on a chair on the narrow deck outside the officers' quarters, trying not to dwell on the worrisome notion that she might be falling for Lucas again.

That would do nothing but complicate her life in the worst possible way.

Sighing, she rubbed her brows. Since when had anything she wanted ever come easily?

Once the *Taliesen* docked in Chicago, Tessa wasted no time in sounding the drill, using the ship's PA system to announce that they were participating in an emergency drill, as required by Coast Guard Regulations.

The passengers still on board were keen to watch as Tessa's crew scrambled for their positions, and she heard jokes about icebergs and devil's triangles, and anxious childish queries answered by soothing adult tones.

She stood at her starboard post while Rob Shea, as second mate, oversaw the portside crew. Once the steward, deck, and engine department crew were in position, she glanced at her stopwatch and said into her two-way: "Lower the boats. Let's go!"

All around her sounded creaking ropes and grunting crewmen. The ratcheting clack of the winches was followed one after another by loud, metal clangs and scrapes as the lifeboats hit the side of the ship on their way down. In a drill, the crew only lowered the boats halfway to the water.

When the last lifeboat was over the side, she raised her two-way. "Inflatable rafts and ladders."

Her team reacted swiftly, and moments later, Rob's voice came over on the radio: "We're deployed portside, over."

"Roger." Tessa clicked the stopwatch, arched a brow at the result and turned to Lucas, who stood beside her, hands clasped behind his back.

"How'd we do?" he asked.

"Fifteen minutes and forty-four seconds."

"Good job."

Tessa frowned. "Theoretically, I'm supposed to evacuate all my passengers and crew in under twenty minutes. Providing nothing goes wrong—like panic. Confusion. A blackout." She raised her two-way radio. "Okay, that was great. We beat our best time by six seconds. Raise the lifeboats and secure them. We'll finish boarding passengers in an hour."

She didn't need to hear the grumbling; she could sense it in the dark stares and irritated expressions. Nothing like an evacuation drill to endear a mate to the crew, no matter what the rules said.

With a critical eye, she watched her crew bring the boats back into position. One of the newer deckhands, a slight fellow, struggled with a winch.

"Hey, Marshall," she called. "We need an extra hand at number three."

Andy raised a hand in acknowledgment and made his way to the lifeboat that dangled at an awkward angle. His white-blond hair flared in the breeze.

"Still favor that kid, I see," Lucas said, leaning toward her.

The touch of his breath on her skin sent a shiver through her. "I don't favor him," she answered, keeping her voice low. "I give him tasks he's capable of carrying out, and it just so happens he's capable of carrying out a lot."

"Uh-huh."

She sighed. "Okay. I like the guy. Sue me."

Lucas grinned, cheeks grooving. "Good thing he's too young for you, not to mention a daddy-to-be, or I might be jealous."

Tessa smiled back, then glanced again at Andy, laughing and joking as he helped crank the winch. "He hardly looks old enough to shave. When I was his age—"

"You were lethal. And you just keep getting better

and better." Lucas gave her a wink as he walked away.

Turning to get in the last word, Tessa caught Jerry eyeing her with interest. "The two of you knew each other before this?"

"Have you heard that old saying about curiosity and the cat, Jerry?"

He grinned. "Uh-huh. Lucky for you, some other cat got my tongue." Jerry moved closer and added in a low voice, "Seriously, whatever's going on with you and the captain, you won't hear me running my mouth off about it. Just be careful. I know a few folks on board who'd enjoy causing you trouble."

Her smile faded, sobered by the genuine concern in his dark eyes. "Careful's my middle name, but thanks. I appreciate it."

With the exercise drill completed, Tessa headed back to her cabin. A fleeting thought of seeking out Lucas crossed her mind, but she quickly discarded it. Watching TV until her watch began was a lot safer.

"Well, now. You got a pretty smile and a hello for me, too?"

Tessa groaned at the taunting voice, not feeling up to sparring with the chief. She turned and said, "Who let you out of your hole?"

"Oh, that hurts, Miss Hot Stuff," Lowery said with an unpleasant smile.

As always, the waves of lust and dislike emanating from him chilled her—but this time, she detected a gloating tone, too.

With a snort of annoyance, she walked past him— only to be brought up short when Lowery grabbed her arm. She didn't pull away. She merely looked at him, at his hand, then at him again. After a moment, he released her.

"But not so smart as you think. I'm watching you.

Yup, that's right, watching your every move, little weasel woman."

"Like I give a damn," she retorted.

"Maybe you don't, but Dee Stanhope sure does," Lowery said with a laugh as she stalked past. "Better remember that."

Tessa continued with forced calm to her cabin and shut the door. She stood in the middle of the room, shaking with fury and dislike, before seizing her pillow and hurling it against the bulkhead.

Knowing she was being watched made her feel violated and sick, and she sat on the bed until the nausea passed.

Did Lowery know she and Lucas were lovers? She didn't see how; they'd been careful—except for Lucas's antics earlier in the pilothouse, but Lowery hadn't been there, and Rob and Dave didn't gossip. Then she recalled Jerry's warning, and wondered if Lowery was only trying to scare her.

Well, it was working.

With a heavy sigh, she leaned back against the bulkhead and pulled her abused pillow onto her lap. Her fear slowly faded as anger replaced it.

Dammit, she wouldn't let pea-brained creeps like Lowery dirty the beauty of what she and Lucas shared. She wouldn't let him frighten her or intimidate her, either.

She sat up straight, lifting her chin. Let the bastard gloat. Let him run and tattle to Dee Stanhope. He had no proof, and she knew Lucas wouldn't sit by and let Dee force her out of a job.

At the moment, she'd like nothing better than to go a round or two with that high-handed, overdressed pink witch, and tell Dee exactly what she thought of her threats. If Lowery wanted to take on both her and Lucas, he was in for the fight of his life.

Besides, even if she left the *Taliesen*, there were other shipping companies. With her work record, she'd find a job, even if it meant going back to working freighters—except then, she and Lucas would hardly see each other, and she didn't want that at all.

A good man was a lot harder to find than a good job.

"God, what a mess," she said with a groan, and fell back on her mattress, hugging her pillow close. "Lucas, when you're around, my life is never going to be dull, is it?"

Seventeen

"I'm driving, Lucas."

He stared at Tessa over the top of her sporty red Grand Prix. The hot sun of a late Saturday afternoon shone down on her face and small round sunglasses, making her look impossibly cute—but his self-preservation instincts kept him from saying so.

"This is a date," he pointed out, even as he considered launching himself over the top of the car, grabbing her, and kissing her until her knees buckled. Then maybe he could talk her back inside and skip this whole dinner idea.

It had been a long, long five days of not touching her. Now, instead of staying inside—preferably in the bedroom and making love until he passed out—they were going out.

"So?" she asked, brow raised.

"So I'm the boy, and that means I drive on dates."

Tessa rolled her eyes as she opened the driver's side

door. "I have two years of payments left on this car. *Nobody* touches it but me. Get in, please."

"Come on, Tess. Let me drive," he said. "It's a great car."

"It is, isn't it?" She grinned. "And I'm driving it. You'll just have to deal with that. Besides, I know where we're going; you don't."

Unwilling to argue further, Lucas slid into the passenger seat, wondering if she didn't trust his driving skills or if she was deliberately forcing him to relinquish control. To loosen up, as she always put it.

"I can't believe I let you talk me into going to dinner at your brother's house," he muttered, buckling his seat belt.

"I didn't expect Steve to be home," Tessa said, and pulled away from her apartment complex. "The *Houghton* had a change of orders, but I'd already told Nina we'd be there. I couldn't very well back out of it."

"I want you to know I think this is a bad idea, in case he shoots me and I don't have a chance to tell you later."

"He won't shoot you," Tessa retorted, her mouth tightening. "At least, not until he shoots me first." Lucas swore under his breath. Glancing quickly at him, Tessa added, "Nina's had a little time to work on him, and she swears it'll be okay."

"I still don't know why you had to include me at all."

"They're my family," she said after a moment, the thrust of her chin determined. "And what you said that night, that we could never have a normal relationship, how I couldn't bring you home to meet my family . . . it bothered me, I guess."

So she'd decided to test the waters, hoping her family could tolerate him. He couldn't argue with that, not if it meant she planned on keeping him around. At least for a while.

After several minutes of silence, curiosity got the better of his pride. "Am I visiting as your boyfriend or a friend?"

She sent him a guilty look, then focused on the busy road. "I thought I'd call you my date."

" 'Date' doesn't have the same meaning as boyfriend."

"Don't you think you're a little old to be a 'boyfriend'?"

"No."

At the next stop sign, she turned to him. "Are you angry?"

"I'm not sure," Lucas said tightly.

For one thing, he liked concrete and identifiable—and measurable—increments of success. He'd gotten used to that in the service: do well, get promoted or a medal. With Tessa, he wasn't getting concrete, much less any inkling of success.

"I've had enough of pretending, and I hate sneaking around."

"I'm not ashamed of you or what we're doing." She glanced at him quickly, then back to the road. "Or what we've done."

Lucas said nothing, not sure what that last part meant. The past tense covered a pretty wide territory.

Fifteen minutes later, Tessa stopped the car on a wide street shaded with stately old oaks, outside a neat, older house with a fenced-in yard. The yard was kid-friendly, littered with rubber balls, toys, a small plastic pool, and a play crib.

Pretty innocent-looking for a potential war zone.

After Tessa switched off the ignition, she turned to him. Lucas made no move to open the car door.

"Well?" she said.

He scrubbed a hand over his face. "I've never dreaded anything more than walking through that door and meeting your brother and his wife."

Leaning over, she kissed him, a soft, warm kiss that ended on a smile as she murmured against his lips, "Come on, hotshot. Let's go."

"Mom! Dad!"

At the strident yell, both he and Tessa startled.

"Auntie Tessie is here with some *man*!"

Despite his tension, Lucas grinned at Tessa's blush. "Guess you don't bring too many men by for dinner. That must make me the main event."

Tessa stuck her tongue out at him, and he laughed. She opened her door and stepped out in time to catch the boy against her in a hug. "Hiya, kiddo."

Steeling himself, Lucas got out of the car.

"Who's that?" the boy demanded.

"My boyfriend," Tessa said, with a quick, mischievous grin at Lucas. "His name's Lucas. And this is my nephew, Tommy."

"Hey, how's it going, Tommy." He smiled, liking the frank curiosity in the kid's dark eyes.

As they headed for the house, the boy tugged at his aunt's shirt, and whispered loudly, "Is he really your boyfriend?"

"Yup."

"But Daddy says you're too busy for boyfriends!"

Unfortunately, the door opened just then, and Lucas didn't get to hear Tessa's answer, although he didn't miss her harried expression. But if Tessa looked harried, the petite, pretty, brown-haired woman in shorts and T-shirt standing in the doorway looked downright nervous. She smiled, but it didn't erase the lines of tension around her eyes.

Tessa performed the introductions, and Nina Jardine squeezed his offered hand, her smile warming.

"Come on in," Nina said. "We were just setting the table."

Lucas followed Tessa and Nina. As Tommy skipped ahead of them, a man walked into the living room, a baby resting on his hip, his dark eyes sparking with barely concealed anger.

Before anyone could speak or act, Lucas did what he did best: take command. He moved forward and extended his hand. "Lucas Hall."

"I know who you are."

An awkward silence followed. Hand still out, Lucas glanced at Tessa, saw her brows pull together in a frown. Only the boy and baby were oblivious to the sudden tension. Tessa shifted restlessly, and the sister-in-law gazed anxiously at her husband.

Finally, after what seemed a forever of a moment, Tessa's brother reached out his free hand and took Lucas's in a firm grip. In a cool, polite voice, he said, "Steve Jardine."

At that moment, Tommy bent and said, "Hey, mister, what happened to your leg? Mommy, look!"

The scar. He'd forgotten about it— and how it might fascinate a small boy.

Tommy's curiosity didn't bother Lucas, but he couldn't miss the increased tension on Steve's face, or Nina's sudden dismay. "I was in an accident. Hurt my leg pretty bad, and the doctors had to put a lot of stitches in it."

"Wow. Was it a car accident?" Tommy squatted to get a better view. "Brenda Potter's cousin was in a car accident and she broke her nose."

"Tommy, that's enough! It's not polite to ask people questions like that," Nina cut in. Reaching for the baby, she added, "Give me Amy. Tommy, you come with me and take care of your sister while I finish setting the table."

"But—"

"Right now, young man."

Grumbling, the boy followed his mother, leaving Lucas alone with Tessa and her brother.

"Well, Steve?" Tessa demanded. "What's it gonna be?"

If it hadn't been for his discomfort, Lucas would've smiled at how quickly she went on the attack. But her eyes always held her emotions close to the surface, and he saw the plea for acceptance beneath her toughness.

Her protectiveness brought his guilt to full force. She'd taken him into her home, to meet her family, and he still couldn't bring himself to tell her about his worst scar, that inner one no one could see.

Steve glanced at Lucas's leg, his brow creased in a frown. Lucas could tell it bothered him. "Any friend of my sister is welcome in my house. C'mon, let's get a beer."

"I'll pass on the beer, but a soda will do me fine."

While Nina hustled about the kitchen and Steve fetched drinks for his guests, Tessa led Lucas to the small, cozy living room. Toys lay scattered almost everywhere, and he had to step over what amounted to a Hot Wheels parking lot.

As Tessa went to turn on the TV, Lucas caught sight of a picture on the far wall. Even this young, he recognized the face from the news reports, one of five he'd know anywhere. Without a word, he walked toward the photograph.

"High-school graduation?" he asked, over the low drone of the television.

When Tessa didn't answer, he turned. Tessa still

stood by the TV, but Steve and Nina had come in, and now stared at him with blank looks.

In the kitchen, Lucas heard the little boy singing to his sister, who babbled away.

"A good-looking kid." He hesitated, then added quietly, "I am very sorry for your loss."

Biting her lip, Tessa looked down, and Nina sent a panicky look at her husband, who hadn't moved a muscle. Obviously, poor Nina had missed the chapter in Miss Manners on dealing with dinner guests who'd been involved in the death of a loved one.

For a moment, Lucas regretted mentioning Matt. But it wasn't as if anybody standing in this room could forget. Maybe if everybody stopped sidestepping the problem and faced it head-on, they could all come to terms with what had happened.

"Thank you, Lucas," Nina finally managed, blinking rapidly. "I have . . . to get out the potato salad. Why don't you all sit and watch TV for a bit?"

Steve watched his wife depart, then handed a beer to Tessa, and a Dr Pepper to Lucas. His motions were stiff, acutely uncomfortable. He cleared his throat. "Yeah. Have a seat. The news will be on soon. Gotta catch the weather, you know."

Tessa took Lucas's arm—her palm moist—and pulled him down beside her on an old tan love seat.

Steve hesitated, then sat across from them on the couch. He popped the top on his beer, took a long swallow, then said, "This is goddamn weird."

"Steve—"

Lucas shook his head sharply, cutting off Tessa. He straightened, and looked over at Steve. "Would you like me to leave?"

A dark flush crept over Steve's sun-browned face, and he shook his head. "It took guts for you to come here, and I respect that. You're my sister's friend—"

Guiltily, Lucas broke eye contact. He was a hell of a lot more than a "friend." When he met Jardine's gaze again, the younger man shook his head, and muttered, "Oh, Christ."

The cat was out of the bag. Lucas glanced at Tessa, who looked equally at a loss.

Finally, Steve said, "Like I said before, for Tessa's sake, you're welcome here."

Tension easing from his muscles, Lucas said, "That's all I ask. Thanks."

Steve nodded, then turned toward the TV, which was showing a car commercial. "So what's it like, running the *Taliesen*? Gotta be something, with an old steam engine like that."

Beside him, Tessa let out a soft sigh, as Lucas answered, "She sails like a dream."

Slowly, the strain eased, although not completely, and Lucas found himself talking shop with Tessa and Steve. Shipping might not have been their only common interest, but it was the safest one.

Lucas had just sat back, relaxed, when the news came on and the anchorwoman's words stopped conversation cold: *Top news tonight—the jury has handed down its verdict in the Yarwood case against Stanhope Shipping Company.*

A familiar, hated knot tightened in his belly.

"We don't have to watch this," Tessa said, her hand closing over his. She rubbed her thumb against his knuckles in a soft, soothing motion.

"Is there a problem?" Steve asked.

Lucas shook his head, but didn't look up. "No," he said, and left it at that.

"—*was a tremendous blow to Joseph Yarwood, whose twenty-two-year-old son died when the tanker exploded and*

sank nearly two years ago. Mr. Yarwood, shouting angrily,
was forcibly removed from the courtroom—"

"He lost," Steve said. "Like he ever had a chance."

Lucas clasped his hands tightly together and stared
down at the pattern of the carpet.

"*—all along, Stanhope Shipping has insisted the tanker*
met all Coast Guard safety standards and it was crew
error—"

"So they always say." Steve snorted in disgust. "And
the greedy bastards keep pushing for more profit,
pushing ships and men until shit like this happens.
And who dies, huh? Not *them*, that's for damn sure."

"Steve, please. Turn it off. None of us needs to see
this."

The TV went silent, and Lucas forced himself to look
up. Tessa's eyes brimmed with worry, and Steve was
frowning again.

"Hey, man, sorry. It's a bad memory for all of us.
Our family . . . we understand you did what you
could." Steve caught Lucas's gaze, and something very
like acceptance flashed briefly between them before he
turned, and called, "Nina? You want any help in the
kitchen, babe?"

"Sure! Tell Tessa I need her outside to watch the kids
while I start the grill, and I need you to chop up this
chicken for me."

"Come with me," Steve said to Lucas. "Something
tells me Nina's dying to corner Tess for some girl talk."

"Is it okay?" Tessa asked.

Lucas nodded, pretending he hadn't seen the worry
in her eyes. "Sure. Go on."

With a last reluctant look at him, Tessa went outside
after Nina, scooping up the babbling baby on her way,
and Lucas followed Steve into the small, bright kitchen.
In silence, he settled against the counter while Steve

slid a large chicken from its package onto a thick wooden cutting board.

Hoisting a huge cleaver, Steve said, "Start talking."

Lucas cleared his throat, suddenly wary. So much for thinking he was in the clear. "About what?"

With one stroke, Steve neatly halved the chicken along the breastbone. "How long have you been seeing my sister, and what are you planning to do about it?"

Nina barely waited until the back screen door slammed behind them before she seized Tessa's arm. "Oh, God, for a minute there, I thought all hell was going to break loose. Believe me when I tell you Steve is *not* happy with you and me about this."

"I figured as much," Tessa said. The humidity closed around her, sticky and hot. "They seem to be doing okay, though?"

"Steve says we ganged up on him, and I think he's mad about that more than anything else. He'll get over it." Nina sent her a sideways look. "Enough of Steve. I want to talk about your Lucas, who is just *gorgeous*! Even better-looking in person than on TV. He's so . . . I don't know what it is, exactly, but—"

"It's called charisma," Tessa interrupted Nina's breathless barrage, shifting Amy in her arms. Tommy made straight for the pool and busied himself by filling squirt guns and shooting bugs.

"That's it! You just want to fall to your knees in adoration or something."

Despite her lingering tension, Tessa smiled. "He has that effect on me, too, but it's not adoration I'm feeling."

"You move fast, girl. I'm still a little shocked by all this myself."

Guilt pricked her at Nina's meaning. "Actually, we have this sort of history between us. I knew him ten years ago. He was . . . well, we spent a summer together."

Nina's eyes widened as she stood next to the grill, hands on her hips. "No."

Tessa shrugged with more nonchalance than she felt.

"Why didn't you say anything? I could just kill you for not telling me this! I need details. Right now. All of them."

"I didn't say anything because he dumped me. I was only nineteen, so my way of dealing with the humiliation was to pretend it never happened. And that's all the details you get."

"He dumped you? Tacky of him." Nina cranked the grill, eyeing Tessa as the flames spurted with a whoosh. "Obviously you've forgiven him. How come?"

"We were both young, with separate interests." Not all that young . . . Lucas had been the same age as Steve was now, and Steve was married and a father of two. She sighed. "Maybe a little immature, and the timing was wrong, anyway."

Nina brightened. "Meaning the timing's right now?"

Cautiously, Tessa answered, "I didn't say that."

"For God's sake, if you're waiting for every little detail to be perfect, you'll die a lonely old lady."

"Oh, come on, Nina, after what you saw in there, how can you say that? Lucas and me . . . it's complicated."

"Seems to me you're working on that."

"There's also the fact that our relationship is against company rules. That's another complication."

"All one of you has to do is get another job. Very simple."

Tessa sighed again. "It's *not* as simple as that."

"Yes, it is. You know what you have to do. Just do it."

Before Tessa could argue, Steve and Lucas came out of the house. Whatever had passed between them inside, they seemed to be getting along well enough. While they weren't joking and slapping each other on the back, at least there was no blood.

Both men headed toward the grill. Lucas smiled at Tessa and the wide-eyed baby, who observed Lucas as she chewed on a finger. "Now here's something I don't see every day: my mate with a baby in her arms."

Tessa smiled back. "Isn't she a sweetie? Say hello, Amy."

"Ba-ba-ba-ba," Amy said around a juicy finger, as Steve handed Nina a platter heaped full of chicken pieces, along with a bottle of barbecue sauce and a brush.

"Daddy!" Tommy ran from the pool. "Mister Lucas, wanna come see my new super soaker? It shoots really far."

"Sure, my man," Steve said cheerfully, and followed Tommy as he skipped back toward the pool, talking nonstop. After a brief hesitation, looking a little lost, Lucas joined them.

Once the men were out of earshot, Nina sidled toward Tessa, and murmured, "I'm assuming Dee Stanhope's out of the picture?"

"She was never in it." Amy began squirming and kicking, so Tessa put her down on the grass. The baby took off after the guys at a fast crawl, her diapered butt wiggling.

While Steve stood talking with Lucas, pumping Tommy's super soaker, Amy pulled herself up on the pool's side. With throaty noises of excitement, she splashed her hands in the water.

Nodding in response to whatever Steve was saying, Lucas hunkered down beside the baby and rested a protective hand on her shoulder to keep her from falling into the pool. His hand looked huge and brown against Amy's tiny back and pink T-shirt.

At his automatic gesture—done without even breaking off from his conversation—Tessa smiled again.

"He's good with kids," Nina said, and Tessa could almost feel waves of approval radiating from her sister-in-law. Then Nina hesitantly asked, "Does he talk much about the accident?"

"Not really." She watched Lucas with Amy a moment longer, and a sharp, almost anxious pang squeezed her heart. "He went into cardiac arrest on the helicopter. Did you know that?"

"No, I didn't," Nina said quietly.

Again, the strength of his presence and vitality struck her. If it hadn't been for a well-trained rescue team, all that vitality would've been lost. The realization that Lucas might have died, and all they'd shared these past few weeks might never have been, sent an icy wave of fear through her, followed by fierce rush of thankfulness.

"And what about you, Tess? How are you dealing with his part in the accident?"

Tessa turned to Nina. "It doesn't feel right to hold it against him. And the thing with the hatch . . . you know nothing was ever proven. I guess that's what's making things work so far."

"He seems like a nice guy. I like him. And I feel sorry for him, too. Being here must be really hard for him."

Tessa didn't answer, only watched Lucas and Amy. Emboldened by the supporting hand at her back, Amy continued splashing, but she'd turned to Lucas and laughed her little baby belly laugh.

"Hey, monkey baby," Steve said, scooping her up. "You're getting our guest all wet. Let's go back to Mommy."

"Do you like kids, Lucas?" Nina called, as Steve transferred the squirming baby back into her arms. Nina promptly returned Amy to the grass before she started howling.

"Yup." Lucas flashed his smile. "The best part of my Coast Guard job was when the school buses rolled in and we'd tour kids through the cutter. Kids are great."

Then Lucas turned to answer some question Tommy asked, and Nina leaned toward Tessa, and whispered, "I really like this one."

"Christ, Nina," Steve muttered in irritation.

Nina sniffed. "Oh, you go away."

"Hey." He peered at her. "You're not crying are you?"

"You know I am. I come from a long, proud line of weepy, emotional women, and just because you don't have a romantic bone in your body doesn't mean—"

Steve kissed her quiet. "Later on, I bet we can find at least one romantic bone on my body, babe."

With that, he strolled off to join Lucas and Tommy, who were now sitting on the grass, deep in discussion over a bug Tommy had captured in his hands.

Tessa folded her arms over her chest and sent a sideways glance at Nina. "You have to admire a man who can turn almost any word into a sexual innuendo. There's raw talent there."

"That's what he is, alright, raw and raunchy." Nina made a noise of disgust, then grinned as she wiped at her eyes. "And I wouldn't trade him for the world."

"Oh, Nina . . . I envy what you and Steve share, and I'm so afraid I'll never have that."

Somehow, admitting her fear brought a tremendous

sense of relief. Tessa glanced at Nina, who carefully arranged chicken pieces on the grill.

"I'm not sure what to say," Nina said at length, plainly flustered by the unexpected change in subject. "Steve and I have a traditional marriage, but traditional isn't how I think of you. I'm not sure it's what you want."

Tessa couldn't deny the truth of that observation. "Sometimes I wonder why I bother trying. The kind of work I do makes it hard to keep a relationship going, and I'm not at all sure things with Lucas will work out any better than they did the first time."

Nina slathered sauce over the chicken. "Do you want it to?"

"I think so." At Nina's arch look, Tessa sighed and admitted, "Yes. Yes, I do."

"Does he treat you right?"

Tessa glanced at Lucas, who was once again acting as baby goalie. That odd little pang blossomed into a warm, sweet ache, and she ran her hands over her arms, suddenly shivery.

"Oh, yes."

"Then make it work. Tessa, I mean it . . . that man is a great catch. Please, please tell me you're not blind."

"Believe me, I'm not blind."

"So reel him in and hold on to him tight. I swear, if you let this one get away, I may have to disown you on behalf of all womankind!"

Eighteen

*I*t was almost ten when they left Nina and Steve's place. As Tessa drove back along quiet residential streets shadowed by nightfall, Lucas stared out the window and tapped his fingers to the beat of a melancholy R.E.M. tune.

She glanced at the gauge panel. "I need to fill up. Is there a gas station on the way to your cabin?"

"Yeah." He turned from the window. "Just up ahead before the next exit."

Tessa met his gaze briefly before returning her attention to the road. "Thank you for coming tonight."

"You have a nice family."

"I thought everything went well." She hesitated, then added, "All things considered."

"Do you think I passed the test?"

"Mostly." She reached over and squeezed his hand. "I want them to like you."

"Why is that, Tessa?"

In the darkness she couldn't make out his expression, and waited until she'd turned into the gas station and pulled up to the pump before answering.

"I don't know if things will work out between us, but I wanted to at least start out on the right foot with my family." She switched off the engine and turned to him. "My family is important to me."

"I don't think your brother is ever going to like me."

"He'll come around. Steve's quick to anger, like me, but I've never known him to hold a grudge for long." She grimaced. "Unlike me."

"Part of your charm." Lucas gave her a quick kiss, then opened the car door and stepped out. "I want to pick up a six-pack of Coke. You want anything while I'm in there?"

"A Snickers bar," she said, stepping up to the pump. "Thanks."

"Got it. I'll pick up the gas tab, too."

"You don't have to do that, I can—" She stopped, because he was already walking away, waving off her protest.

She watched him, so tall and self-confident and purposeful. Even out of uniform, he carried himself in a way that made people notice him. One woman, leaving the convenience store with a gallon of milk and a loaf of bread, did a double take. Gawking back at him, she missed the step from the sidewalk to the tarmac and almost fell.

"And he called me lethal," she murmured, feeling a giddy rush of disbelief that this man was really, truly *hers*.

The pump clicked and she removed the nozzle. Still mooning over Lucas, she didn't pay close enough attention to what she was doing and dribbled gasoline over her shorts and shoes.

Cursing quietly, she grabbed a paper towel and wiped the gas away. Ugh; what a romantic smell . . . eau de unleaded.

Well, she'd just have to take a dip in the cabin's whirlpool tub—and Lucas could help scrub her clean.

Tessa waited in the car, smiling a little dreamily as she imagined where all that scrubbing would probably lead. A minute later, Lucas slid into the seat, whistling, a six-pack of pop in his hand. He tossed the candy bar into her lap as she started the car and pulled away.

"Thanks," she said. "Now how much was the gas?"

His whistling stopped.

When he didn't answer, she glanced at him. "Lucas?"

Slowly sucking in a long breath through his teeth, he turned toward her, his expression tight. "I . . . what?"

"Oh, never mind." After a moment, aware that he still sat with an unnatural stiffness, his breathing rapid, she asked, "Are you okay?"

"Yes." Even his voice sounded different; as if he were speaking through a constriction. "It's hot."

The AC was blasting, and Tessa stared, dumbfounded, as he rolled down his window.

"You're not acting like you're okay." Distracted with concern, she nearly missed the turn to the cabin. She swerved sharply, and he whipped his head around. The look on his face sent a chill clear through her and she braked, a cloud of dust from the dirt road coiling upward.

"What's wrong? Are you sick? Do you need to get—"

"I smell gas."

"Oh, that . . . I spilled some on my clothes back there." Still perplexed, she smiled in an effort to calm him—but her smile froze when she turned on the dome light. His face was gray, his gaze chillingly distant.

"Lucas, stop it. Whatever you're trying to do, it isn't funny. You're scaring me!"

He stared at her for a moment longer, then his eyes focused on her with a sharp, sudden intensity. Without a word, he opened the door and stepped outside.

Speechless, Tessa watched as he walked away, fingers laced behind his head, back arched. Was he in some kind of pain . . . ?

It seemed he intended to walk the rest of the way to the cabin, along this dark, creepy, wood-tangled little road. For a moment longer, she sat in bewildered silence, then snatched the keys from the car and went after him.

"Lucas, what's going on?"

"I can't . . . stand the smell of gasoline." He stopped, still at least ten feet away. When she took a step toward him, he rapidly backed away. Realizing he didn't want her near him, she froze. "Don't! Don't . . . ask questions. Just go to the cabin." His voice was low, harsh. "I'll follow in a minute."

"But I—"

"Just go, goddammit!"

The desperation in his voice left her no choice, although she hated to leave him alone without understanding what was wrong. Reluctantly, she returned to the car and slowly drove past, watching him in the rearview mirror until he faded from view in the darkness.

At the cabin, she quickly showered and disposed of her gas-stained shoes, shorts, and underwear, and slipped on one of Lucas's old Coast Guard T-shirts. After lighting the citronella candles along the length of the porch, she sat in one of the Adirondack chairs with a tall glass of ice water, and waited.

Worried sick, she fretted over possibilities and explanations, none of them comforting. Her hands trembled so badly the ice in the glass rattled.

No more than twenty minutes passed before Lucas showed up, although it seemed she'd waited far longer. When she saw his pronounced limp, worse than usual, she almost sprang up and rushed to help. Uncertain of his response, though, she stayed on the chair.

When he came into the light of the candles, the look in his eyes raised gooseflesh along her arms and legs.

"Why don't you sit down. I'll get you a Coke, then we're going to talk. I think you owe me a few answers."

With a brief nod, he sat heavily in the chair beside hers, legs sprawled, head back, and eyes closed. She was worried by the lines of weariness on his face, carved even deeper by the yellowish light from the candles.

She returned with the six-pack and a glass, poured the fizzing soda over the ice, then handed it to him.

Lucas took it, but a sharp tension radiated outward from him, warning her away. She heard each long breath inward, followed by a slow exhalation. The measured sound of it scraped at her nerves.

"Are you sick?" she asked at length, voicing her deepest fear. Sick, like in cancer. Like in dying.

"Sick," he repeated, as if he didn't understand the word, his expression dark, distant. The silence stretched on until he surprised her by laughing, but the sound of it raised the hair on her arms.

"No, just crazy. A little crazy. Sometimes."

Tessa ached to go to him, to hold him and comfort him—but those taut, defensive lines of his body kept her at a distance. "I don't understand."

"Thank God for that," he muttered. A moment later, his tone weary, he added, "I have a traumatic stress disorder, which sometimes happens to cops or rescue personnel like me." He stopped again, then finished quietly, "Or like I was."

"Traumatic—" Tessa repeated. As the enormity of his words sank in, she fell silent.

"I'm recovering, but now and again something can trigger flashbacks." He looked away, but not before she'd seen the shame, the self-disgust, written on his shadowed face. "Gasoline'll do it for me."

It all fell into place: his nighttime prowling, the ever-present tension, his avoidance of alcohol, his reaction to any mention of Matt, this evening's news report.

And the honorable medical retirement from the Coast Guard which, it would seem, wasn't because of his injured leg.

"The *McKee*?" she whispered.

He made a low noise. "It was a gradual thing, building up over the years. The *McKee* just finished me off."

Tessa reached over and rested her hand lightly on his arm, half-afraid he'd recoil, push her away, or lash out in anger. But Lucas just stared down at the porch, muscles so tense his body vibrated from the force of it.

What now? Her only expectation for the next few days was to lose herself in Lucas's company, to relax with him, indulge in a few hours of blissful, sweet sex and avoid their worries.

But there was no avoiding this. It was as if she'd been sucked into an undertow with nothing to grab on to for support—and if she felt like this, she couldn't imagine what Lucas was going through.

"Does Dee Stanhope know?"

"She knows."

Tessa let that sink in, her heart thudding with such force he must hear it. She wet her dry lips. "Were you planning on telling *me*?"

"When the time was right."

For now, she'd have to ignore the dozens of questions she wanted to ask. She took a short, quick breath, forcing herself to remain calm. She had to; the look of shame in his eyes blared the warning loud and clear as any foghorn: danger ahead, proceed with caution.

Men like Lucas—self-confident, take-charge men; men used to controlling emotions and situations; strong men who were natural-born leaders; men trained to protect; men of action—didn't handle setbacks well.

Without a single word, he'd already told her—in his silence, in his actions—that he felt less a man because of what had happened to him. No matter if she thought that ridiculous; it was what *he* thought that mattered.

"That night you came to my apartment," she said softly. "You told me you needed the *Taliesen*. Is this why?"

He took a drink, then put the glass aside. "I thought that if I could get back on a ship, back in command and in a familiar routine like I'd had in the service, it would be enough. It would mean I'd succeeded in getting my life back, and wearing a uniform is the only measurement of success I've ever known."

"Oh, Lucas, that's your father talking," Tessa said with a sigh. She pulled her chair closer to him and reached for his hand. She asked quietly, "Do you have flashbacks often?"

"Not as much as I used to, and it's been a long time since I had one this bad. I've learned to control my responses. I had a—" he hesitated, then finished tightly "—a therapist who was pretty good."

"I thought stress disorders only happened to people who'd been in combat."

"Sometimes law enforcement *is* combat, and the Coast Guard's the only branch of the military authorized to make civilian arrests, which makes us legitimate targets." He glanced at her, then away. "I've seen the worst one human being can do to another, and seen other things—"

He cut himself off, and Tessa tightened her hand on his.

After a moment, he continued. "You don't want to hear about that, believe me. I was burning out and knew it, which is the main reason I came back to this district after my father's death. I only had to get through a couple more years to retire. Everything should've been alright."

"But the accident wrecked all that?"

"That's a pretty apt way of putting it." He drained his drink, then rolled the ice around in the glass. The monotonous, steady sound had begun to put her nerves on edge when he said, "I have trouble sleeping, but you already knew that, and I still have nightmares. I sometimes have this sense of danger, even though I know nothing's wrong, and I have to trick myself into ignoring it. If something reminds me of the accident, I can get flashbacks so real that I smell the gas, hear the voices. It can make me freeze up for a couple seconds."

Lucas turned his gaze out toward the dark lake. "Sometimes I push people away. Diane and Kevin, they put up with a lot that first year. I'm better than I was, but some days, I'm not easy to live with."

It was a warning, and for a long, quiet moment, Tessa mulled over everything he'd said. "Is it curable?"

"Not like my busted-up leg was curable. It's controllable, though I never really know if the next time I go to the gas station to fill up my car, I'll lose it and think I'm back on that deck, the hatch is opening, and I know—"

Lucas cut himself off, pulling his hand from hers. He

laced his fingers behind his head, arched his back, eyes closed—just as he'd done on the road earlier.

"And I know it's too goddamn late," he finished quietly.

Squeezing back a sudden press of hot tears, Tessa leaned forward, touching his thigh in a gesture of comfort. "You don't have to talk about it, Lucas."

"Yes, I do." Hands still clasped behind his head, he hunched over, elbows on his knees. His voice, when he spoke again, was muffled. "When I climbed on deck, my only thought was to get those guys out alive. But when the ship grounded, the impact damaged the aft hull enough to jam the hatch. The smell of the gas . . . God, it made me sick. I called out, and this guy answered . . . all I could see were his fingers. He kept saying, 'Please, mister, don't let me die,' and I told him . . . I told him I'd get him out."

A long silence followed, and Lucas whispered. "I promised him I wouldn't let him die."

Tessa looked away from his hunched form, fighting tears and trying not to dwell on what it must have been like for Matt and the other men in those final moments—or what had been going through Lucas's mind as he stood on the deck, alone.

"The hatch opened all the way . . . and in that split second, I knew it was all over." He swallowed audibly. "Everybody's best guess is that the open stairway created a massive draft. The fire in the engine-room flashed, ignited the fumes, and blew the aft all to hell."

She knew all that, she'd read the various theories, and the only sticking point had been the hatch. But these other details were new—and at that realization, Tessa went cold with dread.

He *did* remember!

"Lucas, who opened the hatch?"

At her question, he straightened, but again turned from her, and all the answer she needed was in his body's tension, his inability to meet her eyes.

"I think you do remember."

He looked at her then, the orange candle flame reflecting the sheen of his eyes, the stark pain. "Don't ask. Please."

Tessa stood. "You owe me the truth." She paused. "And you owe it to yourself. For the last time, Lucas — did you open the hatch?"

"What happens if I say yes?" His voice was low, his eyes intent, unblinking. "Do you turn around and walk away from me?"

Blood pounded in her ears as she placed her hands on the arms of his chair and leaned toward him. "Did you?"

A short silence followed, stretching on for a long, difficult moment. A muscle in his jaw tightened, then his lids lowered, and he whispered, "I think I did."

Her breath caught in her throat. She stepped away from him, recoiling from the shock of actually hearing him say it.

"Oh, God," he said, still in a whisper. "I'm sure I did."

Time suspended; seconds passed slowly, and Tessa waited for the anger, the sense of betrayal, to rip through her. Lucas looked up, his eyes glittering, unnaturally bright.

And, deep within her, a door left open too long seemed to close with a soft click, and unexpected relief washed over her. An answer. At long, long last, an end to it.

Finally, she met Lucas's gaze as he watched her, waiting for, no doubt, her disdain and censure.

She went to him and slipped her arms around his

neck, feeling his warm, moist skin, the scratchy texture of his hair. He stiffened, as if he couldn't bear her touch, then looped his arms around her hips and pulled her painfully close, his head resting in the valley between her breasts. Tessa closed her eyes.

She couldn't say how long she stood like that, with Lucas still seated, his head against her, their arms wrapped around each other. Seconds, or minutes, it didn't matter.

Then, as another realization shot through her, Tessa opened her eyes. *Fingers—he'd seen fingers in the hatch.*

"It wasn't your fault," she said, pulling back so she could look down.

"I just told you—"

"Somebody was on the other side of the hatch, right?" Tessa interrupted in a rush. "And he was trying to open it?"

Lucas nodded briefly.

"That means it was a no-win situation. Oh, baby, don't you see? Those men were dead before you even came on the scene. It doesn't matter that you opened the hatch. If you hadn't, that other man would have."

Lucas's breath was hot against her skin. "But it matters to me, Tess. I lived. I shouldn't have, but I did. Why?"

It hurt to hear the anguish and anger in his voice, and Tessa was desperately thankful she couldn't see him. No way could she face his grief without falling apart herself.

"I don't know, but there's a reason. There's always a reason." She smoothed back his short hair. "And I am so very thankful that you lived, and that you're here with me right now. If you believe nothing else, Lucas, believe that."

He looked up at her soft, fierce words, and after a

lengthy silence, said quietly, "I didn't lie at the inquiry. I really didn't remember then. The memories started coming back a year ago, but I never told anybody."

"I'm still here," she whispered. "See? I didn't run away. I didn't leave you."

Swallowing back the lump in her throat, she felt humbled by this powerful need to protect and care for him. The strength of it left her shaken.

"Lucas? Do you want to go inside? Go to bed?"

For a long moment he said nothing, only sat very still as she continued to stroke her fingers through his hair, holding his head pillowed against her breasts.

"I'd like you to hold me," he said at last. "That's all."

Tessa tightened her arms around him. So he wouldn't hear the tears in her voice, she managed to whisper one word: "Okay."

Lucas woke at five in the morning and lay still for a few minutes, slowly becoming aware of the warm body pressed against him. To his surprise, he'd slept like a rock after he and Tessa had finally gone to bed. Now, listening to her slow, even breathing, he rubbed his thumb gently against the soft skin under the T-shirt she'd worn to bed.

She hadn't left him. He hadn't really thought she'd stay, after what he'd told her, both about his stress disorder and the *McKee*.

He still felt numb with relief. After days of sweating over her reaction, he wished he'd told her earlier. She'd deserved finding out in a kinder way than she had. God, he must've scared her half to death.

Despite what she'd told him, he didn't believe that the truth about the *McKee* didn't matter to her. Overcome by smoke, the poor bastard behind the hatch probably wouldn't have had the strength to open it without Lucas's help, but in a sense, Tessa was right. It was one fight he couldn't have won; he just hadn't wanted to let go his guilt enough to admit it.

And he still had trouble letting go of that guilt.

With a sigh, Lucas eased out of Tessa's arms and rolled out of bed. He pulled on a pair of boxers, then made his way down the stairs in the dark.

In the main room, he turned on the TV to watch a movie. Kevin had left his collection of old sci-fi and horror movies at the cabin, and Lucas grabbed one that promised bad B-movie satisfaction. He popped a bag of microwave popcorn, grabbed a Coke, and settled back on the overstuffed couch.

"Do I smell popcorn?"

At the sound of Tessa's sleepy voice, Lucas turned and looked up. She leaned against the loft rail, and he could barely make out the pale outline of her face, legs, and T-shirt.

Before he could answer, she said, "It's five in the morning, Lucas."

"I'm okay," he said to her unvoiced concerns. "This is when I usually get up. My internal alarm doesn't always turn off when I'm not working."

She stretched, and the sound of her sigh carried down to him. "What are you watching?"

"An old movie. It's so bad it's good."

"Sounds like predawn logic. Want some company?"

"Sure."

She joined him a moment later, her body still warm from his bed. When she snuggled against him, he pulled her onto his lap and planted a good-morning kiss on her forehead.

No doubt about it; he could get used to this.

For a while, they sat together without talking, watching the movie. He waited, tensed, for the questions to start, or the first hint that she'd now treat him differently—but she only settled more comfortably onto his lap, munching popcorn. He detected no forced cheeriness, or, God forbid, pity, and it seemed she would let him raise the subject on his own.

He loved her all the more for that.

"I wanted to tell you," he said quietly. "But I couldn't seem to force myself to do it. I *am* sorry, Tessa."

"It's okay," she said with a soft smile. "I've learned a thing or two about men by working with them all the time. I won't let you push me away, but I'm not going to hound you, either. I trust you to talk to me when you feel ready."

Something hot burned at the back of his eyes. "Thank you."

She only nodded, reaching for a handful of popcorn. After a moment, she laughed. "There's a man wearing a rubber fish suit. What *is* this movie?"

"Creature from the Black Lagoon." His mood lifted at her laughter, and he smiled. "Check out the woman. You should hear her scream. She's in the same class as Fay Wray."

A moment later, an ear-piercing shriek ripped through the room, and Tessa laughed. Grinning, he fed her a kernel of popcorn, and pretty soon one thing led to another.

Over the sounds of hysterical female shrieks, he kissed Tessa's salty, buttery mouth, then slowly made love to her while the fish-man monster terrorized the lagoon.

Nineteen

*T*he *Taliesen's* next voyage ended as uneventfully as it began, with clear weather, a calm lake, and content passengers, including the company bigwigs Tessa and Lucas had to entertain the entire time. Because of the constant presence of the bigwigs, the sum of her private time with Lucas was a single, fleeting kiss on an empty stairway in the dead of night.

She'd actually welcomed the enforced distance, although she didn't say so to Lucas, fearing he'd misunderstand. But she felt certain they both needed time to get used to all the major changes that had occurred recently between them.

As Lucas docked the ship in Milwaukee with quick efficiency, Tessa stood beside him, beset with sudden jitters. Spending five days on her best behavior, under constant scrutiny by the bigwigs and keeping her crew in hand, was nothing compared to the prospect of being alone again with Lucas.

There was so much she wanted to say, yet all she could seem to do was stand there in silence, only inches from his familiar, comfortable warmth, the earthy scent of his cologne filling her senses. They watched the passengers, then most of the crew except for the security watch, depart the ship. It was better to have him watch something else besides her, with that almost expectant expression on his face, as if he could read the doubts in her mind.

Doubts that she wouldn't be strong enough to deal with what he'd confessed. She was glad he'd told her; glad to no longer feel as if she were flailing about in the dark, trying to understand what was different about him. Still, a traumatic stress syndrome, which might never be cured, wasn't something she could just shrug off.

It was one more complication they surely didn't need.

At that moment, Lucas stepped away from the window, his body brushing hers. In the bright light, his eyes looked more gold than hazel.

"I need to talk to the chief, check in with Jerry, and make a few entries in the ship's log. It'll be another hour before I can get away." He moved closer. "Are you coming out to my place tonight?"

"Do you want me to?"

"Of course I do." He sent her a brief, unreadable glance. "Are you heading to your apartment first?"

Tessa nodded, letting him catch her hand in his and giving his finger a light squeeze.

"Then I'll swing by and pick you up. No sense in both of us driving out to the cabin."

She frowned. "Make sure you park at the next building, in the back."

"Tess, we're off duty and not doing anything illegal,

and like hell am I going to feel guilty about it."

"But what if somebody we know sees us?" she asked.

"Then I'll smile and say hello." He pulled her close. "Now stop arguing and give me a kiss."

"Lucas—"

"Just a kiss."

"Oh, I've heard that before. You never deliver *just* a kiss, you—"

He closed her mouth with his in a deep, hungry kiss; a kiss that said he'd waited long enough. He slid his strong, impatient hands along her back and bottom, stirring in her a sharp, restless need to run her own hands over his bare skin.

When he broke off the kiss seconds later, Tessa grabbed his shoulders to steady her shaky knees. She let out a small sigh, and Lucas's eyes gleamed with humor and healthy lust.

"I'll be at your place within the hour," he murmured, his low, rough voice sending a shiver through her. "Wear something nice. And easy to take off."

With that, leaving her hot with anticipation, he walked out of the pilothouse.

Preoccupied with that kiss full of carnal promises, Tessa hardly noticed the drive to her apartment.

She showered first and then, in a moment of domestic panic, dusted and vacuumed. A quick peek in her refrigerator—not that she expected Lucas to inspect her kitchen the way he inspected the *Taliesen*—revealed that several food items had gone fuzzy. She quickly committed them to the dark deep of the garbage disposal.

With that done, she could no longer put off deciding what to wear. She wanted to look nice, but a little voice whispered it wouldn't matter because Lucas would have her out of her clothes in no time flat.

Still, she wanted something special—something that would make *his* knees go weak for a change—and stared into her open closet, chewing on her lip in vexation as she saw lots of jeans and T-shirts, but nothing knockout sexy.

She really should do something about that. Being practical didn't mean she had to dress in a practical fashion *all* the time.

Searching through the closet again, she paused when she spied something black. "Hello, what's this?"

Pushing aside several sweatshirts, Tessa pulled out a cocktail dress. Remembrance dawned: she'd bought it several years ago for her overly jealous boyfriend in a doomed attempt to persuade him that he was number one in her life, even when she was working with all those other men. But they'd split before she'd ever had the chance to wear it.

She hauled it out—not that there was much to haul out. The dress consisted of a scant, sleeveless scrap of black silk cut to fit a woman's body, with a short skirt, plunging neckline, and low back. No bra with this one.

Oh, yes, the little black dress every woman should have in her arsenal, and she was about to put it to the test. If this didn't make Lucas forget about everything but her, nothing would. And then he could set about making *her* forget everything but him.

In his arms, all through the night, she intended to do a lot of forgetting.

After removing her robe, she donned a pair of high-cut black lace panties, slipped on the dress, and faced the mirror.

She eyed the amount of revealed skin, and homed in on her hips. She smoothed the fabric, and frowned. Panty lines. The dress was a little tighter than she'd hoped.

Well, Marilyn Monroe's lush hips had beguiled an entire generation of men; surely she could manage to tempt just one man—one easily seduced man who'd been celibate nearly a week.

As she eyed her panty lines again, a sly thought bloomed, and she quickly slipped off her underwear.

Still a little shocked at her daring, she headed to the bathroom before she lost her nerve. After brushing her teeth, she combed and fluffed her hair, and dabbed on a bit of racy red lipstick. She surveyed her reflection, and smiled.

Just then, a firm knock sounded on her door. She froze, bravado dissolving. When the insistent knocking came again, she hurried into the living room, and called, "Just a minute!"

A quick peek showed Lucas standing outside her door, wearing a wolfish grin.

Bracing herself, Tessa unchained the door and opened it.

"Hi," she said, in a breathless voice that would've done Marilyn proud—although *hers* was caused by pure nerves.

"Hey yourself. You look . . . great," Lucas said, gaze roaming the length of her with hot appreciation. He still wore his uniform, but he'd taken off his tie and rolled up his sleeves. "No, you look more than great. You look good enough to eat."

Tessa peeked past him. Thank God none of her neighbors were around. "Come in. I haven't had time to pack a bag yet."

"Bag?" Lucas repeated blankly, his gaze focused on her chest. A fine sheen of moisture dotted his upper lip.

Huh. It wasn't weak knees, maybe, but close enough—and *she* did that to him. Smiling, slightly more secure in her feminine power, Tessa turned and walked away from him, putting a dash of wiggle into her walk.

"Yes, an overnighter to take to your place."

She sensed, rather than heard him, come up behind her. His hands slid around her waist, snaring her in mid-stride, and he pulled her back against him. With little separating her body from his, she couldn't miss the press of his erection against her.

"To hell with the bag," Lucas murmured, kissing her just below her ear. She went still with a delicious tension. "To hell with my place."

He let her go, unbuttoning his shirt as she turned to him, eyes gleaming with a sexual intent.

"Lucas—"

"Don't argue, I've been waiting for this for days. Don't tell me to wait," he said, tossing his shirt aside.

"Argue? With a desperate man in a hurry to get naked? No way. You keep on going; I think I'll watch."

Lucas gave her a surprised look, soon replaced by a slow, lazy grin as he began to strip away his uniform. She grew warmer with each piece of clothing shed, and by the time he eased off his underwear, she was more aroused than she'd ever imagined.

Hands on his hips, Lucas studied her. Tessa let her gaze roam, from amused hazel eyes and cheek-slashing dimples to his broad shoulders and chest, where his dark hair narrowed at his hips, pointing down toward neatly muscled legs and an aggressive erection.

Standing completely dressed before a naked man gave her a heady, shivery sense of power.

"Don't take off that dress," he ordered, still grinning. "I like the idea of making love to a beautiful woman in a black dress. Thinking about it turns me on."

Hot desire washed over her as Lucas drew her into

his arms, silk rasping against the rough hairs of his chest. He kissed her eyelid, her cheek, her nose, and then covered her mouth with his. With a low sigh, Tessa slid her arms around his neck, pressing against him as she kissed this wonderfully naked man in her living room.

Minutes passed, and Lucas did nothing more than kiss her, and the more he kissed her, deep and hot and insistent, the more she moved against him, rubbing her hips in a wordless appeal.

With a low groan, Lucas grabbed her bottom in both hands and ground her against him. "Put your legs around me," he said, his voice low.

When she wrapped her legs around his hips, he carried her a few feet into the kitchen and set her on the counter.

Startled, she stared at him. "Here?"

He slid his hands up her thighs. "I want a clear view."

Blushing at his meaning, Tessa leaned back, hands on the counter as his fingers strayed higher, then halted.

His grin turned feral. "You're not wearing any underwear."

"How about that," she managed to answer. "I wonder how that happened?"

Laughing softly, he eased the tight skirt upward along her thighs, inch by inch, watching her reaction. The rapid rise and fall of his chest, however, belied his cool control.

With her dress up around her hips, Tessa sucked in her breath as Lucas moved her legs apart and lightly circled her sex with his fingers. She made a soft sound of contentment and dropped her head back against a cupboard door.

"Don't." His voice was husky, tight. "I want you to watch me love you, Tess."

She opened her eyes, both embarrassed and aroused by what he was doing to her in her kitchen. She caught her lips in her teeth as he slid a finger inside her.

"You are a beautiful, sexy woman, and I want you so bad I can't stand it," he whispered as his fingers coaxed her toward a climax, slick and relentless, tender and demanding. "Definitely never, ever, one of the guys."

Tessa locked her gaze on him. The pressure built, liquid hot and tight as a fist, until he slipped his fingers from her body and lightly fanned her sensitive flesh with his finger. The orgasm broke over her in waves of pleasure so intense her muscles knotted and her bare toes curled in the air.

A moment later, Lucas moved between her legs, and entered her on a long, slick thrust that bumped her head back against the cupboard door.

"Oh, my God," she whispered as he released his breath in a rush. Desire wound sweetly tight again, his every thrust shooting pleasure through her. She stretched her toes, arched her back, taking him deeper—and all the while watching the hard, wholly male part of him play her body.

His penis looked dark against her pale thighs, and just the sight of him like this, so raw and primitive, quickly brought her to climax again. The shuddering pleasure rocked through her, longer this time, and she trembled from the force of it.

Lucas swore harshly, fingers digging into her hips as he pumped into her with a hard, demanding rhythm until his own orgasm shattered the last of his control and he pulled her fully to him, his hips grinding against her.

For a moment, she knew only a hot, breathless sensation of connection, of completeness. Then tenderness swept away the ashes of her spent desire, and she slid to the floor and pulled him against her. She closed her eyes and lost herself to the perspiration-sheened feel of his skin, the roughness of his chest hair against her cheek, the pounding of his heart beneath her ear, and each rapid puff of his breath against her own heated skin.

She couldn't move, speak. All she wanted was to bury her face in the warmth of his neck and stay there, never letting the moment go.

"That," Lucas said, kissing the side of her mouth, "is quality sex." He tipped his head back to look at her, and she caught her breath at the emotion in the depths of his hazel eyes. "There's never been any woman like you, Tessa."

His intense, fierce words left her shaken. "I bet you say that to all the girls you have sex with on kitchen counters." She looked away, unable to face what she saw in his eyes.

He loved her.

It couldn't be anything else, and what he wanted from her ran much deeper than "quality sex." A chill stole over her, chasing away the languid warmth of his lovemaking.

She wasn't ready yet. Not for the risk. She wasn't proud that all the unknowns of his illness scared her, and the specter of the *McKee* still hung between them, though it had faded these past few days. It was only a sad old shadow now.

"You're going too fast, Lucas."

His mouth tightened. "Going where fast? I don't feel like we're making progress here, just sneaking around. I want more."

More? Did he want it all—wife, kids, a little place of their own? So tempting, the thought. Did she want that, too? With him?

Impulsively, she traced the thin scar on his chest with her finger while his hands roved soothingly along her back, up and down along the curve of her spine.

"All week, I've been feeling like you were avoiding me, Tessa, and—"

"We had company reps on the ship! No way was I coming near you, even if I'd had the time."

"That wasn't what I meant. I didn't expect you to come to me, but you *were* avoiding me." He hesitated, and when she looked away, he added, "Does this have to do with the other night? What I told you? Are you afraid of me? Honey, people with stress disorders aren't dangerous, and—"

"Oh, Lucas," she interrupted. "Don't be absurd. I'll never be afraid of you."

"Then are we back where we started, dealing with the fact that I killed your brother?"

"You did *not* kill Matt! And my forgiving you won't do any good if *you* can't forgive yourself." The silence stretched on, and when he didn't respond, she sighed. "You know, you wouldn't be the easiest man to love."

"No," he admitted, his gaze sharpening. "And you're no pushover yourself."

She eyed him warily, but caught the ghost of a smile on his face. "One of us will have to leave the *Taliesen*. You know that, don't you?"

Lucas stepped away, hands on his hips, unconcerned that he wasn't wearing a stitch. Tessa took a long, slow breath, and forced herself to look only at his face, which wore a calm, reflective expression.

"It's no party to start all over again, but it can be done."

"Maybe I don't want to start all over." Tessa glanced away. "Maybe it's not a choice I can make just yet."

"You have to decide what's more important. But take some advice: Don't put off doing something you need to do. None of us is guaranteed a tomorrow." In the following silence, heavy with meaning, he placed his finger on her chin and forced her to look at him. "A lesson I learned a few years ago."

"Oh, Lucas, let's not argue." She pressed against him. "Can't we just forget this for right now and—"

"Tessa," he interrupted, "sex with you is great, but we can't spend the rest of our life in the sack. Sooner or later, you'll have to make your choice."

Lucas stared at her for a moment longer before he turned, grabbed his clothes, and headed toward her bedroom. As a sudden coldness swept through her, she rubbed her hands over her arms. Then, with a sigh, she went after him.

When Tessa stirred the next morning, she lay quietly for a long while, listening to Lucas's quiet, even breathing. He'd fallen asleep around midnight, and as far as she could tell, he hadn't so much as twitched a muscle all night.

No dreams, no flashbacks . . . only a heavy slumber, and it made her happy to think that, in some way, she was good for him, too.

She eased away and stood, smiling. He was as aggressive asleep as he was awake, sprawled over the bed and taking far more space than he should. He'd also won the blanket tug-of-war, leaving her with only the sheets. Not that it had mattered, because he threw off a tremendous amount of heat.

A sudden sadness tugged at her.

Who was she trying to fool? They'd never be together, like an average couple, without one or both of them losing something vital.

The impossibility of it overwhelmed her. Needing to put a distance between herself and the intimacy of this man sleeping in her bed, Tessa quietly pulled her robe from the closet and slipped it on. After closing the bedroom door behind her, she headed for the kitchen to brew a strong pot of coffee.

There, she eyed the counter where Lucas had made love to her. A delicious frisson of desire shimmered through her at the memory. He made it so easy for her to make him the center of her world. If only she could bury her head in the sand and selfishly enjoy what they had at this moment, and not have to face life outside her apartment door.

Sighing, she pushed aside her gloomy thoughts, set the coffee to brewing, wiped down the counter and grounds she'd spilled, then leaned back and waited. She sniffed at the aromatic scent as the pot began gurgling, the smell alone enough to perk her up.

When the pot was half-filled, Tessa reached into the cupboard for two mugs—just as an imperious pounding sounded on her door.

She whipped around, going cold with panic. Shooting a glance toward her bedroom door—still closed, thank God—she hurried to the door before the pounding woke Lucas. Without even checking to see who it was, she yanked it open to find Dee Stanhope on her threshold.

As always, Dee looked polished and sleek, wearing ivory-linen pants and an ice-pink lace shell. In heels, she stood taller than Tessa by several inches.

Clearing her throat, Tessa tightened the ties of her

old terry robe and pushed her bed-messed hair from her eyes. Since millionaire bosses didn't regularly check up on the hired help, this was no social call.

"Hello," Dee said, looking Tessa over from head to toe. "Did I wake you?"

"It's seven-thirty in the morning and I'm off duty." Tessa kept her body firmly in the doorway, blocking Dee's entrance, as well as any view of Lucas should he come wandering down the hall.

"Sorry," Dee said, but her tone didn't ring sincere. "I needed to ask you a question."

Despite her alarm, Tessa arched her brow. "You could've used the telephone."

A slow smile curved Dee's pink mouth. "I did, actually. I'm looking for Lucas. I called his cabin and left several messages, but for some reason, he hasn't called me back. So I thought I'd drop by and ask if you've seen your captain."

"Not since I left the *Taliesen* in port yesterday," Tessa answered, her tone calm.

"You're sure about that?"

"Is there something wrong, Mrs. Stanhope?"

The woman's gaze shifted beyond Tessa's shoulder. "I need to talk to Lucas."

"You're not going to find him in my apartment at seven-thirty in the morning."

"Then you won't have a problem inviting me inside, will you?"

As if she had a choice. Tessa stepped aside and motioned Dee through the door with exaggerated politeness.

"I was just making coffee." Tessa headed toward the kitchen. She spoke a little louder than usual, hoping that if Lucas was awake, he'd heard her warning loud and clear and had by now crammed his phenomenally hot, naked body under her bed.

Dread settled over her as she remembered that she'd stored all her unpacked boxes under her bed and in her closet—there was no way he could fit in either one.

"What a quaint little place you have," Dee said as she followed behind. "It's not quite what I'd expected of you."

"Really?" Tessa turned. "And what were you expecting?"

"Something a little more . . . mannish, I think."

Tightening her lips, Tessa reached for the coffeepot. She would not let this woman goad her.

"A full pot? You must really like your coffee. And look, here's a second cup on the counter. Expecting someone?"

Her hand jerked as she poured, spilling a little. Without turning to face Dee, she asked, "Do you take cream or sugar?"

"Both, please. Thank you, Tessa. You're a dear."

Tessa handed the steaming cup to Dee, who stood watching her with a hard glint of anger in her eyes and a smile on her pink lips. "Where is he?"

Tessa returned Dee's stare evenly, not about to endure a browbeating. "Mrs. Stanhope, I have to tell you that this early in the morning, my patience is a little short, and I'd appreciate it if you'd tell me exactly why you're here."

"Nice love bites on your neck, by the way."

Tessa could do nothing to halt the heated flush slowly seeping up along her chest to her face. "My private life off the ship is none of your concern."

"I could care less who you're screwing, but it had better not be the man I've been trying to call all night and all morning."

Dee put her cup on the counter, untouched, and before Tessa could stop her, she'd whirled around and stalked down the hall toward the bedroom.

"Hey!" Tessa yelled in shock, slamming down her own cup with such force that the coffee sloshed over her hand. "What the *hell* do you think you're doing!"

She scrambled after Dee, but wasn't quick enough. Dee had the bedroom door open by the time Tessa reached her.

Twenty

*L*ucas landed in the juniper bushes with a low, pained curse. With only his unzipped trousers on, nothing protected his chest, arms, or face from the scratching, poking branches.

He touched a burning sting on his cheek, and his finger came away red with blood.

"Dammit," he muttered, and glanced up at Tessa's balcony, listening to her outraged voice arguing with Dee. He'd barely had time to swing over the balcony, the bundle of his telltale clothes under one arm, before Dee had barged into Tessa's bedroom like Attila the Hun.

This was too much. He was a grown man, for Christ's sake! He'd run down drug smugglers and commanded ships; he didn't skulk in bushes like a disobedient child and—

A sudden, high-pitched yapping erupted next to him. He leaped to a defensive crouch within a split second, instinctively reaching for the sidearm he no longer carried—and found himself facing a patio door and, on the other side of the glass, an animate furball with a red bow tied in its hair.

Lucas bared his teeth at the mutt, hoping to shut it up, but it only yapped louder. At that moment, a pair of fuzzy pink slippers materialized behind the dog. He looked up.

An elderly woman in a print-flowered housedress and rollers in her gray hair stared at him, her face pressed in astonishment against the glass.

His first thought was relief that she didn't have a shotgun. His second was that he'd better zip his pants and put on his shirt before the woman went hysterical.

He rose from the bushes. The old lady's eyes widened, and he was sure that at any minute now, her dog would come apart at the seams. Grimacing, he zipped his trousers, then grabbed his shirt, all the while keeping his eyes on his unwelcome audience.

As he pulled on his shirt, the woman's gaze darted toward his shoulder boards, and her mouth dropped open. A second later, she scuttled away. He could see her on the phone, staring at him, talking a mile a minute.

Lucas glanced back up at the balcony, torn between wanting to put himself between Tessa and Dee, or making a dash for his car, parked behind the next building, to lie low.

It sounded as if Tessa was holding her own, but he wanted to stay close. Just in case; and it wasn't as if he was doing anything illegal. By all rights, he should be sitting up there with the woman he'd made love to last night. Slinking was bad enough; like hell was he going to turn tail and run.

*   *   *

Heart pounding, blood roaring in her ears, Tessa slammed her fist against her bedroom wall. This was it—good-bye job, good-bye everything.

"You have no right to do this," she snapped.

"What are you going to do about it? Call the cops?" Dee asked, her tone mocking as she walked into the bedroom.

Tessa followed, holding her breath—and nearly sat down on the floor, with relief, at the sight of her empty bed.

Thank you, Lucas!

"What a charming room. You have quite a romantic streak in you, Tessa. I'm shocked."

With this temporary reprieve, anger outpaced her anxiety. "I think you owe me an apology, Mrs. Stanhope."

"You do? What a marvelous notion."

Dee walked around the bed, trailing a painted nail over the bedspread that Lucas had hastily thrown over the rumpled sheets. Tessa saw no sign of his clothing, but with a sinking feeling saw that he hadn't covered the pillows. Each pillow was marked with an unmistakable indention. Dee didn't miss it; Tessa could tell by the arched look on the woman's face.

"Again, where is he?"

"There's nobody in the apartment but me."

It was true enough. Her bedroom window, which led to a narrow balcony, gaped open, curtains fluttering. And a dog was yapping below. It could only be Mrs. Dalton's high-strung Shih Tzu, barking at Lucas.

Dee drifted toward the window, and as she pushed the curtain aside, Tessa held her breath again, heart hammering. The yapping had risen to a nearly hysterical pitch.

Dee peered outside. "That dog doesn't sound happy."

"It never does," Tessa said tightly. "Now, if you've seen everything . . . ?"

"Yes, yes, I'm on my way, even though I think you're lying through your teeth. And just so we're clear on this, I'm watching you, and if I find that you're having an affair with the captain of my ship, I'll see to it you'll never work for a reputable shipping company ever again."

"You're welcome to try, but don't expect me to roll over and play dead." Fear pulsed, icy cold, at the threat, but Tessa planted her hands on her hips and forced herself to appear calm. God, she wanted to grab this pink-tinted creature and slap her silly. "Have you always been such a manipulative bitch?"

"Well. That was direct." Dee's pale brows arched. "Oh, don't give me that holier-than-thou look. I know what you're thinking. You look at me and jump to the same clichéd conclusions everybody else does. You see exactly what I want you to see, because by the time you narrow-minded fools figure out how wrong you are, it's too late."

Dee sat on the bed and crossed her legs, and Tessa, surprised by the woman's brass, only stared as Lucas's warning echoed in her memory: *Don't underestimate her*.

"You don't think I loved my husband, and that I married him for his money and used him."

"Mrs. Stanhope, I don't see where this has anything to—"

"It so happens I loved him very much. So much so that even though he couldn't give me children, I didn't care. When you're twenty-two, being childless seems a minor thing when your husband can give you the world." Dee tipped her head to one side, wearing her maddening smile. "This changed as the years passed, but I loved Rolly too much to leave him. He felt guilty that we couldn't have children, so when I asked for the *Taliesen*, he gave her to me. That ship's the only baby I'm likely to ever have, unless a decent male specimen comes along very soon."

The *Taliesen* was Dee's way of making up for being *childless*? God, give her a direct male any day, even one of Amos Lowery's variety. When it came to Dee Stanhope, she just didn't understand.

She cleared her throat. "Captain Hall doesn't strike me as the type to dole out stud service."

"I'm sure he can be persuaded to consider it, if there are no extraneous distractions." Dee pushed herself to her feet. "I've misjudged you, Tessa. We're more alike than I thought."

A more disgusting suggestion, Tessa couldn't imagine. "I don't think so."

Instead of being angry—as any other normal woman would've been—Dee laughed. As if she were actually enjoying herself. "Open your eyes. You only see what you want to see."

"What I want to see, Mrs. Stanhope, is you walking out my door right now. I'll show you out."

"Don't strain your hospitality. I can find my own way. Tell Lucas I expect him in my office within the hour."

Dee walked to the living room, and Tessa followed, faltering when she saw a tall man in a suit lounging against the doorframe.

"What the hell is this," Tessa demanded, pulling her robe closed tighter. "Open house?"

The man eyed her with interest. "Detective John

Burton, ma'am. Sorry. Mrs. Stanhope slipped her leash."

"Leash?" Dee stepped close to the cop. Her eyes glinted as she wound his tie around her fist and pulled him down. "I wonder who's on a leash here. Shall we see if I can make you bark like the dog you are?"

The cop grinned. "Woof."

Dee stepped back, releasing his tie. For a moment, Tessa swore a flustered look crossed her face.

"Mrs. Stanhope," Burton said, still grinning. "One of my men is waiting for you downstairs. Be a good girl and go with him."

Without a single word, Dee slammed the door behind her, and Tessa winced as the picture frames rattled on her walls.

"You know, not that it's any of my business," Burton said, scratching his nose, "but I suggest that either you or the captain find another job, and pretty damn quick."

Tessa shot him a look of irritation. "Detective, is there something you wanted?"

"Yeah. Hall."

"What do I look like, his baby-sitter?"

Burton rubbed his jaw as he surveyed her robe and bare feet. "Not exactly. Ms. Jardine, is he here?"

"He'd better be." Tessa marched back to her bedroom. Behind her, she heard the dead bolt click into place. Obviously, Burton didn't trust Dee not to make an encore performance.

Leaning out her window, she called, "Lucas, where are you?"

"Down here."

Burton joined her at the window, not even bothering to hide his grin. "Hey, Captain. It's Detective Burton."

"Oh, Christ," came the muttered response.

Burton's grin widened. "Do you need an ambulance?"

"No, I don't," Lucas retorted over the sound of snapping branches and snarling yaps.

"You're not, uh, doing anything illegal down there, are you? Indecent exposure?"

"What do you want, Burton?"

"I need to talk to you about these messages."

"Now?" Tessa demanded, as Lucas swore again.

"It's important," Burton said. "Sorry."

"Tell him to wait inside. I'm coming up," Lucas ordered. "And Burton, there's an old lady staring at me through her patio door. I'm betting she's called the police. I'd appreciate it if you'd take care of that."

Burton, with a sound that sounded suspiciously like a snort of laughter, left the window. Tessa stepped out onto the balcony, and as she leaned over the rail a pair of socks sailed upward and hit her in the face.

Briefs, shoes, and a duffel followed—all of which she caught—and those items were followed a moment later by Lucas himself.

Unable to hold back her grin, Tessa watched Lucas jump and catch the bottom rails of her balcony. The dog went berserk as Lucas's bare feet dangled inches from the first floor's patio door. Tessa imagined old Mrs. Dalton pressing her face to the glass, soaking up the most excitement she'd had in years.

Not that Tessa wouldn't get a little excited if she saw a man who looked like Lucas doing a Tarzan impersonation off an upper-story balcony.

Her lips twitched. "Romeo, Romeo, thou art one smart dude."

With a grunt of effort, Lucas swung his body until he'd gained enough momentum to push himself upward, muscles bulking like the day at the pier, and vaulted over the rail as if there wasn't eight feet of air below him.

Dazzled by the raw power he'd so casually exhibited, she gave a low whistle. "That was kinda sexy. Can I push you back over and watch you climb up here again?"

He gave her a dark look as he stood before her, tensed, half-dressed, face scratched and oozing blood.

"Well," she said after a brief silence, "you sure know how to show a girl a good time."

Letting out his breath, he said, "Tessa, I'm sorry you had to go through that."

"I was terrified she'd find you."

He brushed his knuckles over her cheek. "You okay?"

"I don't know if I can keep this up," Tessa said, the admission tumbling out before she could stop herself. "The stress, and everything else, is a little more than I bargained for."

Lucas studied her face, then said quietly, "Let me see what Burton wants. After that, we can talk."

She nodded, already aware of an odd, hollow feeling that came of knowing talk would do little good. Voicing the doubt she'd held close for so long only made it more concrete: This relationship wasn't working for her. And he knew it, too.

In silence they returned to the living room, and found Burton sitting on the couch inspecting his fingernails. The detective looked up as they entered and took in Lucas's rumpled uniform and scratches. "You want to go somewhere else for this?"

Lucas glanced at Tessa as he took the chair opposite Burton. "We can talk here. She knows about the notes."

Tessa sank down at the opposite end of the couch as Burton gave a short nod.

"Okay, I'll get to the point. Whoever's leaving the notes either works for Stanhope Shipping or is familiar with the company. Mrs. Stanhope's schedule isn't secret, but our riddle-happy friend knows when she's in Milwaukee. Mrs. Stanhope plans on staying here for the next few weeks, so I expect we'll get more of these little gems." He shifted on the couch, leaning toward Lucas, gaze intent. "And let's not forget the *McKee*."

Lucas's mouth thinned. "I'm not likely to forget it anytime soon."

"Could be somebody else feels that way," Burton said. "I've asked an FBI profiler to look at the evidence, but I've got a few thoughts about what might be going on here."

Confused, Tessa caught Lucas's wary gaze . . . and thought he looked guilty, too. How had a threat to Dee Stanhope suddenly ended up involving the *McKee*?

"I bet there's hard feelings toward Stanhope Shipping, especially after this recent court verdict. Maybe somebody wants to do something about those hard feelings. Maybe somebody feels they didn't get justice." Burton rubbed at his chin, his attention never wavering from Lucas. "You remember the first note Mrs. Stanhope showed you?"

"The knock-knock joke about ice," Lucas said—then swore softly. "Not *just ice* . . . but *justice*! God, I can't believe I missed that."

"Hey, I didn't catch it right off, either. Now, the *McKee* accident is being blamed on crew error. I'm thinking this pissed off somebody. I feel the suspect believes events have left him no other alternative but to strike back. The clues are taunts, but I also think he wants us to figure them out. He wants to be stopped."

Tessa glanced at Lucas, wondering if he was remembering the TV news showing a furious, red-faced Joseph Yarwood being dragged from the courtroom.

"The second note directly refers to the *McKee*, I'm sure of it," Burton continued. "The phrase *blows away* could mean an explosion, and *down will go baby* is suggestive of a sinking ship. What do you think?"

Lucas frowned and leaned forward. "Could be. The *bough-wow* bothered me, but if this refers to a ship, the guy's trying to tell us that B-O-U-G-H should be read as B-O-W."

Burton's brows shot upward. "I didn't think of that. Good catch. You're a sharp guy."

"I've had run-ins with criminal minds," Lucas said wryly.

"I know," Burton said quietly. "Why do you think I'm telling you this?"

"Because you don't have enough evidence to make an arrest, but you want to be sure—"

"—that you're watching your back," Burton finished.

Tessa had heard enough. "Hold on. You've lost me here, and you're scaring the hell out of me. I thought Dee Stanhope was being threatened. Where does *Lucas* fit into this? I think I deserve some answers. You know my brother died on the *McKee*."

Burton nodded, and Tessa wondered if this was another reason why he was sitting in her living room—a reason having little to do with Dee slipping her "leash."

"Then you know my family settled with the company out of court and we split the money among Matt's nieces and nephews. I don't like Dee Stanhope, but I don't blame her for my brother's death. Nor does anyone in my family."

"Others might not feel that way." Burton continued to watch her with a sharp, assessing gaze. "Besides yourself, do you know if any of the victims' family members still work for Stanhope Shipping? Or if any of them live in the area?"

"I'm not sure on the first question." Tessa frowned. "On the second, I'd guess there are quite a few family members in the area. Ask the legal department. They can tell you."

Burton gave another brief nod. Tessa had a feeling he'd already done so, and was now only following protocol. "As Matt Jardine's sister, has anyone approached you to express anger at his death? Or anger that you still work for Stanhope?"

"No! Now would you please answer my questions about Lucas?"

"Dee's third note may be a reference to me," Lucas said.

"Why didn't you tell me?" Tessa demanded. "You're a potential target, and you don't think this is important enough to mention?"

"I didn't because it was only a guess at the time."

"It's more than that," Burton cut in, looking between the two of them. "I've spent hours staring at these notes. I kept thinking the third one read more like a list, and realized yesterday the first letter of each word in the list part spells L-T-C-D-R. That ring a bell, Hall?"

"Lieutenant commander," Lucas said, mouth grim. "My rank when I left the service."

"Exactly. This guy's asking *you* a question: Are you ready?"

Tessa went cold at the familiar phrase. "Lucas, what's going on here?"

He looked at her, his expression grim. "Justice. If Burton's right, somebody blames Dee and me for what happened on the *McKee* and means to make us pay for it."

"And we know who that somebody is." Outrage replacing her fear, she turned to Burton. "Joseph Yarwood. He made threats on public TV just days ago. Arrest him."

"A bereaved father's angry outbursts aren't evidence enough," Burton said.

"What more do you need?" Tessa demanded. "Dead bodies? By then, it'll be too late!"

"There are laws I have to follow, Ms. Jardine, and those laws say I don't have enough evidence to request an arrest warrant." Burton glanced at Lucas. "But nobody says I can't watch the man. What kind of security measures do you have on your ship?"

"Nothing too impressive, but federal antiterrorist regulations forbid anyone but the crew and ticketed passengers aboard the *Taliesen* when she's under way or in port."

"That's a plus. Do passengers go through any security when they board the ship?"

Lucas shook his head. "No. It's not like an airport."

A tense silence fell over the room.

"So what you're getting at is that nothing can stop someone with a gun from buying a ticket and going on a shooting spree on our ship," Tessa said at length.

Burton nodded. "I believe it's a legitimate concern."

"I'll alert the ticket office," Lucas said. "I don't suppose you have a picture of Yarwood I can pass around to my officers?"

"He's not a suspect; I can't do that. But his outburst in court the other day landed him on the front page of the papers."

A look of understanding passed between Lucas and Burton, and Tessa's anxiety increased. "God. I can't believe this."

"Look, I could be wrong, but if you encounter any suspicious behavior on the ship, in port, or anywhere else, get in touch with me. I don't care what time it is. You call."

Lucas nodded, then said, "You mentioned another note?"

"Yeah. Here's an extra copy for you. I want to know what you think." Burton handed Lucas a piece of paper, then glanced at Tessa. "You can read it, too."

Damn right she would. Tessa immediately moved to stand behind Lucas and read over his shoulder:

Remember the Alamo, remember the Maine.
Ah, Bobby, we hardly knew ye.
Hickory, dickory dock, rock around the clock.
The cat looked at the clock.
The clock struck two, and away she blew.

Goose bumps prickled along the flesh of her arms and legs. "What does it mean?"

"Not sure," Burton answered. "It's code, like all the others. But you can bet it's not something nice."

She stared at the note, trying to relate the menacing hints to the *McKee.*

"The *Maine* was a battleship blown up in the Spanish-American war," Burton said. "Again, another reference to the *McKee.* The guy's obsessed about it— keeps returning to it, like a broken record. What a fort in Texas and dead Kennedys have to do with it, I don't know. When did the *McKee* sink?"

"A little after eight in the evening," Lucas said. "Nowhere near two. But Bobby's a derivative of Robert, and you're right; it's still the *McKee.*"

"The Alamo fell under siege," Tessa added. "Detective, could this person be threatening a hostage situation?"

"I wouldn't dismiss the possibility, though that

might be a bit much for one person to pull off, and I don't have reason to believe this involves more than one person." Burton pinched the bridge of his nose. He looked less the part of the dispassionate cop than a man who'd gone too long without sleep. "I'll see what we can do about security at the port. I've got Yarwood under surveillance. I've talked with him, but so far he checks out. He's angry and bitter, but there's no law against that. And it might not be Yarwood. It could be somebody else. It could also be somebody's idea of a sick joke."

"Maybe we should ground the *Taliesen*," Lucas said.

"Already suggested it. Mrs. Stanhope said no. Says she can't afford to take a loss like that, and she thinks the threat is against only you and her. She's likely right."

Tessa glanced at Lucas, her unease deepening at the frustration and indecision in his eyes. "She could also be wrong."

"I want to see what the FBI says, but I'm fairly certain this guy is fixated on the two people he feels responsible for his son's death. He's not interested in hurting anybody else. I don't think you need to worry about your ship, Hall, but I do think you need to worry that you're a walking target. I don't suppose I can persuade you to take a long vacation."

A chill of sheer, black terror washed over her, and she knew Lucas's response even before he said, "No."

Burton grunted, not looking surprised. "I'm suggesting to Mrs. Stanhope that she stay within the secure confines of her estate. Hopefully she'll listen to me. If you don't mind, since she seems to think a lot of you, I'd appreciate it if you could talk some sense into her."

"Why not suggest she leave town?" Tessa asked pointedly.

"I did. The woman says she's on vacation and she's not letting some wacko scare her away." Burton stood. "I admire her courage, but personally, I think she's crazy, and she's giving me heartburn. Call if you need me."

With Burton's departure, Tessa shut the door and twisted the dead bolt into place. Silence fell heavily over the room, and she slowly turned. "Well—this has been an interesting morning."

Lucas eased onto the couch, dropping his head back on the cushions, looking exhausted. "The good news is that from here on out, the day can only get better."

She folded her arms across her chest. "You should've told me."

Lucas straightened, his expression impatient. "If I'd known then what I know now, I would've. At the time, I figured the police had it under control."

Again, silence fell between them—and this time, brought with it an undeniable distance.

"Lucas, about what I said, that I don't think I can keep this up—"

"I have to go see Dee," he interrupted. Pushing up from the sofa, he brushed past her and headed toward the bedroom.

"Lucas, wait! We . . . we have a problem here, and I—"

He whirled, eyes snapping with anger, mouth tight. "No."

"No? No what?"

"I am not giving up on us!"

At the shock of Lucas shouting at her—he'd never so much as raised his voice to her before—Tessa flinched, then looked away as a sudden despair engulfed her. "I wish I were stronger for you. I wish I could be what you need me to be, but I can't. It's too much. It's just too much."

To her shock and dismay, she started crying. At once, she covered her eyes with a hand, trying to hide her tears. She sensed Lucas move closer, and at the touch of his fingers on her hair, she went stiff and turned away.

"Don't touch me. Oh, please, don't."

He dropped his hand to his side, and at that her tears turned to noisy sobs. Once she'd let go, she couldn't stop the torrent. The tears kept coming and coming.

Without a word, Lucas turned and walked away. Moments later, she heard the door slam behind him.

Miserable, hating herself for being so weak and scared to death of this strange new threat to Lucas, Tessa sat on the floor and buried her face in her shaking hands. "I'm sorry," she whispered. "I'm so sorry . . ."

Twenty-one

When Lucas returned to his cabin, he saw Tessa's car parked out front. He sat behind the wheel for what seemed like ages, already on edge from the morning's events and his recent argument with Dee, then finally opened the door and stepped out.

No use putting off the inevitable.

When he didn't find Tessa in the cabin, he walked down to the pier. She was sitting on a lawn chair, reading a book, and wore a pair of shorts over a plain one-piece black swimsuit that looked anything but plain on her curves. As the pier creaked beneath his feet, she looked up. Sunglasses hid her eyes, and she didn't smile.

After a moment, she put the book down on the pier. "How'd it go with Dee?"

"We had words," he answered evenly. "And she won't be dropping by your place anymore."

"Did you talk to her about the ship and Yarwood?"

It appeared she intended to deal with the little stuff first. He almost smiled at the thought, as if a threat against his life was "little stuff."

"I told her to ground the *Taliesen* until the police cleared things up," he said. "But she went on about crewmen with families to support and bills to pay, cargo to be delivered, contracts to be honored. Maybe she's right."

"What are you going to do?"

This he could answer. It had taken him a minute or two to come up with a workable plan to deal with Yarwood's possible threat. Coming up with a plan to soothe Tessa's fears, on the other hand, was proving to be damn near impossible.

"I made copies of Yarwood's picture, and I'll hand them out to the officers when I meet with them. We'll keep a tight watch. Burton's talking with port security in Milwaukee, and I'll call ahead to our other ports to do the same. I don't want this going beyond the officers yet. We don't need a panic on board ship."

Tessa nodded. "Sounds like you've got everything under control."

Not quite everything.

"Yeah . . . taking control is what I do best, isn't it?" She looked down at her book, and after a moment, he added, "If it's Yarwood, Burton has the noose in place, and at the first suspicious move, he'll pull it tight."

"Are you sure you won't take some time off? We could get a relief captain, and—"

"No," he interrupted. "I'm not letting fear rule any part of my life. I've been down that road and won't go back."

As her gaze met his, understanding—and guilt— flashed briefly. "Fine, but do me a favor and don't go prowling off the ship, okay? Especially in uniform.

That's just painting a big bull's-eye on your back."

"I told Burton I'd stay aboard the *Taliesen* until this all shakes out."

She regarded him a while longer before pushing up from the chair. "Lucas, I've been thinking about what happened this morning, and how Dee could've found out about us so quickly. I bet someone on the ship is watching us."

"Coded messages and now spies." Lucas made a sound of disgust. "It sounds like something Dee would pull. Who do you think it is?"

"Amos Lowery. The man hates my guts. He doesn't like you, either. He actually told me he was watching me . . . he said: 'I'm watching you, weasely woman.' Or something like that."

" 'Weasely woman'?" Lucas repeated, anger rising on Tessa's behalf. Damn, he wanted to punch Lowery out.

She folded her arms across her chest, doing incredible things to her cleavage beneath the taut lycra. "Nice, huh?"

Very nice. Lucas forced his gaze away from her breasts. In trouble up to his eyebrows, and he couldn't keep his mind off sex. "I'll talk with him once we're under way. Although I can't see him kissing up to Dee."

"He'd do anything to stay on the *Taliesen*. He loves that engine more than anything else." Tessa retrieved her book and started for the cabin. After a moment, Lucas followed.

"Are you spending the night?" he asked, even though he already knew the answer.

She glanced back over her shoulder, and shook her head.

He let out a long breath. "I guess you decided you

want a man who's less trouble than I am, after all, and one who didn't kill your brother."

Tessa turned, looking furious. "Is that what you think?"

Shoving his hands in his pockets, Lucas said, "Is there another reason?"

"Lucas, I meant what I said that night, and I can't blame you for Matt's death. But it's not something I can just ignore, any more than I can ignore the seriousness of your . . . your—"

"Condition?" he said quietly. "That's what Dee calls it."

"It's not something to make light of, is it?"

"No," he agreed.

"And then I find out your life is in danger, and Dee is threatening to not only fire me but ruin any other chance I might have of finding work with a reputable company—and I can't quite seem to figure out how to deal with all of this."

"What exactly is it you're afraid of, Tessa?" he asked at length.

"Afraid? I'm not afraid, Lucas, I'm simply overwhelmed! I don't think I can deal with all this without it affecting my job performance, and over four hundred people on that ship depend on us to keep our heads straight. Especially now." An uneasy look crossed her face as she stopped in front of the porch. "Lucas, you're in danger. How do you feel? Are you okay?"

Lucas glanced away, the heat of anger and shame seeping through him. It was a good question; and as first mate, she needed to ask it. After all, the first mate needed to know if her captain was going to fall to pieces in a moment of stress.

"Don't you trust me not to freeze up in a crisis situation?"

"I trust you," she said. "The question is, do you trust yourself?"

"I can handle it."

He wanted to believe that if some nutcase with a gun started shooting away on his ship, he'd do whatever was necessary to protect his passengers and crew—but he couldn't be sure, and it scared the hell out of him.

Tessa sighed. "I believe in you, Lucas. Breaking things off between us doesn't mean I wouldn't trust you with my life."

She stood before him, beautiful and proud, and he loved her for her belief in him, for her confidence and honesty, even if what she was telling him wasn't what he wanted to hear. His anger faded.

Well, what could he expect? Blaming her for panicking, for feeling overwhelmed by everything he'd dragged her into, wasn't an option. He'd spent years dealing with crisis situations as a matter of daily business—she was just a sailor, and rarely had to worry about anything beyond bad weather.

Lucas moved closer. She smelled like sunshine and wind, and the heat of her skin radiated toward him like a touch.

"Give us a chance. You're no quitter, and what we have between us is worth fighting for. It's easy to walk away when the going gets rough. Don't make the same mistake I did ten years ago." He paused, then said quietly, "I love you, Tessa."

Her eyes widened, and she stared at him as the wind ruffled her dark hair. Then she turned, and slowly headed up the steps to the porch. "Oh, Lucas."

Her tone sounded sad, rather than surprised or happy or anything else he'd expected. He sat beside her on the porch steps and took a deep breath, smelling the sharp tang of pine needles and lake. The silence stretched on, but she still didn't say the words he wanted to hear.

After several moments passed, he said, "I've been thinking of leaving the *Taliesen* after the season's over. I can always find a job on another ship, if that's what I want."

Tessa turned to him with an expression of incredulity. "You can't be serious. I know how important it is for you to be able to command the *Taliesen*. I can't . . . you don't have to give her up for me. That wouldn't be right."

"Who says I'd be giving it up for you?" He leaned forward, leaning his elbows on his knees as he gazed out toward the sparkling water of the lake. "You know . . . the Coast Guard taught me a lot. It gave me a purpose, daily routines, a code of conduct as an officer, and a way to measure my success that everybody could see. After the *McKee*, I lost all that."

Tessa watched him with a small frown.

"You're right that I wanted the *Taliesen* to prove to myself I wasn't a failure," he admitted quietly. "And she gave me the purpose I thought I needed. Lately, I've been thinking I had the right idea, but I went about it all wrong."

"I don't get what you're saying."

"I'm not real sure myself." He shifted, so he could face her. "Tessa, I've lived my whole life trying to measure up to somebody else's idea of success—first my father's, then the service. I don't need that anymore. The *Taliesen* is a grand old ship. When she's under way, I'm proud as hell to command her. But the job of captain . . . I can live without it."

Tessa let out a long sigh. "Even if one of us were to transfer to another ship, what kind of life would we have together, with both of us at sea for months on end and rarely seeing each other? It'd never work, Lucas. We may as well admit that now, before we get in any deeper."

He stared down at his dress shoes, hiding a small smile. Ah, here was real success: Tessa wavering, weakening.

"What if I were to leave shipping altogether?" he asked. "Would that make a difference to you?"

For a long moment, she regarded him with a mixture of wariness and hope, then looked away, shaking her head.

"It's a nice thought, Lucas," she said softly. "But what it really comes down to is that ten years ago we went our separate ways because life got in the way. I'm not so sure it won't happen again. And I saw what it was like for my parents, all the bitterness and anger and blame they heaped on each other. I guess . . . that's what I'm afraid of."

And afraid of taking the risk—he could hear that fear in everything she didn't say. God, he could understand that.

"I can't promise perfect. I can't promise a traditional relationship, but I'll give you everything I've got. That much I can, and do, promise you."

She flung him a look brimming with sudden panic. "Lucas, I came here to finish our conversation from this morning, not to negotiate. I've made my decision, and that's it!"

She started to rise, but Lucas shot out his hand to halt her. Instinct warned him he'd pushed far enough. Any more, and she'd bolt for good.

"Okay . . . okay. Calm down," he said in his most soothing voice, and she slowly sank back down onto the step.

Another long, uncomfortable silence followed, until

Tessa murmured, "I'd like **us to be** friends."

Lucas glanced at her. "I **thought** we were friends all along."

She didn't look at him. "**You know** what I mean."

Frowning, Lucas stared down at his hands, held clenched between his knees. "I never took what you gave me for granted. If something should happen to me—"

"Lucas, please!" Tessa swung toward him, her expression frightened. "Don't say things like that. You promise me you'll be careful and not get yourself shot. I mean it, Lucas, I want your promise!"

"I managed not to get shot in all the years I worked drug interdiction. I sure as hell don't intend to get shot now." Then, as if she hadn't interrupted, he added, "But there are some things I can't control, and if something should happen to me, I want you to know that I love you."

She returned his steady gaze for a moment, then turned away—but not before he saw the glimmer of tears in her eyes.

And, again, no *I love you* in return.

His stomach clenched hard, and doubt washed over him. For the first time, he faced the truth that she didn't feel the same way toward him as he did toward her. For the first time, he realized that he might fail to win her back.

"I always seem to make you cry," he murmured.

Tessa sniffed. "It's okay. You're still the only man I can cry in front of and not feel like a total fool."

"Well," he said, feeling a need to make some sort of response, "that's something."

Silence fell between them, and somewhere out on the lake a jet skier sped past, motor whining like a giant mosquito.

"So," Tessa said at length, with a forced cheerfulness. "If you were to leave shipping, what would you do?"

Lucas didn't answer right away. Finally, he said, "If I tell you, don't laugh."

"I would never laugh at you. You know better than that."

Lucas leaned back, elbows on the step behind him, and stared back out across the lake again. "See, I have this dream. It's not much, really, but I want to buy a boat and hire myself out for fishing charters. Like I told you that night at Mackinac Island. I want to have my own company. Be my own man."

Without looking to see her reaction, he added, "I want to let my hair grow and not have to shave every day. I'm tired of wearing a uniform that sets me apart from everybody else. I want to walk into a room and not have conversations stop cold."

She lightly touched his arm in a gesture of comfort.

"And I don't want to be responsible for hundreds of people. I know it's not ambitious, but I don't want procedure anymore." He looked down. "My old man's been dead for over two years. It's time I stopped living my life to please him."

He looked up, and she tipped her head to one side, her gaze searching his. The wind blew a strand of hair across her mouth, and it was all he could do not to reach out and brush it away, to touch her.

"And this would make you happy?" Tessa asked slowly.

"Yes," he said without hesitation.

"Then that's all that matters, isn't it?" she asked with a sudden, quiet intensity, almost as if she were trying to convince herself of something as well.

He shifted on the hard wood of the porch. "Are you

still planning on working relief after the *Taliesen* goes into winter layup?"

Tessa nodded. "With vacations and sick leaves, there's steady work for an officer. Not that I like shuttling from one freighter to another, but I haven't any other options. Not unless I go back to working on the lakers full-time."

Which would take her out of his life for weeks on end, March through December. If he worked on a freighter—which he sure as hell had no desire to do— they'd rarely be on the same schedule. She was right; the odds weren't in their favor if they both stayed in shipping. It made him even more determined to get off the *Taliesen*, and the sooner the better.

But first things first. He still had to win back Tessa.

This time he wasn't walking away from the challenge.

So he'd go slow, careful not to rush her. He'd shower her with flowers and attention, show her he loved her and needed her in his life. After he left the *Taliesen*, he'd have all the time he needed to prove they could make a life together.

"Will you at least stay for dinner?" he asked abruptly. "Just dinner. Nothing else, I swear it."

He waited tensely, one long second after another, as Tessa hesitated, plainly torn. "As friends?"

If it was all he could have now, then so be it. "Friends."

Tessa smiled. "Then I'd love to stay for dinner."

Twenty-two

*L*ucas arrived at the port before dawn on Friday, nodding at the dockworkers and yawning crewmen stirring along the quiet corridors and decks of the *Taliesen*. The old girl was still asleep, engine humming quietly.

He took his time with the inspection, lingering in the dark, cavernlike hold and the hot, cramped spaces of the engine-room. He even walked along the catwalks, nodding once at Amos Lowery, who watched him suspiciously.

He'd have to deal with Lowery, but later.

Walking the length of both berth decks, Lucas ran his fingers along the bulkhead, as he always did, feeling the comforting thrum of his ship's pulse. This early, in the shadows, the ivory, aqua, and chrome looked softly welcoming, instead of so relentlessly open and airy.

On the main deck, he smelled the mouth-watering

scents of breakfast from the galley, heard the clink and clang of metal, the low buzz of voices. The tall, blond bartender named Scott was romancing one of the gift-shop clerks, and he looked tired as he buttoned his vest.

From the main deck, Lucas climbed the ladder to the narrow deck outside the pilothouse and looked out across the port. Tessa hadn't arrived yet, and the pilothouse was empty except for the night watchman and Dave Compton, chatting over coffee and donuts. When she did arrive, things between them were bound to be awkward.

The breeze was sharp and light, a whispery touch against his skin, and Lucas turned his face to the sky. He listened to the slosh of water against the hull and shore, the ever-present racket of the gulls.

It promised to be a beautiful day, and not even his restlessness, or the gray emptiness that had dogged him since Tessa had broken off their relationship, could diminish the sight of Lake Michigan at sunrise.

He didn't want to think danger could be hiding somewhere out there on such a beautiful day, and it seemed profane to bring it within this graceful old ship. But bring it he would, when he met with his officers.

When the morning sun still rode low in the hazy sky, Lucas guided the *Taliesen* out of Milwaukee and sent the old girl steaming along familiar territory toward Chicago.

Tessa avoided him, of course, and although he still caught her eye often, he kept his distance. But because he wanted to be near her, he stayed in the pilothouse when he would've otherwise left. As he roamed the room, trying to keep out of everybody's way and look like he had a reason to remain, Lucas spied the red wooden yo-yo on the chart desk and picked it up.

A day rarely passed that he didn't see the toy attached to a finger of one of his mates. Compton, Shea, and Tessa constantly tried to outdo each other with tricks.

To keep his hands—and mind—busy, Lucas slipped the string on his finger and dropped the yo-yo. With a low hum, it sprang back into his hand. He raised a brow. "Ingenious thing."

Glancing up, he caught Tessa, the watchman, and the lookout staring at him. For the first time that morning, Tessa smiled.

"This should be interesting," she murmured.

It was a challenge Lucas couldn't pass by. Of course, she knew it. Remembering what he'd observed, he spun the yo-yo down, suspended it, and then rocked it slowly back and forth.

He gave her a smug look. "I believe this is rock-the-baby."

"If only the deck gang could see what you guys are doing up here in the brain box," said the lookout, shaking his head. "They'd be wondering just who's the yo-yo."

Lucas grinned at the good-natured dig, but didn't stop playing. The thing was addictive. "What's the latest weather report?"

"Clear skies, lots of sunshine. Breezy, but nothing out of the ordinary. Perfect cruise weather," Tessa said.

"Just what the captain wants to hear. I'm heading to the officers' mess for the morning meeting." He read the sudden worry shadowing her face, along with a flash of regret and longing in her eyes. Knowing she missed him lightened his mood. "I'll fill you in afterward."

She only nodded. On impulse, he tossed her the yo-yo, and she neatly caught it. "There's something to keep you busy." Again, their eyes met. He smiled. "Easy on the old girl."

"Never fear. The lady and I understand each other. She won't pull any funny stuff. She knows who's the boss."

The men laughed, but Lucas wasn't fooled by her light words. He'd seen the concern and fear in her eyes.

That fear shadowed him as he headed to the officers' mess. The room was packed, and an immediate silence fell over the room as he walked in. Some days, he wasn't bothered by the change in atmosphere, the halted conversations. Today wasn't one of them.

He nodded a greeting, caught Jerry's smile, and noted that Lowery hadn't bothered to show up yet. No surprise there.

The stewards had set up a breakfast buffet, and Lucas made his choices, then sat down at the head of the table as conversation returned to normal. He'd barely tucked into his breakfast when the chief ambled in.

Lowery sat down without a word of acknowledgment at the opposite end of the table from Lucas, who didn't miss the silent statement of Lowery's position.

"Everything in order in the engine department?" Lucas asked.

"Yes, sir."

Lucas hesitated, a fork of steaming omelet halfway to his mouth. The chief never called him sir. What the hell?

"Is there a problem, Mr. Lowery?"

The smirk elongated. "No, sir. Not at all."

With that, the older man began whistling. It took a few seconds before Lucas recognized it, "Pop Goes the Weasel."

Lucas narrowed his eyes as understanding dawned. "It's time to get this meeting in order," he said sharply.

Within five minutes, he'd updated his officers on the possible threat and need for security. By the time he'd finished speaking, everybody sat in stunned silence—even Lowery.

"My God," Jerry said at length.

"You all have the photo. Every forty- to fifty-year-old white male who leaves or boards the ship is suspect. I don't want this guy slipping past us. Jerry, your people deal most with the passengers, and I need you to keep sharp. You or one of the other pursers accompany the housekeepers. You can't search rooms, but you can keep an eye out for trouble. Report any suspicious behavior directly to me, but I don't want the passengers alarmed. That's it for now. I'll update you as the need arises."

Slowly, their faces grim, his officers filed out of the room. Only Lowery remained behind.

"Do you have something to say to me, Chief?"

Lowery pushed his plate away, sat back in his chair, and started whistling "Pop Goes the Weasel" again. Then, in a rusty, off-tune baritone, he sang: " 'All around the mulberry bush, the monkey chased the weasel . . . the monkey thought it was all in fun. Pop goes the weasel!' " Lowery wheezed out a laugh. "Poor little weasel, eh?"

Lucas stood. Back straight, face expressionless, he walked toward the grinning chief engineer. Lowery didn't bother to stand, so Lucas grabbed the front of Lowery's coveralls and hauled him to his feet.

"Is that a threat, Mr. Lowery?" he asked softly.

Malice sparked in the man's eyes. "Maybe."

"Dee Stanhope asked you to spy on me and Tessa Jardine."

Surprise flared, then quickly iced over again with malice. "Reckon you're smarter than you look."

With great effort, Lucas resisted a powerful, intense urge to slam the man back against the wall. "Dee won't need your reports anymore," he said. "Is that clear?"

Lowery shook free of Lucas's grip, and as he left the room, he said, "Clear as a bell. Hope nailin' her tail is worth the trouble it's gonna cost you—big, *big* trouble."

Lucas stood for a moment in the empty room, reining in his rage, then spun and headed toward his cabin.

He'd warned Dee that he'd quit if she didn't stop playing her stupid games, but she was so certain of her power over him that she refused to take him seriously.

Time to call her bluff.

For too long, he'd been on the fence about leaving the *Taliesen*, but the memory of his last conversation with Tessa made him realize he couldn't delay his decision any longer. He'd take care of Dee first, then he'd make a few other calls and put all those long-held, half-formed plans into motion.

He was going to make his little dream a reality. And nothing—not Dee, not any goddamn threats to his life—would stop him.

After he shut the door, he picked up his cell phone and dialed Dee's private Milwaukee number. After four rings, she picked up. "Dee? It's Lucas. You have some explaining to do."

A surprised pause, then, "My, aren't we grouchy today. Is there a problem?"

"How about I start with Amos Lowery?"

Dee sighed. "He's a jerk, but he's a damn good engineer. Sorry, Lucas. I won't get rid of him. If he's causing trouble, I'll have another talk with him."

"You ordered him to spy on Tessa and me."

A long silence followed on the other end. "Well, not exactly. He offered, I'm assuming as a way to make up for the fact he's been such a pain to deal with, and I didn't say no. Sorry if he's gotten a little overzealous, but all's fair in love and war, darling."

Lucas's gaze fell on a business card on his desk: *Sturgeon Bay Yacht and Specialty Boats.*

He smiled. "Not this time. You've got two weeks to find yourself another captain. I quit."

Twenty-three

*B*y the time the *Taliesen* steamed away after picking up passengers and cargo in Grand Haven, the officers had grown increasingly short-tempered and tense, and an edgy awareness of danger seeped through Lucas's every thought—but this time the danger was real.

Standing at the window bay, staring out at the vast darkness before him, Lucas listened to Shea and the wheelsman chatting about recipes for banana bread.

Idly, he spun the yo-yo in his hand and walked-the-dog. Fooling with the toy kept his edginess at bay and helped him concentrate. He did his best thinking while his hands were busy.

"Hey, you're getting pretty good at that," Shea said.

Lucas turned, but before he could answer, the telephone rang and Shea went to answer. "Yeah, the skipper's on the bridge. Who's calling?" Lucas was already walking forward when Shea's eyes went round. "Sure thing, Detective. Here he is."

Lucas took the phone. "Hall."

"It's Burton. I've got bad news."

Lucas met Shea's worried gaze. "I'm putting you on hold. I'll pick up again in my office."

He punched the hold button, replaced the receiver and, with one last look at Shea, headed to his office. He shut the door, then picked up his phone. "Is Dee alright?"

"Mrs. S is fine, if going stir-crazy. But Joe Yarwood is missing." Burton's voice was terse.

Lucas swore softly. "Wasn't he under surveillance?"

"He was. When he didn't show up at work, my men asked for him. The wife claimed he'd left to meet a friend to go fishing up north. Said he was upset and needed to get away."

"Is she telling the truth?"

"She thinks so. We checked with the friend. They met at a neighborhood bar and Yarwood told his friend he was having car trouble and needed a lift downtown. The friend dropped him off, but didn't see where he went after that."

"When was this?"

"Just before you put into Grand Haven. Any trouble there?"

"No. We boarded passengers and some cargo. All the passengers checked out, as far as we can determine."

"You're heading toward Mackinac Island next?" Burton asked after a moment.

"Yes. We'll put in tomorrow, and leave the next morning."

"And I don't suppose you noticed what day it is, that's coming up the day after tomorrow."

Lucas cut his gaze toward his calendar, and a chill dread washed over him. "Oh, shit."

"Right. The second anniversary of the *McKee's* sinking," Burton said, his voice tight. "I'm hazarding a guess here, but if this guy's going to try something, I'm betting it's at the island. The area is separate from the mainland, and it's a short distance to Canada, right?"

"Right."

"How easy would it be for him to disappear into Canada?"

"It's possible to slip past the U.S. and Canadian Coast Guard by water, if that's what you're asking."

"Damn," Burton said with a sigh. "I'm real sorry about this. We've put out an alert on Yarwood, and I'll keep you posted."

"That's all you've got? A friend was the last to see him?"

"Nope, there's one more thing. Since he left without his car, we checked rentals in Milwaukee. Yarwood apparently rented a car the day he left. We've got a trace on the plates, and I've alerted both the Mackinac Island and Mackinaw City police departments. Try not to make yourself a target, okay?"

"I'll try," Lucas said. "Thanks."

After hanging up, Lucas sat for a moment longer, mulling over this ominous shift in the status quo. He needed to update his officers, but he'd talk to Tessa first as a matter of course.

He stood, shaking his head ruefully. Who the hell was he fooling? He wanted to see her, alone, and this was a good excuse.

He left his cabin and knocked on Tessa's door. She answered after a moment, eyes sleepy.

"What's wrong?" she asked as he shut the door behind her, her gaze searching his. "Something's wrong, isn't it?"

Lucas clasped his hands behind his back, because if he didn't, he'd yank her close and kiss her soft mouth, then run his hands over that warm, curving body he missed so badly he could taste it.

"Yarwood's pulled a disappearing act," he said, and her faced paled. "Burton thinks he's headed for Mackinac Island."

"Oh, God," she whispered.

"I want you to double the watch while we're at anchor. The police have been alerted and will be on hand to help out, but this guy's already given Burton the slip. He's smart."

For a moment, wanting to give her good news to take off the sting of the bad news, he considered telling her what he'd found out about Lowery and Dee—and that he'd told Dee to take a hike. But, again, he decided to wait until they'd docked in Milwaukee. She had enough on her mind, and he needed to keep her focused on the immediate problem.

Tessa nodded. "How are you doing? Holding up okay?"

His gaze met hers, and it was all he could do to keep himself from touching her. Just one touch.

"I miss you, Tess." She sighed, and when she opened her mouth to speak, he held up his hand. "Forget I said that. I shouldn't have."

Now what? He should leave. Open the door and walk out. But he couldn't seem to move. "Sorry I woke you up."

"I wasn't really sleeping. God, I'm a nervous wreck."

"It'll be over soon. Go back to bed. At least we're safe out on the water." He opened the door, and despite his best intentions not to press her, he said, "If you've changed your mind about you and me, I'd be happy to tuck you back into bed."

"Oh, Lucas . . ." Tessa gazed up at him, dark indecision in her gaze. Then she shook her head, but tempered her rejection with a sweet smile.

"I had to ask," he said, trying not to look disappointed. "I'll go round up the other officers. See you later."

After updating his officers, he headed back to the pilothouse. He retrieved the yo-yo and stood lost in thought by the window bay, snapping the yo-yo up and down, up and down, as the *Taliesen* glided along the Michigan shore in the darkness.

The daylong layover at Mackinac Island passed without incident, if not without tension. When passengers grumbled about having to show a photo ID to reboard the ship, in addition to their tickets, Jerry Jackson smoothed ruffled feathers with his easy smile, his quiet and firm strength, and the words: "Federal regulations."

Police officers patrolled the harbor around the clock, but if anybody from the ship or the island thought it odd, nobody mentioned it. Even the regular crew soon shrugged off the suddenly stricter rules as just some bureaucratic hassle.

The morning of departure dawned clear but windy, and the *Taliesen* balked a little leaving port until Lucas turned her into the wind. During the entire time at Mackinac Island, Tessa kept her distance. When he came into the mess, she'd leave. In the pilothouse, she stayed as far from him as possible without being too obvious about it. Beyond his issuing orders and her passing on information, they barely talked.

He'd never been more miserable in his life.

As his ship steamed away from the island, Lucas left the awkward tension of the pilothouse behind and returned to his office. He sat at his desk, rubbing his tired eyes. Lack of sleep and Tessa's ongoing distance had given him an edgy buzz, and he'd awakened that morning before dawn with that familiar sense of danger and foreboding—only worse.

Despite all expectations and logic, Yarwood hadn't made his move. Perhaps the security measures he'd taken had been enough to deter trouble. Maybe it really *was* all a sick joke.

But he didn't think so.

Something was wrong. Very, very wrong. Something they were all missing.

He tapped a pencil against his desk, resisting an urge to let his worst fear slip from his cage of control. But if there ever was a time to be afraid, that time was now.

Into the silence of the room, he whispered, "What if I've guessed wrong?"

What if they'd *all* guessed wrong from the beginning, and this wasn't about the *McKee*? What if Yarwood was talking about the *Taliesen*?

Frowning, he grabbed a notebook and from memory wrote down all the notes Dee had received. Then he sat back and read them over through the filter of not the *McKee*, but the *Taliesen*.

Knock, knock. Who's there? Ice. Ice who? Just ice.

No ambiguity here. He had to give Yarwood credit for a twisted sense of humor in knowing how to knock on the door and introduce himself.

Rock-a-bye pretty baby on the sea-saw. When the wind BLOWS AWAY the cradle will crack. When the bough-wow breaks, the cradle will fall, and down will go baby, cradle and all.

Here was ambiguity. He'd thought *pretty baby* referred to Dee Stanhope—so had Burton—and these preconceived assumptions had kept him from seeing the obvious. In his memory, Dee's breathless voice echoed: *This is my baby I'm placing in your hands . . .*

He'd lost track of the number of times she'd referred to the *Taliesen* as her *baby* in the newspapers and on TV. Certainly often enough for someone obsessed with her to have noticed and written, in essence: *rock-a-bye pretty baby on the sea . . . when she's blown away, the bow will break, and down will go baby . . .*

"Jesus," Lucas muttered, perspiration prickling his skin.

TIGRESS, TIGRESS BURNING BRIGHT. NINE LIVES HAS YOUR   TOMCAT?   LYNX . . . TIGER . . . COUGAR . . . DEADLY . . . R.I.P. ARE YOU READY?

A taunt directed at him. Newspapers and TV had linked him with Dee, and it seemed likely Yarwood also blamed him for what happened to the *McKee*.

To Yarwood, it must seem as if Lucas were the proverbial cat with nine lives, and now that he commanded the *Taliesen*, no wonder Yarwood was asking: *Lieutenant Commander, are you ready this time . . . ?*

Remember the Alamo, remember the Maine. *Ah, Bobby, we hardly knew ye. Hickory, dickory dock, rock around the clock. The cat looked at the clock. The clock struck two, and away she blew.*

Alarm hammered at him, even though he could make no sense of this last threat.

Remember . . .

Was it a demand to remember the dead? Anger echoed in these references to violent death, and grief rang in the allusion to assassinated Kennedys, men cut down in their prime. Was Yarwood using the *Maine*'s rallying cry as a warning to remember the *McKee*, or to remind them why he was seeking so-called justice?

Maybe it was a defense, or even an excuse.

Lucas didn't doubt the *cat* referred to him, but the clock and reference to two . . . was this a specific warning?

Rock . . . the *McKee* had foundered on a rocky shoal, but what did the two o'clock mean?

He sat straight, going cold. "Not two o'clock, dammit; he means two *years*!"

There was no denying the obvious conclusion: The threat wasn't against Dee or himself. Not directly, anyway.

The target was the *Taliesen*.

An eye for an eye, the oldest kind of justice.

With that realization, the pieces rapidly fell into place and he knew at once that Yarwood had made no attempt to board the *Taliesen* because he didn't need to.

Quickly, mouth set in a grim line, he pushed away from his desk and went to Tessa's cabin. He pounded on her door. She answered immediately, still in uniform though off watch, her gaze clear-eyed and sharp.

"I need to talk to you now. Come with me."

Without a word, she followed him to his office. As soon as he'd closed the door behind them, Lucas demanded, "Did we take on any cargo at Mackinac?"

She shook her head. "No. We let off a number of

passengers and took on another forty or so. They all checked out."

He frowned. "What about Grand Haven?"

"Let me get the paperwork." She left for the pilot-house and a moment later came back with a stack of papers, thumbing through them. "Nothing unusual. Let off passengers, took on new. Again, all the passengers checked out."

"Vehicles?"

"Yes, and all legally registered to ticketed passengers."

"What else did we take on?"

There had to be something he was missing. He yanked at his tie, feeling his shirt cling to his skin with perspiration.

"What's wrong?"

"Answer the question, Tessa, dammit!"

Her face paled. "We took on some crates of gears for delivery in Milwaukee, and a number of boxes of electronic parts. Replenished the food larders." She quickly skimmed through the bills of lading. "Oh, wait. Here's another two vehicles . . . I remember now, they weren't listed with any passengers, but as cargo. Two rental cars, one bound for Green Bay and—"

"Rental cars?" Lucas moved closer. He still had the pencil in his hand, and ran it down the paper—until he stabbed the point at the middle of the page. "There it is. A rental car from Alamo."

"I don't—" Tessa stopped, her eyes widening. "Oh, God, Lucas. You're not—"

A knock pounded at the door—the closed door.

Lucas and Tessa exchanged looks; and fear flashed in her eyes a split moment before Shea dashed into the room without even waiting for Lucas's permission to enter.

"I just got a call on the radio from someone who wouldn't identify himself. Sir, I think you need to see this now."

Lucas took the paper, Tessa beside him, and read:

Focus. Hocus pocus locus. Jack be nimble, Jack be quick. What rhymes with doom?

"What rhymes with doom?" Tessa whispered.

The pencil in Lucas's hand snapped. "Boom."

Twenty-four

*T*essa stood frozen in shock, staring after Lucas as he ran for the pilothouse; then she scrambled after him, Rob at her heels.

"Locus. He means place." At the wheel, Lucas spun toward Rob. "How far are we from Garden Island?"

Rob blinked. "Thirty, forty minutes, maybe."

"That fits. He wants the bomb to go off as we pass where the *McKee* sank. He gets points for style," Lucas finished, mouth in a grim line. "The son of a bitch."

"*Bomb?* Jesus Christ," Rob whispered, going white.

"I don't have time to explain," Lucas glanced at her, Rob, and the wheelsman, who sat staring open-mouthed. "All along, Yarwood's been telling us he plans to blow up the *Taliesen* on the second anniversary of the *McKee*'s sinking. I just didn't see it until five minutes ago!"

"Oh, my God," Tessa said, heart pounding, palms sweating at the chilling realization that the lives of nearly five hundred passengers and crew were in danger. "What are we going to do?"

"Abandon ship. I can't risk any other option."

She caught his gaze. "Lucas, what if you're wrong?"

"If I'm wrong, then I look like an idiot and we have a lot of pissed-off passengers and Coasties. But I'd rather have pissed-off passengers than dead ones."

"Oh, Jesus," Rob said again.

"This is no time to panic," Lucas snapped. "Get me the water depth. I need to know if we can drop anchor."

Rob ran for the chart table and called back, "Looks like it's shallow enough."

"Good. The last thing I want is a drifting bomb."

Bringing her burgeoning fear back under control, Tessa said, "There'll be a panic—"

"It can't be helped," Lucas interrupted. His eyes locked with hers. "I'm giving you five minutes to get as many of your crew in place before I sound the abandon ship alarm. Go. Both of you. I'll order the engine to full stop. Tell Compton I need him on emergency detail . . . and get everybody out of the cargo hold stat! When I sound the alarm, I'll send out a mayday."

With a quick glance at Rob, Tessa ran down the hall of the officers' deck, banging on starboard doors while Rob banged portside. When they were halfway down the hall, the ship shuddered as Lucas cut her engine. Off-duty officers milled in the hall, in uniform and out, demanding to know what the hell was going on, why the ship was stopping.

"Get the steward personnel to their emergency positions," Tessa ordered Rob. "I'll brief the officers. I want as many crew as possible available to keep the panic to a minimum. And stay on the two-way!"

Rob nodded and ran to carry out her orders.

"Listen up!" Tessa called over the din of demanding and questioning voices. "We have a critical situation. The captain has every reason to believe we have a bomb on board ship. In less than five minutes, he's going to sound the abandon ship alarm." A collective gasp sounded, punctured by curses. "I don't know how much time we have to get the passengers to safety, but we move as fast as we can. Dave, clear the hold stat and drop anchor. The rest of you, get to your stations now!"

For a split second, no one moved. Then her officers scrambled at once—and in grim silence.

Tessa spun and ran back to the pilothouse. Lucas stood alone at the wheel, hand on the chadburn.

He turned as she came beside him. She seized his shirt in her fists, forcing him to meet her gaze directly as she burst out, "I don't want to leave you!"

The worst fear pounding at her, amid all the others, was that she couldn't lose him—not like this. She couldn't bear it.

"You don't have a choice," he said tightly. "Get to your station. That's an order."

He was right; but even knowing the needs of passengers and crew outweighed her need to stay with Lucas did nothing to cut through her pain. She stood on tiptoe and pressed a kiss against his rough cheek. Lucas kissed her back, hard and brief.

"Keep safe," she whispered. "I'll hold a place for you in the last raft, and I won't leave this ship without you."

"I'll be there, I promise. You do your job, and let me do mine. And be careful, Tessa."

At the sight of him standing alone on his bridge, a rush of pride and grief overwhelmed her—and something else she denied for too long.

"I love you," she said, holding his gaze.

His eyes darkened. "Hell of a time to tell me, Tess."

"Lucas, I—"

"You need to go now," he interrupted, and turned away from her, holding the wheel in a white-knuckled grip.

With one last look at his rigid back, hating that she had to leave him, she ran for the boat deck.

As she stepped out into the bright, sunny day, the *Taliesen*'s whistle blared seven short blasts and one long—the unmistakable signal to abandon ship.

The whistle's echo lingered in the air for a split second, and then a woman screamed.

Lucas had already sweated through his shirt as he fought to control the spikes of fear and tried not to worry about the woman he loved—out of his reach and out of his protection. If something were to happen to her . . .

He stopped the thought cold, and hurried to the radio as the *Taliesen* shuddered beneath him, her anchor dragging. "Mayday, mayday . . . this is the SS *Taliesen*. Please respond, over."

Static crackled for several long, tense seconds, then a voice answered: "Taliesen, *this is the* Ellen Sherman. *We read you. What is the nature of your emergency and your position, over.*"

The coal freighter *Ellen Sherman*—good. The radar showed her five miles away, sailing downbound.

"We have a car bomb on board and I'm abandoning ship," Lucas answered calmly. "Our current position is forty-five-point-thirty North and eighty-five-point-thirty West, off Garden Island. We require immediate assistance. I have nearly five hundred people on this ship. I'd appreciate it, *Sherman*, if you'd fly."

"*Roger . . . we're on our way,* Taliesen. Hold on!"

Immediately following the *Sherman*'s response, a new voice sounded over the radio: "Taliesen, *this is Coast Guard Air Station Traverse City. We have received your mayday and we are routing all available assets to your assistance, over.*"

"Roger," Lucas said. "How long will it take your people to get here?"

"*Two rescue helicopters will be on scene in forty minutes, sir. The cutter* Acacia *is out on buoy patrol and turning back. The* Sherman *will be on-scene first. Sir, get your passengers and crew as far away from your ship as possible.*"

"We're working on it, Traverse City, over."

Lucas turned. In the distance, he could see the green, wooded shoreline of Garden Island, seeming so close, yet it might as well be on another planet, considering how little time he had. On the radar, multiple blips headed his way—the *Ellen Sherman* closest, and his old cutter, the *Acacia,* farthest, along with several fishing boats from the islands. The helicopters were in the air, speeding at 140 mph toward him.

Still not fast enough.

Evacuating a ship was the last thing any captain wanted. On board ship, he had control, but once his crew and passengers were off the ship and in the water, that control vanished. This situation left him no other choice.

His two-way radio hummed with activity. Tessa's voice was still calm, but he could hear the undertone of fear as she ordered a lifeboat lowered. He could see boats and rafts already in the water, but not nearly as many as he wanted to see.

Fear sluiced through him, but he fought it back with

deep, steady breaths and one fierce, hammering thought: *This time nobody is dying on my watch.*

Nobody.

He glanced at his wristwatch. In ten minutes' time, they would've passed alongside the site of the *McKee* wreck. Ten lousy minutes was all he had.

Outside, he heard the cries and shouts, the rising panic. No matter how many drills a crew performed, the real thing never went as smoothly as planned.

"Taliesen, *this is Traverse City requesting an update of your status, over.*"

"Status unchanged. We're continuing to evacuate the ship. Approximately three-quarters of the passengers are away."

"*Roger,* Taliesen. *Get your crew on deck.*"

"We're at a full stop and at anchor. The chief engineer has shut down the engine and I have all my people on deck. I'll man the bridge as long as I can."

"*Excellent, sir. It's good to know we have one of our own on board and in control of the situation.*"

Tessa stood at her starboard post, moving to the last lifeboat. "Count them off, Jerry! The next sixty!"

Jerry Jackson stood like a beacon of calm amid the remaining swarm of passengers. Towering over most everybody, his physical strength and presence commanded attention.

The first passengers she'd evacuated were children, the elderly, and handicapped. Most of the adults had remained calm, and she'd hustled the hysterical ones onto a boat before they could incite a panic in the others.

But so many still remained on the ship! So many men

and women, their faces all blurred together. Tessa forced herself not to register their fear, their pleas. She couldn't afford to give in to her own fear or worries.

"Move along now," Jerry was hollering. "Stay calm. Everything's gonna be fine."

As each passenger ran toward her, Tessa directed them through the embarkation gate and into the boat, where her trained lifeboatmen quickly positioned them tightly together.

In five minutes, the lifeboat was filled to capacity.

Tessa glanced up toward the pilothouse. Lucas was near the radio, where he had to be, and she silently prayed he was holding his own up there.

"Okay, let her go!" she ordered, signaling to the crew above her manning the winch. She locked her gaze on a teenage girl with huge, fear-filled eyes. "Everybody hold on and stay close together. Don't grab the side of the boat as we lower you; we don't want any crushed fingers!"

Or worse.

Lowering a lifeboat from an old winch was a tricky affair, and Tessa forced herself to ignore the screams and shouts as the passengers jerked and swung on their way down, bumping against the *Taliesen*'s hull.

Oh, God, please don't let any of them fall!

Farther on down the deck, the crew had thrown ladders over the side of the ship. Inflatable rafts bobbed in the dark water. Scott the bartender stood calmly evacuating passengers who were able to climb down the ladder into the rafts, and at his side were two young women from the ship's gift shop, responding with equal calm and efficiency.

All passengers wore life vests—at least that part of the drill had gone without a hitch.

But there were still too many people on deck.

She glanced at her watch.

Five minutes. They only had five minutes!

Tessa looked up again—and a split second later, the *Taliesen* exploded.

Twenty-five

*I*n the pilothouse, Lucas slammed hard against the bulkhead. A sharp pain lanced his chest as the ship heaved again, throwing him back against the wheel and ramming it under his ribs.

With a hiss of pain, he dragged himself to his feet—and at once registered the steep angle of the deck.

He lunged for the radio. "This is the *Taliesen*! We've had an explosion. I repeat, we've had an explosion and the ship is taking on water . . . I've got a severe list to port. Traverse City, I need a miracle here!"

"Secure that lifeboat," Tessa yelled over the frantic screams of the passengers in the half-launched lifeboat, dangling at a precarious angle. The crew inside desperately tried to prevent passengers from tumbling out.

The explosion had knocked a number of crew and passengers overboard, while tumbling everyone else against the bulkhead and each other amid screams of panic.

As she pushed her way toward the rail, she saw that Jerry had the bartender's hand, his face straining with effort as he pulled Scott over the rail and back onto the deck.

Something big had blown on the car deck, below the waterline, and this sudden list was very, very bad news.

"Rob, what's happening?" she demanded over the two-way. The port side had taken the worst of the explosion. If Rob hadn't launched all his boats, he might not be able to now. "Rob!"

No response.

She tried not to think of why Rob wasn't answering. He'd lost his radio overboard. Dropped it, broke it, something . . .

"Lucas, I can't get Rob . . . tell me what it looks like portside!"

As she waited, one agonizing second after another for Lucas to respond—he had to be alright!—she watched as her crew safely lowered the last, dangling lifeboat.

"Move faster," she yelled, and she heard the fear in her voice.

An explosion on the car deck meant it was only a matter of time before the fire ignited other fuel tanks.

"Get all the rafts into the water . . . I want everybody off the ship now!" She raised her two-way. "Lucas, dammit, answer me!"

But it was Rob who answered, "Tess! We've got people in the water. We're listing bad . . . I can't launch the last boat!"

"Get the rafts in and tell everybody to jump and swim for it. We're running out of time!"

From the corner of her eye, she saw a little girl break free of her mother to follow after a tiny, dark darting form.

What the hell? A dog? And how had they missed evacuating a child?

As the girl slipped through an open hatch, the mother screamed and turned to follow, but a crewman grabbed her and lifted her overboard.

"Marshall," she yelled. "Grab that kid now!"

Andy turned, followed her finger jabbing at a flash of bright yellow. He nodded, pushed his way through the press of bodies at the rail, and ducked through the hatch where the little girl had gone—a hatch that led to a crew-only area of the ship.

Lucas heard Tessa's frantic questions, but couldn't respond. Braced against his ship's list, he was on the radio to the Coast Guard: "We're taking on water. She's going down. We have most of the passengers safely away, but I see hundreds in the water."

"*Hold on, sir. The* Ellen Sherman *is within visual range and all available assets are alerted to your position. Concentrate on getting everybody off the ship and as far away as possible.*"

The sound of something hitting the deck caught his attention. Turning, he saw the yo-yo fall from the chart table and roll to the far side of the tilting bridge.

For moment, he stared at it. Someday, a diver would glide down the murky depths and through the ruins of this pilothouse, quiet and dark, and wonder at that little red toy lying on the deck: how it had come to be there, and who it had belonged to.

"Roger," he said quietly. "We're doing the best we can."

"*I know you are, sir. Stand by.*"

"I'm not going anywhere." Lucas glanced down at the portside deck, where Rob Shea and his team struggled to evacuate the remaining passengers and crew. "I'm with the old girl right until the end."

Minutes later, all passengers were off the ship. With the threat of other explosions looming, it hadn't taken long to convince even the most fearful to jump into the cold, choppy waters of Lake Michigan. Lifeboats and rafts, spilling over with people, bobbed on the waves. In the distance, Tessa made out the dark bulk of the *Sherman*. Rob, with a shout, pointed out a motorboat speeding their way, going so fast the bow never seemed to touch the water.

Only four officers remained on board—Lucas, Lowery, Rob, and herself. In the last raft, Jerry Jackson stood by the emergency radio, surrounded by crew and passengers.

Tessa glanced up at the pilothouse and lifted her two-way. "Lucas, all the passengers are away. We're ready on the last raft. We're waiting for you."

Lucas leaned out a window, and she gasped at the blood on his face. "Don't wait for me," he shouted down. "I've got one more call to make to the Coast Guard, then I'm grabbing the log. Climb into the raft and get those people away from the *Taliesen*. I'll swim out to you!"

She had maintained her control for these last hellish minutes; now it snapped.

"I will not leave this ship without you!"

"That's an order, Jardine!"

Through a sudden sheen of tears, she stared up at

the pilothouse and Lucas. Hundreds of lives depended on her. *Hundreds.* She could not disobey Lucas, but leaving him behind . . . She swallowed a scream, knowing if she let it out she wouldn't be able to stop.

She hesitated a split second longer, then obeyed her captain's orders and climbed down the ladder.

"Pull yourself together," snapped Lowery. "You're a goddamned officer. Act like one!"

Fury cut through the numbing panic, and she shot him a hateful glare before she dived into the cold water, gasping from the shock of it.

Moments later Jerry and Rob had pulled her into the raft. At the rail, Lowery seemed to hesitate. He glanced up at the empty pilothouse window, then swore pungently. He clambered over the side, agile as a monkey, and dropped beside the raft.

"Row," the old man barked as he climbed inside. "This bitch is gonna blow, and we don't want to be anywhere near it when she does. Hall's on his own!"

In the pilothouse, Lucas stumbled along the slanting deck toward his desk. He grabbed the logbook, shoved it inside his shirt, then fought his way back to the radio.

The list had worsened, and the ship was on auxiliary power. Soon, even that would go.

Setting his mouth in a grim line, he hailed the Coast Guard for the last time: "Traverse City, we have evacuated passengers and crew. This is Captain Lucas Hall signing off from the *Taliesen*, over."

"Roger, sir. Get yourself to safety and hang tight."

It was time to leave his ship. With his hand on the bulkhead, he could feel her every wounded shudder, straining as her hull structure began to fail. Soon she'd roll turtle, and it would only be a matter of minutes before she slipped beneath the water.

"This is it, old girl," he whispered, on a rush of anger and grief. "So long."

Lucas quickly made his way out of the bridge and toward the deck hatch, pulling himself along with grim determination and by whatever handholds he could find.

He'd reached the rail when another powerful explosion tore through the *Taliesen*.

Like a living thing, she pitched in her agony, spewing black smoke into the sky and rolling until she lay at a slippery twenty-degree angle.

Cursing, Lucas grabbed the rail and held on, sliding as the ship heaved. An orange raft bobbed not far from him, and he could see Tessa and the others waving their arms. He couldn't hear what they were saying, but he didn't have to.

Jump, those frantic gestures told him. *Get off the ship!*

He climbed onto the ladder that swung wildly over the hull, losing his foothold several times before he jumped into the cold, dark water. With fast, powerful strokes, he finally put distance between himself and his dying ship.

Every wave that slapped against him made the pain in his chest burn. The stiff, sharp logbook he'd shoved in his shirt didn't help any.

As he approached the raft, Tessa and Jerry reached for him. He steadied himself by grasping the raft's side, then pulled the logbook from his shirt and tossed it inside.

Tessa, her face white and eyes huge with fear, took his face in her hands and kissed him like there was no tomorrow, not giving a damn who could see.

He broke free and hauled himself into the raft, and

Tessa at once seized his hand and held it tightly.

He managed a smile for her, gasping for breath. "Thanks for holding me a spot."

A quick scan showed every lifeboat and raft stuffed full, and a number of people bobbing on the waves, most of them men. A fishing boat was hauling passengers out of the water, as was the newly arrived island ferryboat. Lucas could barely make out the *Acacia*, coming at top speed. The *Sherman* had closed the distance, her lifeboats already lowered.

But a sense of foreboding still hounded him.

"Are you sure we got everybody?" he demanded.

"Not everybody." Rob leaned forward, face pale as he lowered his two-way. "Tessa, we're missing a little girl. Name's Rachel. She's about ten, wearing a yellow jacket."

Tessa's face lost all color. "She ran through the forward hatch leading to the officers' quarters. I sent Andy after her. Oh, God, Lucas . . . Andy and that little girl are still on the *Taliesen*!"

Twenty-six

*F**ingers, grasping his through a door.*
The cloying, sweet stink of gasoline.
Please mister . . . don't let me die. Don't let me die . . .

Fury and despair slammed through him, and Lucas squeezed his eyes shut, sucking in his breath.

"No," he hissed, fighting it back.

He opened his eyes to the confused stares of those in the raft—all except Tessa. The terrified light in her eyes told him she knew what he was about to do.

Dear, sweet, strong Tessa; in her capable hands, his passengers and crew would be safe.

"Nobody dies," he said quietly as he took her face between his palms. "Not this time."

"Lucas, I can't let you go back—"

He silenced her with a quick, hard kiss—and, God, pulling away was the single hardest thing he'd ever had to do. This could be the last time he'd ever kiss her, but he refused to accept that. She made a grab for him, but he shook free of her and dived from the raft. The next wave carried him beyond her reach, and he heard her anguished cry.

Forcing himself to ignore it, and the burning pain in his chest, he swam fast and hard back toward the *Taliesen*. She lay awkward in the water, slipping beneath the waves, but while she was afloat he could still hope to find that little girl and Andy Marshall alive.

His first obstacle was getting onto the ladder dangling above him. When the ship rocked on the waves, the ladder dipped low enough for him to barely reach.

Lucas intently studied the roll, catching the rhythm, and when the hull bobbed down toward him again, he grabbed for the dangling ladder.

And missed.

Cursing, he waited until it dipped within in reach again, the seconds seeming to pass like hours, then lunged—and caught it.

Dangling over water, Lucas climbed upward, hand over hand, focusing all his attention, all his strength, on getting to the rail looming so far above him.

The odds of finding two people—providing they were alive—before the *Taliesen* sank were slim, but he didn't stop to think about it as years of training kicked back in and the adrenaline rush took over.

He vaulted over the railing and promptly slid into the bulkhead. Then, wrenching open the hatch to the officers' quarters, he went inside the ship.

Murky darkness filled the companionway, the only light coming through the portholes now that the auxiliary generator had failed. Water swirled around his legs. He smelled smoke—oh, God, smoke—thick and acrid.

"Andy!" he shouted. "Andy, where are you?"

No answer. He'd have to do this the hard way, by

trying to get inside the mind of a little girl. Why would she have run off in the first place? Where? To get something left behind in her cabin, no doubt. Typical human response—house on fire, go back for money or some memento.

Except the kid found herself on the wrong deck, disoriented and scared—and scared kids almost always tried to hide. She could be in a stairwell, or even a cabin.

Lucas crawled and slid along, hoping Marshall had at least caught up with the kid before things had gone wrong. And he hoped to God that Marshall had been on his way to the deck with the kid when that last explosion hit.

"Andy!" he shouted again. His voice echoed eerily, but no answer came back.

Then, very faint—a sound. Lucas stopped, listening. It came again, sharp, high-pitched. A dog barking?

But the barking was suddenly drowned out by a chilling, grinding scream of metal, the sound of the ship tearing apart.

More time, dammit. He needed more time!

"Hey," he yelled when the noise subsided. "If you can't talk, bang on something!"

Again, he heard yipping and then—unmistakably— a frantic, metallic banging. Ahead. Or below? With the echo and the sounds of his dying ship, he couldn't get a clear fix.

Lucas continued, almost falling into a port cabin as its door gaped open beneath him. He had to inch his way across the open door, careful not to let the pitch of the ship knock him down inside the flooding room.

Sweating, he kept moving, one hand after another, until he was clear. The banging and barking suddenly grew louder, clearer.

"Keep making noise, I'm coming!"

"Help!"

A young voice; a terribly young and frightened voice.

"Help me, please!"

Lucas stopped, shuddering, and sucked in a long breath through his teeth to clear out the coiling, icy fear.

"I don't have time for this shit," he muttered angrily.

"He's hurt," a girl cried. "I can't move him!"

He had to be close; she sounded right under him. He crawled toward the next cabin. Obviously Marshall was in no shape to respond . . . unless the kid was talking about the dog. But an injured dog wouldn't be barking like that.

Finally, from the next cabin and behind its closed door, clearly sounded the clanging, yipping, and loud sobs.

Lucas reached over and turned the latch. It swung open and slammed back. The girl screamed over the dog's barking.

"Howdy there," Lucas said, in his calmest possible voice, he was near breathless from his exertions.

"Get me out!" The girl's voice was high-pitched with terror. "Help!"

He had to calm her down fast, and said in a soothing voice, "What's your name, sweetheart?"

"Ra-Rachel . . . Rachel Williams."

He could hardly see anything in the cabin, but could make out two huddled forms. One small, one big. The big one wasn't moving. Lucas went cold.

"I'm Lucas, Rachel. What's your dog's name?" Thinking fast, he unbuckled his belt and yanked it off.

"Beanie." The girl sniffed, but she sounded a little

calmer, although her voice was tremulous. "He's scared, too."

"We all are, Rachel."

"This guy is hurt real bad," Rachel said. "His name is Andy. There's water all over!"

"Andy, it's Hall. Can you answer me?"

"Wake up!" The girl shook Andy. "Somebody's here . . . you have to wake up now!"

A low groan responded, then a painful gasp. "Captain?"

"Where are you hurt?"

"Leg's busted . . . maybe my arm, too. The kid . . . she's okay. We were almost to the deck when the explosion hit . . . and I fell. I'm sorry, sir . . . I'm sorry."

Lucas set his jaw. "It's not your fault, Andy. Now, Rachel, I'm going to lower my belt. I want you to grab on to it and hold on real tight. Pretend it's a rope. I'll pull you out. Okay?"

"Okay."

"Andy, I'm going to need you to support her."

"I can do it, sir."

"Good. You're going to be okay, Andy. I'll get you out."

He'd said that before, and five men had gone to the bottom of Lake Michigan.

But not this time.

"Up you go, Rachel." Andy's voice was thick with pain, even though he tried to sound cheerful. "Got it?"

"Yeah."

"Hold tight," Lucas warned. "I'm pulling you up now."

Bracing himself, he started pulling. Pain shot through his ribs, but he ignored it. Nothing mattered but getting this kid out of that dark death pit.

"Get a foothold on the wall," Andy said over the

dog's nonstop yipping. "Attagirl. Pretend you're climbing a mountain."

"I'm okay," Rachel said. He could see her face. Lots of curly dark hair, huge eyes. A bright yellow jacket.

Andy heaved Rachel upward with a hiss of pain, and Lucas grabbed Rachel's arm and pulled her through the door. Her arms locked tightly around his neck, and she pressed her tear-streaked cheek to his face.

Muffled yips of outrage erupted from her jacket. Lucas looked down to see a puppy poke its head out of her jacket. It wore a red collar.

Jesus. The girl had gone after her dog, which shouldn't have been on the ship in the first place. They might all die, because this kid's parents had broken one small rule.

"Okay, Rachel, you need to let me go now," Lucas said, prying her arms away. "I have to get Andy. I need you to be brave—"

"Sir," came Andy's weak voice. "You get her out. Please. Don't worry about me. I can wait."

Lucas hesitated. He could carry Rachel outside to safety, then come back for Andy before the *Taliesen* rolled. Maybe. But it wasn't a chance he was willing to risk.

"We're not leaving you behind. We're in this together. Can you be brave for me a little longer, Rachel?"

Sniffing, Rachel nodded. She squatted, her arms tight around her squirming dog, and whispered, "You better hurry."

"There's the helicopters!"

At Rob's yell, Tessa looked up where two blessed,

bright spots of orange blazed **against** the cloud-streaked sky.

Oh, God, thank you!

Another quick glance showed **the immense** bulk of the *Ellen Sherman* upon them, and **the** *Acacia* closing. The freighter had her lifeboats in **the water**, her crew at the rails, waiting. Another few minutes, and they'd be loading passengers onto the solid, if inelegant, safety of her deck. More boats from the nearby island range had arrived and were taking passengers on board.

Tessa turned her anxious gaze back to the *Taliesen*.

If she rolled, with her upper decks below water, Lucas, Andy, and little Rachel wouldn't make it out alive.

And this lake would claim someone else she loved.

"Lucas, damn you," she whispered, shaking. "Don't you dare die on me."

A hand settled on her shoulder, and squeezed. "He'll make it out," Jerry murmured. "If he promised you he'd be here, then he'll be here."

Fear threatened to overrun all her defenses again, but none of them were out of danger yet, and she hadn't time for any emotion at all. She had a job to do. She stayed on the radio with the Coast Guard and the *Sherman*, directing the rescue of her passengers and crew.

But all the time, inside, she kept up a constant litany: *Please, God, please let him be safe.*

Inside the cabin, water swirling darkly around his thighs, Lucas grunted as he tried to shove Andy up through the open door. Andy wasn't big, but he was at least a solid 150 pounds of wiry muscle.

"Grab the doorframe," Lucas ordered. "Can you do that?"

"I think so." Andy's voice was quiet, determined. Lucas wouldn't let himself think of the pain the young deckhand was going through, or how cold and clammy his skin felt.

"Rachel, when I push him up, grab the back of his shirt, okay?"

"Okay, Lucas."

The kid was incredible. Either she had no idea how close they were to dying, or she had more courage than both he and Andy combined.

Precious seconds ticked by before Andy finally cleared the door, rolling away in pain and exhaustion.

Now Lucas had to get himself out of the cabin.

Knowing he wouldn't get much help from Andy, Lucas used the bunk for leverage. He jumped for the doorframe, and caught it. His muscles shook with the effort to pull himself up, sweat dripping down his face, pain shooting through his chest.

Two small hands grabbed his head, holding firmly, then a larger, stronger hand grasped the waistband of his trousers and pulled. A moment later, Lucas heaved himself from the cabin, gasping for breath.

The puppy wasn't barking, but its head peeped from inside Rachel's jacket, ears cocked forward, eyes bright with interest.

At least the dog was having fun.

"Okay," Lucas said when he'd caught his breath. "Now we gotta crawl out of here, and we have to move fast. Andy, I'll carry Rachel. Can you follow me?"

"Yeah," Andy said, rolling to his knees. A grin split his battered face. "What's a couple of busted bones, eh?"

Lucas grinned back, giving the deckhand's shoulder a quick, reassuring squeeze. Taking Rachel's arm, he said, "Climb up on my back. Pretend I'm just a big horse and you hold on tight, honey. Got that?"

Rachel nodded and climbed onto Lucas, and he bit back a groan as her legs clamped tightly around his lower ribs.

He crawled carefully back the way he'd come, going as fast as he dared, checking over his shoulder on Andy's progress. By now, with natural endorphins kicking in, the kid had probably blanked out the pain.

Each minute dragged as Lucas crawled closer to the bright rectangle of light that was the open hatch to the deck. Andy's breathing sounded harsh and labored. Rachel held on to him with a painful grip, her dog whimpering. The *Taliesen* groaned and creaked and shuddered.

"Hold on, old girl," Lucas muttered after one loud shrieking sound left Rachel whimpering with fear. "We're almost there."

At the hatchway, Lucas hoisted Rachel outside, then reached behind him and pulled Andy closer. "You're next. Ready?"

Andy nodded. Lucas didn't like the way the kid looked. With an effort, he shoved Andy through the hatch, then pulled himself up into the wind and beautiful sunshine.

"Look!" Jerry stood, pointing. "It's Hall! They're on deck, and he's got Marshall and the girl!"

Relief flooded Tessa as she twisted, frantically seeking him out. "Thank God!" To her radio, she said, "We have people on the starboard deck! Coast Guard, do you copy?"

"Roger, we see 'em," a crackling voice answered.

Tessa looked up. One of the orange Dolphin helicopters swung in low, sleek and swift. The pilot maneuvered the helicopter with deceptive ease. Two figures squatted in the helo's open bay: the mechanic and rescue swimmer, preparing to descend and airlift Rachel, Andy, and Lucas to safety.

When she looked back at the listing *Taliesen*, Tessa saw Lucas signaling the rescue swimmer with his hands, telling them to evacuate the child first. The second helicopter, hovering at a safe distance away from the first, would sweep in as soon as Rachel was clear.

"Marshall looks bad," Jerry said quietly.

Tessa shifted her gaze to Andy, who slumped on the deck, hunched over in pain. Lucas huddled over both the girl and the young deckhand, protecting them with his body.

"The little girl looks okay . . . there goes the swimmer," Tessa said. "He's coming out of the helo now."

With a practiced efficiency that made it look easy, the mechanic lowered the rescue swimmer while the pilot and copilot kept the helicopter hovering as still as possible, high enough to keep the rotors from whipping the water into a frenzy. But even so, the prop wash rippled the water in great, ever-widening concentric circles.

Tessa, in the closest raft, sat down quickly before the next rolling wave knocked her overboard.

Jerry leaned toward her. "I've got a count from Compton and the *Sherman*'s skipper. We have four hundred eighty-four passengers and crew accounted for, and with Hall, Marshall, and Rachel on the *Taliesen*, that makes a complete passenger and crew list of four eighty-seven. Everybody is off the ship."

Tessa nodded, faint with relief. But the ordeal wouldn't be over until the last man was off that ship—and she knew who that last man would be.

As she watched, the rescue swimmer landed on the *Taliesen*'s deck, harness in hand. Lucas immediately handed Rachel over, helping to secure the harness.

Scant moments later, Rachel embarked upon the ride of her life. Safe in the swimmer's embrace, she dangled above the water as she was lifted toward the helicopter. Tessa heard a faint cheer, even over the noise of the rotors. A quick glance showed everybody in the life-boats and rafts, and all those on the fishing boats, ferry, and the *Ellen Sherman*, cheering in triumph.

Don't be too thankful yet, people.

Tessa turned anxiously toward the *Taliesen*. Her list had grown steadily worse—now near a dangerous forty-five degrees. Lucas struggled to stay in place while crouched protectively over Andy to keep him from sliding into the water.

Tears stung her eyes at his selfless bravery, and the force of her love for him burned through her. She pressed against the side of the raft, her fingers white on its edge.

God, she had been the worst kind of coward!

She couldn't lose him—not now. Not with so many unsaid words between them, with so many years to look forward to.

"Hurry," she whispered to the helicopter above. "Hurry!"

Listening to the *Taliesen*'s groans, feeling her shudders beneath him, Lucas knew his time had all but run out.

Hunkering down, he wedged his leg against the bulkhead to keep Andy as motionless as possible. He'd gone into shock. Lucas recognized the signs, and with mounting desperation, he glanced up. Rachel twirled high above him, one arm clutching the rescue swimmer, her other clutching her little mutt.

She released one hand just long enough to wave.

Lucas waved back.

"She's going to b-be okay?" Andy mumbled, shivering.

"Yes," Lucas answered with a smile. "And so are you. It's your turn next. Just hang on."

"I'm c-cold."

"I know," Lucas said. "They'll get you warmed up."

The *Taliesen* lurched, and Lucas grabbed Andy's shirt as they both slid hard into the bulkhead. Lucas twisted, taking the brunt of the hit himself. He bit his lip until he tasted blood so that he wouldn't cry out in pain.

"You boys better move it," he muttered as he glared up at the helicopter. "Or we're going to get wet again."

Finally, the mechanic lifted both the rescue swimmer and Rachel into the open bay and immediately the pilot made way for the second helicopter.

"Here they come for you," Lucas said, trying to gain some sort of foothold on the shifting ship as he watched the next rescue swimmer spiraling down toward him.

Lucas raised his arm, signaling a need to hurry. It seemed to take forever for the swimmer to reach him.

"How badly is he hurt, sir?" the swimmer yelled over the roar of the rotors.

"Pretty bad. A broken leg for sure. He's shocky," Lucas shouted back. "We don't have time for the basket . . . this ship's gonna roll!"

The swimmer nodded, legs braced on the deck, hands on the bulkhead and rail. Even with the harness and rope supporting him, he could hardly keep steady. "Come on, buddy. Let's go."

Lucas helped the swimmer secure the harness

around Andy, fighting against the unpredictable pitch of the ship. Finally, the swimmer gave the signal for the mechanic to lift him.

"You're next, sir!"

Lucas only nodded. He helped steady Andy until they were out of reach, then let his hand fall to his side and closed his eyes.

Safe. They were both safe.

But he didn't have time for relief. The *Taliesen* pitched again, settling on her side.

This was it. The beginning of the end.

Lucas grabbed the rail with both hands to keep from sliding into the water. He had to remain on the ship as long as possible; otherwise, he risked being pulled under with the *Taliesen*. He no longer had the strength to swim. Realizing the urgency of the moment, the pilot of the second helicopter carefully eased away before Andy was on board, and the first helicopter lowered into position to retrieve Lucas.

He prayed Tessa was right, and that every single one of his passengers and crew were accounted for. God, let no one be alive inside this ship. Everything but the starboard deck was below water now.

Above him, the rescue swimmer began his descent.

Lucas looked for Tessa, and saw her standing in the raft. Both Jackson and Shea struggled to hold her in place. Leave it to his Tessa not to take anything sitting down, not even disaster.

He wanted to wave, to give her a signal and let her know he'd make it back to her, but he didn't dare let go of the rail. No stupid heroics. He just wanted off this ship before she went under.

Glancing up again, Lucas could see the swimmer clearly. His eyes were hidden by the visor of his helmet, but the line of his mouth looked grim. He extended his hand toward Lucas.

The *Taliesen* began her final roll.

"Sir, grab my hand!"

Lucas jumped. He caught the extended hand and held on as the man's fingers dug painfully into his skin. Pain lanced through him, white-hot, at the strain. His feet cleared the ship. The swimmer's mouth opened, but Lucas couldn't hear what he said, only saw the man frantically grabbing for Lucas's other arm.

A gust of wind slammed into them and ripped Lucas from the swimmer's grip.

For a forever of a second, he fell as the wet, dark keel hurtled closer and closer. The instant before he slammed into cold steel, Lucas thought: *Shit, this'll hurt like hell . . .*

Twenty-seven

Cries of horror rose above the thunder of rotors and powerful diesel engines. Tessa barely heard it over the sound of her own scream as she watched Lucas fall and the rescue swimmer make a desperate grab, only to miss. Lucas hit the *Taliesen*'s upturned keel hard, then disappeared into the water.

"I have to get him!" She stood to dive over the raft, but arms closed around her, holding her back.

"Stop it," Rob yelled in her ear, his arms tightening. "Dammit, you'll capsize the raft, Tess!"

"Then let me go . . . I have to get to him!"

"Let the Coast Guard do their job. They're getting ready to drop the rescue swimmer in the water and . . . oooph!"

Elbowing Rob in the gut, Tessa freed herself and dived into the water, the liquid cold stealing her breath.

"Tessa, it's too dangerous to go near the ship," Jerry yelled after her. "It'll pull you under!"

Shaking her head violently, although she knew her danger, she pushed off. Like hell would she sit by helplessly and watch Lucas die.

As she swam, one thought pierced through her focused intensity: She wouldn't let him down when he needed her most. Not this time.

A spot of bright orange splashed down some twenty feet in front of her: the rescue swimmer, dropped from the helicopter at a safe distance from the *Taliesen*. Wordlessly, the swimmer slid a float toward her and then swam with faster, more powerful strokes than hers toward the place where Lucas had gone under.

Tessa followed, grabbing the life preserver. An engine purred behind her, and she looked over her shoulder to see a Coast Guard utility boat approaching. A young Guardsman, in work blues and an orange life vest, leaned down from the deck and held out his hand toward her.

"Take my hand!"

She shook her head, treading water. "Not until I find him!"

"You have to come on the boat now, ma'am!" Another Coastie joined the first—neither looked much older than eighteen or nineteen—and they snagged her by the back of her shirt and belt and hauled her, struggling and cursing, onto the boat.

"We got him!"

The shout came from the front of the boat, where the boatswain's mate stood at the wheel.

Panting and shivering, Tessa turned. The rescue swimmer waved his hand, his other holding on to a limp form in the water beside him.

"Oh, Lucas . . . no," Tessa whispered as the utility boat's motor roared to life and sped toward the rescue swimmer.

Within minutes, she knelt with a group of Coasties, helping them drag both the swimmer and Lucas's body onto the deck.

"Is he breathing?" she demanded.

"No," the swimmer gasped out.

The boatswain quickly backed the boat away from the sinking ship as the rescue swimmer and another guardsman began CPR. Tessa held on to the rail, fingernails digging into the palms of her hands. She couldn't see Lucas through the huddle of bodies, only glimpsed a limp, long-fingered hand on the deck.

"Breathe," she whispered. "Come on, baby . . . please!"

Above, the rescue helicopter hovered, the mechanic poised in the open bay, waiting for a signal to send down the basket.

Then Lucas's hand jerked and both men bending over him reared back as he coughed, then rolled over and violently retched.

The rescue swimmer flashed Tessa a weary grin. "Now, that's music to my ears."

"Lucas!" Tessa slid across the small deck, taking his shoulders in her hands. His body shook with tremors and his skin felt cold as death. She turned to call for a blanket, but a Coastie was one step ahead of her and handed one over. Tessa wrapped the blanket around Lucas, pressing kisses against his icy cheek.

Still coughing, he looked up. He had a large gash across his forehead, and blood stained his ripped shirt-sleeve.

Her gaze locked with his in a suspended moment of stillness, before another coughing spasm rocked him. She gathered him close, running a comforting hand over his back.

"You did it," she whispered, understanding that

dark fear in his eyes. "You didn't lose anyone."

He shuddered, his arms closing around her with smothering strength. "Everybody got out?" he asked, his voice muffled.

"Everybody. Nobody died."

She held tightly on to him until a voice from above said, "I'm sorry, ma'am, but I gotta check him over."

Tessa scooted back, letting the rescue swimmer hunker down to do a quick vitals check.

"Where does it hurt?"

"Everywhere," Lucas said, wincing.

"I bet. Does anything feel broken?"

"Ribs, maybe . . . hurts when I breathe. My head feels like it's ready to split in two."

"You took a bad fall, and you might have a concussion. That's a nasty cut on your head." The man dabbed at it. "It'll need stitches. Let's get you up in the helicopter and to a hospital."

"I'm going with him," Tessa said firmly. "Don't even try to stop me."

Suddenly, a shout sounded from somewhere close: "There she goes! She's going under!"

Lucas twisted around. Tessa turned more slowly, noticing as she did so that everyone on the *Sherman* and the fishing boats, the newly arrived *Acacia*, and all those still in the lifeboats and on the utility boat, now faced the *Taliesen*.

She didn't want to see it, but forced herself to watch as water churned around the sinking ship and exploded outward with violent force as the sleek, gray hull slipped beneath the water.

"Oh, my God," said the swimmer beside her, his voice thick.

Lucas dragged himself to the rail and stood, his muscles taut with strain as he watched his ship sink, the shadowy hull beneath the water growing dimmer and dimmer.

Tessa came to stand beside him, lending him her silent support.

A moment later, the *Taliesen* was gone, leaving only the waves and receding, rippling circles to mark where she had been.

The last of her kind; and lost forever.

The *Sherman*'s mighty whistle blared: one long, two short—a final master's salute.

As the last echo faded, Lucas turned. Tears filled her eyes at the pain on his face, as he whispered, "I couldn't save her."

A tear slipped free as she held him tight. The rescue swimmer laid a hand on Lucas's shoulder and squeezed it.

"I'm sorry, sir. You did everything you could. The important thing was to save your passengers and crew." He paused, then added, "But she was a little beauty of a ship."

Lucas, eyes squeezed tight, only nodded. Then he stood straight, the captain once again, and opened his eyes, seeing as she did, the passengers and crew silently crowding the rails of the *Sherman*. Silence hung over the water. One burly crewman on the *Sherman* wiped the back of his hand over his eyes.

Lucas turned away. "Let's get the hell out of here."

Twenty-eight

*T*essa lost track of how many hellish, chaotic hours had passed since Lucas and Andy were airlifted to a Milwaukee hospital. After much wrangling, she'd been allowed to go along—though she'd hardly seen Lucas except for a few brief moments between tests, procedures, and question sessions.

She'd endured an endless line of doctors and nurses, reporters, and the police, including Detective Burton. Her voice was raw and her throat hurt.

By nightfall, the hordes had dispersed and Lucas was sleeping in his room, still under observation. Since she wasn't allowed in his room, she'd bummed a cup of bad coffee off one of the nurses and prepared to camp out in the waiting area until the next morning.

The hospital was amazingly quiet after hours, and she couldn't miss hearing the clipped, aggressive rhythm of high heels coming down the hall. Tessa had prepared herself for the confrontation before she even glimpsed a flash of pink.

"Well. What a surprise to see you still here," Dee said in a tone of cool sarcasm as she walked closer. She wore a Chanel suit in soft pink with navy trim—the perfect outfit for a hospital invasion.

Tessa wasn't up to verbal sparring. "It's nearly midnight. What are you doing here?"

"Checking on the victims of the latest disaster to hit my company." Despite her wry voice, the hospital's harsh artificial light revealed the lines of strain around her eyes and mouth. "Andy Marshall will need surgery to pin together his broken leg, but he'll go home soon. I understand Lucas will be discharged in the morning. But you'd know more about that than I would."

Tessa sighed. "What do you want, Dee?"

"It was such wonderful news footage, you and Lucas kissing like that by the helicopter. So romantic. I don't think I've ever seen you cry, Tessa."

"I save it up for all my really good Hallmark moments." Tessa faced Dee squarely. "If you're here to tell me I'm out of a job, save your breath. I quit."

"Quit?" Dee laughed as if it were a joke. "There seems to be a lot of that going around lately."

Tessa frowned at her response. "I'd appreciate if you'd just talk straight for a change. It's been a tiring day."

Dee's pale eyes shone with an odd brightness. "It hasn't exactly been a banner day for me, either. Six years I've worked on the *Taliesen*. Six years of putting my heart and soul—"

Dee abruptly turned away, and Tessa couldn't help feeling a rush of compassion, no matter how much she disliked the woman. They'd all lost something when the *Taliesen* had slipped below the waves, perhaps Dee Stanhope most of all.

Standing, she lightly touched Dee's shoulder. "She was a beautiful old ship. I'm so sorry."

After a moment, when Dee glanced back up, her eyes were dry, but nothing could disguise her very real grief. "Silly, isn't it? To feel like this over a steel hulk and a bit of paint."

Before Tessa could respond—still struggling with this unfamiliar sensation of feeling sorry for Dee—the woman produced another one of her blinding smiles. A little confused by this rapid shift, not to mention wary, Tessa sat back down and grabbed her cold coffee.

"Now, what's this nonsense about quitting or getting fired? What an absurd idea! Why would I be so foolish as to let go such a heroic officer?"

Tessa stared at Dee, stunned. "I can't believe you said that."

"Why so shocked? I'm a businesswoman. I take opportunities where I find them, even in defeat."

"This is worse than defeat. Somebody sank your ship. She's gone. The bar and dance floor, all the musician's instruments, the cars and cargo, everything." Her purple sundress, and her last picture of Matt. "It's all at the bottom of Lake Michigan."

"I'm well aware of that." Dee smoothed back her hair, and Tessa could've sworn the woman's hand shook ever so slightly. "And once the dust from this settles, I'm sure there'll be a number of people who won't be sorry that Old Rolly's Folly made an absolute fool of herself. Won't they be surprised to find that I'm not giving up?"

In spite of herself, Tessa felt a twinge of respect for the woman. She'd never like her, but she could understand tenacity like this.

Dee crossed her legs, swinging a foot. The rest of her appearance was cool, elegant—except for the nervous energy escaping in that swinging foot. "Nobody knows this yet, but two months ago, I bought an old schooner. I'm converting her to a dinner cruise ship to sail outside Milwaukee, and she'll be ready next May. I have another lined up for the following year, in Chicago, and I have my eye on an old car ferry." At Tessa's surprised stare, Dee shrugged her shoulders. "Some people dedicate themselves to saving the whales or rain forests. Me, I save old ships."

On a sudden suspicion, Tessa asked, "What does any of this have to do with me?"

"Officers like you and Lucas aren't exactly a dime a dozen, and I'm looking for a captain. Lucas quit on me a few days ago, so I'm asking you."

Tessa straightened so quickly that the coffee in her cup sloshed onto her hand. "Lucas *quit*?"

"He didn't tell you? Oh, dear. I hope I haven't caused a little problem." Again, she shrugged, her foot circling ever faster. "He was, shall we say, a mite perturbed with me at the time. I'm rather hoping I can change his mind."

"Why ask me?" Tessa asked bluntly. "Or are you figuring you can get a little extra mileage out of the notoriety of having a captain who survived the *Taliesen*'s sinking?"

"Well, of course."

"You want to use me—"

"We can use each other. That's the beauty of it, because we both have something the other wants."

Tessa narrowed her eyes. Had she actually, for a moment there, *liked* this creature? "That's disgusting."

Dee recrossed her legs. "Oh, enough with the drama. I want to make money. You want to be a captain . . .

and something tells me you'll want a job that won't keep you away from hearth and home. What I'm proposing means one cruise per day, six days a week, April through October. You'd be home every night."

The offer held an undeniable appeal. She couldn't really get this lucky, could she? There had to be a catch.

"I'll think about it," she said, her tone grudging.

"Good enough. I'm not about to let a little personal pride stand in the way of profit. I'm hoping you'll feel the same."

Putting aside her coffee, Tessa leaned toward Dee. "You're here for another reason than to offer me a job. What is it?"

"Ships sink, but life goes on," Dee said, her smile fading. "I'm heading back to Cleveland to tie up a few loose ends before the lawyers and investigators descend upon me. I have a message I'd wanted to deliver personally to Lucas, but I can't wait. I'd like you to give him the message for me."

Suddenly wary, Tessa said, "Depends on what it is."

"I just learned Joseph Yarwood turned himself over to the authorities in Michigan a few hours ago. He's confessed to placing the car bomb on the *Taliesen*. Lucas might like to know that he's no longer a walking, talking target."

Relieved, Tessa slumped back in her chair. A moment passed before she trusted herself to speak. "Thank you."

"With all due respect to that man's poor family, I hope they'll lock up Yarwood for the rest of his natural life. And then some."

"I'm just glad it's over."

"So am I." A strained silence settled over the room, and finally Dee stood. "I'd better be on my way. I'm sure John's tired of waiting."

"John?" Tessa repeated, puzzled. "John who?"

"Burton. You know—my guard dog."

"But you don't need a guard dog anymore." She paused. "And I didn't know you two were on a first-name basis."

The smile was back. "Life is full of surprises isn't it?" Dee walked away a short distance—in a stride far more graceful than Tessa ever could've managed in four-inch heels—then turned. "I wanted to thank you and Lucas for all you did. And tell Lucas . . . I know how hard it must've been for him to go back after Marshall and that little girl. In my eyes, he'll always be a hero—even if he had the poor taste to choose you over me."

With a laugh, Dee walked away with her hips swinging, heels clicking—getting in the last word, as usual.

Tessa stared after her until she was gone, then leaned back in her chair. After a moment, she shook her head and laughed quietly.

After a week of more talks with the police, Coast Guard, and investigators from the NTSB, Tessa was heartily sick of covering the same territory over and over again. The only thing that had seen her through these latest long hours was knowing Lucas waited for her at the cabin that afternoon.

Between meetings, doctor appointments, and concerned family members dropping by on a daily basis—including her father!—she'd had little time alone with Lucas. That, combined with her exhaustion and his injuries, made it easy to avoid certain issues . . . such as how she'd gradually moved into his cabin over the week. First her favorite coffee mug found its way into his cupboards, then an extra shirt and bra into his dresser, and finally more clothing in his closet, and her toothbrush, toiletries, and personal items in his bathroom.

Not once had he asked her what she was doing, and she hadn't been anxious to bring up the subject, either, at a total loss how to explain her feelings. But foremost in her mind was a single thought: What next? She suspected, from the glances Lucas had sent her way, and his sometimes hesitant touch, he was wondering the same thing.

Tessa pulled up beside Lucas's car and switched off the engine, but didn't go into the cabin right away.

She couldn't help feeling guilty. One day, she was telling Lucas it was all over between them, and the next their ship had sunk and now she was sleeping in his bed again.

He had to be a little uncertain about her intentions. Yet he hadn't asked her a single question, just went about as if nothing had changed.

Of course, everything had changed. As if she could forget, with the sight of his bruised and battered body a constant reminder of how close she'd come to losing him. She repeatedly found herself placing her hand on his chest, over his heart, as if still needing reassurance that he was truly well and with her.

Sighing, she pulled the keys from the ignition.

Time to stop being chickenhearted. She kept rationalizing her heel-dragging as worry over Lucas, although physically, he was strong and healing. Mentally, he didn't seem any worse for his ordeal. This entire week, he'd slept like a rock, and she'd had to shake him awake several mornings. He shrugged this off as being doped up on painkillers, but she couldn't help wonder if those harrowing moments on the *Tal-*

iesen had, in some way, helped him heal his older, inner wounds.

Oddly, *she'd* recently suffered nightmares and awakened, terrified, to seek comfort in Lucas's arms. She now understood, rather more than she liked, why his recovery would be a long, slow one. Some things simply needed to be dealt with one day at a time. He might always suffer from symptoms of traumatic stress; he might not. Only time would tell.

But after what she and Lucas had survived, no obstacles existed that they couldn't overcome together.

Well. Enough delaying.

She stared at the cabin a moment longer, then swung out of the car, blinking against the afternoon sun, and headed up the steps. There, she found a Post-it note affixed to the screen door with a piece of duct tape. On it, Lucas had scrawled: *Gone fishing.*

Gone fishing? In *what*?

A quick look didn't reveal any other car parked nearby, and she doubted his fisherman brother-in-law, Kevin, would be around at this time of day; he'd be out on the lake, working.

Had Lucas gone with him? He hadn't mentioned doing so this morning.

Frowning, Tessa headed down to the pier, her pace brisk. When she passed the grove of pines that sheltered the pier from the cabin, she stopped short.

Lucas sat on the pier in shorts and his faded old USCG T-shirt—and looming above him was a forty-five-foot cabin cruiser so new its paint still sparkled in the light.

"Lucas," she shouted. He turned slowly, a smile crossing his face. Shaking her head in disbelief, she jabbed her finger at the cruiser and demanded, "What is *that*?"

His grin widened. "It's a boat, Tess. You know, a vessel that floats on water and—"

"I can see it's a boat," she interrupted, closing the brief distance between them at a run. "Where did it come from? Whose is it? God, it's *beautiful!*"

Laughter sparkled in Lucas's eyes. "It's all mine."

Understanding dawned, and she smiled. "You did it."

"Was there ever any doubt?"

"No," she admitted, walking the length of the pier and admiring the sleek craft. It must've cost him a bundle. "Really nice. Are you going to let me drive?"

"No way. It's my boat. But tell you what: if you're a real good girl, I might let you touch the keys."

She grinned. "I want to go for a ride. Right now."

"I'll take you for a ride. Later."

Tessa caught the purely predatory gleam in his eyes, which made her wonder what exactly he meant by *ride.* Then Lucas opened his arms and, without a word, she sat on his lap, head against his chest, and listened to his heart beat its steady, comforting rhythm.

"Mmmm . . . you smell wonderful, Lucas."

His chest shook with silent laughter, and she glanced up to find him watching her, a lazy grin on his face.

Careful of the stiff sutures, she touched the cut on his forehead, then trailed her finger down to the yellowing bruise beside his mouth. "I'd kiss you, but I'm still afraid there's no spot on you that won't hurt."

"So how about kissing all the spots and making them better?"

Brow arched, Tessa surveyed the cuts and contusions covering him from head to foot. "That'd take a while."

"We have the rest of the afternoon. That ought to do it."

Tessa eyed him, still not sure he meant what she

hoped he meant. Though she'd shared Lucas's bed since he came home from the hospital, with all the stress and commotion and his injuries and well-meaning relatives underfoot, making love had taken a backseat to other needs.

"How are you feeling?"

"Like I'm a week postexplosion, postheader onto a steel hull, and postswallowing more of Lake Michigan than I should've."

"I'm serious, Lucas."

"So am I. I feel fine." He grinned. "Although it'll be a while before I do any swimming. Or any push-ups."

Oh, yes; there was definitely a frisky sparkle in those hazel eyes. "Hmmm . . . I've been thinking lately I could use some upper body toning. What do you think?"

A slow smile curved his lips—and a sweet, languorous ache spread within her. "All in good time," he murmured. "First things first."

Curiosity roused, she asked, "What do you mean?"

"Just things," he said, grinning, and Tessa rolled her eyes at his mysterious manner. "Sherri called an hour ago. Andy's surgery went well. He's going home in a couple of days."

"That's great news. I ran into Rob and Jerry at the police station earlier. Rob's already got a relief job lined up, and Jerry said he's taking off a few months because his wife and daughters won't let him out of the house. I guess life's getting back to normal." After a moment, she added, "I also checked in with the office about working relief. As much as I'm enjoying myself, I can't sit here with you the rest of the season. Bills to pay, you know."

"I bet they'll round up some work for you pretty quick. Have you talked to Dee about her schooner offer yet?"

"I'm still thinking it over. It wouldn't be a bad job, I guess. Have you thought about taking it on yourself?"

He shook his head. "No more ships for me. I've nearly died twice. I'm not superstitious, but I don't want to find out if the third time's the charm." He glanced at her. "Are you going to take it?"

"Depends."

"You wanted to be a captain, Tess. Here's your chance. All you have to do is get your master's license, and that'll be no problem with your skills and experience."

She looked away, her gaze falling on the spanking-new cruiser bobbing at the pier beside her. "I know, but it wouldn't be like working on a real ship—like a freighter or even the *Taliesen*."

"No," Lucas agreed, "but she'll have sails. Captaining her will take real, old-fashioned sailing skills. Think about what a challenge that would be."

It *would* be a challenge, and a flutter of excitement filled her at the thought.

Tessa sent him another quick peek, remembering she'd come after him with a specific intention before this new cabin cruiser—and Lucas's mysteriousness—distracted her.

Clearing her throat, she said, "I'd also have regular hours. I'm thinking that might come in handy?"

"Are you trying to tell me something, Tess?"

She sighed. "You're not going to make this easy for me, are you?"

"Should I?"

She shook her head. "I was pretty hard on you. About Matt, and work. Dee gave me quite a scare, but I shouldn't have acted like such a hysterical twit."

"We're all clear on Matt?"

"You know, he'd be mad as hell at me for using him

as an excuse not to be with you. I loved him so much, Lucas, and losing him without having a chance to say good-bye was so hard." She reached out and took his hand in hers. "But maybe I was using your part in his death as a way to avoid being with you, because I was afraid of falling in love with you, and having it not work out between us again. That was wrong of me, and I'm sorry."

Lucas nodded, but said nothing.

"When the *Taliesen* went down, I was terrified I'd lost you. And afterward, when I was holding your hand in the helicopter, I kept thinking that I'd been such a fool. It wasn't your fault Matt died." She met his watchful gaze. "And as much as I love working on ships, it's just a job. It can't hold me close at night, or go for a swim with me, or a walk in the woods. A ship can't give me children. I want children, Lucas. I want a family."

He smiled. "According to Nina, I'm good with kids."

Tessa smiled back. "But I would like to stay in shipping. How are we going to deal with that?"

Here it was: the big question, the point where every one of her past relationships had foundered.

Lucas shrugged. "So we won't have the average American family life, whatever that means. Can't say that it matters. I know what makes you tick, Tessa, because it's the same way for me. I'd never ask you to give up something so important. We'll work around it."

Tessa squeezed her eyes shut. She hadn't realized how tense she'd become, until relief rushed through her with such power that it left her weak and light-headed.

"Thank you," she whispered, leaning against his shoulder.

Shifting, he kissed the top of her head. "Kids will

mean an adjustment, but I figure we'll tackle that when the time comes. One good thing about a charter business is that when I'm not out on the water, I can be with our kids."

Our kids.

Tessa turned into his chest, smiling.

"And between Nina and my sisters and mother," he continued, "baby-sitters shouldn't be hard to find. How does all that sound?"

Like a proposal.

Tessa looked up at him, expectant.

He scratched his chin. "You like this place?"

Startled by the abrupt change of conversation—and a little disappointed that he hadn't popped the question she'd hoped for—Tessa blinked, then looked around at the cabin and quiet lake, the trees and blue sky.

"Well, sure. It's beautiful and peaceful here."

"I've been looking at a place like it up by Port Washington. I'm thinking of buying it. For us."

"Us?" she repeated.

"Yeah," he murmured, his mouth just inches from hers. "It's a good place to raise kids. Big pier with room for a forty-five-footer. Close to the highway for commuting. Two bedrooms, a fireplace, and a porch. Room for a big dog to run."

Love for him rushed through her, filling her with happiness, and Tessa leaned against him. "I'm sold."

"Good. That leaves only one thing left to do." With a look of amused innocence that instantly made her suspicious, he fished an envelope from his pocket and handed it to her. "Open it."

Still regarding him narrowly, Tessa took the envelope. She peeked inside.

"These are plane tickets. Two of them." She stared at Lucas in bemusement, then looked back in the envelope. "They're dated for tomorrow to . . . *Las Vegas*?"

"That's right." He pulled a small black-velvet box from his pocket and placed it in her hand, wrapping her fingers around it. "Maybe this'll help you make sense of it."

Tessa's heart pounded with a sudden understanding, and an odd breathlessness stole over her as she slowly opened the box. Sunlight glinted against gold, and a diamond flashed in the sunlight. "Oh, Lucas . . . it's beautiful!"

His lips brushed against her ear as he whispered, "So . . . do you wanna run off to Vegas with me tomorrow and get married?"

"Tomorrow?" she gasped.

"My schedule's clear. You have anything better to do?"

"You've been a busy boy," Tessa murmured as Lucas took her hand and slipped the ring on her finger. She stared at it, as if she couldn't quite believe it was real.

"When I know what I want, I go after it."

Glancing at him, she raised a brow. "You didn't do this all today. You can't buy a boat, plane tickets, and an engagement ring in one morning. You've been planning this all along."

He grinned, his cheeks creasing in that way that made her knees go weak and her heart skip a beat. "Maybe."

"You were pretty damn sure of yourself!"

"Yeah." He leaned back, looking far too confident and cocky. "And I was pretty damn sure of you, too."

"How long?"

"How long what?"

She gave him a poke with her elbow. "How long have you been planning this?"

"A while. I bought the boat a couple days ago. I

bought the ring the morning you left your toothbrush in the bathroom."

Tessa started laughing.

"I just bought the plane tickets today, though." He looped his arm around her waist and pulled close for a long, lazy kiss.

After a moment, she broke it off with a sigh of contentment, first looking at him, then the ring. "I can't believe you were so sneaky."

"So what's the answer, Tess?"

She looked at him blankly. "Answer?"

Lucas grinned, shaking his head. "Are you going to say yes and marry me, or am I going to have to resort to something drastic, like get down on my knees and beg? I'm so stiff I don't think I could get back up," he added wryly, "so I'm hoping you'll feel guilty for teasing me like this, and just say yes."

Tessa laughed, then squealed: "Yes!"

She had to kiss him again, and meant it to be short and sweet, but he held on to her tightly and it ended up long and hot and sweet.

Breaking away again, she admired her ring for a moment longer. "Well, if we're going to be untraditional, seems to me we may as well start out on the right foot. Eloping to Vegas works for me."

Lucas, his eyes gleaming with an unmistakably seductive intent, came to his feet and pulled her up with him. "Hell, if you like untraditional that much, how about we have the honeymoon first?"

Before she could protest, he scooped her up in his arms, wincing as the effort strained his bruised ribs.

"Lucas, put me down!"

But he ignored her. He headed instead for the cabin cruiser—just as the sound of laughter carried toward them from behind.

"Ah, shit," Lucas said in disgust, turning. "Not again."

Over his shoulder, Tessa could see Nina and Lucas's sister, Diane, standing at the pier, their kids in tow. All six of them.

"I like my sister," he muttered. "Really, I do. But I wish to hell she'd call ahead first."

"Hellooo!" Nina warbled, waving, as the group came to a sudden halt at the foot of the pier. "Whoopsies! We were looking for Tessa. Didn't expect to find you both here. Your note said you'd gone fishing, Lucas."

"I *am* going fishing," Lucas called back.

Nina and Diana exchanged glances, and Tessa could feel one of those hot, creeping blushes steal up toward her cheeks.

Nina grinned. "It looks like you already caught something. You gonna keep her, or throw her back in?"

Tessa stiffened in Lucas's arms as she darted a look toward the water, gently lapping at the pier. "Don't you even think about it, Lucas Hall, or I swear—"

"I thought I'd keep this one," Lucas interrupted, grinning. "We were just going for a ride."

Again, Nina and Diane exchanged looks as the kids fidgeted and talked excitedly about the big, brand-new boat. With an effort, the two women kept them from racing down the pier.

"You want us to leave?" Diane asked.

"Nah," Lucas said. "Make yourself at home; it's your cabin. But Tessa and I plan on being away for the rest of the day."

Nina laughed. "Fishing?"

"Yeah. I know all the good spots." Lucas gazed down at her, and winked. "I thought I'd show her just how good they are."

Author's Note

*T*his book wouldn't have been possible without the many people who helped me sort out details regarding the Great Lakes maritime community. So, thanks to Rich Beckman, dock agent at Marquette, Michigan, for letting me watch as taconite was loaded onto the freighters and not laughing whenever I slipped on the pellets (it's not easy walking on marble-sized bits of ore). Thanks to Tom Hawley of the Lake Michigan Carferry Company for arranging my stay on the SS *Badger*, and a big THANK YOU!!! to Captain Dean Hobbs and Second Mate Justin Pierson for touring me around the ship and answering my questions—and to Karin, the cruise director, for all her running around on my behalf. A warm thanks to two great guys—pilot LTJG Daniel Leary and rescue swimmer AST1 John Donohue of the U.S. Coast Guard Air Station, Traverse City, who let me tour their facility and answered my questions on rescue operations in the Great Lakes (and for putting up with four kids climbing inside the helicopter!). Finally, thank you, Mary Louise Plant of the SS *Milwaukee Clipper Preservation Inc.*, for talking with me about the *Milwaukee Clipper*, the ship that inspired the *Taliesen*.

If I've made any mistakes in my story or taken excessive dramatic liberties, the blame is entirely my own.

The only steam-fired passenger ship on the Great Lakes today is the SS *Badger*, which runs daily from May through October between Mantiowoc, Wisconsin, and Ludington, Michigan. If you're ever in the area and have time to spare, hop on board. Sailing the *Badger* will give you a whole new perspective on, and appreciation of, our inland seas (especially when the winds are running north–south and churning up waves big enough to raise your body off the bunk and leave your stomach stranded in midair for a second . . .).

Modern cruise ships do sail the Great Lakes, namely the German-owned *Columbus*. Not so long ago, a cruise ship ran aground in the St. Lawrence River and all her thousand-plus passengers had to be evacuated—which only proves you don't need an ocean for a ship to get into trouble. So be nice to your local Coasties . . . you never know when you might need their help!

The Valley Camp Maritime Museum and Soo Locks in Sault Sainte Marie, Michigan, also contributed to this book. The Valley Camp Maritime Museum is housed in an old freighter. Among its many displays are the *Edmund Fitzgerald*'s two lifeboats, their sturdy aluminum hulls torn like paper—a chilling reminder of how dangerous these inland seas can be. And while I was following a local news story about the disappearance of a veteran three-man crew of the fishing boat *Linda E*—which vanished on Lake Michigan without a trace, or even a call for help, on a clear, calm December day in 1998—I discovered that the captain was married to my mother's cousin. This bit of research ended up hitting a little closer to home.

I can't forget to thank to my husband, Bob, for playing photographer and explaining various technobabble that generally makes my eyes glaze over ("Hon, can you explain that quadruple expansion steam engine thingamajiggie again?"). As always, love and kisses to my son, Jerott, for thinking a book-writing mom is pretty awesome, and hugs to my many wonderful cyber pals (yeah, Gail, this includes you!) for their humor and support. You guys are the best! Last, but not least, thanks to my agent, Pam Ahearn, and my editor, Micki Nuding, for trusting me to write a book like this in the first place.

Michelle Jerott

She's the *USA TODAY* bestselling author popularly known as Rachel Lee

Now, don't miss the latest sassy, sexy contemporary romance
by
Sue Civil-Brown

❧ Tempting Mr. Wright ☙

Coming in October from Avon Books

Tess Morrow and Jack Wright have always struck sparks . . . and they're about to find out that sometimes someone who's all wrong can be just right!

Discover Contemporary Romances
at Their Sizzling Hot Best
from Avon Books

SLEEPLESS IN MONTANA by Cait London
80038-1/$5.99 US/$7.99 Can

A KISS TO DREAM ON by Neesa Hart
80787-4/$5.99 US/$7.99 Can

CATCHING KELLY by Sue Civil-Brown
80061-6/$5.99 US/$7.99 Can

WISH YOU WERE HERE by Christie Ridgway
81255-X/$5.99 US/$7.99 Can

IT MUST BE LOVE by Rachel Gibson
80715-7/$5.99 US/$7.99 Can

ONE SUMMER'S NIGHT by Mary Alice Kruesi
79887-5/$5.99 US/$7.99 Can

BRIDE FOR A NIGHT by Patti Berg
80736-X/$5.99 US/$7.99 Can

HOW TO TRAP A TYCOON by Elizabeth Bevarly
81048-4/$5.99 US/$7.99 Can

WISHIN' ON A STAR by Eboni Snoe
81395-5/$5.99 US/$7.99 Can